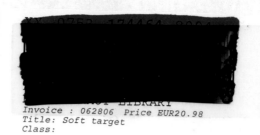

Soft Target

STEPHEN LEATHER

LARGE PRINT

Oxford

First published in Great Britain 2005
by
Hodder & Stoughton
a division of Hodder Headline

Published in Large Print 2005 by ISIS Publishing Ltd,
7 Centremead, Osney Mead, Oxford OX2 0ES
by arrangement with
Hodder & Stoughton,
a division of Hodder Headline

British Library Cataloguing in Publication Data
Leather, Stephen
    Soft target. – Large print ed.
    1. Undercover operations – Fiction
    2. Police corruption – Fiction 3. Suspense fiction
    4. Large type books
    I. Title
    823.9'14 [F]

            ISBN 0–7531–7445–6 (hb)
            ISBN 0–7531–7446–4 (pb)

Printed and bound in Great Britain by
T. J. International Ltd., Padstow, Cornwall

For Charlotte

I am indebted to Terry O'Connor for his help and advice on the workings of the Metropolitan Police's SO19 Firearms Unit. Mick Joyce, Peter Mardle and Alistair Cumming of the British Transport Police were generous with their time and expertise while explaining how the London Underground would deal with a terrorist incident. Any errors of fact are mine and not theirs.

Denis O'Donoghue, Barbara Schmeling and Matt Richards helped me get the manuscript into shape, and I was fortunate once again to have the benefits of Hazel Orme's editing skills.

Producing a novel can be a long, arduous process, and having an editor of the calibre of Carolyn Mays makes the journey a more pleasant one. I'll always be grateful for her input and support.

The heroin had come a long way. It had started its journey as opium in Afghanistan, carried on the backs of donkeys to Jalalabad where it sold for a hundred US dollars a kilo. Sealed in polythene and wrapped in burlap sacking, it was carried over the border into Pakistan, under the eye of former Taliban fighters, and from there to Uzbekistan, where Chinese technicians converted it into heroin.

Bribes were paid to Customs officers, and it was dispatched by rail in a consignment of flour to Poland. There, it was transferred to hidden compartments in a containerload of tinned plums and driven to Germany. Customs officials in the European Union were harder to bribe than those in the former Soviet Union, but the truck crossed without hindrance. A German truck driver took the container to France, where a Turk drove it on to a cross-Channel ferry. He had a British passport and was a regular on the ferry. Customs at Dover didn't give him a second glance.

Three hours later the heroin was being driven on the M2 towards London and had increased in wholesale value to £30,000 a kilo. There were two hundred kilos in the container, six million pounds' worth. Once it had been cut, the street value would be around fifteen million.

Twice when the truck drove under footbridges across the motorway it was monitored by spotters, men with mobile phones who checked that it wasn't being followed. Both were satisfied that it was not and phoned ahead to say that everything was as it should be.

As the Turk drove into Central London he was shadowed by two high-powered motorcycles. Once they were certain that the truck still wasn't being followed he was told where to make his delivery. He went to a warehouse in North London where the plums were unloaded, to be sold on to a legitimate supermarket chain. Four Turkish Cypriots unbolted a metal plate that ran the width of the rear of the container. Behind the plate, steel trays were packed with the white plastic parcels of brown powder, each the size of a small loaf of bread. They checked the purity and weight of the heroin, and sent the driver on his way.

The consignment was divided into four. The Turks took the lion's share and, for a week or so, the street price of heroin fell by ten per cent in North London. Forty kilos were sold to a group of former IRA activists who took it on the ferry to Belfast where they were arrested by the Northern Irish police. Another thirty kilos ended up on the streets of Liverpool. The dealers usually used milk powder to bulk out the drug but the heroin arrived on a Sunday and their local shop was shut. They substituted quinine but the dealer who did

2

the mixing used too much and twenty-seven heroin addicts ended up in hospital. Three died.

The Turks sold ten kilos to a Yardie gang in Harlesden. They didn't like doing business with the Jamaicans, but the Yardies were keen to buy for cash. Customs had seized one of their deliveries in the suitcases of a mother of three at Heathrow Airport. Twelve kilos. She had been unlucky: she didn't fit the profile of a mule but an officer had seen her fumbling nervously for her mobile phone as she pushed her trolley through the green channel. The heroin hadn't even been well hidden — the false compartments in the bottom of her oversized suitcases were discovered within minutes. The woman had broken down in tears and told the officer that a gang in Kingston had threatened to castrate her two sons if she didn't do as they wanted, and had promised her a thousand dollars if she did. The investigators told her she'd get a lighter sentence if she gave evidence against the gang, but she cried all the harder.

The handover between the Turks and the Yardies took place on a petrol-station forecourt in Wood Lane. A Turkish godfather owned it, so the CCTV cameras were switched off and the Turks had three heavies with submachine pistols hidden in the toilets in case the Yardies tried to take the drugs for free.

The Yardies, too, were armed but they brought three hundred thousand pounds with them, mainly in fifty-pound notes. The Turks counted the bundles of money and examined three closely. Satisfied, they handed over the drugs. The Yardies had brought a

3

chemical kit and tested two packages, then pronounced themselves satisfied. The deal was done. The Yardies piled into a BMW and drove into the night with their heroin.

"I hate the Yardies," said one of the Turks, as he watched the BMW disappear into the distance. "You can't trust them. Give me the Bangladeshis every time." He lit a small cigar and drew the smoke deep into his lungs. "You know where you are with a Bangladeshi."

"I hate the Turks," said Delroy Moran. He was sitting in the front passenger seat of the 7 Series BMW. Gangly, with shoulder-length dreadlocks, he'd flown into London six months earlier to escape a murder investigation in Jamaica. He was wearing a tight T-shirt, and a gold medallion featuring a cannabis plant dangled round his neck. The deal he'd just done was his biggest to date and the adrenaline was still flooding through his veins. He planned to cut the heroin with milk powder and sell it in Harlesden at seventy pounds a gram. Seventy thousand a kilo.

"Yeah, well, they hate us," said Chas Eaton, the driver. He didn't have a licence or insurance but he did have three convictions for dangerous driving, under different names, and had once run over and killed a thirteen-year-old girl at a zebra crossing in South London. He had left the scene, abandoned and torched the car, and hadn't suffered a moment's guilt. "But money's money, innit?"

4

"I'm just saying, given the chance they'd rob us blind. You've gotta count your fingers every time you shake their hands, know what I mean?"

The two heavies sat in the back of the BMW. Their knees were wide apart but still pressed against the front seats. "Starvin'" Marvin Dexter and Lewis "Jacko" Jackson. Both were London born and bred of Jamaican parents, and when they weren't riding shotgun for Delroy Moran they were in either the gym or the boxing ring. The duffel bags were stuffed under their legs and they were holding their guns down. There were enough drugs in the car to ensure that they would go down for a double-digit prison sentence so they had no intention of going quietly if they were stopped by the police.

Eaton brought the BMW to a halt in front of a row of shops: a hardware store, an "everything for a pound" shop, a cut-price supermarket, a minicab company, a betting shop, an off-licence — everything that was necessary for inner-city life. There were two storeys of flats above them. The entrance to Moran's apartment was between the betting shop and the off-licence, both now closed for the night. Three young women were huddled in front of the minicab office. Dyed blondes, short skirts, cheap jewellery. If Moran hadn't been working he'd have gone over and asked if they wanted to party. One of the blondes, who couldn't have been more than sixteen, smiled at him hopefully through the windscreen but he ignored her. "It's gonna rain, innit?" he said. "Put the car away, yeah?" There was a line of lock-up garages behind the shops and he rented two.

He twisted in his seat and nodded at Dexter and Jackson. "Swift, yeah?"

Dexter and Jackson opened the rear doors, heaved themselves out of the car and shouldered the duffel bags, their guns inside their jackets.

Moran hurried to the front door, jabbed at an intercom on the wall to warn the two men inside the apartment that they were on the way up, and opened the door. A small CCTV camera was pointing down at the doorway and Moran flashed it a grin, then stepped aside to let Dexter and Jackson head up the stairs. The intercom was still buzzing, then went silent, and the door closed before Moran could follow the others. He cursed the two men upstairs. Probably spaced out of their skulls. He stabbed at it again and heard a sleepy voice: "Yeah?"

"We're on the way up, everything okay?"

"Yeah."

Moran glared up the CCTV camera. "If they've been at the crack I'm gonna do for them, innit," said Moran. He followed Dexter and Jackson inside, then closed the front door. It had been reinforced with a metal sheet and the door frame was lined with strips of metal. It would take the police minutes with their ram even to dent it. Moran exhaled. He was home and dry. Three hundred thousand pounds they'd paid the Turks. Cut and on the street, the heroin was worth almost three-quarters of a million. Easy money.

Chas Eaton drove the BMW slowly down the road, turned left, then left again down the alley that ran behind the shops. The lock-up garages were brick-built with corrugated metal roofs and most had wooden doors, but Moran's two had metal shutters, heavy-duty padlocks and alarms. They kept the BMW in one of the garages and four stolen high-powered motorcycles in the other.

Eaton stopped and climbed out of the car. From where he was standing he could see the rear of the apartments above the shops. Most of the windows that overlooked the alley were bathrooms and several times Eaton had glimpsed naked flesh while he parked the car at night. The light in Moran's bathroom was off but Eaton frowned when he saw that the window was half open and a ladder was propped under it against the wall. He cursed. There'd be hell to pay if the flat had been burgled. If there had been a break-in, it wouldn't have been a local. Delroy Moran was feared for miles around.

As Eaton headed for the door he fished the padlock key from his trouser pocket. He heard a muffled footstep behind him and started to turn. "Say goodnight, Sooty," said a voice, and something hard crashed into the back of Eaton's head. He was unconscious before he hit the ground.

Moran headed up the stairs, after Dexter and Jackson, to a second door, also reinforced with metal. Above it was a second CCTV camera. The door opened and the two men carried the bags inside. Jackson stopped on the threshold. Moran pushed him in the small of the back but he seemed reluctant to move. When Moran peered over his shoulder, he saw why.

A man wearing a rubber Alien mask with teardrop-shaped black eyes was standing in the middle of the room, holding a large automatic in both hands. Dexter was kneeling on the floor, the duffel bag still on his shoulder. "Inside!" hissed Alien.

Moran reached for the Glock tucked into the back of his trousers but a second masked man appeared at the side of the gunman, wearing a Frankenstein mask and holding a Magnum revolver. He was wearing a dark blue anorak with the hood up over the mask, black leather gloves, dark blue jeans and black boots. Frankenstein waved his weapon. "Touch that gun and you'll be one sorry nigger," he shouted. "Now get inside."

The man in the Alien mask grabbed Jackson's coat collar, pulled him into the room and forced him to his knees.

Moran moved his hand away from the butt of the Glock. "You don't know who you're fucking with," he said.

"Delroy Moran, drug-dealing scumbag, molester of underage girls and murderer of a taxi-driver in Kingston," said the Alien. "I know exactly who I'm dealing with, and nothing would make me happier than to put a bullet in your sorry excuse for a face. Now, take three steps forward and get down on your knees." He was wearing identical clothing to Frankenstein.

"This is fucked-up, man," said Moran.

"Yeah, life's a bitch," said Frankenstein.

"Fire that motherfucker and the cops'll be over you like a rash," snarled Moran.

"Oh, right, Delroy. The cops rush over to Harlesden every time they hear a gun go off, do they? And just how are they gonna get through the two steel doors?" He gestured with the Magnum. "I'll keep it simple, you being educationally challenged and all. In. Now."

Moran swore and stepped into the room.

Frankenstein kicked the door shut. "Knees. Down. Now," he said.

Moran dropped to his knees, his eyes never leaving the gunman's face. "You are dead meat," he said.

"Sticks and stones, Delroy."

Frankenstein grabbed the duffel bag from Dexter and ripped open the top. He examined the contents. "Heroin," he said to Alien, then took Jackson's duffel bag and checked it. "Ten kilos, I'd say."

"Heading for the big time, hey, Delroy?" said Alien. "Now, everyone put their hands behind their heads, fingers interlinked, nice and slowly."

The three Yardies did as they were told. Frankenstein took the Glock from Moran and tucked it into his belt. "Nice gun, the Glock," said Frankenstein. "Never jams. But me, I prefer the good old Colt. Can't go wrong with a Colt, that's what I always say."

"You've got the gear, man," said Moran. "Do I have to listen to a lecture on guns?"

Alien took a step towards Moran and pointed his gun at the man's face. "You're a very funny nigger, Delroy. But it's the cash we want, not your drugs."

"There's no money. And the racial slurs are wearing thin," said Moran.

Alien whipped his gun across Moran's face. Blood spurted and Moran's head spun to the left. He saw the two men he'd left to guard his flat, lying face down with strips of tape across their mouths, their hands bound behind them with plastic strips.

Frankenstein stepped in front of Moran. "When did you get the safe?" he asked.

Moran's eyes flicked to the left, to the door that led into the main bedroom. "Three days ago."

"Open it."

"It's empty."

"So open it and show me."

"It's empty. We used the cash to buy the gear."

"I'm not going to tell you again."

"Fuck you."

Frankenstein lashed out and whipped the gun barrel across Moran's cheek. More blood flowed. "Open the fucking safe."

"Open it yourself."

Frankenstein grabbed Moran by the shirt collar and pulled him along the floor towards the bedroom.

A shot rang out, the noise deafening in the small room. Frankenstein let go of Moran's shirt and whirled round, cursing. Jackson was still on his knees but he was holding a small gun in his right hand. Alien staggered against the door. Jackson fired again and a second bullet thwacked into the wall above Alien's head.

Moran rolled over towards a red plastic sofa. Jackson fired again and hit Alien in the chest. Everyone was staring at the gun in Jackson's hand. Alien straightened up, then grunted and levelled his gun at Jackson.

"They're wearing vests!" screamed Moran. "Shoot him in the head, man! Shoot the fucker!"

Jackson pointed his gun at Alien's head but before his finger could tighten on the trigger Frankenstein fired and a bullet slammed into Jackson's chest. Jackson pitched forwards, his face screwed up with pain.

Moran rolled again and slammed up against the sofa. He groped underneath for the loaded submachine pistol he kept there. An Ingram MAC 10 with a bulbous silencer and thirty rounds in the clip. His fingers found the butt and he pulled it out.

Frankenstein whirled round as Moran rolled on to his back, ducked low and fired twice, hitting him in the head both times. The Ingram fell from Moran's hand and clattered on to the floor.

"Shit, shit, shit," cursed Frankenstein.

Another shot rang out and a bullet thudded into the ceiling. Bang! Another. Frankenstein flinched but it was Alien who screamed. He dropped his automatic and clasped his hands to his groin. "I'm hit!" he shrieked. Jackson was lying on his side, his .22 still pointing at Alien. He was grinning in triumph, blood seeping between his teeth. Frankenstein fired the Magnum again and Jackson lay still.

Blood seeped through Alien's fingers. He looked at Frankenstein. "I'm hit," he said again, quieter this time.

"I'm fucking hit." Then his legs buckled and he fell to the ground.

Frankenstein ran over to him and crouched to examine the wound. The bullet had gone in under the vest, missing the Kevlar by less than an inch.

The intercom buzzed. Frankenstein hurried across the room and answered it. "What the hell's going on up there?" said a voice.

"Get up here," said Frankenstein, and pressed the button to open the door down below. Footsteps pounded up the stairs and a man in a werewolf mask came in, holding a gun. "What the fuck's going on?" he said.

"Andy's been hit."

"Shit." Werewolf pointed his gun at Dexter. "How do we play it?"

Dexter held his hands high in the air. "Don't shoot, man!"

Frankenstein looked around the room. Two men, bound and gagged. Two dead. Another on his knees, pleading not to be killed.

"How do we play it?" repeated Werewolf. "It's your call."

Frankenstein's mind raced. "Let me think," he said.

The driver pulled the van to the side of the road, switched off the engine and killed the lights. The werewolf mask was in the glove compartment, along with the short length of lead pipe bound with masking tape that he'd used to club Eaton unconscious. Eaton was bound and gagged, lying face down in the lock-up.

12

The van had been stolen: it was fitted with false plates and had the name of an emergency plumbing firm on the sides. Werewolf had wanted to drive to the nearest Accident and Emergency Unit but Frankenstein had told him to drive out of London. Now they sat in the darkened lane, the nearest house half a mile away, the engine clicking as it cooled.

"This has turned to shit," said Werewolf.

"Yeah," said Frankenstein, in the passenger seat. He had taken off his mask and pulled back his anorak hood. His hair was cropped close to his skull and he was balding on top. He had a curving Mexican-style moustache. "What the hell are we going to do?" He twisted in his seat to look at Alien, who was curled up on the floor in a foetal ball.

"You know what we have to do," said Werewolf, drumming his palms on the steering-wheel. "We've got to get Andy to a hospital."

"And what do we tell them?" said Frankenstein.

"We leave him outside. We don't have to say anything."

"Get real," said Frankenstein. "As soon as they identify him, they'll come looking for us."

Werewolf slammed his hands down hard on the wheel. "So we deny everything," he said. "What can they do?"

Frankenstein glared at Werewolf. "Don't be so naïve," he said. "They'll dig out the bullet, and if they can match it to any in Moran's flat that puts Andy at a murder scene — in a gunfight with a Yardie posse." He

13

slapped the dashboard with his gloved hand. "God damn it, we should have slotted them all."

"Rosie, listen to yourself," said Werewolf.

Frankenstein stared through the windscreen. "They're witnesses," he said. "They started the bloody fireworks, we should have ended it. They know how many of us there were. If they identify Andy, they go looking for two others. How long do you think it'll be before they come knocking on our doors?"

"We can alibi each other," said Werewolf. "What are they gonna do? Call us liars?"

"I'm not doing a twenty stretch," said Frankenstein. "Before we went into this we knew what the downside was, and we agreed to take the risk."

"We said that if one of us got killed, the rest of us would cover it up," said Werewolf. "Andy isn't dead."

"He's got a slug in the guts," said Frankenstein.

"But he's not dead."

Alien groaned. Frankenstein had given him an anorak to clutch against the wound but blood was pooling around him.

"Let's take this outside," said Frankenstein. He climbed out of the van and waited for Werewolf to join him. Their breath feathered from their mouths in the cold night air. Somewhere in the distance an owl hooted and high overhead the green and red lights of an airliner were heading for Heathrow.

"Let's look at this logically," said Frankenstein, his voice just above a whisper. "The way I see it, Andy's a goner anyway. It was a bloody .22 so the slug'll have

14

spun round in his guts and done God only knows how much damage."

"Best will in the world, you're not a doctor, Rosie," said Werewolf.

"But I've seen enough people shot to know what's bad and what isn't," said Frankenstein. "And Andy's bad."

"He's not going to get any better lying in the van, that's for sure."

"Agreed," said Frankenstein. "So, what are the options? We take him to hospital, then hold up our hands to shooting two Yardies and stealing their heroin? What if Andy goes and dies anyway? Where does that leave us? Looking like twats staring at twenty years behind bars for nothing."

"So we wait for him to die, is that what you're saying?" said Werewolf.

Frankenstein shrugged.

"Why don't you spit it out?" said Werewolf.

"I shouldn't have to," said Frankenstein.

"You want to finish him," said Werewolf flatly. "You want to put a bullet in his head. What if it was me lying on the floor of the van bleeding? Would you put a bullet in me? Look me in the eyes and tell me that's what you'd do."

"If it was me, I'd expect you to do the same," said Frankenstein.

"Easy for you to say, standing there while Andy's bleeding to death," said Werewolf. "Look, maybe there's another way. We take him to a doctor instead of a hospital."

"They've all got to report gunshot wounds."

"A hookie one," said Werewolf. "Someone who'll take the bullet out and not say anything."

"You know someone?"

"There's a guy in Peckham. We could be there in thirty minutes at this time of night."

"He needs major surgery, not a couple of stitches," said Frankenstein, "and blood. Lots of it."

"At least we can try," said Werewolf.

"Then what?" asked Frankenstein. "Your quack patches Andy up, then what? Andy goes on sick leave for six months to recuperate? For God's sake, how's he going to explain away a bullet wound? And what about the quack? Does he know you? Are you going to spend the rest of your life waiting for him to grass you up?"

"We pay him enough he'll keep schtum."

Frankenstein threw up his hands. "You're mad," he said.

"Maybe," said Werewolf. "But if it was you, Rosie, I'd be out here saying the same."

"He'll probably die anyway," said Frankenstein.

"But at least I'd know I tried," said Werewolf. "Let's just get him to the quack and see what the quack says."

Frankenstein took a deep breath and exhaled. "Okay. Just don't expect me not to say I told you so when the shit hits the fan."

"The shit has already hit the fan," said Werewolf, but Frankenstein was walking back to the van. Werewolf hurried after him.

As Werewolf got into the front, Frankenstein climbed through the rear door and knelt down beside Alien. "It's okay, Andy, we're going to get you to hospital."

Alien didn't respond. Frankenstein took the glove off his right hand and felt for a pulse in his neck, but as soon as he touched it he knew the man was dead. He looked up at Werewolf. "You might think I'm a callous bastard, but thank heaven for small mercies is what I say."

"What now?" asked Werewolf.

"We bury him where he'll never be found. Then it's back to life as normal."

"What about the gear?" asked Werewolf, gesturing at the two bloodstained duffel bags.

"Leave that to me," said Frankenstein.

"We didn't go into this to steal drugs," said Werewolf.

"You think we should have left with nothing?" snapped Frankenstein.

"I'm just saying we went there for cash, that's all."

"And there wasn't any. And Andy took a bullet in the gut. You want us to go through all that for nothing?"

Werewolf pointed at the MAC 10, which was lying on the floor of the van next to Alien. "What the hell did you bring that for?"

"Souvenir," said Frankenstein.

"It's a bloody liability, a weapon like that," said Werewolf. "Spray and pray."

"Looks the business, though, doesn't it?" said Frankenstein. "A gun like that could be useful."

"You're not thinking of doing this again, are you?" asked Werewolf. "After what's just happened?"

"I'll sort it," said Frankenstein. "Don't worry." He sounded a lot more confident than he felt. Werewolf was right. Cash was one thing — even dirty money could be cleaned, moved and spent. Drugs were trouble, plain and simple.

The man stared through the windscreen at the rainswept supermarket car park. Housewives were pushing trolleys towards hatchbacks, their shoulders hunched against the rain. Office workers on their way home huddled together at the entrance, their frozen meals-for-one thawing as they waited in vain for a break in the downpour. The sky overhead was gunmetal grey and the forecast had been for rain all night. Every few seconds the wipers flicked across the windscreen.

It occurred to the man that a murder should always be discussed after the sun had gone down, ideally when it was raining. A storm added atmosphere — a flash of lightning, a roll of thunder. It could be planned just as easily on a beach under a blazing midday sun or on a pleasant spring afternoon, but there wasn't the same sense of menace.

He tapped his fingers on the steering-wheel. He didn't need to wear gloves but they were part of the image. Hired killers wore gloves. It was expected. His were black leather, moulded to his hands like a second skin. A strangler's gloves. The man had been many things in his life, but he liked being a hired killer best of all. It was probably the job satisfaction, he thought, and smiled. It was okay to smile when he was on his own but he'd have to watch it when he was with Hendrickson. Hired killers didn't smile.

He spotted the man driving into the car park. It was a convertible Mercedes with a personalised number-plate. A flash car, designed to impress. It would be noticed and remembered. The hired killer drove a grey Volvo: a nondescript car in a nondescript colour with a nondescript registration number. In his business it was important to blend into the background. It was the same with his clothes. He never wore designer clothes when he was working, or anything other than a plastic wristwatch. He had no tattoos, his hair was cut short, but not too short, and he spoke with no discernible accent. His clothes were simple, off-the-peg, and the black wool jacket he wore was one of thousands sold through a mail-order company.

Larry Hendrickson climbed out of his Mercedes. He was wearing a dark suit, well cut, with three buttons on the jacket. Probably Armani and certainly expensive. He unfurled a red, green and white golfing umbrella. His gleaming black shoes were made-to-measure.

The man knew that on Hendrickson's wrist there was an expensive Gucci watch. His hair was expensively cut, his fingernails manicured, and on the two occasions that the man had met him, Hendrickson had used the same aftershave.

Hendrickson walked across the car park, taking care to avoid the deeper puddles on the tarmac. He was carrying a slim briefcase made from the skin of some exotic animal. He looked over his shoulder, so quickly that the man knew he wouldn't have spotted a tail even if there had been one.

He hurried to the Volvo and climbed in, shaking the rain off his umbrella and dropping it behind the front seats before he flashed the man a smile. A frightened smile.

"Great day for ducks," said Hendrickson.

"I guess," said the man flatly.

"Did everything go okay?" asked Hendrickson. He put his briefcase on his knees. Sweat beaded his forehead and there was a nervous tic at the side of his left eye.

"Of course," said the man. He reached into his jacket and Hendrickson flinched. "You wanted pictures," said the man.

Hendrickson nodded. He was wearing wire-framed Gucci glasses and he pushed them up the bridge of his nose. The man's hand reappeared with four Polaroids. He gave them to Hendrickson.

"Did he say anything?" Hendrickson asked, as he flicked through the photographs, then put them into his jacket pocket.

"He said, 'Don't,' and 'Please,' but generally I try to get it over with as quickly as possible," said the man. "Conversations tend to slow the process."

"Did you tell him who was paying you?"

The man's eyes narrowed. "Did you want me to?"

20

Hendrickson's cheeks reddened. "No, no," he said hurriedly. "I just wondered, that's all."

"I did exactly as you asked," said the man. "I killed him and I buried him where he'll never be found. That's what you wanted, right?"

"Of course."

"So, now it's time to pay the piper." The man held out his hand.

Hendrickson opened the briefcase, took out a bulky brown envelope and gave it to the man, who slid open the flap and ran his fingernail along the block of fifty-pound notes.

"It's all there," said Hendrickson. "Fifteen thousand pounds." He closed the case and snapped the two locks shut.

"I'm sure it is."

"Aren't you going to count it?"

"Do I need to?"

"I just meant . . . you know . . ." Hendrickson's voice tailed off.

"If we don't trust each other now, we're both in deep shit," said the man. He put the envelope inside his coat. "This is all about trust. You trust me to do the job, I trust you to pay me in full. We trust each other not to go to the cops."

"Oh, God," said Hendrickson. "The cops." He pushed the glasses up his nose again. The smell of his aftershave was almost overpowering.

"Don't worry about the cops," said the man. "They're stupid."

"I hope so."

"They're too busy hassling motorists to worry about a businessman who's gone AWOL. They won't even investigate."

"They'll want to know where he's gone at some point."

"They might talk to you, but it'll be routine. He's a grown man, and without a body they won't make it a murder inquiry."

"And the body won't ever be found?"

The man grinned. "Not in a million years."

"And the gun? You've disposed of it?"

"I know what I'm doing, Larry."

Hendrickson swallowed nervously.

"Relax," said the man. "You asked me to kill your partner. I did. You asked me to dispose of the body. I did. The company's now yours to do with as you like. You've got what you wanted. I've got my money." He patted his coat pocket. "Now we go our separate ways."

"It was when you mentioned the police — I panicked."

"There's no need. Even if the cops do suspect that Sewell's been killed, you have an alibi for when I did it. All you have to do is to keep your head."

Hendrickson nodded slowly. "You must think I'm stupid."

"You haven't done this before. I have."

"How many times?"

The man frowned. "What?"

"How many times have you . . . killed someone?"

"Enough to know that it's best not to talk about it."

"But you don't . . . feel anything . . . do you?"

22

The man's eyes hardened. "You don't know what you're talking about," he said.

Hendrickson held up his hands defensively. "I'm sorry, I didn't mean to offend you."

"You're not offending me, you're annoying me."

The rain thundered down on the roof of the blue Transit van but the three men inside were wearing headphones and barely aware of the noise.

"What's he waiting for?" asked the youngest. He had been with the undercover unit for just two months and this was his first time in the van. He'd arrived with two cans of Red Bull and a Tupperware container filled with ham and cheese sandwiches.

"It's his call," said Superintendent Sam Hargrove, adjusting his headphones. "Has to be."

Two digital tape-recorders were recording everything that was said in the Volvo, and two CCTV monitors showed visuals — the tops of the two men's heads and a shot from the front passenger footwell.

"But we've got everything we need. A confession on tape and the money in his hands."

"It's his call," repeated the superintendent.

A sheet of paper was stuck to the wall of the van with "WE LIVE AND LEARN" typed on it. Until the man in the car said the magic words, the three men in the van wouldn't be going anywhere. Nor would the half-dozen uniformed officers crammed into the back of the van on the other side of the car park.

Hargrove ran his thumb over the transmit button of his transceiver. He was as impatient as the youngster to have the target in custody, but he'd meant what he said: it was the undercover operative's call. It always was. He was the man on the spot, the man whose life was on the line. Until Hargrove was sure it was safe to move in, the operation continued to run.

Hendrickson's face was bathed in sweat. He took a large white handkerchief from his jacket pocket and wiped it. "You couldn't turn the heater down, could you?" he asked. "It's like an oven in here."

The man adjusted the temperature. It wasn't especially hot in the car.

"Are you okay?" asked the man.

"I haven't done this sort of thing before," said Hendrickson.

"There's always a first time."

"It's just that I might have more work for you."

"You want someone else killed?"

"Not me." He swallowed and licked his lips. "Someone I know."

"So, now you're touting for business for me, is that it?"

Hendrickson dabbed his lips with the handkerchief. "It's someone at my health club. They have a problem, and I got the feeling they could use you."

"Close friend, is it? I wouldn't want you bandying my name around to all and sundry."

"I didn't tell her who you were. I just said I knew someone who might be able to help, that's all."

"Who is she?"

Hendrickson glanced out of the rear window.

"What's wrong?" asked the man.

"I feel like we're being watched."

"That's guilt kicking in."

Hendrickson wiped his forehead again. "What about you? Don't you feel any guilt?"

The man shrugged carelessly. "If I did, I wouldn't do what I do, would I?"

"I guess not." Hendrickson held out his hands in front of him, palms down. "Look at me. I'm shaking."

"Go home and have a cup of tea. Plenty of sugar. You'll be fine."

Hendrickson folded his arms. "He was a bastard," he said.

"Who?"

"Sewell. He was running the company into the ground."

"Better off without him, then," said the man. "This woman, who is she?"

Hendrickson grimaced. "I'm not sure I should tell you. Just in case."

"In case what?"

"In case she changes her mind."

"Give me her number and I'll phone her."

Hendrickson shook his head. "I'd rather pass your number to her. She can call you if she decides to go ahead."

The man put his hands on the steering-wheel and gripped it. "That's not how it works," he said. "I don't hand out my number to strangers. I'm not a plumber."

"I rang you, though, didn't I?"

"My number was passed to you because you'd been asking around for someone to take care of your problem. I knew who you were before you called. I don't know who this woman is. For all I know, she could be an undercover cop."

Hendrickson snorted. "No way she's a cop."

"You know her well, do you?"

"Well enough. Her husband knocks her around."

"And that's who she wants killed? Her husband?"

Hendrickson nodded. "She came to the club with bruises on her arm. Didn't want to talk about it at first. We had a few drinks in the bar and it all came tumbling out."

"So you're having an affair with her, is that it? And with the husband out of the way you'll be free to move in."

"It's not like that," Hendrickson said. "She's just a friend."

"Got to be a pretty close friend if you're talking murder with her."

"I didn't say murder. She just said she wished her husband was dead and I said I might know someone who could help her."

"There's a hell of a jump from wishing he was dead to paying someone to kill him."

Hendrickson shuddered. "Not that big a jump."

"It was different for you," said the man. "You wanted Sewell out of the picture so that you could control the company. Killing him made financial sense."

"Her husband's rich," said Hendrickson.

"So all she has to do is get a decent lawyer. If her husband's been abusive, she'll take him to the cleaners."

A middle-aged housewife rattled a trolley past the car with one hand as she held a plastic carrier-bag over her head. She looked at them through the windscreen. Hendrickson turned away his face and didn't speak until she'd gone. "Her husband isn't the sort of man you can divorce," he said.

"Spit it out, Larry," said the man. "What's the story? Tell me now or get out of the car and we can go our separate ways."

Hendrickson hesitated, then spoke quickly. "Her husband's violent, that's all I know. A real hard bastard. He's already told her that if she ever leaves him he'll put her in the ground. She says he means it. Divorce is out of the question."

"And what's her name?"

"Angie."

"Angie what?"

"I just know her as Angie."

The man's eyes widened in surprise. "You don't even know her full name and you're talking about hired killers with her?"

"I've known her for months."

"But not her name?"

"You know what it's like in the gym. You nod and say hello — you don't exchange business cards. We were just talking, that's all."

"About killing her husband?"

"I think she feels she can open up to me because I'm not a close friend. I don't know her husband, only what she's told me. And all I said was that maybe I knew someone she could talk to who might help."

"What does she look like?"

"She's pretty, blonde, late twenties. A bit tarty, a bit flash — no bra when she exercises, you know the sort."

The man studied Hendrickson with unblinking pale blue eyes.

Hendrickson looked away nervously. "I just thought . . ." he said, then mumbled incoherently.

"You call that thinking?" said the man. "Did you tell her I was offing your partner?"

"Of course not."

"Don't you think she's going to put two and two together when she discovers he's out of the picture?"

"She doesn't know what I do. I didn't tell her I was paying you. It was just a general conversation, that's all." He leaned forward, his arms round his stomach. "I feel sick," he said.

"Not in the car," said the man. "If you're going to throw up, open the door." He flicked the air-conditioning control and cold air blasted across their faces. "Deep breaths," he said.

"I'm sorry," said Hendrickson, still bent double.

"It's the stress," said the man.

"I mean about Angie. I shouldn't have mentioned it. You're right, it's none of my business."

The man tapped his gloved fingers on the steering-wheel. "You think she's serious? About wanting him dead?"

Hendrickson took several deep breaths. "I'm sure of it."

The man's fingers continued to tap the steering-wheel.

"Do you want me to give her your number?" asked Hendrickson.

"Take the bird in the hand, Spider. For God's sake — take the bird in the hand!" There was no way that Shepherd could hear the superintendent: radio communication could only be one way as transmission noise would blow an operative's cover. Hargrove closed his eyes and massaged the back of his neck. The tendons were as taut as steel wires.

"He's going to let it run, isn't he?" said the young officer. He had a video camera trained on the car in the distance but the rain meant that the footage would be virtually unusable. Not that the exterior video mattered. The two video cameras in the Volvo had recorded everything, and the audio was all they needed to put Hendrickson away on conspiracy to commit murder.

Hargrove ignored the officer but he knew he was right: Shepherd *was* going to let it run. The rain continued to beat down on the roof of the van as Hargrove strained to hear what was going on inside the car. "Okay," said Shepherd, through his headphones. "Tell her to call me. But if it turns to shit, I'll come looking for you."

Hargrove cursed under his breath. He reached for his bottle of Evian water and took a long swig, then cursed again.

The young officer watched through the viewfinder of his video-camera as Hendrickson climbed out of the car and ran across the car park, the umbrella low over his head. "What do we do, sir?" he asked.

Hargrove sighed. He opened his eyes, put his transceiver to his mouth and clicked the transmit button. "Alpha One, everyone stand down. Repeat, everyone stand down."

Hargrove paid for the drinks and carried them to the corner table of the pub. Shepherd was taking off his black leather gloves and nodded his thanks as the superintendent placed the Jameson's and soda in front of him. His hair was wet and the shoulders of his coat flecked with water.

"It's not how I'd have played it, Spider. That's all I'm saying."

"I had seconds to make up my mind," said Shepherd, stuffing the gloves into his coat pocket. "What did you expect me to do? Tell him I had to check with my boss?" He took a sip of his whiskey.

"No one's saying it wasn't your call," said Hargrove. He sat down on the bench seat next to Shepherd and stretched out his legs. He had been in the back of the Transit van for the best part of four hours. "I'm just reminding you that we've spent two months setting up Hendrickson and I wouldn't want to put that at risk for the sake of a maybe down the line. Plus, we've got Hendrickson's partner tucked away in a safe-house. He'll be none too happy when I tell him he's got to stay there for the foreseeable future."

"I figure it'll take a few days at most. I'll fix up a meet to see if she's serious. I'll go in wired up, get her to pay a deposit and we can leave it at that. If her husband's knocking her around the court'll probably go easy on her so there's no point in busting a gut."

Hargrove cupped his hands round his brandy glass. "You'll be going in blind," he said. "All we have is a first name."

"She's a battered wife," said Shepherd. "I doubt I'll be in any danger."

"I don't like it, Spider. There are too many ifs, buts and maybes."

Shepherd leaned forward. "Boss, if she doesn't talk to me, she might find someone else."

Hargrove nodded thoughtfully. "Forty-eight hours, that's all I can give you."

Shepherd looked pained, but the time frame wasn't up to him. "The ball's in her court," he said. "Hendrickson wouldn't give me her number."

"If she's serious she'll call. If she isn't, it's a waste of time anyway. Forty-eight hours, Spider. Then we arrest Hendrickson."

Shepherd opened his mouth to argue but the superintendent silenced him with a wave. Shepherd had worked with Hargrove long enough to know when he'd reached his limit. Forty-eight hours was all the time he had.

Roger Sewell was a big man, a good three inches taller than the superintendent, and thirty kilograms heavier. He had receding hair that he'd grown long and tied back in a ponytail, and a goatee beard. He was wearing a grey suit but had taken off his tie and thrown it on to the hotel bed.

"No bloody way am I spending another night in this shit-hole," he said. "I was promised a safe-house not a two-star bloody hotel."

"It's forty-eight hours," said Hargrove, patiently. "Two days."

"Two days during which that bastard Hendrickson is going to be ripping my company apart," said Sewell. He pointed an accusing finger at the superintendent. "Are you going to reimburse me for any money I lose on this?" He didn't give the superintendent time to reply. "Of course you're bloody not. What if he empties the bank accounts and transfers the money off-shore. Then I'm fucked with a capital F, aren't I?"

"Today's Friday," said Hargrove. "You have my word that by Monday your partner will be in custody and you'll be free to do whatever you want. Just give me the weekend, Mr Sewell."

Sewell paced over to the window. "They won't even let me go to the bloody pub. This is Leeds, for God's sake. No one knows me in Leeds. I wouldn't be seen dead in Leeds."

"It's too much of a risk, Mr Sewell," said Hargrove. "If anyone recognises you and mentions it to Hendrickson, he'll know he's been set up and he'll run."

"So put him under surveillance."

"We have. Two men are watching him round the clock. But we can't account for phone calls or emails."

Sewell slammed his hand against the window-frame. "I'm the innocent party here, yet I'm the one being held prisoner. That bastard Hendrickson should be behind bars and he's living it up on the outside while I'm eating off a tray." He turned to face the superintendent. "I've done everything you've asked of me. I even lay down in that hole in the ground with fake blood on my face while you took photographs. But I've reached my limit."

"Forty-eight hours, Mr Sewell. It's not much to ask."

"That's easy for you to say. You don't have to sleep on a lumpy mattress and watch a fourteen-inch TV. And have you seen the bloody room-service menu? Chips with everything."

"Mr Sewell, let's not lose sight of what was happening. Your partner was looking to have you killed. If we hadn't intervened there was a good chance he'd have succeeded and we wouldn't be having this conversation."

Sewell dropped into an overstuffed armchair and swung his feet up on to the bed. He ran a hand over his thinning hair and down the ponytail. "Bastard," he said. "I can't believe he'd have me killed. He's a vegetarian, for God's sake."

"People have killed for a lot less than he stands to gain with you out of the picture," said Hargrove.

"Yeah, but it's only bloody money."

"We do appreciate the help you've given us," said the superintendent. "By Monday you can be back in the office and you'll have the satisfaction of knowing that your partner is going to prison for a long time."

"I hope so," said Sewell. "I bloody well hope so." He looked across at the superintendent. "Can you at least tell me why?"

"It's an ongoing operation," said Hargrove. "That's all I can tell you."

"Involving Hendrickson?"

Hargrove nodded. He didn't like lying to Sewell, but he knew that the man was a lot less likely to co-operate if he knew that the operation had been extended to include a second party. Besides, it was a white lie. Hendrickson *was* involved. Up to a point. "You'll be doing us a great service," said the superintendent.

"You'll owe me one," said Sewell.

"Indeed," said Hargrove.

"I want my laptop," said Sewell. "And my mobile phone."

"I don't think that's a good idea," said Hargrove.

"I won't call anyone. I won't send emails. I just need to know what's happening."

"Computers leave traces. So do mobile phones. We can't afford the risk of anyone finding out you're still alive."

Sewell threw up his hands in disgust.

"Two days, Mr Sewell," said Hargrove. "You have my word."

The local police had assigned three uniformed officers to babysit Sewell, taking it in turns to sit in the hotel's reception area in plain clothes. They weren't there to guard him, merely to ensure that he stayed in the hotel. The only threat to Sewell's life was Hendrickson, and

34

Hendrickson was under the impression that his business partner was dead and buried in the New Forest.

The officer on duty was a fifty-something sergeant with a thickening waistline and thinning hair. He began to get to his feet as Hargrove walked out of the lift but the superintendent waved at him to stay seated and sat in the adjacent armchair. "How's he been?" he asked.

"Grumpy, sir," said the sergeant. "Keeps asking if he can go out for a walk. Complains about the food, the TV, the bed."

"He's not to go out," said Hargrove.

"I understand, sir."

"We're having to extend his stay over the weekend," said Hargrove. "I'll be clearing it with your bosses. But the longer he's here, the more likely he is to slip the leash, so I'm going to have to ask you to set up shop in the corridor outside his room."

The sergeant looked fed up but said nothing. The superintendent sympathised. Sitting in a hotel corridor wasn't the most entertaining way to pass an eight-hour shift. "If he's still unhappy about the hotel food he can order in from restaurants but make sure he pays cash. On no account is he to use his credit card."

"Understood, sir."

"Pass on the instructions to the rest of the team," said the superintendent. "If you want to break it up into four-hour shifts, that's fine by me. So long as he's covered round the clock, you can work it any way you want."

"It's all overtime," said the sergeant. "You won't be hearing any complaints."

Shepherd sat in his car and looked at the front of the house: a neat semi, the garden lovingly tended, the paintwork less than a year old, a TV dish over the garage. Tom and Moira Wintour had put a lot of work into their Hereford home and it showed. A year-old Lexus was parked in front of the garage, freshly waxed.

Shepherd had driven down from Manchester in his own car, a dark green Honda CRV. He'd left the Volvo in the car park below the city-centre loft where his *alter ego* Tony Nelson lived. Once the operation was over and he had Angie on tape, the surveillance equipment would be removed and the Volvo would go back into the police pool with new licence plates and registration details.

On the back seat of the CRV a carrier-bag contained two PlayStation cartridges that he'd bought in a toy shop in Manchester. He'd spent the best part of an hour there but hadn't been able to think of anything else to buy his son. He climbed out, walked to the front door and rang the bell. He saw a blurred figure through the frosted glass, then Moira opened the door, smiling brightly. As always, her makeup was immaculate. "Daniel, you made it," she said.

Shepherd smiled back and forced himself to ignore the implied criticism. He felt bad enough that he had had to cancel his last two visits at short notice without his mother-in-law reminding him of his shortcomings.

Moira was the only person who used his full name. She always had, ever since they'd first met. He'd asked her to call him Dan but she'd paid no attention and Daniel he had remained. Friends and colleagues alike used Dan or his army nickname, Spider.

"Liam's in the garden," she said.

"How is he?"

"Fine."

"He sleeping okay?"

"Daniel, he's fine. Really. Can I get you a cup of tea?"

Shepherd declined her offer and went through the kitchen into the garden. Liam was kicking a football against a low brick wall. His face broke into a grin as he saw his father walking across the lawn. "Dad!" he yelled, and rushed over, grabbed him round the waist and hugged him hard. "I wasn't sure if you'd really come."

"I said I would, didn't I?" said Shepherd, but he felt guilty. He never deliberately set out to let his son down, but the nature of his work meant that he rarely knew what he'd be doing or where he'd be from one week to the next. He gave his son the carrier-bag. "I got you these," he said.

Liam let out a whoop as he saw the PlayStation cartridges. Then his face fell. "Gran doesn't let me play video games," he said.

"Never?"

"An hour a day," said Liam, grimly.

"That sounds reasonable," said Shepherd.

"Mum always let me play as long as I wanted."

37

"No, she didn't, and you know it," said Shepherd. "She said it was bad for your eyes."

"Can I play them now?"

"Let's go to the park for a kickabout."

Liam picked up his ball and they went back into the kitchen. Moira was standing by the kettle, waiting for it to boil. "I've got cake," she said.

"Liam and I are off to the park. We won't be long," said Shepherd.

For a moment she looked as if she was going to protest, but then she forced a smile.

The park was a five-minute walk from the house. Liam bounced the ball as they walked.

"So, are you okay?" asked Shepherd.

Liam shrugged.

"You know your gran and granddad love you, right?"

Another shrug.

"And the school here is okay, right?" Tom and Moira had arranged for Liam to attend the local school until Shepherd had things sorted in London.

"It's okay."

"It's not for ever."

Liam was clutching the ball to his chest. "Are you sure?"

Shepherd stopped walking, put his hands on his son's shoulders, then knelt down in front of him. "What do you mean?"

"Are you dumping me?" He was close to tears.

"Dumping you?"

"With Gran and Granddad."

"Of course not."

"They say I can stay with them for ever."

"They're just being nice."

"They keep saying it's my room. But it's not my room. My room's in our house, isn't it?" His lower lip trembled.

"No question about that." Shepherd ruffled his son's hair.

"Why aren't I living with you?"

The question's blunt simplicity was like a knife in Shepherd's chest. He pulled Liam into his arms and buried his face in the boy's neck. Liam dropped the football. "You'll come home soon, I promise."

"I miss you, Dad."

"I miss you, too."

"Why *aren't* I living with you?"

"Because I've got to find someone to take care of us."

"I can take care of us," said Liam earnestly.

"There's a lot to do, Liam. Cooking, cleaning, laundry, shopping. I've got work, you've got school. We need someone to do that sort of thing for us."

"Like a maid?"

"Yeah. An au pair they call them. She'll take care of the house and us."

"Like Mum used to do?"

"Yeah."

"But she won't be my mum, right?"

"Right."

"Because I don't want a new mum."

"I know."

"I keep dreaming about her."

"Me too."

Liam sniffed. "Where's my ball?"

Shepherd released the child and looked around. The ball had rolled into the gutter. He retrieved it and gave it to his son. They walked in silence to the park. Shepherd didn't know what to say to him. Yes, he wanted him back in London, but there was no way he could take care of Liam and carry on working without domestic help. Liam was only eight, too young to be a latch-key kid, and public transport where they lived was so unreliable that he'd have to be driven to and from school every day. There was no way Shepherd could make that sort of commitment while he worked for Hargrove.

There was a football pitch at the park and they wandered over to the closest set of goalposts, passing the ball back and forth between them. Shepherd stood in the goalmouth and Liam took penalty shots but his heart clearly wasn't in it. There was no power in any of his kicks and he didn't seem to care whether he got the ball past his father or not.

Shepherd tossed the ball back to his son. "Give it some stick, Liam."

Liam placed the ball on the penalty spot, took a few steps back, then tapped it towards him. The ball rolled across the ground and stopped at Shepherd's feet. "That's terrible." Shepherd laughed. "The worst shot I've ever seen."

"This is stupid," said Liam.

"What's stupid?"

"This."

"Football? You like football." Shepherd picked up the ball and threw it back to the boy.

Liam caught it and held it to his chest. "You don't really want to play."

"I wouldn't be here if I didn't want to play with you," said Shepherd.

"Remember when you were in prison?" asked Liam.

"Sure." Shepherd had been working undercover on the remand wing of HMP Shelton, trying to get close to a major drugs importer who was sabotaging the case against him from behind bars. Sue had brought Liam to visit him. It was against all the rules, but Shepherd had needed to see them both.

"Well, that's what this is like," said Liam. "It's like I'm in prison and you're visiting me. And once visiting time's over you'll go and I'll be here on my own."

"You're not on your own. You're with your gran and granddad."

"You know what I mean," said Liam. "You don't want me."

"Liam!" protested Shepherd.

"It's true! You never wanted me!" Liam dropped the ball and ran away.

"Liam, come here!" Shepherd shouted. One of his mobile phones rang and he pulled it out of his pocket. "Liam, wait for me!" It was the Tony Nelson phone. The caller had blocked their number. "Liam, God damn it, stay where you are!" Shepherd yelled.

Liam stopped and turned to look at him. Tears were running down his cheeks. Shepherd pointed a warning finger at him, then pressed the button to accept the call. It was a woman. "Is that Tony Nelson?"

"Yeah," said Shepherd.

"Larry said I should call you."

"He told me I might be able to help you," said Shepherd. "What do you want?"

"I think you know," she said.

"I hope you're not a time-waster."

"It's just difficult. On the phone."

"Do you want to meet?"

Liam stood with his hands on his hips, glaring at Shepherd. "Dad!" he shouted.

Shepherd pointed at him, then pressed a finger to his own lips, telling him to be quiet.

"I think so," she said.

"You're Angie, right?"

She caught her breath. "Larry told you my name?"

"Just that you were Angie, that's all. Look, Angie, you called me so that means you've already put a lot of thought into this. If we're going to go through with it there are things to discuss and that's best done face to face."

"I'm not stupid," said the woman.

"I'm not saying you are," said Shepherd, "but this is outside your normal experience so you're anxious. I understand that. But I can't afford to have my time wasted so you have to decide if you want to move forward or forget the whole thing. And to move forward, we have to meet."

"Okay," she said.

"So, do you need my help or not?"

"Yes," she said. "Yes, I do."

"I hate you!" Liam shouted. He turned and ran across the playing-field in the direction of Tom and Moira's house.

"Where are you?" asked Angie, suddenly suspicious.

"In a park. There are kids here but no one's listening."

"Who was that shouting?"

"Just a kid. Where do you live?"

She didn't reply.

"Are you there?" asked Shepherd, wondering if he'd lost the connection. Liam left the playing-field and ran along the pavement, arms pumping furiously. Shepherd wanted to run after him but he knew that if he spooked Angie there was a good chance she wouldn't call back. It was like reeling in a fish: he had to keep just the right amount of tension on the line. Any hint that there was a problem and he'd lose her. He forced himself to ignore Liam and concentrate on the voice at the end of the line.

"I'm here. I just don't like you knowing too much about me."

"If I don't know where you are, I'm not going to be able to help you, am I?"

"I guess not."

"So tell me where you are and we'll arrange a meeting."

He heard her take a deep breath. "You know Piccadilly Gardens?"

"Of course." It was the square in the city centre, terminus for the city's tram system.

"We'll meet there. This evening. Five o'clock."

"It's too crowded," he said. "Too many people." He looked at his watch. It was eleven thirty. Plenty of time to drive back to Manchester.

"I want there to be people around," she said. "Safety in numbers."

"Look, Angie, this is my field of expertise. We need a place where we can talk. Piccadilly Gardens will be mobbed."

"That's why it'll be safe. No one will pay us any attention."

Shepherd cursed under his breath. He wanted her in his car so that he could record their conversation. If they were in a square filled with trams, daytrippers and shoppers, he'd have to wear a wire, and personal wires were unreliable at the best of times. But if he pressed the point too far she'd get suspicious.

"It's my way or we forget the whole thing," she said, more confidence in her voice.

"Okay," said Shepherd. "Piccadilly Gardens, five o'clock. How will I recognise you?"

"You won't," she said. "I want to take a good look at you first."

"What are you worried about, Angie? Didn't your friend vouch for me?"

"Larry thinks the sun shines out of your arse, but I want to see who I'm dealing with."

"Fine," said Shepherd. "I'll be wearing a black leather jacket, grey pullover, black jeans, and carrying a copy of the *Financial Times*."

"This is like a blind date, isn't it?"

"Not really," said Shepherd, coldly. He had to stay in character and Tony Nelson didn't flirt, didn't joke, didn't make small-talk. He was a stone-cold professional killer. "I'll be by the fountain at five on the dot. If you haven't contacted me by ten past, I'm out of there."

"I understand, Mr Nelson. And, believe me, I'm not wasting your time."

She cut the connection and Shepherd put the phone back into his pocket. "Game on," he muttered. He picked up Liam's football and headed for Tom and Moira's house.

Moira was waiting for him at the door. "Daniel, what on earth happened?"

"Nothing," said Shepherd.

"Liam came back crying his eyes out."

"Where is he?" asked Shepherd, squeezing past her.

"In his room."

Shepherd went upstairs, carrying the football, and knocked on Liam's door. When there was no reply he tried to open it, but it was locked. "Let me in, Liam."

"Go away."

"Please, Liam, I want to talk to you." Shepherd pressed his ear to the door.

"Go away."

"Look, I have to go back to Manchester."

"So go."

"It's work."

"I don't care."

Shepherd sighed. He looked at his watch again. "I've got time for a coffee. Or we could have a go on the PlayStation."

Moira came up the stairs. "Daniel, maybe you should leave him be for a while," she said quietly.

"He's *my* son, Moira," said Shepherd. "I know how to handle him."

"Do you?" said Moira archly. "Well if that's the case, why's he in there with the door locked, sobbing his eyes out?"

Shepherd glared at her, then turned back to the door. He knocked on it gently. "Come on, Liam. Let's not be silly. I don't have long."

"I hate you. I just want you to leave me alone."

"Daniel . . ." said Moira.

Shepherd ignored her. "I didn't want to answer the phone, but it was important. I had to take the call. I wanted to talk to you, but this person might not have called back and it was important."

There was no answer from Liam, but Shepherd heard a sniff.

"Liam, I love you more than anything. I'm sorry if I'm a bad father at the moment but I've a lot on my plate and this is all new territory for me."

Shepherd put his ear against the door but Liam didn't say anything. "I'll count to ten, okay? Then you can come out and we'll be friends again."

Moira went back downstairs. Shepherd was ashamed at the way he'd spoken to her, but there were times when his mother-in-law's holier-than-thou attitude got on his nerves. She meant well, but she hadn't worked

46

since the day she'd married Tom, and the grand total of her life experience came down to her suburban friends, a weekly game of bridge and an annual holiday to either France, Spain or Italy. She had no idea of what Shepherd's life was like or the pressures he was under. Yes, he wanted to be a good father. Yes, he wanted to do the right thing by his son. But it was easy for her: she had Tom, his bank manager's salary and an index-linked pension a few years away. Shepherd had a job to do, a living to earn, and a woman in Manchester who wanted her husband dead.

Shepherd started counting. When he got to five he tapped on the door in time with the numbers. "Six. Seven. Eight. Nine. Ten." Shepherd took a deep breath. "Liam?" The door was so flimsy he could have knocked it down with one kick. "Liam, please. At least give me a hug before I go." He rested his forehead against the door and sighed. "Okay. Look, I have to go, but I'll phone you this evening. I promise."

Shepherd started downstairs but he had only gone a few steps when the bedroom door opened. Liam stood on the landing, his cheeks wet. Shepherd rushed back upstairs, bent down and picked up his son. "I'm sorry I'm such a rubbish father," he said.

"It's okay," said Liam.

"I'm trying, I really am. Bear with me, until I get things sorted."

"I just want to be with you, Dad."

"I know you do." He kissed Liam, then sniffed his hair. "You need a bath," he said.

"I know."

"And wash behind your ears."

"I always do."

Shepherd lowered his boy to the floor. "I'll be back as soon as I can."

"Cross your heart?"

Shepherd solemnly crossed his heart.

"And you'll phone tonight before I go to sleep?"

Shepherd crossed his heart again. Liam nodded, satisfied. Shepherd went downstairs.

Moira was in the kitchen, filling an earthenware teapot. "Have you got time for tea, at least?" she asked.

"I've got to go, Moira. I'm sorry I snapped."

"You didn't, Daniel. You just told an interfering old woman to mind her own business. Nothing wrong with that." She finished pouring water into the teapot and replaced the lid.

She wanted to be mollified, Shepherd could tell. Self-criticism was one of the overused weapons in Moira's extensive psychological armoury. "You're not interfering, and I know you've only got his best interests at heart," he said.

"We all have," said Moira. She began wiping down the worktop, even though it was spotless. "He's been through a lot and what he needs now, more than anything, is stability."

"I'm getting there," said Shepherd.

Moira opened her mouth, then evidently decided not to say anything. She carried on wiping.

"I'll phone tonight from Manchester," he said.

"What's happening up there?"

"Just a job. It should be over this afternoon, then I'll be back in London."

"What about Sue's things? I could come down one weekend. Help you sort out the clothing and shoes. There are charity shops that will take them."

"I'll do it," said Shepherd. He kissed her left cheek awkwardly, then hurried down the hallway and out of the front door. She was right, of course. It was time to clear out Sue's clothes. Four months was a long time. He'd tried several times. He'd opened her side of the fitted wardrobe in the bedroom and even gone as far as taking out some of her clothes, but he'd never managed to throw any away. Somehow it seemed disloyal. They weren't just clothes, they were Sue's clothes. Everything she had, everything she'd touched, everything she'd worn — it was all a part of her and he wasn't prepared yet to discard anything. Or her.

He looked up as he climbed into the car and saw Liam standing at a bedroom window. Shepherd waved and flashed him a thumbs-up. Liam did the same and Shepherd grinned. At least his visit hadn't been a complete disaster.

Shepherd parked on the top floor of a multi-storey car park close to Piccadilly Gardens and sat for ten minutes to see who drove up. There were housewives, families with children, young couples out for a Saturday's shopping in the city centre. Eventually he locked the car and walked down to the third floor. The blue Transit surveillance van was in the corner furthest away from the stairs and lifts. Shepherd tapped the rolled-up copy of the *Financial Times* against his leg as he walked over to it, knocked twice on the rear door and climbed inside. Hargrove was there with Jimmy Faley, the young officer who'd been on the Hendrickson surveillance, and an Asian technician whom Shepherd hadn't met before.

Hargrove took a swig from his plastic bottle of Evian water. "This is Amar Singh," he said. "He's on attachment from the National Criminal Intelligence Service with some state-of-the-art surveillance gear." Shepherd shook Singh's hand.

"I can't imagine a worse place to record a conversation," said Singh.

"Yeah, it wasn't my choice," said Shepherd. He nodded at Faley and sat down on a plastic stool.

Singh pushed a black attaché case across the metal floor. "Make sure the briefcase is as close to her as possible," he said.

"You don't have to teach me to suck eggs," said Shepherd.

"I'm not teaching you to suck anything," said the technician, "but its effective range is down to three feet on the outside and I wouldn't want you blaming me if all we pick up is traffic. I'd be happier if you were wearing a wire, too."

"She's jumpy enough to pat me down," said Shepherd.

"In a crowded square?"

"A lover's hug, hands down my back, a quick grope between the legs, all she's got to do is touch something hard and she'll be off."

50

"She might just think you're pleased to see her," said Singh.

Shepherd gave him a tight smile. "I've got better things to be doing on a Saturday afternoon, believe me," he said. He looked at Hargrove. "Long-range mikes?"

"We'll have two guys on top of the office blocks overlooking the square, but I don't hold out much hope. There's a lot of noise out there." He pointed at the case. "That's our best hope."

Shepherd clicked the twin combination locks and examined the interior. It was lined with a light brown fake suede material and had pockets for pens, business cards and a small calculator. He took out the calculator and examined it. There was nothing unusual about it. He put it back into its pocket, then inspected the exterior. It looked like an ordinary attaché case. "Okay, I give in," he said. "How does it work?"

Singh grinned. "The batteries and transmitter are built into the body of the case, and there's a recording chip in there as back-up in case we lose transmission. There's no way anyone will find it, short of cutting the leather. There are two microphones, one in each lock. You set the combinations to nine-nine-eight to open, nine-nine-nine to start transmitting."

"The three nines would be your idea, I guess," said Shepherd.

"The whole gizmo's my baby," said Singh.

Shepherd closed the case and clicked the locks shut. "Nice piece of kit," he said.

Singh beamed.

"Anything on her?" Shepherd asked Hargrove.

"Not enough," said Hargrove. "We contacted the health club first thing this morning but the admin staff are away until Monday. I decided against calling the centre manager at home because there's an outside chance that he might be a friend and I didn't want to start raising red flags. We did a check on the electoral register for Angie and Angela, but without a surname or address it threw up hundreds of possibilities within twenty miles of the fitness centre."

"So I go in blind? I hate that." Usually when Shepherd went undercover he was fully briefed on his target. He had time to memorise photographs and background details and knew exactly who he was dealing with. But this time all he had was a name. Angie. And a brief description that Hendrickson had given him. Blonde, pretty, late twenties. A bit tarty, a bit flash. "No bra when she exercises, you know the sort," Hendrickson had said. Shepherd didn't. He looked at his watch. "I said I'd be there at five and wait ten minutes."

"Did she sound serious?" asked Hargrove. "I'd hate to think we're on a wild goose chase."

"She sounded worried," said Shepherd. "Easily spooked."

"All we need is the offer," said Hargrove. "We can't give it the full monty, like we did with Hendrickson. Sewell's been on ice long enough. Just get the offer and tell her you need the money by Monday. The offer and the down-payment are all we'll need. I'll get her to roll over."

Shepherd let himself out of the rear door. Singh reached over and pulled it shut.

Shepherd ran down the stairs to the ground floor and pushed open the double doors that led out of the building and on to a side-street. It was a warm afternoon but he'd told her he'd be wearing his leather jacket so he couldn't take it off. The attaché case was in his right hand, the *Financial Times* in the left.

The narrow street opened into Piccadilly Gardens. The flowerbeds were full of yellow and purple blooms. There was a hi-tech fountain to the left, small jets of water that leaped and curved through the air, then splashed into metal-lined holes in the ground. Half a dozen small children rushed around, trying to avoid the water but shrieking with pleasure each time they got drenched.

Shepherd walked round the edge of the square towards the fountain. He looked at his watch. Five o'clock exactly. There was an empty wooden bench a dozen paces from the fountain and he sat down, swung the case on to his knees, and placed the newspaper on top. There was no point in scanning the crowds so he read through the paper's headlines. Not that he cared a jot for the fate of the nation's businesses. He had no shares, and only a few thousand pounds in his one and only bank account. When he had been in the SAS his salary had been the same as a regular paratrooper drew, and a police officer's wasn't much better. No one joined the military or the police to get rich.

"Tony? Tony Nelson?"

Shepherd looked up and squinted in the bright sunlight. He shaded his eyes with the flat of his hand. Slim. Blonde. Pretty. Cute upturned nose. Pale blue eyes. Naturally blonde hair, loose around her face. Lips that curved easily into a smile. "Angie?"

The smile widened, but Shepherd could see nervousness in her eyes and the furrowing of her brow. "Shall we walk and talk?" she suggested.

"I'm okay here," said Shepherd.

"I'm a bit restless, truth be told," she said. "I don't think I can sit still at the moment." She was wearing a loose-cut white linen jacket and Versace denim jeans, with high-heeled open-toe shoes and a Louis Vuitton shoulder-bag. There was a gold Rolex on her left wrist.

"Okay." Shepherd opened the case, put the newspaper inside, and clicked the locks shut. He flicked the combinations to nine-nine-nine, then transferred the case to his left hand as he stood up. "We could go for a coffee, or something stronger." He wanted her inside, away from the noise of the traffic.

"I'm driving," she said, "and caffeine's the last thing I want." She held out her left hand, palm downwards. It was trembling. Shepherd noted the large diamond engagement ring and the thick gold band on her wedding finger. "See?"

"Nervous?"

"Shouldn't I be?" she said. She glanced around, as if she feared that someone might be watching them. "Come on, let's walk."

They moved away from the fountain. Shepherd kept the attaché case between them, but there was a lot of noise: children squealing, engines rumbling, couples arguing, two black teenagers break-dancing next to a boom box. Shepherd doubted that the hidden microphones would pick up much more than background sounds.

"You're not from Manchester, are you?" she asked.

"I move around a lot," said Shepherd. "It doesn't pay to stay too long in one place, doing what I do."

"How much do you charge?" she whispered.

"Didn't Hendrickson tell you?"

"He just said you weren't cheap. And you did what you were paid for."

"I'm not cheap," said Shepherd, "but for what you want, you don't want cheap. You want it done right, without repercussions."

"He said you were professional."

"I am. Thirty thousand pounds. Half when you decide you want to go ahead. Half on completion."

She took a packet of Marlboro menthol out of her bag, put one between her lips and lit it with a gold Dunhill lighter, then offered one to Shepherd. He shook his head.

"How do I know you won't just take the fifteen thousand and disappear?" she asked.

"Because I'm a professional."

"So I have to trust you?"

Shepherd stopped. "I didn't come here to be insulted," he said. "I don't know who you are or where you're from. I'm the one taking things on trust here. For all I know you could be a cop."

"Do look like the filth?" She flicked ash on the ground.

"Cops come in all shapes and sizes," said Shepherd. "Just because you've got a double-D cleavage and fuck-me high heels doesn't mean you haven't walked a beat."

"They're Cs," she said, "and they're real."

"I didn't doubt it for a second," said Shepherd. "And so am I. Do you have thirty thousand pounds?"

She smiled sarcastically. "Not on me, no, but I can get it." She started walking again. Shepherd caught her up.

"When?"

"When do you want it?"

"The sooner you pay me, the sooner I can do the job."

"Just like that?"

"You give me the down-payment. We fix up a time and a place. You establish an alibi. I do the job. You pay me the rest of the money. We go our separate ways."

"No guilt? No recriminations?"

"For me? Or for you?"

Angie smiled tightly. "Oh, don't worry about me," she said. "I won't lose a minute's sleep, believe me."

"Hendrickson said he beats you."

She blew smoke at the sky. "And the rest."

"Why don't you just go to the cops?" said Shepherd. "They don't look kindly on wife-beaters. When he's locked away, you can get a divorce."

"You don't know my husband," she said.

56

"I'm going to have to, though. To get the job done I'll need to know everything about him."

She blew more smoke at the sky, then stopped and looked at him through narrowed eyes. "This is where the whole trust thing comes into play," she said. "Suppose I tell you, and suppose you decide you'll make more money by talking to him?"

"I wouldn't have lasted as long as I have if I'd gone around double-crossing clients," said Shepherd. "Word gets about."

"Can we talk hypothetically?" she said.

"I'd rather talk specifics," said Shepherd.

She dropped what was left of her cigarette and stubbed it out with her toe. "This is such a bad idea," she muttered.

Shepherd said nothing. The approach had to come from her. If he pressed her in any way he risked becoming an *agent provocateur*.

She lit another cigarette. "They can kill you, those things," said Shepherd.

"My husband smokes two packs a day and he's as healthy as a horse," she said, and shivered.

"How did you get so scared of him?" asked Shepherd.

"It's what he does," she said. "He scares people. He makes them so afraid of him that they do what he wants."

"And he scared you into marrying him, did he?"

"He's charming with it," she said. "He can charm the birds down from the bloody trees when he puts his mind to it. I didn't realise then that sociopaths can turn on the charm at will." She took a long pull on the cigarette, then let the smoke seep slowly through her pursed lips. "Have you ever turned a job down?"

"I've had people who couldn't raise the money," said Shepherd.

"I meant, once you've found out who the target is, have you ever refused to go ahead?"

"I don't care who the target is," Shepherd said. "All I care about is getting paid. I'm not a vigilante. I don't care why or who. Just when, where and how much."

"Have gun, will travel?"

"I'm a professional. It's what I do." Shepherd was replaying the conversation in his mind, trying to work out if he had enough. He was pretty sure he hadn't. It was akin to nailing a prostitute. He needed Angie to tell him exactly what she wanted him to do, and how much she was prepared to pay him. And in an ideal world, he needed her to hand him an envelope full of cash. He looked at his watch.

"Have you got somewhere else to go?" asked Angie.

"I get the feeling I'm wasting my time here," he said.

Angie sighed. "I want him dead," she whispered.

She had spoken so softly that Shepherd doubted the microphone had caught it. "And you're prepared to pay me thirty grand to do it?"

She opened her eyes, nodded and started walking again. Shepherd cursed inwardly and hurried after her. Whispers and nods wouldn't count for anything in court.

"Who is it you want me to kill?" he asked, as he drew level with her.

"I told you. My husband."

"I need his name, Angie."

"Charlie. Charlie Kerr."

"I'm going to need a photograph. You can give me one with the down-payment."

She nodded again.

"You can get it?"

Another nod. Shepherd gritted his teeth. The only proof of the conversation would be the recording, and so far, when it came to specifics, he had done all the talking.

"Tell me about him," he said.

"Like what?"

"What he does, where he goes, how he spends his time."

She held the cigarette inches from her mouth and stared at the filter. It was smeared with lipstick. Her eyes remained fixed on it as she answered his question. "A gangster," she hissed. "He's a fucking gangster."

"Literally?"

"Literally. Drugs. Protection. He used to rob building societies, but that was way back when."

Shepherd ran the name through his mental database but drew a blank. It wasn't a name he'd come across before. His memory was virtually perfect so if he'd so much as read the name in a file or heard it mentioned in conversation he would have remembered. "Where do you live?"

Angie gave him their address. Hale Barnes. An affluent suburb of Manchester.

"I guess he doesn't have an office," said Shepherd.

"He owns a nightclub in the north of the city, Aces. His little in-joke. Aces. AC's — Angela and Charlie's. Sweet, huh? Now he uses it to pick up a succession of teenage tramps. And he has the cheek to tell me that if he ever catches me with another guy he'll break my legs."

"He's there every night?"

"He says he is. He tells me to call him on his mobile so he could be anywhere."

"Any associates I should know about?"

"Do you want a list?"

"I need to know who's likely to be in the vicinity. Does he have bodyguards, for instance?"

She dropped the half-smoked cigarette and stamped on it as if she was stamping on her husband's throat. "There's Ray and Eddie. He sees more of them than he does of me, but I wouldn't call them bodyguards. Eddie drives him around."

"Do they carry?"

"Carry?"

"Guns. Are they armed?"

"I don't think so. I've never seen Charlie with a gun."

"You said he deals in drugs. What sort?"

"He doesn't deal, exactly. He imports. Cocaine, mainly."

"From where?"

"He never says. But we've a place in Spain and whenever we go to Morocco he disappears with the guys for hours at a time. He goes to Miami a couple of times a year and that's business, he says." She took out the packet of Marlboro and toyed with it. "You're having second thoughts, aren't you?"

"What do you mean?"

"Now you know it's Charlie Kerr, big-time gangster, I need taking out, you're getting cold feet."

"Says who?"

"I can see it in your face."

Shepherd looked at her, his face blank. "I'm not scared of your husband, no matter who he is."

"I didn't say you were. I said you were having second thoughts. My husband's a dangerous man. Not the sort you'd normally come across, I bet."

"I come across all sorts," said Shepherd.

"We'll see," said Angie. She stopped walking and stared at him. "So you'll do it? You'll kill him for thirty thousand pounds?"

Shepherd held her look. Her eyes were burning with a fierce intensity and she was leaning towards him, so close he could smell her perfume.

"Is that what you want?" he asked.

"Yes," she said. "Yes, it is."

So that was it. Caught on tape. What she wanted doing and how much she was prepared to pay. Conspiracy to commit murder. Life imprisonment. The fact that she was young and pretty and had an abusive husband meant that she'd probably get away with seven years, maybe six. She'd still be pretty when she got out, just not as young. "I'll need a number to call you," he said. "You blocked your mobile when you called me last time."

Angie took out her phone and tapped out his number. His phone rang and he took it out of his pocket. Her number was on the screen. "Got it?" she asked. Shepherd nodded, and she cancelled the call. "You're better texting me than calling," she said. "Every time my phone rings he wants to know who it is."

Shepherd put away his phone. "Worst possible scenario and he wants to know whose number it is, tell him you clipped my car and it's an insurance job. No damage to yours but I lost a tail-light. Use the name I gave you. Tony Nelson."

"That's your real name?"

"It's the name I'm using. That's what you'll call me. And when this is over, Tony Nelson will no longer exist."

"And I'll never see you again?"

"Why would you want to? The reason I can get away with what I do is because no one knows who I am. Even if you decide to go to the police, what can you tell them? That you paid a man called Tony Nelson to kill your husband. A man who doesn't exist."

"Why would I go to the police?"

"Guilt. Remorse."

"There'll be no guilt," she said vehemently. "He's made my life a misery."

"No kids?"

"He can't." She smiled coldly. "Low sperm count, the doctors said, but he won't accept it. Blames me. That's probably why he screws around as much as he does." She wrapped her arms round herself. "More information than you need, right?" she said.

"Anything you tell me helps," said Shepherd. "When can you get the money?"

"I'll have to withdraw it from one of my accounts. That's a problem, isn't it?"

"Because?"

"The cops might check for withdrawals in the days up to . . ." She hesitated, then finished the sentence. ". . . up to the day it happens."

"You just need a cover story," said Shepherd. She was right, of course, Shepherd knew, but he didn't want her dragging things out while she withdrew the cash in dribs and drabs. He already had enough on tape to charge her with conspiracy, but the cash would be proof positive. "Say you were going gambling. Are you a member of any casinos?"

"A couple in Manchester. Charlie likes to play blackjack."

"Perfect," said Shepherd. "Worst comes to the worst, you say you went gambling."

"The casinos keep records," she said.

"So make sure you go a few times before I do the job. In fact, as alibis go, you could do a lot worse than be in a casino — lots of witnesses, and you have a story for where the cash went."

"Do you think the police will suspect me?"

"I'll make it look like a gangland hit," said Shepherd. "The police will put it down to a drugs war and do the bare minimum."

"Good riddance to bad rubbish?"

"Something like that," said Shepherd.

She shivered again. "It's funny, isn't it? It's just another day, the sun is shining, the birds are singing, people are living their lives, and we're talking about murder."

"We have to talk about it. It has to be planned down to the last detail because if we make one mistake they catch us. Can you get the fifteen grand by Monday morning?"

She nodded.

"And pictures. The more the merrier. We'll talk about his schedule once you've paid me the deposit."

They stood in silence for a while. "That's it?" Angie said eventually.

"That's it."

"I feel like I've just made a deal with the devil."

"In a way you have."

She forced a smile, then walked away. Shepherd saw two of Hargrove's men, both dressed casually, moving parallel to her as she left the square. They'd follow her back to her car and would be in radio contact with two motorcyclists who had parked close by. By nightfall they would know all there was to know about Angie Kerr and her gangster husband.

Shepherd headed back to the multi-storey car park, checking reflections in office windows and car wing mirrors to make sure he wasn't being followed. Angie Kerr was the suspicious type and he wouldn't put it past her to have someone tail him. Just as he had satisfied himself that no one was behind him, his mobile rang. "Looking good, Spider," said the superintendent.

"You heard everything?"

"We lost you a few times but we got the gist," said Hargrove. "That plus the fifteen grand will nail it for us. Our guys are on her tail as we speak."

"I'm on my way back now," said Shepherd.

"Don't bother. We're in a side-street overlooking the square — we'll pick you up. Where are you?"

Shepherd gave him directions, and five minutes later the Transit pulled up. Shepherd climbed into the back. Singh pulled the attaché case out of his hands. The superintendent took a swig of Evian water. "We didn't get much from the directional microphones but the case worked a treat."

"Of course it did," said Singh, caressing it as if it were a favourite cat.

Shepherd grinned at his enthusiasm and patted him on the back. "We're done?" he asked.

"Absolutely," said Hargrove.

Shepherd climbed out of the van. He took a circuitous route to the warehouse conversion and used his swipe card to open the outer door. His flat was on the second floor. He kept nothing of himself in it. If anyone should become suspicious of Tony Nelson, they could search it for hours and never find a clue as to his real identity. The utility bills were in Nelson's name, paid for by direct debit from a bank account that would stand up to any scrutiny. The flat had been decorated and furnished by the landlord: white walls, light oak floors, pine furniture ordered from the Habitat catalogue. Shepherd took a bottle of lager from the stainless-steel fridge in the kitchen and sat down on the white canvas square-armed sofa in front of the television.

He looked at the clock on top of the empty bookcase. Six thirty. He'd finish the beer, have a shower, then phone Liam. He took the two mobiles from his jacket pocket and put them on the glass-topped coffee-table. He sipped his lager. If all went to plan he'd be back in London on Monday afternoon. Hargrove hadn't mentioned a new assignment so there was a chance that he could take a few days off. It would give him time to fix up an au pair and get the house ready for Liam's return. He took a drink from the bottle. He might even make a start on clearing out Sue's things. It was about time.

He lay back on the sofa and rested the bottle on his stomach. It had been a hell of a day. Driving from Manchester to Hereford and back, then straight into the Angie Kerr sting. One hell of a day.

Keith Rose couldn't help smiling as he drove west on the M25. Here he was, fifteen years into a career with the Metropolitan Police, two awards for bravery on the living-room wall, and he had ten kilos of heroin in the boot of his car on the way to his very own drugs deal. "Funny old world," he whispered.

He'd thought long and hard about what he should do with the heroin they'd taken from the crack house in Harlesden. In a perfect world he'd have dumped the polythene-wrapped packages in the nearest landfill or lake, but the world wasn't perfect and ten kilos of grade-four heroin was worth more than three-quarters of a million pounds on the street. Not that he would get anywhere near that amount. Three-quarters of a million was what the drug was worth when it was cut with whatever the dealers had to hand and sold on to addicts in single-dose wraps. The Yardies had probably paid about three hundred grand for it. The only way Rose could get that sort of money for the heroin was if he were to sell it on to street dealers and that was too much of a risk. The only way to sell it safely was to pass it on to an importer at a price below the cost of bringing it into the country. It was a simple matter of economics. A street dealer had to pay between twenty and thirty thousand pounds a kilo. An importer bringing it in from the Continent would pay half that. So, to an importer in the UK, the heroin in Rose's boot was worth a maximum of fifteen thousand pounds a kilo. And it would have to be even cheaper than that for them to risk doing business with someone they didn't know.

The problem for Rose was that most of the major drugs importers were under surveillance by the Drugs Squad or MI5. And the smart ones were so cagey that they would only do business with people they knew. Which meant that Rose would be putting his career, if not his life, on the line for a hundred and fifty grand at best. And he had to split that two ways. Seventy-five grand wasn't much in the grand scheme of things. Two years' salary, give or take. Which meant plan B: take the drugs to Ireland. Irish prices were generally twenty or thirty per cent higher than in Britain — a reflection of the Celtic Tiger's healthy economy and the fact that most of the drugs sold on there were brought from England — and the Garda Siochana, the Irish police force, was about as efficient as the Keystone Cops on a bad day. Also there was no real equivalent of MI5. The Irish Defence Forces Military Intelligence G2 Branch and the Garda's Special Branch C3 Section concentrated on terrorism and counter-intelligence, so drugs were left to the boys in blue.

Half an hour on the Police National Computer was all it had taken for Rose to compile a list of the top three drug barons in the Irish Republic with their addresses. All had done business at one time or another with an Irish crime family in North London and were known to the Drugs Squad. All were put under surveillance whenever they set foot on British soil, but they weren't stupid: they rarely visited the UK and even avoided stopovers at Heathrow *en route* to their villas in Spain.

They were ex-directory, but Rose's method of contacting them had been simplicity itself. He had sent a one-ounce package of his heroin by regular mail to each man, with a laser-printed note saying he had ten kilos for sale at twenty thousand euros a kilo, delivery in Ireland, and the number of a pay-as-you-go mobile that he'd bought in a shop on the Edgware Road. Two had replied. One had sent a text message in two words, one of which was an obscenity. The other had phoned late at night and started by telling Rose of all the terrible things that would happen to him if he was messing them around. Then he said they wanted to see the gear. He promised to call when he was in Dublin and the man had given him a mobile number. Game on. You didn't have to be especially clever to be a drugs dealer, just careful. And, as gamekeeper-turned-poacher, Keith Rose knew how careful to be.

The heroin they'd taken from the Harlesden flat was double-wrapped in thick polythene so a drugs dog wouldn't so much as wag its tail if it stumbled across it, but Rose knew that the chances of him being checked when he drove his car off the ferry from Holyhead to Dublin were next to zero. And, in the unlikely event that he was stopped, he'd produce his warrant card before they even thought about giving his car the once-over. If plan B went as well as he expected, he'd be back in London with two hundred thousand euros within twenty-four hours. Having taken the opportunity to down a couple of pints of the genuine black stuff.

A band was playing, far off in the distance. Shepherd groaned and opened his eyes. There was a bitter taste in his mouth. One of his mobiles was ringing. He groped for it. Hargrove's phone. He swung his feet off the sofa and took the call. "What's wrong?" he asked.

"Nothing, but we need to meet tomorrow," said the superintendent. "Charlie Kerr's a bit out of the ordinary. I have to run some things by you before Monday."

Shepherd rubbed a hand over his face. The lager bottle lay on its side by one of the sofa legs. He must have fallen asleep with it in his hand. "Fine. Where and when?"

"I'll let you have a lie-in," said Hargrove. "Let's say three o'clock. There's a rugby field in Trafford by a pub called the Golden Fleece."

"I'll be there. Everything's okay, right?" He looked out of the floor-to-ceiling window that took up most of the left-hand side of the apartment. It was dark outside. A full moon hung in the pitch black sky, the night so clear that he could see the craters that pockmarked its surface.

"Everything's fine. I'll brief you tomorrow."

Shepherd cut the connection and stared at the phone. It was half past eleven. He cursed. He dialled Moira's number and groaned inwardly when Tom answered the phone. He apologised for phoning so late.

"It's almost midnight," Tom groaned.

"I promised to call Liam before he went to sleep."

"He's been in bed for hours."

Shepherd apologised again, but before he'd finished Moira had taken the phone from her husband. "Daniel, this isn't good enough, it really isn't."

"I fell asleep," said Shepherd, lamely.

"And your son cried himself to sleep," said Moira. "I let him stay up until ten and that's an hour past his weekend bedtime. You promised, Daniel, and you shouldn't make promises you can't keep."

"It wasn't a question of not keeping a promise," said Shepherd. "I fell asleep, that's all. It wasn't deliberate."

70

"Whatever, he's asleep now. Call again tomorrow. And think of how much your thoughtlessness has hurt him."

She cut the connection. Shepherd lay back on the sofa and stared up at the ceiling. His mother-in-law was right. He'd let his son down yet again. His stomach churned and he felt like throwing up. He'd cut short his promised visit, he'd fallen asleep when he'd promised to phone and he'd left his son in storage, like unwanted furniture. If there had been a prize for worst father of the year, he'd win it. He made a silent promise to himself: as soon as the Angie Kerr job was tucked away, he'd make it up to Liam. He'd show his son just how good a father he could be.

Rose spent two hours driving around the north of Dublin looking for a suitable place to hand over the drugs, then spent the night in a cheap bed-and-breakfast. Before he went to sleep he phoned his wife and told her he was on a surveillance operation at Gatwick Airport and that he loved her. He spent five minutes talking to his daughter, then he phoned the Irish mobile number and told the man who answered that he would show him the heroin at eleven o'clock in the morning. He had the venue already planned and the Irishman didn't argue. After making the second call he slept a dreamless sleep.

Breakfast was a full Irish — eggs, bacon, sausage, white pudding, black pudding, potato scone, fried bread — and Rose cleared his plate before he drove to the airport. He left his car in the short-term car park and walked to the arrivals terminal where he picked up the keys to a rental. He drove it to the short-term car park, and when he was sure he wasn't being watched he switched the drugs and a cloth-wrapped bundle to the new car, then drove out of the airport whistling to himself.

The place he'd chosen for the handover was the car park of a pub on the edge of a rough housing scheme — blocks of flats with broken windows and graffiti, shopfronts protected by roll-down metal shutters. It didn't look the sort of place that was regularly visited by the Garda, and he doubted that any of the locals would be members of a Neighbourhood Watch scheme. There were no CCTV cameras and the nearest police station was five miles away. According to the Police National Computer, it was slap in the middle of the area controlled by the gang that was going to buy the heroin. Rose had thought they'd be more relaxed on their home turf, less likely to be trigger happy.

He arrived half an hour before the time he'd told the Irishman. He parked with the front of his car facing the road and slid the cloth-wrapped bundle between his legs. He was wearing sunglasses and leather gloves, with a baseball cap pulled down over his face. A ten-year-old Mercedes pulled into the car park at a quarter to eleven. There were four men in it and Rose recognised two of the faces from the computer files. They were enforcers. The man who ran the gang was keeping his distance, but Rose had expected as much. He flashed his headlights and the Mercedes rolled slowly across the car park.

72

Rose stayed in his car. The rear doors of the Mercedes opened and two men walked towards him. They wore long coats that flapped in the wind, and had their hands in the pockets. Rose wound down the window. "Can you guys do me a favour and stop where you are?" he called.

The two men halted, a dozen paces from the car. "Have youse got the gear?" said the taller of the two. Six feet two, maybe, with wide shoulders hunched against the wind that blew between the blocks of flats. His nose was almost flattened against his face. A boxer's nose.

"Have you got the money?"

"We're gonna have to see the gear before youse gets to see the cash."

"I've no problem with that, but just so we know where we stand, what are you carrying?"

The boxer frowned. "What?"

Rose smiled patiently. "What sort of weaponry have you got under your coats? I'm guessing handguns or a sawn-off at most." He raised the gun he was holding, just enough so that they could see what it was. "I've got an Ingram MAC 10, which fires eleven hundred rounds per minute and holds thirty in the magazine so I don't want you making me nervous — if my trigger finger gets jumpy I could accidentally empty the whole clip in less time than you could say . . . well, before you could open your mouth, actually." He glanced at the weapon in his hand. "Recoil-operated, select-fire submachine-gun, fires from an open bolt. Nice, but not especially accurate beyond twenty-five metres. And in case you're wondering, yes, it would shoot right through the panel of this door. And with the silencer, not too many people would hear it. Not that they'd give a shit around here anyway."

The two men looked at each other, then back at Rose, whose smile widened. "I'm not trying to pull a fast one on you," he added. "I just want us to know where we all stand. Let's see what you've got."

The boxer slid his right hand out of his pocket. An automatic, probably a Colt. The other pulled back his coat: a Kalashnikov assault rifle with a folding stock hung from a nylon sling.

"Nice," said Rose. The file had mentioned the gang's links to former paramilitaries so the Kalashnikov wasn't a surprise. "So, if the shit does hit the proverbial, it's going to get very noisy and very messy. I'm just here to sell the gear and get back over the water. It's good stuff, and it's pure as the driven, so you're getting a hell of a good deal."

"Youse could be the cops," said the boxer.

"I could be, but my accent alone should let you know that I'm not working for the Garda. And the fact that I'm cradling a MAC 10 in my hot little hands sort of puts paid to any undercover police operation, doesn't it?"

The boxer nodded slowly. "So now what do we do?"

"I show you the gear. You show me the money. When we're both happy, we exchange and go our separate ways."

"Where is it?"

"The boot. Where's the money?"

74

"Back seat."

"Okay. Why don't you get into the seat here next to me while your mate with the heavy artillery checks the gear?"

"Youse wouldn't have an itchy trigger finger, would you?"

"I know what I'm doing," said Rose.

The boxer sighed, opened the passenger door and climbed in. He had his gun in his lap, the barrel pointing at the dash-board. Rose popped open the boot and watched in his rear-view mirror as the guy with the Kalashnikov went to the back of the car.

"Youse came alone?" mused the boxer.

"I just want to sell the merchandise," said Rose. "I don't want to start a gang war. I thought if I turned up mob-handed you'd get jumpy and that's the last thing we need."

"Where did youse get it from?"

Rose tapped the side of his nose with a forefinger. "Need to know," he said.

The guy with the Kalashnikov bent down and disappeared from Rose's view. Rose was relaxed, but he kept his finger on the trigger.

"Youse look like a cop."

"Yeah, everyone says that."

"Except you're as nervous as a cat in a kennel right now, which you wouldn't be if youse had back-up."

"I've no back-up. Trust me on that. But I do have a gun that can fire eleven hundred bullets a second so tell your mate to get a move on, will you?"

The boxer gave him a curt nod and shouted something in Gaelic to his colleague.

"English," said Rose. "If you don't mind."

"How does it look, Kieran?" shouted the boxer.

Rose took his eyes off the rear-view mirror and checked out the Mercedes. The driver had his hands on the steering-wheel. The front passenger was sitting stony-faced, chewing gum.

"Looks good," said Kieran. He walked to the passenger side of Rose's car. "Ten kilos. Good stuff. The man walks the walk."

"So far so good," said the boxer. "Now, how do youse want to play it?"

"You and I walk over to your car and check the money. Kieran stays in front of us and keeps his hands away from the Kalashnikov."

The boxer climbed slowly out of the car. Rose did the same, sliding the MAC 10 under his jacket as he closed the door. Kieran walked to the Mercedes, his long coat flapping behind him. Rose accompanied the boxer, his finger still on the MAC 10 trigger. He scanned the windows of the flats overlooking the car park but no one was watching. Two plump teenage girls pushed prams away from the block entrance, smoking and swearing.

They reached the Mercedes and Kieran pulled open the rear doors. There were two black Adidas gym bags on the back seat. He pulled them out and swung them on to the boot.

"Watch the paintwork, will youse?" snarled the boxer.

Kieran unzipped one of the bags and stepped to the side. He kept his hands free, a faint smile on his face. Rose peered inside the bag. It was full of bundles of fifty-euro notes. He pulled one out at random and flicked through it. Then he sniffed it.

The boxer laughed. "Think we printed them ourselves?"

Rose put back the bundle and unzipped the second bag. He checked another bundle at random. It seemed genuine, and all the notes were used. If they had been counterfeit they would all have been new, Rose thought. He stepped back from the car. "Everything looks cool," he said.

"Youse don't want to count it?"

"I trust you," said Rose, deadpan. "Plus, you rip me off for a few grand, so what? I didn't see you weighing the gear to see if I'm a few ounces short. It's all based on trust at the end of the day. Trust and artillery."

"Trust and artillery," said the boxer. "I like that."

"Kieran can put the bags in my boot, and take the gear."

The boxer nodded at Kieran, who transferred the money and carried the heroin to the boot of the Mercedes and slammed it shut.

Rose backed towards his car, ready to swing out the MAC 10 at the first sign of a double-cross, but Kieran slid into the back seat of the Mercedes. "It's been a pleasure doing business with youse," said the boxer, throwing Rose an ironic salute. "Have a safe trip home." He got into the back of the car, slammed the door and the vehicle rolled slowly out of the car park.

Rose watched as it drove away, white plumes feathering from the exhaust. His heart was hammering in his chest but he wanted to throw back his head and howl in triumph. He'd done it. He'd bloody well done it.

The bad guy popped his head up from behind a crate and Liam fired twice with the shotgun. The man's skull exploded with a satisfying pop and brains splattered over the wall behind him. Two more bad guys appeared from behind a row of oil barrels, brandishing axes. Liam reloaded smoothly and blew them away.

"Don't those things carry parental warnings?" asked Moira. She was carrying a tray with a glass of orange juice and some fig rolls on it.

"Parents don't play video games, Gran," said Liam, his eyes never leaving the screen. His thumbs flashed over the handset and two more villains slumped to the ground.

"You know what I mean, young man. Don't be cheeky," she admonished him, as she placed the tray on the coffee-table.

"Sorry, Gran," said Liam. He reloaded and waited for a bad guy to appear at the top of the stairs, then shot him in the chest.

Moira sat down on the sofa next to Liam. "Did your father buy you that?"

"Nah, he got me two racing games. I got this with my pocket money."

"An hour we said, remember? An hour a day."

"Okay."

"Would you mind switching it off and talking to me?"

"Gran . . ."

"I'd like to talk to you."

Liam sighed and switched off the console. He reached for his orange juice and gulped it down.

"You know your granddad and I love having you here," she said.

Liam wiped his mouth on the back of his hand.

"And you're happy at school?"

"It's okay."

"But it's a good school, isn't it? And there's a better mix of children in your class. Not as many . . . well, you know what I mean, don't you? It's not like London."

"The teachers are nice," said Liam, "and I like walking to school."

"There you are, then," said Moira. "You like your room here, too, don't you?"

Liam nodded, and bit into a biscuit.

"Your granddad and I were thinking that perhaps you'd like to stay with us."

Liam frowned. "For ever?"

"Not necessarily, no," said Moira, hurriedly. "But your father's very busy at work, you know that. And remember what happened last night. He said he'd phone but he didn't. He isn't very reliable, so Granddad and I think you might be better off here with us."

"Is this Dad's idea?" asked Liam. Tears sprang to his eyes.

Moira put her arm round his shoulders. "No, it's not. He's still talking about you going to London to be with him. But it's going to be difficult, and it might be better for him if you stayed here."

Liam wiped his eyes on his sleeve. "It isn't fair."

"What do you mean?" asked Moira.

"It's like you're all trying to force me to do something I don't want to do."

"No one's trying to force you to do anything, Liam."

"Dad never asked me if I wanted to come and stay here. He just dumped me."

"Now you're being silly."

"He doesn't want me. That's why he left me here and it's why he didn't call."

"He does want you, Liam, of course he does. We want you, too — and we all want what's best for you."

"I want to be with my mum!"

"Liam!" Moira protested. "Calm down."

"I don't want to! I wish I was with Mum right now. I wish I was dead like her!"

Liam rushed out of the room, knocking over his glass with what remained of the juice.

Tom came in from the garden as Moira was dabbing at the carpet with a damp cloth. "I heard shouting, what's wrong?"

Moira shook her head. "Nothing," she said. "Nothing's wrong."

Even from the far side of the field Shepherd could hear the crunch of bone against bone as the two men collided at full pelt. The rugby ball bounced into touch

80

and the two men helped each other up, grins on their mud-splattered faces.

Hargrove was sitting on a wooden bench outside the pub, which overlooked the rugby pitch. Shepherd sat down next to him, wearing his black leather jacket and blue jeans. He hadn't shaved. The superintendent was immaculately dressed as always, in a pristine blue blazer, grey flannels and gleaming brogues. He sipped his shandy. "Can I get you a drink, Spider?"

"I'm okay," said Shepherd. He stretched out his legs and sighed.

"Not a rugby player, are you?" asked the superintendent.

"Not really, no."

"Too many rules?" said Hargrove.

"Something like that."

"I'm a cricket man myself," said Hargrove. "Never understood why it isn't played all year round."

"The weather, maybe," said Shepherd.

"The thing I like about it is that it's a team game," said Hargrove, ignoring Shepherd's comment. "But at the same time you function as an individual. When you're batting, it's all down to you. No back-up, no support. When you're fielding, you're working as a team."

Play restarted on the pitch, but after a few seconds there was another juddering crunch, three players went down and the referee blew his whistle.

"You're a runner, right?" asked Hargrove.

"It's a way of keeping fit," Shepherd said. "I don't run for fun."

"What do you do for fun?"

Shepherd ran a hand through his unkempt hair. It was a good question. He used to go to the cinema and for long walks. He used to eat, drink and make merry. But that was before Sue had died. He still tried to have fun with Liam, but more out of parental duty than from the desire to enjoy himself. He'd kick a football with his son, play video games and take him to matches, but no matter how much he loved Liam, the boy was an ever-present reminder of the wife he'd lost. Fun hadn't been a major part of his life in recent months.

Hargrove took a sip of his shandy. "Charlie Kerr," he said. "We've opened a real can of worms."

Shepherd looked across at him. "He's known?"

Hargrove smiled. "Oh, yes. Not Premier Division yet, but on the way. Greater Manchester Drugs Squad have been on to him for a while. The Firm and the Church have been keeping a watching brief."

The Firm: MI5. It had been tasked with targeting big-time drugs-dealers and career criminals after the fall of the Soviet Union and the IRA's decision to start peace talks had left the Security Service with little to do. And the Church: Customs and Excise.

"Why just a watching brief?" asked Shepherd.

"Kerr's one of the smart ones. Doesn't go near the gear, doesn't touch the cash. It's a question of resources. It would cost millions to put him away. They've been hoping that eventually he'll deal with someone they've turned."

Hargrove took a CD Rom in a plastic case from his blazer pocket and handed it to Shepherd. "Those are

82

the files on him. Surveillance pictures, known associates, all the intel we have."

Shepherd pocketed the disk. He knew that the nature of the investigation was about to change, but he waited for the superintendent to continue. Spectators cheered as a bald, burly player ran a good fifty yards down the pitch and hurled himself between the posts. The referee's whistle blew long and hard.

"He runs a sideline in protection rackets but that's a hangover from his old days. Now he leaves that pretty much up to one of his heavies, Eddie Anderson. His nightclubs are busy, but they're money-laundering set-ups more than anything."

And a source of eager young girls, Angie had said. The woman scorned. The woman whose life was about to change for ever, and not for the better, thought Shepherd.

"Kerr's father was an old-school villain, Billy Kerr. Armed robber who got involved in the drugs trade in the late eighties. Got shot on the Costa del Crime a few years back. Professional hit, but there was never anyone in the frame for it."

"So Charlie's following in his father's footsteps?"

"Seems that way. But he's self-made. He was only a teenager when his dad was killed. He was living with his mother. She and Kerr had separated not long after he was born and Kerr had almost no hand in raising him. Must have been in his genes." Play started again on the pitch. "This could be a godsend, Spider."

"Maybe," said Shepherd.

"We've got her on tape, conspiracy to murder. If she turns up with the cash tomorrow, that's the icing on the cake. If we offer her a way out, there's a good chance she'll take it."

"She's scared to death of him."

"She doesn't have a choice," said Hargrove. "No real choice, anyway. If she goes down he'll know exactly what she was planning. He might decide that life behind bars is punishment enough, but a guy with his resources can have someone killed in prison just as easily as on the outside. If she gives evidence against him, though, he'll be the one behind bars."

"Yeah, but she's not stupid. She'll know that just because he's banged up doesn't mean he can't have her killed," said Shepherd.

"So she's damned if she does and damned if she doesn't," said Hargrove. "At least we can offer her protection. A new identity. The works."

"Plus she gets to keep his money?"

"Anything that's not confiscated as the proceeds of crime," agreed Hargrove. "That's got to sound more attractive than life behind bars."

Shepherd stretched out his legs. If it had been a simple matter of offering Angie Kerr the choice of two evils, there would have been no need to give him the files on her husband. Hargrove obviously wanted him to make the approach.

"We'll only get one shot," said Shepherd. "If she turns us down, Kerr will know we're on to him and go to ground."

"Which means we're no worse off than we are now," said Hargrove.

"And we've no idea how much she knows about her husband's operation."

"Exactly," said Hargrove.

"Which is where I come in?"

Hargrove looked at Shepherd. "Are you okay about this?"

"It's messy," said Shepherd, "getting close to the wife to get to the husband."

"No one's asking you to get into bed with her, Spider," said the superintendent. "Just find out how much she knows about his business. It could be that he keeps her in the dark, in which case she's no use to us."

"And we charge her with conspiracy anyway? Even though there's a good chance he'll have her killed?"

"She's the one who's hired a killer. We can't let her walk just because her husband's a villain."

"A drugs baron who knocks her around, who terrorises her and screws anything in a short skirt?"

The superintendent raised an eyebrow quizzically. "You're not going soft on me, are you?"

"It's not about being soft. It's about justice. You're saying that if we can't put him away, even though he's a grade-A villain, we'll make do with wifey."

"If you feel that strongly about it, make sure there's enough to put him away. And if wifey helps, wifey walks. Look, there's a whole series of imponderables we have to nail down. We have to find out how much she knows about Kerr's wrong-doing, then see if she's prepared to give evidence against him — as his wife she's entitled to refuse. And if she *is* prepared to help, we'll need evidence to back it up."

"What about Sewell?" asked Shepherd. "He's not going to be happy about being kept under wraps."

"Leave Sewell to me."

"What about resources?"

"Whatever we need. Greater Manchester Police will be footing the bill."

And taking the credit if we bring Kerr down, thought Shepherd, ruefully. It was always that way. Hargrove's undercover unit had a roving brief: forces around the country put in a request to the Home Office whenever they needed the unit's services, and Hargrove reported to the Home Secretary. The members of the unit never took credit for their successes and never appeared in court. They simply amassed the evidence, put the case together and moved on. Taking credit would mean blowing their cover, and the last thing an undercover policeman needed was publicity.

Shepherd stood up. "I'll make a call, tell her I need more info."

"And get the deposit. We need it on video."

Shepherd walked away, hands in his pockets. He didn't look back, but could feel Hargrove watching him. He cursed under his breath. The Angie Kerr job wasn't going to be as cut and dried as he'd hoped, and every day in Manchester was a day away from his son.

Rose drove back to the airport and parked the rental car next to his own vehicle. He checked that no one was around, then transferred the MAC 10 to the boot of his car. Customs checks into the UK were as cursory as those into Ireland so he had no qualms about taking it back to London.

He took the rental back to its drop-off point, then retrieved his own car and drove it to the ferry terminal. He had an hour's wait before boarding. His mobile rang as he was getting out of his car. "It's good gear you've sold us," said a voice. A guttural Irish accent. Not the boxer and not the man to whom Rose had spoken on the phone before.

"I told you so," said Rose. He headed up the metal stairway to the main deck.

"And your price was fair. Would you be able to get us more?"

"Maybe," said Rose.

"You know where we are," said the man.

"Yes," said Rose. He cut the connection and walked up on to the deck. He watched as the remaining cars drove on to the ferry. As they left Dublin port and headed across the Irish Sea, he took the Sim card out of the phone and flicked it out over the waves.

Shepherd made himself a cup of coffee, then slotted the CD into his laptop. The information on the disk was password protected and Shepherd keyed in the eight-digit number that would give him access. It was one of the perks of having a near-photographic memory: he never had to remember a password or phone number.

The files were split into three sections: MI5, Customs and Excise, and the Greater Manchester

Police Drugs Squad. The MI5 file was the largest but contained little intelligence. It consisted mainly of copies of wire-tap authorisations and transcripts of conversations that Charlie Kerr had made over the previous eighteen months, none of which appeared to have had anything to do with drugs. Hargrove had been right: the Security Service had nothing more than a watching brief, and if all they were doing was monitoring his phone traffic then they didn't stand a chance of getting anything on him. A criminal of Kerr's calibre would hardly start organising cocaine shipments by phone, even using pay-as-you-go mobiles. MI5 had access to the Echelon eavesdropping system, a joint venture between the United States, Great Britain and New Zealand, which allowed for the world-wide monitoring of all phone and email conversations. It was also equipped with voice-recognition so accurate it could identify a target from among millions of conversations. But listening to Kerr and catching him in the act of setting up a major drugs deal were two different things. The only way to get him would be to use an undercover agent, or persuade a family member or associate to inform on him.

The Customs and Excise file was a tenth the size of MI5's, but it contained surveillance photographs of Charlie and Angie arriving at Heathrow airport and leaving Málaga airport. Kerr was balding, a big man with broad shoulders. He was a head taller than Angie and in several of the photographs he had an arm round her as if he wanted to establish ownership. There were also photographs of them at their villa in Spain, and at various restaurants with several Costa del Crime faces. There was nothing wrong with the Kerrs wining and dining with major criminals, of course, drinking Dom Pérignon and tipping with fifty-euro notes. It wasn't a criminal offence to associate with villains. Yet. There were reports of Kerr's trips to the United States, Drug Enforcement Administration and FBI reports on whom he had met in Miami. There was no information on any pending US investigations in the file, so either they weren't telling the Church or the Church was playing Secret Squirrel with its overseas information.

In theory, the intelligence services, Customs and the police were supposed to co-operate on major cases, but in practice they guarded their turf jealously. There was a lot of resentment on behalf of the police and Customs that MI5 had moved into anti-drugs work. The Security Service had shown little interest in catching drugs barons until their own jobs were on the line and now whenever they were involved in a major seizure their press-relations people went into overdrive, trumpeting every drugs bust as a major victory for MI5. Also the spies were able to operate in decidedly grey areas, while the police had to follow the Police and Criminal Evidence Act to the letter. And while Customs had to fight for every penny of its budget, it seemed that MI5 had a blank cheque book to play with.

Customs had tried using an undercover agent to infiltrate Kerr's circle in Marbella, but two weeks into the investigation he'd been sussed and had made a rapid withdrawal. He was only identified by his cover name in the reports he'd filed. There was nothing in them that would have resulted in charges: he had met with Kerr three times in various nightclubs but the only conversations they'd had were social chit-chat. According to the agent, Charlie Kerr was notoriously unfaithful to his wife, and on the nights he was out without her he usually ended up bedding one pretty girl or another, although he was always back in his villa by dawn. The agent had suggested sending in a pretty female undercover agent but the head of Drugs Operations had vetoed a honey trap. Charlie Kerr was too dangerous: a borderline psychopath.

The Marbella operation had been aborted one night after the agent had been out in a group with two of Kerr's associates, Ray Wates and Eddie Anderson — the men Angie had talked about. They'd sat on either side of the agent and plied him with drink. When Charlie had left with a young Spanish waitress they'd suggested they move on to another club. The agent had had a bad feeling about the way the men were smiling at him. He'd pretended to be more drunk than he was and said he had to go to the bathroom. He'd broken a window, climbed down a drainpipe and caught a plane back to London. Shepherd understood the man's decision. Sometimes you had to go with your instincts. If a situation felt wrong it probably was.

The police file contained more hard intelligence than those of MI5 and the Church put together. In his mid-twenties Charlie Kerr had been charged with armed robbery three times. Each time the case had collapsed before it had got to court. Witnesses were intimidated or paid off; evidence mysteriously disap-peared. In one case CCTV footage was wiped in police custody. Kerr was thought to have been responsible for more than two dozen building-society and bank robberies over a five-year period, netting, according to police estimates, close to a quarter of a million pounds. Sometimes he worked alone, sometimes with a partner, and he hadn't served a day in prison. He had a criminal record, though, for an assault on his eighteenth birthday: he'd bitten the ear off a middle-aged man in a pub and had been given a year's probation after three witnesses swore that he had been provoked. It was the only time he had been in court but it meant that his fingerprints, teeth impressions and DNA were in the system.

Kerr had channelled the profits from the robberies into drugs but, because of his record, he took more care than most to cover his tracks. He was paranoid about phones and did virtually all his business outdoors, face to face. There were hundreds of surveillance photographs in his police file, but no hard evidence of drugs-dealing. The police had looked into Kerr's nightclubs, and while they were sure he was using them to launder his drugs profits, they hadn't been able to prove it. There were also rumours that his men were extorting money from other nightclubs in the Manchester area, but only one owner had ever complained officially — his club had burned down the next day and he left the city shortly afterwards.

Shepherd read the file with a heavy heart. It was always the really nasty pieces of work who got away with it. Petty thieves, small-time pimps, street-corner drugs-dealers were rounded up, tried and packed off to prison. But the real villains were virtually untouchable. They surrounded themselves with physical and legal protection, intimidated or bought their way out of trouble, and caused untold misery to the population at large. Time and again, in police and Customs files he saw appeals for major investigations turned down because the resources weren't available: it was too expensive to put together a case that was guaranteed to result in a conviction. And the powers-that-be couldn't afford to move against the likes of Kerr without a guarantee of success. If the case collapsed they would look incompetent, so it was easier, and safer, not to try.

The Drugs Squad had tried working its way up the chain, picking up dealers on the street with balloons of heroin in their mouths, then using the threat of a jail sentence to get them to roll over on their supplier. They'd had some success, putting two major wholesalers away, but they couldn't get near Kerr or his associates. People were simply too scared to give evidence against him.

Shepherd sat back and ran his hands through his hair. What about Angie? She, more than anyone, must know what her husband was capable of. Would she be prepared to go into the witness box and tell a court how he brought hundreds of kilos of heroin and cocaine into the country? And what about afterwards? If the Crown could find a non-corruptible jury and a judge who couldn't be paid off or intimidated, and if Charlie Kerr was sent down for ten or fifteen years, what would happen to her? A lifetime in witness protection? Or a bullet in the head from the contract killer that Kerr would surely put on her trail to show the world that you never went up against Charlie Kerr?

Angie Kerr's life as she knew it was about to end. If she refused to help the police she'd go to prison on conspiracy to murder. If she co-operated, she'd be in hiding for the rest of her life. And Shepherd knew that anyone could be found eventually, providing you had time and money. And Charlie Kerr had plenty of both.

Roger Sewell finished drying himself and tried to pull on the hotel robe. It would barely have fitted a man half his size and he couldn't get it across his shoulders. He swore and flung it away from him. The hotel room was eight paces from door to window, and six from the bed's headboard to the TV cabinet. Sewell knew this because he had spent the best part of the day pacing up and down, cursing Larry Hendrickson for wanting him dead, and the police for keeping him locked in a room the size of a cell. He'd only agreed to co-operate in the first place because he wanted to see Hendrickson behind bars, but right now Hendrickson was probably wining and dining a couple of escort girls in one of Manchester's top clubs.

Sewell glared at the half-eaten cheeseburger and chips on the dressing-table. He hadn't stayed in anything below four stars since his teenage years. The food was terrible and they didn't have a bottle of wine for more than twenty pounds. Sewell wouldn't ask a dog to live in the place, but the cops seemed to think it was acceptable to ask him to stay put for another two days. And Sewell hadn't been fooled by the smooth-talking Superintendent Hargrove. Something had obviously gone wrong and they wanted to keep him on ice until they'd covered their arses. He didn't believe Hargrove's story about there being another contract. They'd screwed up their investigation and Sewell was paying the price.

He wrapped a towel around his waist, picked up the remote control and flicked through the TV channels. Nothing but soap operas and quiz shows. There were at least three policemen downstairs so there was no way he could leave the hotel. When they'd first told him about Hendrickson's plan, they'd asked him not to tell anyone else, not even his family. Not that Sewell had much in the way of family. A mother in a nursing-home in North Wales, a sister who'd got halfway round the world during her gap year, married an Australian and never come home, and a couple of elderly aunts. If Sewell died, the only people at his funeral would be business acquaintances — he had fewer friends than he had relatives. He had followed instructions and no one knew where he was. But that meant he didn't know what Hendrickson was doing with the company, or its money. If Hendrickson was sure he'd got away with murdering Sewell, he wouldn't hurry to take over the company. He would probably wait a few days before he reported him missing, then bring in his own man as co-signatory on the bank accounts and sell the company. He had been pestering Sewell to sell for the past three years but he had always refused. Sewell owned seventy per cent of the shares so there was no way Hendrickson could sell without his agreement. Or death.

Everything depended on Hendrickson being convinced that no one suspected he had murdered his partner. If Hendrickson knew the police were closing in on him, he'd probably empty the bank accounts and make a run for it. Some offshore accounts could be accessed 24/7, and it wouldn't take more than a few phone calls to transfer around half a million pounds out of the business. If Hendrickson realised the police were on to him, that would be more than enough running-away money.

Sewell picked up the hotel phone and pressed nine for an outside line. He smiled as he got a dial tone. He was fed up to the back teeth of following instructions. He could call his lawyer, John Garden, and at least check up on the bank accounts to see if Hendrickson had been making unexpected withdrawals. A few minutes on the phone would either put his mind at rest or confirm his worst fears. Garden had been on Sewell's payroll for almost ten years and he trusted him as much as he trusted anyone.

Sewell tapped out the number of his lawyer, but before he'd hit the fifth digit a brusque voice was on the line: "Sir, who are you trying to call?"

"That's none of your business," said Sewell.

"I've been instructed not to let you make any phone calls," said the man.

Sewell recognised the voice of the sergeant who'd brought him to the hotel in the first place. "I want my laptop brought in, and I need cash."

"No visitors, sir. Those are my orders."

"You tell me I can order food to be brought in, but I have to use cash and I'm down to my last twenty quid."

"I'll speak to the superintendent," said the sergeant.

"I've had enough of this," said Sewell. "I'm co-operating, I'm doing everything you ask — all I want is my laptop and some cash."

"Like I said, sir, I'll speak to the superintendent."

"I want to talk to my lawyer," said Sewell, forcefully.

"I can't allow that, sir," said the sergeant, "without the superintendent's say-so."

"Isn't there something called habeas corpus?" said Sewell. "A lawyer has the right of access to his client?"

"That applies to people in custody, sir," said the sergeant.

"Well what do you call this?" asked Sewell. "It's worse than prison."

"I think that's an exaggeration, sir," said the sergeant. "I've visited a few in my time and I don't remember one with room service."

"Listen, you sarcastic piece of shit, either I talk to my lawyer tonight or I set fire to my room. There's no way you'll be able to keep me here if the place burns down."

"That would be a very foolish thing to do, sir."

"Tell Hargrove I want to talk to my lawyer or I start lighting matches." Sewell slammed down the phone. He picked up his room-service tray and threw it against the wall.

It was just after nine o'clock when Keith Rose got home. As he pulled into the drive he saw his wife at the sitting-room window. She waved and disappeared. He drove into the garage and went through the internal door to the kitchen. Tracey was in her pink dressing-gown, pouring boiling water into two mugs. "Sorry I'm late, love," he said, putting his hands on her hips and nuzzling her neck.

"You need a bath," she said, stirring sugar into one of the mugs of coffee.

"How was she today?" he asked, stroking his wife's long auburn hair.

"Not good," said Tracey. She turned and linked her arms round his neck, kissing him hard on the lips.

Rose broke away first. "Is she asleep?"

"Just dropped off."

"I'll go up and see her."

Tracey released him. "Was it bad?" she asked.

Rose frowned, not understanding what she meant.

"Gatwick. The surveillance."

"Waste of a weekend," he said. "All foreplay and no orgasm."

Tracey smiled coyly. "I'll see if I can remedy that," she said. "Go and see your little girl, then come to bed."

Rose went upstairs. Kelly's bedroom door was ajar and a nightlight cast shadows from the toys scattered around the room. He sat down on the bed, taking care not to disturb the drip line that ran across the sheet and into her left forearm. He ran his hand down the side of her face. There were dark patches under her eyes and her chest barely moved as she breathed.

"It's going to be okay, sweetheart," Rose whispered. "Daddy's going to do whatever it takes to make you better."

The phone rang. Sewell slid off the bed and padded over to answer it.

It was Superintendent Hargrove. "I gather you're not happy, Mr Sewell."

"Damn right I'm not," said Sewell. "Your Rottweilers won't even let me talk to my lawyer."

"What do you intend to talk to him about?" asked Hargrove.

"No one knows where I am and I need someone on my side." Sewell thought it best not to mention that he wanted Garden to check up on his firm's financial status.

"As we prevented your murder, you can assume we're on your side, Mr Sewell. Your partner was looking for a hitman. If we hadn't presented him with our man, you'd be lying in a shallow grave in the New Forest with a bullet in your skull."

Sewell sighed. Every conversation he had with the superintendent went around in circles. "Fine. I'm grateful. But I need to know my legal position."

"You're helping us put a criminal behind bars."

"But I'm the one who's being held at the moment."

"It won't be for long, Mr Sewell."

"Two days, you said. Which means one more day to go." Sewell sensed hesitation in the superintendent. "One more day to go, right?" he pressed. "I'm out tomorrow?"

"I hope so," said Hargrove.

"You'd better do more than hope," said Sewell. "Look, I can go at any time, can I?"

"I'd rather you didn't, but I can't stop you. You don't need a lawyer to tell you that."

"You're saying I can go home now?"

"Yes, Mr Sewell, but I'd rather you didn't. As soon as Hendrickson sees you he'll know he's been set up."

"So you'll have to arrest him?"

"Probably. Which means that our secondary investigation gets blown out of the water."

"So?"

"Another potential murderer will get away with it."

"Like I said, so?"

"What if you were the potential victim, Mr Sewell? What if we needed someone else to stay hidden for a few days so that we could catch Hendrickson in the act? Wouldn't you want that person to co-operate?"

"There you go again," said Sewell. "Now it's a few days. You said two before."

The superintendent sighed. "I'm as unhappy about this as you are," he said, "but we now have a second ongoing investigation. Another contract has come to light, and we want the same man who nailed your partner to go after this person. If you surface, Hendrickson will tip off the other person and all hell will break loose. And you will put my man at risk."

"Have you got Hendrickson under surveillance?"

"We know where he is."

Sewell pounced on the evasion. "Do you have men watching him?"

"We don't have a car outside his house, but we have him red-flagged at all ports and airports. If he was going to run, we'd know. We're watching his credit-card activity so we'll know if he buys a ticket to go anywhere. He doesn't suspect anything so there's no reason for him to run. He thinks he got away with murdering you. Provided you stay where you are, that won't change."

"I want my laptop," said Sewell. "I've got work to do."

"I can't allow you to send emails," said Hargrove.

"You're monitoring all calls so you'd hear if I fired up the modem. Look, I'm not asking for much. My laptop — and I need cash. Someone told the Rottweilers I can't use my credit cards and I'm running low on funds."

"I'll sort that out," said Hargrove.

"And my computer?"

"Where is it?" asked Hargrove.

"In the boot of my car."

"The car in your garage? The BMW?"

"That's it."

"Okay. Give your keys to the sergeant on duty and I'll pick it up for you. I'll drop it round tomorrow."

"If you don't, I'm walking."

"The sergeant says you were threatening arson."

"That's still a possibility," said Sewell, and hung up before the superintendent could respond.

Shepherd was making himself a cup of coffee when one of his mobile phones rang. He had three lined up on

100

the kitchen table. One was personal, one was the phone Hargrove used to contact him, the third, which was ringing, was for his current operation. He picked it up. It was Angie Kerr. He pressed the green button to take the call. "Yeah," he said.

"Is that Tony?"

"Yeah. Have you got the money?"

"Yes. And the photographs. Can you see me today?"

"The sooner the better," said Shepherd. He looked at his watch. It was ten thirty. His car was already wired for sound and vision but it would take at least an hour for the surveillance team to get into position. "How about midday?"

"Okay. Piccadilly Gardens again?"

"No," said Shepherd. "From now on I call the shots. You're not handing money to me in a crowded square. We do it where no one can see us." He wanted it captured on video and the only way to do that was in his car. "Where are you now?"

"Home. Charlie went out and said he wouldn't be back all day."

"And there's no problem with you leaving the house?"

"No, I'm here on my own."

"Better make it some distance away," said Shepherd. "Do you know Altrincham? There's a Safeway supermarket there." It was a ten-minute drive from Hale Barnes, a small town that had long ago been engulfed by Greater Manchester.

"I know it."

"I'll be in a grey Volvo. Drive around the car park until you see me, then park away from me. Don't look at me. Get out of your car and go into the supermarket. That'll give me a chance to check that you're not being followed. Wait two minutes, then walk out. If I'm sitting with both hands on the steering-wheel, it's safe to come to my car. If my hands aren't on the wheel the meeting's cancelled and you wait for me to call you. Have you got that?"

"Yes, but who do you think'll be following me?"

"Better safe than sorry," he said curtly. "Just do as I say. Be there at noon." He cut the connection.

Hargrove parked down the road from Sewell's house, then sat in the car to check that he hadn't been followed — from force of habit rather than genuine concern. He got out of the car, turned up the collar of his coat and kept his head down as he walked to the garage door. He unlocked it and pushed it upwards, slipped inside, flicked the light switch and pulled the door down.

The laptop was on the back seat of the car in a black nylon case. Hargrove picked it up and was heading to the garage door when he saw the door that led through to the house. He stopped and looked at it, then tried the handle. It opened. Hargrove smiled to himself. He had no authority to search Sewell's house, but the man had given him the keys. He went through into the kitchen and put the laptop on the table.

All the equipment and appliances were stainless steel and didn't appear to have been used. The refrigerator contained bottles of Bollinger and imported lager. There was a stainless-steel bread bin, but it was empty, and Hargrove couldn't find any food in the cupboards. Menus from various local restaurants hung on a hook by the oven and a carrier-bag containing the remnants of a Chinese takeaway was in the steel bin by the door.

There was a big-screen plasma television on the sitting-room wall and a state-of-the-art sound system with DVD recorder and satellite receiver. The furniture was black leather, the coffee-tables mainly glass, and there was a black-wood sideboard loaded with bottles of spirits. Hargrove could see why Sewell wasn't enjoying his stay in the hotel.

He went back into the kitchen and switched on the laptop. It was a new model Sony with wi-fi to connect it to the Internet via wireless. There was also a modem. Hargrove found a connecting cable in the nylon case and slipped it into his pocket. He couldn't afford to have Sewell prowling around the Internet. There was nothing he could do about the wi-fi other than to check there was no signal in the hotel. He doubted there would be — it didn't have satellite TV or a business centre.

Hargrove's fingers played across the keyboard. He ran Sewell's Outlook Express program, then went through his Inbox and Sent Items folders. His mail seemed to consist of two sections: office correspondence and contacts from an adult matchmaking service. Hargrove read through more than fifty replies from women who thought that Sewell was a handsome twenty-five-year-old with blond hair, a six-pack abdomen and a sexual organ that would put an elephant's to shame. He had clearly posted someone else's photograph on the website and was reaping the benefits. Many of the emails in his Inbox had photographs attached, and in most of the pictures the women were naked. Hargrove didn't know if Sewell ever met any of them or if he just got a kick from reading their replies, but he'd have some explaining to do if they met him. The real Sewell was neither handsome nor twenty-five; he didn't have a six-pack or blond hair.

The office correspondence was far less racy but even more interesting. There were emails going back nine months from Larry Hendrickson, pressing Sewell to agree to sell his company to a London firm. The offer had been raised from an initial £750,000 to just under two million. There were no copies of the replies Sewell had sent, but it was obvious that Hendrickson had been getting increasingly desperate. His emails initially detailed the financial reasons for a sale, then practically begged Sewell to accept the deal. The last few were terse. Not threatening, nothing that could be used in court, but it was clear that the two men were no longer friends. The bigger chunk of the shares was owned by Sewell, who had founded the company, but Hendrickson would still be in line for almost half a million pounds. That alone was worth killing for, but with Sewell out of the way Hendrickson stood to gain control of the whole company.

Hargrove switched off the laptop, closed it and put it back into the case. He drove to Altrincham and dropped off the laptop at the local police station with a chief inspector who owed him a few favours. The man promised to get the laptop to the Leeds hotel by nightfall. Hargrove thanked him and headed off to meet the surveillance van. It would soon be time for Shepherd's meeting with Angie Kerr.

Shepherd parked his Volvo in a space well away from the building. Supermarket car parks were his favourite place for a meeting. No one was surprised to see a man sitting alone in his car: they assumed that he was waiting for his wife. There were always plenty of people about, which meant that faces tended not to be recognised.

Hargrove's surveillance van drove slowly round the car park, then reversed into a space in the far corner.

"Check for sound," said Shepherd. The van's lights flashed once. There were two microphones, one in the passenger-side ventilation duct, the other in the hands-free telephone.

"Check for vision," he said. The van's lights flashed again. There were two tiny video cameras in the car, one down in the passenger-side footwell, the other in the overhead light fitting. Both microphones and cameras were linked to a transmitter in the boot of the Volvo and the sound and images could be heard and seen up to a mile away. Shepherd had a gun under the passenger seat, a SIG-Sauer with seven cartridges in the clip. He wasn't expecting trouble from Angie, but her husband was a different matter.

He scanned the vehicles in the car park. Nothing out of the ordinary. He slid into character. He was Tony Nelson, hitman for hire. Former paratrooper turned mercenary who'd fought for the highest bidder in the Balkans before moving into private practice. No wife, no children, parents long since dead, in a car accident caused by a drunk driver, and a sister he hadn't seen for ten years. There was nothing about Tony Nelson that Shepherd didn't know; there was no question that could be asked of him to which he didn't know the answer. That was the way it had to be.

Shepherd saw Angie at the wheel of a Jaguar, crawling between the ranks of parked cars. A large red motorcycle peeled away from the supermarket entrance and headed down the road. A woman in a Mini sounded her horn impatiently, but Angie continued to drive slowly until she spotted Shepherd at the wheel of the Volvo. She smiled instinctively, then bit her lower lip and looked away as she remembered she wasn't supposed to acknowledge him until she'd been inside the supermarket.

She found a parking space and walked into the shop. She was wearing a well-cut blazer over a white polo-neck sweater, faded blue denims and high-heeled boots. Her body language screamed that she knew Shepherd was watching her: her back was ramrod straight and her right hand gripped the strap of her shoulder-bag as if her life depended on it. Shepherd knew that looking relaxed when you were scared was one of the hardest things to pull off. Feigning anger, aggression, fear or any strong emotion was easy, but being normal when your life was on the line was a skill that came only with years of experience.

Shepherd placed his gloved hands on the steering-wheel and waited for her to reappear. He glanced at the surveillance van. The cab was empty. The driver had moved into the back and was probably waiting to snap Angie with a long lens. Hargrove would be sitting with his headphones on and sipping the Evian water he always had by his side on surveillance operations.

When Shepherd looked back at the supermarket. Angie was already heading his way. He avoided eye-contact until she slid into the passenger seat. "It's the last car I'd expect you to have," she said.

"That's why I drive it," said Shepherd. "It's a family car so anyone driving one is assumed to be a family man."

"Your whole life is like that, I suppose," she said. "Layers and layers of disguise. Do you even know who you are?"

It was a good question, thought Shepherd, one that got to the heart of his undercover work. He had assumed so many identities over the years that sometimes even he wondered who Dan Shepherd really was. Or if he existed any more. But it wasn't a question he wanted to address now. He was Tony Nelson, hired killer. "Do you have the money?" he asked.

Angie reached into her bag and took out a thick envelope. It wasn't sealed and Shepherd ran his thumb along the stack of fifty-pound notes. He slid it into his jacket pocket.

"You said you wanted a photograph," she said, taking another envelope from her bag. "I brought a few."

Shepherd flicked through them: Kerr lying on a sofa, grinning at the camera, Kerr sitting under a beach umbrella raising a bottle of Spanish beer, Kerr kneeling next to a golden retriever. "What's the dog's name?" asked Shepherd.

"Brinks," said Angie. "After Brinks Mat. All that gold bullion stolen from the airport. I wanted to call her Goldie but he said she was Brinks and that was the end of it."

"He wasn't involved in the Brinks Mat robbery, was he? He'd only have been a teenager."

"His dad was," said Angie.

"A family business, then?"

Angie shrugged. "Not really. Charlie didn't have much to do with his father."

"Maybe that's the problem," said Shepherd. "Maybe he's spent his life trying to prove that he's as big a man as his father was. Trying to win his approval through imitation."

Angie tilted her head to one side. "That's very perceptive, considering you've never met him," she said.

"It's common enough," said Shepherd.

"What about you? Was your father a hired killer?"

"My father was a baker. All I remember of him was the smell of flour."

She smiled. "Don't tell me you both needed the dough," she said.

Despite himself Shepherd laughed, and felt himself slip out of character. As Dan Shepherd, he liked the woman. But Tony Nelson wasn't sitting in the Volvo with fifteen thousand pounds in his jacket pocket because he liked her. He was there to do a job. "Does he walk the dog on his own?"

Angie's hand went up to her mouth. Her nails were a deep pink, Shepherd noticed. "Don't do it in front of Brinks," she said. "Oh, God, that would be terrible."

"I need him to be on his own." Shepherd continued to flick through the photographs. Kerr standing with two men. Shepherd recognised them as Eddie Anderson and Ray Wates. Anderson was small and wiry with tight black curls. Wates was as tall as Kerr but broader, his head shaved. "Who are these guys?" he asked Angie. One of the hardest things to do undercover was to compartmentalise what he knew and what others thought he knew. As Dan Shepherd he knew everything the police knew about Eddie Anderson and Ray Wates, but as Tony Nelson they were just faces in a photograph.

"Eddie and Ray," she said. "They're practically joined at the hip to Charlie these days." She tapped a fingernail on Anderson's face. "That's Eddie. He's Charlie's yes man. Everything Charlie says, Eddie agrees with him. He thinks the sun shines out of Charlie's arse." She pointed to Wates's burly chest. "Ray's Charlie's muscle. You wouldn't want to meet him in a dark alley."

Shepherd nodded. Wates was a hard case, all right. He'd been sent down in his twenties on a seven stretch for GBH but had been released after four. Since he'd started working for Kerr he'd been charged by the police half a dozen times for threatening behaviour and assault, but witnesses had always failed to make it to court and Wates had walked each time.

"They don't stay at the house, though?"

"Bloody right they don't," said Angie. "But they're there first thing in the morning and usually in for a nightcap last thing."

"Who drives your husband?"

"Eddie."

Shepherd took a pen and a notepad from his jacket pocket. He scribbled down the names. For her benefit, not his. "What's your address?"

She told him and Shepherd wrote it down. It was a five-bedroom house with a double garage standing in almost an acre of gardens. There was a swimming-pool at the back and a tennis court. Shepherd had seen surveillance photographs and a floor plan of the internal layout.

"And what car does he drive?"

He knew it was a black Range Rover, but Tony Nelson had to be spoon-fed the details.

Her mobile phone rang and she jumped as if she'd been stung. She fished it out of her bag and swore. "It's him," she said. "Christ!"

"Don't answer it," he said.

"He gets stroppy if he has to leave a message," she said. "Accuses me of all sorts." She pressed the button to take the call and put the phone to her ear. "Hiya," she said. Shepherd heard the stress in her voice. "At the supermarket," she said. "We needed wine." A pause. "That Frascati I like. We're out of it." Another pause. "I know but I just felt like the Frascati." She bit her lower lip, her right hand clenched into fist. "Half an hour," she said. "I was going to get some seafood, too. Make a paella. Is that okay?" The fist clenched and unclenched. "What time?" She screwed up her face. "I'm not nagging," she said eventually. "I was just asking what . . . Hello? Charlie?"

She looked at Shepherd. "Hung up on me," she said, as she put her phone away. "He does that a lot."

"Was he giving you a hard time?"

"He wanted to know why I wasn't at home. Then when I asked what time he'd get back he went ballistic. Accused me of spying on him."

"How late does he stay out?"

"Late. He comes back stinking of cheap perfume and thinks I won't notice."

"The guys he does business with, do you know who they are?"

"Why?"

"I want to muddy the waters as much as possible," said Shepherd. "If I shoot him in the head in your back garden, the police will want to know where you were and if you and your husband had been rowing. If he gets shot in a Moss Side council block full of crack-heads and gang-bangers they'll put it down to a business deal gone wrong. You said he dealt in cocaine. Does he sell it to crack dealers?"

"He hates blacks," said Angie. "No way would he ever do business with them. Says they'd kill their own mothers for a tenner."

"What about South Americans? Last time we met you said he went to Miami twice a year. I figure it wasn't for the sun, so who does he meet there?"

"He never takes me," she said. "He says it's business and I don't know who he sees."

Shepherd did. There were DEA files on the CD Hargrove had given him, along with photographs of Kerr meeting representatives of Carlos Rodriguez, one of Colombia's most successful cocaine and heroin dealers. The DEA surveillance hadn't produced any concrete evidence, but Shepherd doubted that the three-thousand-mile trip had been a social visit.

"Does he take you to Spain?" Kerr had a large villa overlooking Marbella. Six bedrooms, six bathrooms, and a pool twice the size of the one in Hale Barnes.

"Three or four times a year," she said.

"Does he go on his own?"

"Why?"

"I could do it there. If you were in the UK, no way would the police be looking at you. Shootings are ten a penny on the Costa del Crime."

"Usually I go with him, but I could come up with an excuse next time." She frowned. "Problem is, I don't know when he'll be going next. And I'd rather you did it sooner than later."

"Is there a rush?"

She shook her head. "It's just that now I've decided I want it done, I want it done. I don't want it hanging over me. Is it okay if I smoke?"

Shepherd nodded and she took a packet of Marlboro menthol out of her bag. She lit one and put the packet back. "Do you always ask this many questions?" she asked. She opened the window and blew smoke through the gap.

"The better prepared I am, the less chance there is of something going wrong," he said, "and from what you've told me, Charlie Kerr isn't the typical target."

"What is typical?" she asked.

"Usually it's a business disagreement that can't be solved any other way. Or a way of teaching somebody a lesson."

She chuckled throatily. "You don't teach somebody a lesson by killing them," she said.

"No, but you can kill someone as a warning to others," he said.

"And you've done that?"

"I do what I'm paid to do," he said. "You asked what a typical job was."

"You don't have many wronged wives contacting you, then?"

"Most wronged wives head for a solicitor," said Shepherd.

"You think I'm being a bit drastic, don't you?"

Shepherd didn't reply.

Angie turned to him and pulled down the neck of her sweater. Just below the collar bone, on her right breast, was a circular scab. A cigarette burn, healing nicely. "Last time we had an argument, he did this to me. He'd had a bit to drink. Said he was sorry afterwards, said he only did it because he loves me so much, but it wasn't the first time and I doubt it'll be the last." She let go of the sweater and took a drag on the cigarette. "Bastard," she hissed.

"How much is he worth, your husband?"

"Not planning to raise your price, are you?" she asked.

"Just background," he said.

"Forewarned is forearmed?"

"Something like that."

"Seven million, give or take," she said.

"And do you know where it all is?"

"It's not buried under the swimming-pool, if that's what you mean."

"What I mean is that, once he's dead, you'll have to make sure you can get your hands on his assets. Most heavy criminals hide their ill-gotten gains and if your husband's done that you might find you're penniless when he's gone."

Angie smiled thinly. "Most of the bank accounts are in my name," she said. "I'm the majority owner of most of his businesses. In fact, nothing's in his name. He doesn't even have a credit card. Says the filth can track you anywhere you go if you use plastic."

He was right. One of the easiest ways to keep someone under surveillance was to watch their credit-card spending. Restaurants, hotels, plane tickets. It was indelible proof of where a target had been. The

114

smart ones stuck to cash. And the really smart ones made sure that no assets were in their name.

"So, you're going to do it?" she asked. She flicked the stub of her cigarette through the window.

"I've taken your money," he said. "It's as good as done."

"When?"

"Give me a day or two. I'll have to watch him for a while, get used to his habits."

"What if he sees you?"

"He won't."

"He's edgy. Thinks the cops are watching him. Doesn't discuss business on a land line, only uses pay-as-you-go mobiles."

"If the cops are watching him, I'll spot them," said Shepherd. He knew they weren't. Hargrove had checked with the head of the Greater Manchester Police Drugs Squad and been told that Kerr wasn't under active surveillance.

"And if they are?"

"It'll make it more difficult, that's all. Once I've accepted a job, Mrs Kerr, I follow it through, come what may."

"Angie," she said. "You and I are about as close to each other as two people can get without having sex, right?"

Shepherd laughed again, then forced himself to straighten his face.

"You look different when you smile," she said.

"Everybody does," he replied.

"No, you look like a totally different person."

"I don't have too much to smile about in this line of work," said Shepherd. "It's not like I get to see people in their best light. I'll call you once I've decided when and where."

"And I fix up an alibi?"

"The more people the better. Ideally somewhere with CCTV. You mentioned the casino last time. That's the perfect place."

"Will I see you again?"

"Afterwards. To pay me the rest of the money."

"So that's it, then?"

"That's it," said Shepherd.

She opened the door and climbed out of the Volvo, then leaned back in. "I'm not a hard-hearted bitch, you know."

"I never said you were," he said.

"And it's not about the money. I couldn't give a shit about how much he's got. It's just . . ."

"You're scared," he finished for her. "You're scared of what he might do to you."

"He's always said he'd rather I was dead than with someone else." She slammed the door and walked towards the supermarket.

Shepherd leaned his head on the rest. So that was that. He had the money in his pocket and she'd handed it to him with bare hands so her fingerprints would be on the envelope. He had her on video discussing the murder of her husband. Life behind bars. Unless she co-operated.

One of his mobiles rang. He was carrying two, the one used by Tony Nelson and the other to take calls

116

from Hargrove. It was the latter. "Excellent, Spider," said Hargrove. "Perfect sound and vision."

"Now what?"

"I'll run it by the CPS."

"Are we going to use her to get the husband?"

"Doesn't sound like she's got much to offer," said the superintendent.

"She knows where the money is," said Shepherd. "And we could use her in Spain."

"You heard what she said, Spider. She doesn't know when he'll be over there again."

"So she gets thrown to the wolves?"

"She's conspiring to commit murder, not shoplifting a can of catfood," said Hargrove. "Look, it's been a stressful couple of days. Take an early bath, you've earned it."

"Thanks," said Shepherd. He cut the connection and tapped the phone against his chin. He wasn't proud of himself. Angie Kerr was a victim, yet the full weight of the law would be used against her. If there had been any justice in the world the authorities would have moved against her husband years ago. But it was always easier to go for the soft targets.

He drove back to the rented flat and changed into his running gear. At the bottom of the wardrobe there was an old canvas rucksack containing half a dozen housebricks wrapped in newspaper, a habit from his SAS days. A run without weight on his back wasn't a challenge. And he didn't wear state-of-the-art nylon trainers stitched together by Chinese juveniles earning a dollar a day: he ran in army boots. For Shepherd running wasn't a fashion statement, it was a way of keeping his body at the level of fitness his job required.

He took the stairs down to the ground floor and pushed through the double glass doors that led out to the pavement. It didn't matter whether he ran in the city or through woodland. After the first ten minutes he wasn't aware of his surroundings. Now he ran on automatic pilot, his thoughts never far from Angie Kerr and the unfairness of it all.

Angie parked next to her husband's Range Rover. She picked up the supermarket carrier-bags from the passenger seat — the ingredients for paella and three bottles of Frascati. She liked the Italian wine. Her husband was always getting her to drink expensive champagne when they were out but she preferred Frascati. It was smoother and didn't have the acidic aftertaste she always got from champagne.

She unlocked the front door. "Charlie, it's me," she called, but there was no reply. She went through to the kitchen and put the wine in the fridge.

"Where were you?" said her husband. She jumped. She hadn't heard him come up behind her. He was leaning against the doorway, a smile on his face.

"I told you. Shopping."

"You were gone almost two hours." He enunciated each word as if he was speaking to someone who had to lip-read.

"Charlie, I had to park, I had to get the food. The supermarket was busy."

"It's Monday. It's never busy on a Monday. And you went to the supermarket on Saturday."

"For general food shopping. But I wanted more Frascati. And I said I'd make paella, right?"

Kerr nodded at the carrier-bag on the kitchen table. "So that's why you were gone so long, yeah? For paella and cheap Italian plonk."

"And petrol."

Kerr lit a cigarette and blew smoke at her. "So you filled up the Jag?"

Angie nodded.

Kerr took another long drag on his cigarette, held the smoke in his lungs, then exhaled through clenched teeth, all the time watching his wife's face. "So," he said, "if we go outside and check, the tank'll be full, will it?"

"Charlie, why are you doing this?" she whispered.

"Because I don't like being lied to. In fact, I hate it — hate it more than anything. And you know why?"

Angie knew. He'd told her a hundred times or more.

"Tell me why I hate being lied to."

"Because it means people think they're smarter than you. When they're not."

Kerr smiled. "That's right. And do you think you're smarter than me?"

"No," she said. "I don't."

He pushed himself away from the door and walked across the kitchen, passing so close that she could smell his aftershave. She stiffened when he drew level with her but she forced herself not to flinch because she knew he would take that as a sign of guilt. Her heart pounded and her mouth was dry, but she tried not to swallow. He picked up the carrier-bag and looked inside. "Paella," he said.

"I know you like paella."

"You like paella," he said. "I'm more of a lobster man."

"You know you can't get decent lobster in Manchester," she said.

"Not a patch on Spanish lobster, you're right there," he said. He put the carrier-bag down on the work surface. "So, let's go and have a look at the Jag, shall we?"

"Charlie . . ."

"What?" he said, raising his eyebrows. "Want to change your story? A last-minute amendment to the details of where the hell you've been for the last two hours?"

Angie felt tears spring to her eyes and blinked them away. He took a perverse pleasure in making her cry, then having sex with her as the tears ran down her face. It wasn't making love — it wasn't even sex. It was rape. Without love, without tenderness, just grunts, curses and threats of what he wanted to do to her. It was hardly ever in bed, either. It was in the kitchen, over the back of one of the sofas in the sitting room, or against a bathroom wall. He was always sorry afterwards. Or he said he was. He'd stroke her hair and kiss her neck and say he really loved her, that it was only because he loved her so much that he hurt her. And he made her a promise as he stroked her hair and kissed her neck: if she ever left him, if he ever thought she was going to leave him, he'd kill her. Because he loved her so much.

"I went to the supermarket for the shopping and I got petrol," she said, fighting to keep her voice steady. She kept smiling at him because he'd take any other facial expression as an excuse to get physical — a push, a pinch, a slap. Then her tears and the violence.

He took a step towards her and raised his cigarette. She flinched. He grinned and put the cigarette slowly to his lips. He inhaled slowly and the tip went bright red. Then he took it out of his mouth and held it a few inches from her left cheek. Her face ached from smiling. She knew he wouldn't stub it out on her face. He was too clever for that. When he marked her it was on a place no one else would see.

"Let's have a look, shall we?" he said. He blew smoke into her face. "Got the keys?"

"Sure," said Angie.

He walked into the hallway. Angie followed him. Kerr opened the front door and headed for the Jaguar. He stopped when he reached the driver's side and held out his hand. Angie gave him the keys. He pressed the electronic tag and the locks clicked open. "You okay?" he asked her.

"Fine," she said.

"Anything you want to say?"

Angie shook her head.

Kerr opened the door and the internal light winked on. He slid on to the driver's seat and inserted the ignition key. He peered at the fuel gauge. The needle swung up to the full position. Kerr stared at it for several seconds, then pulled out the key and climbed out of the car. He closed the door and tossed the keys to his wife. "Come on, let's have a drink," he said. "I'll open a bottle of Dom."

He went into the house. Angie stared after him, her hands trembling.

The phone woke Shepherd from a dreamless sleep and he fumbled for it. "Are you awake, Spider?"

"I am now," said Shepherd, rubbing his face.

"I've had a word with the CPS and NCIS. They're all getting very hot over Angie Kerr."

"Yeah, well, she's a sexy girl."

"The initial response is that they want her turned," said Hargrove. "They don't feel they've any other way of nailing her husband."

"Which says a lot about the sad state of policing in this country, doesn't it?"

"Now, now, Spider, you're getting all bitter and twisted."

"He's a criminal, right? I've read the files you gave me. MI5, the Church, the Manchester cops, they all know he's bad. Even the DEA's been on his case in Miami. But no one does anything."

"It's a question of resources, you know that. Even we have to choose whom we assist. My unit gets hundreds of requests every year, but we take on a couple of dozen at most."

"A guy like Kerr should be a priority, that's all I'm saying."

"There are hundreds of Kerrs in the UK. Thousands, maybe. We have to choose our targets carefully."

"We take the cases we know we'll win, is that what you're saying?"

"What's the alternative? We spend our time chasing dead ends? There's no point in mounting an investigation if we know we're going to fail. You have to play the odds. A guy like Hendrickson, we know we can put him away. Kerr's a bigger fish and you need a bigger hook to catch him."

"And Angie Kerr is the hook?"

"Hopefully," said Hargrove. "The Drugs Squad and the Church can act on anything she gives them."

"He'll kill her," said Shepherd grimly.

"She'll be protected," said Hargrove. "Look, this isn't a conversation for the phone, and I need to run something else by you. You know the pub by the canal, the place where we first discussed the Hendrickson case?"

"Sure."

"Can you be there at eleven?"

Shepherd squinted at the alarm clock on the bedside table. It was just after nine. Plenty of time. "Yeah."

"See you, then," said the superintendent. "And remember, we're on the same side here. I'm no happier about using Angie Kerr than you are, but sometimes the end justifies the means."

Shepherd pulled on an old pair of shorts and a tattered T-shirt and went for a short run, a quick two kilometres without the rucksack, then shaved, showered and changed into a pullover and jeans. He retrieved his leather jacket from the sofa where he'd thrown it the previous night and headed out, picking up a coffee from his local Starbucks as he walked to the meeting-place. The pub was only fifteen minutes from his apartment, on the edge of the city's vibrant Canal Street gay area.

Hargrove was sitting on a wooden bench outside the pub. He stood up as Shepherd approached, and the two men walked along the canal path.

"Two guys taking an early-morning stroll, people will get the wrong idea," said Shepherd.

"Since when have you cared what people think?" said Hargrove. "Besides, you're not my type."

As ever, the superintendent was immaculately dressed: a well-cut cashmere overcoat over a blue Savile Row pinstripe suit, starched white shirt with cufflinks in the shape of cricket bats, and an MCC tie. "I could be your bit of rough," said Shepherd.

"You've been up north too long," said Hargrove. "You're developing the northern sarcasm."

"Aye, and I've started eating mushy peas, too. But you're right, I wouldn't mind being closer to home."

"That's good, because I need you on another job in London, ASAP."

Shepherd grimaced. "I was hoping for a few days off. It's been a while since I saw Liam."

"This is urgent, I'm afraid."

"It always is," said Shepherd, and regretted it. No one forced him to do the work he did. He was an undercover cop by choice and could walk away any

124

time he wanted to. "Sorry," he said. "I've been in Tony Nelson's skin too long."

"Well, you'll be leaving him behind for this next case," said the superintendent. "You'll be a cop. Investigating cops."

Shepherd groaned. An operation against other cops was dirty work at best, dangerous at worst, and he'd tried to steer clear of it. "Can't IIC handle it?"

"Not this one. We need someone with your specialist knowledge."

"Specifically?"

"Your ability to handle automatic weapons. No one in the Internal Investigation Command has your military background, and while most of my people are proficient with handguns, I need someone familiar with carbines. Especially the MP5, which is what the SO19 guys use."

The Heckler & Koch was the weapon of choice in the SAS, and Hargrove was right. Even four years after leaving the regiment, Shepherd knew he could take apart and reassemble the weapon blindfold, and it wouldn't take him more than a few hours on the range to be as accurate as he ever was. The MP5 was a simple enough weapon, but few police officers were trained in its use. The Diplomatic Protection Group used them. So did the Met's armed-response units.

"We think the Met might have a rogue armed-response unit," said Hargrove. "Rogue as in they've either gone vigilante or they're ripping off drugs-dealers at gunpoint."

"Bloody hell," said Shepherd.

"Yeah, tell me about it," said Hargrove. "The commissioner's one unhappy bunny."

"If it's cut and dried, why do they need us?"

"Because it isn't. All the Met has is circumstantial."

"No smoking gun?" said Shepherd.

"Just a roomful of dead drugs-dealers and a cop who's disappeared."

"So you want me to do what? Infiltrate the gang and get them to take me on their next heist?"

"Your intuition never ceases to amaze me, Spider."

Shepherd's eyebrows headed skywards. "You're serious, aren't you?"

"I'm afraid I am."

Shepherd put his hands into his jacket pockets. "Investigating cops is always messy."

"It doesn't come messier."

"Plus, they can spot undercover cops. They know the signs."

"You'll be in as a cop. We can stick close to your true background."

"Not my name, though. Shit hits the fan, I want to disappear."

"I'll get a legend sorted by tomorrow evening. We can use the SAS background but say you left because you couldn't hack it, then seven years up in Scotland. Strathclyde, maybe. The three men we're looking at are all London boys, never been north of the border."

"They can pick up a phone," said Shepherd.

"I'll have it covered," said Hargrove. "You don't go in unless your legend's watertight."

126

"I'd rather we didn't use the SAS. I don't want them asking for war stories. Let's say I was in the Paras."

"Agreed," said Hargrove. "I'll get our background boys to draw something up and run it by you at the end of the week. I'll get a car sorted. We'll play you having money problems and looking to make a fast buck."

"So they ask me to take part in the robberies? How likely is that?"

"I want you looking corruptible. It might get them talking."

Shepherd wasn't convinced it would be that easy to get maverick cops to open up to him. "So, what's the story?" he asked.

"Last week two drugs-dealers were shot dead in a Harlesden crack house. It took the police the best part of an hour to force their way in and by then the shooters had gone out the back way. There was a witness alive in the house and another in a lock-up. All they can tell us is that the robbers were white and that there were three, two in the house and one who was outside most of the time. They wore dark clothing and rubber masks. When the shooting started two of the witnesses were bound, gagged and face down, so they don't know what happened. But one of the dead Yardies had a .22 that had been fired five times. Only two of the bullets have been accounted for."

"So one or more of them was hit?"

"The witnesses say that one of the Yardies who died screamed something about a vest. Then one of the robbers yelled that he was hit."

"Why do you think it was cops?" asked Shepherd.

"The forensics boys got hold of a decent slug from one of the dead Yardies, ran it through the Scotland Yard database, and that's when it all got interesting."

"In what way?"

"The bullet came from a .45 Python that was used in a robbery in South London last year. They got the guy, a Clapham blagger by the name of Joey Davies. He's doing a fifteen stretch in Parkhurst. They never found the gun."

"Guns are bought and sold."

"Of course they are. But Davies always claimed that the Python was in his flat when he was busted. The police found two other guns, but not the Python. First guys into the flat were an SO19 Trojan unit, which included one of the guys we think has gone bad. Keith Rose."

"So this Rose picks up a gun last year and saves it for a rainy day?"

"Looks that way."

"So why don't the rubber-heels boys pick him up and sweat him?"

"Because he's been a cop for fifteen years so he's not going to sweat, and because all we've got is circumstantial and hypothesis. We have a bullet, we don't have a gun. And we have witnesses who can only remember Frankenstein and Alien masks and dark clothing."

"It's possible that the gun was stolen but sold on to a gang with a grudge against the Yardies."

"It's possible, but this doesn't feel like a gang fight to me. If it was, they'd have killed everyone. It's more like a robbery that went wrong. The way we see it, the robbers got in and overpowered the two Yardies, then waited for the rest of the guys to come back. One of the Yardies pulled a gun and all hell broke loose. Then the robbers bailed out."

"Presumably the Yardies won't say what was taken?"

"They deny there were drugs in the flat. There was crack-processing equipment in the attic and a safe with twenty grand in it. Twenty grand doesn't seem much, so I think it's safe to assume that the robbers got away with drugs or cash. Maybe both."

A narrow boat put-putted past them. A big man wearing a brown-leather jerkin and a floppy felt hat waved a can of Carlsberg in salute, his other hand on the tiller. Hargrove smiled back.

"I'm missing the obvious, aren't I?" said Shepherd.

"Maybe," said the superintendent.

Shepherd ran through everything Hargrove had told him. "One of the robbers was hit," he said eventually.

The superintendent smiled. "Exactly."

"Do any of the SO19 guys have any unexplained injuries?"

"One has disappeared. Andy Ormsby had only been with them six months. Didn't turn up for work the day after the robbery. After three days the police broke into his flat and it looked as if he'd just packed a suitcase and left."

"No note?"

"Nothing. And no one's heard from him since."

"So the Yardies killed him, then?"

"Maybe," said Hargrove. "Maybe not."

Shepherd's brow furrowed as he realised what the superintendent had suggested. "His mates killed him? He was wounded but they couldn't take him to a hospital so they topped him?"

"Or waited for him to die. Only they know what happened. But there wasn't any blood in the flat, not from the robber. If there was we'd have done a match with Ormsby's DNA and we wouldn't be having this conversation."

"That's my way in, then? I replace Ormsby?"

"It's the way I see it," said Hargrove.

"Isn't it a bit obvious?"

"They probably won't realise we traced the bullet. There's no reason for them to think they're suspects. People do have nervous breakdowns and disappear, and jobs don't get more stressful than serving with an armed-response unit."

"How about an undercover cop pretending to be a member of an ARV? I'd be trying to set up cops with guns. How stressful is that?"

"Are you saying you don't want the assignment?"

Shepherd flashed Hargrove a tight smile. It was always up to an undercover operative to decide whether or not they would accept a job. It had to be that way. But Shepherd had never turned down an assignment and he had no intention of starting now. "I'll need a couple of days on the range. If I'm rusty, they'll spot it."

"We can fix you up on a police range here. Or in Scotland."

"I'll get it sorted."

"Hereford?"

Shepherd nodded. "It'll give me a chance to see Liam, too."

"Can you be ready to go in on Monday?"

That gave Shepherd six days to prepare. Six days in which to wipe away the persona of Tony Nelson and step into his new character. "If you can have the legend ready by then," he said. He took a deep breath. "No rest for the wicked."

"Are you okay?"

"It never ends, does it?" said Shepherd. "At first you think you're making a difference, but for every villain we put away, there's another two waiting to take his place."

"That doesn't mean we stop trying, Spider. You've put some dangerous men behind bars. You can be proud of what you've achieved."

"Yeah, but in the grand scheme of things, what difference do we really make?"

"Ah, now you're getting all metaphysical. The meaning of life."

"I know what life's about," said Shepherd. "It's about raising children. First time I held Liam in my arms I knew that. Nothing else matters. But how do babies grow up to be rapists, drugs-dealers and murderers? I look at Liam and I just know he's going to turn out okay. He's only eight but you can already see he's a good kid. He's polite, he's considerate, he doesn't get into fights. Everybody likes him."

"He's got you as a role model, Spider. And he couldn't have asked for a better mother than Sue."

"I don't think it's down to that. I don't remember teaching him the difference between right and wrong," said Shepherd, "but there isn't an ounce of badness in him. Then you look at the kids prowling in packs doing drugs and mugging other kids for their mobiles and you wonder why they went bad. It's not too big a step from playing truant to dealing drugs, and the next thing you know they're shooting each other with automatic weapons."

"Kids go bad," said Hargrove, "and bad kids grow into bad adults, and our job is to put away as many of the bad guys as possible."

"Treat the symptoms, not the disease?"

"Hell's bells, Spider, are you having a crisis of confidence?"

Shepherd didn't reply.

"Do you want to see our psychologist?" said Hargrove quietly. "Talk things through?"

"I'm not crazy."

"It's not about being crazy," said the superintendent. "It's about stress and how you deal with it. That's why we have a psychologist as part of the team, to nip problems in the bud. The last twelve months you've been through a lot."

"I know."

"Knowing it and dealing with it are two different things. You never really grieved for Sue."

Shepherd stopped walking and glared at Hargrove. "Bullshit," he said. "Bull-fucking-shit."

Hargrove put up his hands defensively. "I'm just saying, when it happened you were in prison undercover. You didn't have time to deal with it. When you got out you had Liam to take care of. Then you wanted to get back into harness. You needed to work, you said. I thought maybe you were right, but you've gone from one job to the next and maybe you need time to grieve."

"I'm not the crying sort."

"Again, crying and grieving aren't the same thing."

"I'm not seeing a shrink. End of story."

"Right. I'm just saying it's an option."

"This isn't about Sue. Or Liam. Or my stress levels. It's about pissing on a forest fire."

"If we don't try, if we let them get away with it, how does that make the world a better place? You were in Afghanistan with the SAS and we were supposed to have won that one, but did it really solve anything? That doesn't stop us fighting for what we think is right."

"And now I'm going up against other cops?"

"Cops who've gone bad, Spider. And in my book they're worse than dyed-in-the-wool villains. Is that what this is about? Going after cops?"

Shepherd started walking again. "I'll be fine. Trust me."

Shepherd drove his CRV towards London at a steady seventy miles an hour, resisting the urge to join the stream of executive cars whizzing by in the outside lane. He used his hands-free to phone an au pair agency in Ealing and arranged an appointment for the following morning at ten o'clock. He'd already filled in their questionnaire, but they required a personal interview before they would send a woman to his house. From the sound of it, it was easier to get into the SAS than on to the agency's books.

His second phone call was to Major Allan Gannon, who answered on the third ring.

"Not caught you at a bad time, have I?" said Shepherd.

"Spider! Business, social, or are your nuts in the fire again?"

It was a fair enough question. Usually when Shepherd phoned the major he needed a favour. He explained that he was about to join a police armed-response unit and that he needed a refresher course in the equipment and tactics he'd be using.

Gannon chuckled. "Guess you're a little rusty," he said. "When?"

"Soon as possible," said Shepherd.

"What are you doing over the next couple of days?"

"I'm on my way to London and I've a few things to do in the morning, but then I'm yours."

"Come to the Duke of York barracks at noon," said Gannon. "Bring an overnight bag." He cut the connection, leaving Shepherd to wonder what he had planned. One thing he was certain of: he was putting himself in good hands. He'd served with the major in Ireland, the former Yugoslavia, Sierra Leone and Afghanistan, and trained with him everywhere from the jungles of Brunei to the Arctic wastelands of northern Norway. There wasn't a man he trusted more.

★   ★   ★

There was a double-knock on the hotel-room door. Sewell was staring at a spreadsheet on his laptop. "Go away," he said. "I don't need the bed turning down."

"It's not Housekeeping, Mr Sewell," said a man's voice. It was the superintendent.

Sewell got up and walked to the door. He was naked except for a hotel towel wrapped round his waist.

Superintendent Hargrove was wearing an immaculate pinstripe suit, a crisp white shirt and a blue tie with red cricket balls on it. He was holding two bottles of Bollinger. "I gather this is your tipple."

"Does this mean we're celebrating that shit Hendrickson being arrested?" asked Sewell.

Hargrove looked pained. "Not exactly." He closed the door.

"We said Monday. Today's Tuesday. Forty-eight hours has become four days."

"I'm sorry," said Hargrove, "I really am. It's just that this is bigger than we first thought."

"Bigger than attempted murder?"

Hargrove looked around for somewhere to sit. Sewell had the only chair, facing his computer. "Do you mind if I sit on the bed?" he asked.

"Suit yourself," said Sewell. He popped the cork out of one of the bottles of champagne, went to the cramped bathroom and took two plastic cups off the glass shelf by the basin. He poured champagne into them and gave one to the superintendent. That Hargrove knew Bollinger was his favourite champagne suggested that he had done more than get the laptop from his car when he visited Sewell's house, but Sewell wasn't up to picking a fight. "You realise you're running out of any goodwill you might have had?" he said.

"I don't know what to say," said Hargrove.

Sewell doubted that was true. The superintendent had obviously come to the hotel with something on his mind, and he'd never been lost for words during their previous conversations. "Enough is enough," he said. "I've given you four days, which is twice as long as you said it would take. You said you had all you needed to arrest Hendrickson."

"We do," said Hargrove.

"So arrest him. Throw the shit into a cell and let me get back to running my company."

"I wish it was as simple as that," said Hargrove. He sipped his champagne. "I don't suppose there's any whiskey in the minibar is there?" he asked.

"There isn't a minibar. Hendrickson will have better facilities in prison than I've got here," Sewell said.

"But you've got your computer. And I've given the sergeant cash for any food you want bringing in."

"I want to go home," said Sewell flatly.

"We need more time," said Hargrove.

Sewell swore.

"Possibly the rest of this week."

"I told you already, Hendrickson could be bleeding my company dry. By the time I get back into my office there might be nothing left. What then, Superintendent? The police will come up with three million quid, will they? Out of petty cash?"

"Actually . . ." Hargrove took an envelope out of his jacket pocket and handed it to Sewell, who put down his beaker and opened it. It was from the chief constable of Greater Manchester, agreeing to reimburse him for any money he lost as a result of his co-operation with the ongoing investigation. He would also guarantee a consultancy fee of twenty-five thousand pounds, whatever the outcome of either case.

"He can do that?" asked Sewell.

"He can do whatever he wants with police funds," said Hargrove.

"This guy you're after, the second investigation, he's big, yeah?"

"Oh, yes," said Hargrove. "He's big."

"Big kudos for you if you get him, commendations all round, the chief constable looks good?"

"If it wasn't important, we wouldn't have put your case on hold," said Hargrove.

"So he's bigger than me, is that what you mean?" Sewell bristled. "I sit here in this pokey hell-hole while you find bigger fish to fry?"

"No one's saying your case isn't important, Mr Sewell. Larry Hendrickson will go to prison for a long time, and rightly so. But what we're working on now is a different sort of case. I wish I could go into details, but I can't. What I can tell you is that the guy we're going after is a nasty son-of-a-bitch and the police here have had all sorts of problems with him. You'll win all sorts of Brownie points if you help take him out."

Sewell reread the chief constable's letter. "The twenty-five grand's mine whatever happens?"

"Providing you co-operate."

"And if I come to you after this is over and tell you that as a result of that shit Hendrickson being in charge of my company I'm a hundred grand down, the Greater Manchester Police will write me a cheque to cover the loss?"

"That's what the letter says," said Hargrove. "The chief constable might want to see a breakdown of your losses, but I can't see him going back on his word."

"All right, then."

"You're okay to lie low for the rest of this week?" asked Hargrove.

"Yes, but not here," said Sewell. "I want an upgrade."

"I don't think that'll be a problem. We'll move you tomorrow."

"Five stars."

"Agreed," said Hargrove wearily.

"A suite. Not a room."

Hargrove nodded.

"And sex," Sewell added.

"I'm going to have to draw the line there, Mr Sewell," said the superintendent.

"I've had nothing but my right hand for company," said Sewell. "That's a cruel and unusual punishment in my book."

"I can't risk you meeting a girlfriend," said Hargrove. "It's only four or five more days."

"It wouldn't have to be a girlfriend," said Sewell. "I'd use an escort agency. They'll send a girl round. I'll make sure it's not one I've had before."

138

Hargrove rubbed the back of his neck. "Okay," he said wearily.

"And the sergeant uses his money to pay for it."

"For God's sake, man!" said Hargrove.

Sewell shrugged. "I can't use my credit cards, can I?" he said. "Besides, if the chief constable wants me to be happy, he'll pay."

Hargrove stood up. "I think I'd better go before you take the shirt off my back," he said.

"It wouldn't fit," said Sewell, grinning, "but I'll have the tie."

Angie Kerr climbed out of the shower and stood watching her reflection in the floor-to-ceiling mirror as she towelled herself dry. The scab on her breast was about to come off and she dabbed it carefully with the edge of her towel. It wasn't the first time her husband had burned her, but if everything went to plan it would be the last. No more burns, no more slaps, no more punches to the stomach that he knew would hurt but not leave a permanent mark. All his friends knew how he treated her. Sometimes when he abused her in public, she got a sympathetic glance or some small acknowledgement that they knew what she was going through, but they were all too scared of Charlie to say anything.

Eddie Anderson had come closest to talking to him about it. Charlie had punched her in the stomach while they were in the VIP section of Aces after she'd asked him to stop flirting with one of the waitresses. The girl was a tall, leggy blonde, barely out of her teens, and

Charlie had had his hand on her backside, squeezing it as if he was checking a melon for ripeness. The girl was leading him on, flashing her eyes and flicking her hair, and she had known full well that Angie was his wife.

Angie had waited until she and her husband were alone before she told him she didn't like him making a fool of her. He'd smiled coldly, then slammed his fist into her belly. She'd been unable to breathe for a minute or so, gasping as tears streamed down her face. Charlie had stood up and walked over to the bar where Eddie and Ray were drinking. Angie had just about recovered her breath when Eddie came over and told her he was to drive her home. Angie didn't argue. She knew that if she did, her husband would hurt her all the more.

He had given her his arm, she had taken it gratefully and they had walked out together. Angie would never forget the look of triumph on the waitress's face. She wondered if the girl knew what Charlie was like, if he ever showed her his violent side. Maybe he only needed one woman to dominate, and it was her bad luck that he'd chosen her. Eddie had helped her into the back of the car, but he didn't say anything until he was sitting in the front with the engine running. He'd looked at her in the rear-view mirror. "Are you all right, Mrs Kerr?" he'd asked.

He'd kept looking at her, waiting for her to answer. Angie had wondered what he expected her to say. If she'd said no, she wasn't, that her husband had hit her one time too many, would he have taken her to hospital? To the police station? Had Charlie asked

Eddie to pretend to be concerned to see how she'd react? And if she had told Eddie that she was sick to death of the beatings and the verbal abuse, would he have told Charlie, and would Charlie have made her life more of a misery than it already was?

"The way he treats you, it's not right," Eddie said quietly. This time she had seen concern in his eyes.

Angie had found herself smiling, even though her stomach felt as if it had burst. "I'm okay, Eddie," she'd said. "I know he loves me really."

Eddie had stared at her for several seconds, then put the car into gear. He hadn't spoken again all the way home, even when he'd walked her to the door.

Angie towelled her hair dry, brushed it, and sprayed Kenzo perfume around her neck. Charlie liked her to smell good when she got into bed. She turned off the light and walked into the bedroom.

He was standing by the window, looking up at the moonlit sky. "I love you, Peaches," he said, without turning.

She knew he meant it. But "love" didn't mean the same to Charlie Kerr as it meant to most people. It meant control. It meant ownership. He loved his car. He loved his house. He loved his villa in Spain. And he loved her.

"Come here," he said.

He was naked — he never wore anything in bed and insisted that she didn't either. She padded across the carpet and slid her arms round his waist, pressing her breasts to his back.

"You'll never leave me, will you?" he said.

The moon was full and looked so close that Angie felt she could almost reach up and grab it. "No, Charlie. I'll never leave you," she said.

"You know what would happen if you did?"

Angie swallowed. She kissed the back of his neck.

"I'd find you," he said. "I'd track you down and I'd kill you with my bare hands."

"I know you would," she whispered.

He reached behind and stroked the insides of her thighs. "You're my wife and I love you," he said.

"I know."

"If I didn't love you, I wouldn't lose my temper," he said. "I'd just walk away. I wouldn't care." He turned and pressed his lips against hers, his tongue forcing its way into her mouth so quickly that she didn't have time to breathe. She felt herself gag and fought it. The times when he was having sex with her were the most dangerous. If she did the wrong thing, said the wrong thing, even moaned in the wrong way, his caresses turned to punches, his kisses to bites. She let him kiss her hard, and moaned softly, the way he liked. She had to make him think she was enjoying it. He stopped kissing her and held her head in his hands, staring into her eyes. "I love you, Angie," he said.

"I love you too," she said, although it had been a long time since she'd loved him. Now there was just contempt for him in her heart, and hatred. She didn't want to leave him. She wanted him dead. And Tony Nelson was going to kill him for her.

Charlie grinned, then turned her so that she was facing the window. He grabbed her wrists and put her arms up against the glass. "Open your legs," he said.

Angie did as she was told, and he forced himself inside her.

"Yes," she said, "yes, yes, yes." She stared up at the moon and imagined Tony Nelson shooting him in the back of the head with a large handgun. "Yes," she moaned. "Yes, yes, yes."

Shepherd walked around the ground floor of the house, checking the locks on the windows and doors. He was only going to be away for a couple of days but there had been several opportunistic break-ins in the area, according to a flyer put through his letterbox by the local crime-prevention officer.

He'd considered selling the house after Sue's accident but Liam had protested vociferously. It was Mum's house and he didn't want to live anywhere else. Shepherd knew what the boy meant. He'd been the one who'd paid the mortgage but Sue had decided on the décor and furniture and there wasn't a room that didn't have her presence in it. Saying goodbye to the house would mean saying goodbye to Sue, and neither he nor Liam was prepared to do that.

Most of the books on the shelves in the sitting room had been Sue's and her magazines were in the bathroom. After he'd got back from Manchester he'd cleared Sue's clothes out of his bedroom into black plastic bags, then left them in the spare room. He couldn't throw them away.

One of his mobiles rang and he hurried to the kitchen. It was the one Hargrove used, but a woman's voice spoke. She introduced herself as Kathy Gift and said that Superintendent Hargrove had suggested she call to arrange an appointment.

"Why?" he asked. Hargrove hadn't mentioned her.

"Sorry, I should have said. I'm a psychologist attached to Superintendent Hargrove's unit," she said.

"I said I didn't want a shrink," he said. "Anyway, I'm just about to leave for a training exercise."

"When are you back?"

"A couple of days."

"Friday?"

"I'm not sure, but I'll be away from London at the weekend whatever happens."

"Will you call me when you're back so that we can schedule an appointment?"

"Of course," said Shepherd, and cut the connection. He had no intention of meeting her or any other psychologist.

He looked at his watch and cursed. He'd told the au pair agency he'd be there at ten and he was already a few minutes late. He carried his bags out to the CRV and drove half a mile to the neat row of shops where the agency had its offices above a veterinary surgeon. He parked on a meter, buzzed the intercom and hurried up the stairs.

The office consisted of two rooms, one with two secretaries surrounded by filing cabinets and a window overlooking the rear yards of the shops, and a larger office for the owner, Sheila Malcolm, BSc. Shepherd knew about the academic qualification as it was on the agency's letterhead and on the metal plate on the door.

Shepherd apologised for being late and the secretaries made him wait while Miss Malcolm rearranged her schedule to accommodate him. She was alone in her office when Shepherd was ushered in and he assumed that either she had been on the phone or she was punishing him. He apologised again as he sat down in front of her desk.

Miss Malcolm tapped on her computer keyboard and looked at the screen over the top of her glasses. "You need someone to live in and take care of your home and your young son." She was archly elegant in a well-cut two-piece tweed suit. Her dyed auburn hair was perfectly coiffured and her pale pink lipstick had been applied with a surgeon's precision.

Shepherd nodded.

"A lot of our girls are reluctant to live in when there isn't a lady of the house," said Miss Malcolm.

"My wife died," said Shepherd.

Miss Malcolm had the grace to blush. She removed her spectacles and let them hang round her neck on a thin silver chain. "I'm sorry to hear that," she said. "It's usually divorced husbands who come to us, and they're sometimes more trouble than they're worth." She flashed him a smile. "I'm sure you understand."

"My wife died," repeated Shepherd, "and, as you can see from the form I filled in, I'm a police officer. I think it's fair to say that I'm a safe bet."

"Absolutely, Mr Shepherd."

"My boy is with his grandparents at the moment, but I want live-in help so that he can be with me."

"A boy should be with his father," said Miss Malcolm. She looked at her terminal. "You have a room for her, which is good, and a car. How does your son get to school?"

"Car," said Shepherd.

"And will you be responsible for the school-run, or will the girl?"

Shepherd swallowed. Images flashed through his mind. Sue at the wheel of her black VW Golf. Liam in the back seat. Sue twisting to pick up Liam's backpack. The traffic lights on red. The Golf accelerating. The supermarket lorry.

"Mr Shepherd?"

Shepherd shook his head. "I'd do it when I was in London, but from time to time I'll be away."

"You travel a lot?"

"Some."

"So you'd want someone a bit more mature, who could take responsibility for everything in your absence."

"That sounds good," said Shepherd. "If possible, I'd prefer them to be British."

"Ah, these days we have few British girls on our books," Miss Malcolm said. "It wasn't always like that, of course. Some of our best girls were filling in time before university. We had Cheltenham Ladies' College girls, but now they're either working in Switzerland or trekking across South East Asia. The bulk of our girls are from the new entrants to the EU, Poland, Hungary,

146

Slovenia. I can wholeheartedly recommend the Polish girls. They're hard workers and trustworthy. We've had a few negative experiences with the Slovenians, but we now have them thoroughly checked before we bring them over."

Shepherd would have preferred a girl from the UK so that he could run his own check through the Police National Computer, but it sounded as if he wasn't going to get the chance. "Do you have anyone who could start immediately?"

"I have three Polish girls arriving tomorrow, two from Estonia, and I'm having half a dozen applicants interviewed in Slovenia later this week. Nurses. They can earn five times as much in London as au pairs." She raised her eyebrows. "Now, I'll have to check whether they have international driving licences, and I'm not sure whether they want live-in positions. Sometimes they like to stay together. We try to discourage sharing — bad habits spread. But we should have several likely candidates for you to see before the end of the week."

"And they're all screened for criminal records?" asked Shepherd.

"Absolutely," said Miss Malcolm. "We insist on a letter from the local police authority saying they haven't committed any offences, and an HIV-status certificate. We prefer them to have references from previous employers, ideally in the UK. That's not always possible, of course, as many are coming here for the first time."

Shepherd stood up. "I'm going to be away for a few days," he said. "You can get me on my mobile."

"Going anywhere nice?" asked Miss Malcolm.

"Not really," said Shepherd. "Business rather than pleasure."

"Well, hopefully by the time you get back we'll have fixed up the perfect young lady for you," she said brightly.

The phone rang and Sewell frowned. He wasn't allowed to call out and since he'd been in the hotel no one had rung him. He picked up the receiver. "Yes?"

"Mr Sewell, this is Sergeant Beattie, downstairs."

Sewell sighed, expecting bad news.

"If you could have your bag packed, we'd like to move you in about fifteen minutes."

Sewell thanked him, then threw his clothes and washbag into the holdall he'd brought with him when the police had picked him up from home on Friday morning. He switched off his laptop, closed it and put it into its nylon bag with the unopened bottle of Bollinger.

The sergeant knocked on his door and took him downstairs to where a younger officer in plain clothes was waiting at the wheel of a green Rover. Sewell and the sergeant climbed into the back. There was no small-talk during the short drive across the city, but Sewell wasn't trying to make friends with his custodians.

The lobby of the hotel to which they took him was a big improvement on his previous accommodation. It was bright and airy, and there were three pretty girls behind the desk who greeted them with smiles. The sergeant handled the check-in, the younger plain-clothes officer carried Sewell's holdall.

A porter showed them to Sewell's suite. There was a large sitting room with a sofa, two armchairs and a television set three times the size of the one in the previous hotel. There was a DVD player, too. Sewell opened the minibar and grinned. There was a full range of beer, spirits and mixers, and two half-bottles of champagne. It wasn't Bollinger, but it was drinkable.

There was another big-screen TV in the bedroom and a king-size bed. The bathroom contained a Jacuzzi and a shower big enough for a rugby team. Sewell's smile widened. Things were getting better by the minute.

"Is there anything we can get you, sir?" asked the sergeant.

Sewell picked up a copy of the room-service menu and flicked through it. Oysters, fillet steak, Dover sole, a full range of French and Italian wines. "Hookers," he said. "Lots and lots of hookers."

The guard checked Shepherd's ID against the computer printout on his clipboard and waved to the far end of the parade-ground. "If you'd park in bay thirty-two, sir, and head on through the door over there. Major Gannon's expecting you."

Shepherd edged the CRV over the metal teeth that would rip into the tyres of vehicles going the wrong way. He appreciated the "sir" but it didn't apply to his former rank in the SAS or to his present status as a detective constable with the police.

He locked the car and went through the door with his overnight bag. Two soldiers in fatigues were standing behind a reception desk. Shepherd showed his ID and one took him down a corridor and knocked on a mahogany door. As he walked in, Major Gannon was already striding across the room, his arm outstretched. "You're looking good, Spider," he said.

"Thanks, sir. You're in no bad shape yourself." The major was a big man with a strong chin, wide shoulders and a nose that looked as if it had been broken at least once. He had the appearance of an enlisted man rather than the high-flying officer that he was. In all the years Shepherd had known him he had never heard him referred to as a Rupert, the derogatory term troopers used to describe their officers. The major was always "the Boss". Shepherd had gone into battle with him twice, and would have died for him without a second thought.

Gannon shook his hand and slapped him on the back. "Tea?" he asked. "Staff's got a brew on."

"Thanks," said Shepherd. "Two sugars."

The staff sergeant poured a mug of thick, treacly tea, splashed in a little milk and used a dessertspoon to heap in two mounds of sugar. Gannon sat down behind his desk. Behind him was a large window overlooking the parade-ground. There were three phones on the desk, and the briefcase containing the secure satellite phone they called the Almighty lay on a table. It never left Gannon's side. The only people who had access to it were the prime minister, the Cabinet Office, and the chiefs of MI5 and MI6. When it rang it meant that all hell was breaking loose somewhere. The major was head of the Increment, an *ad hoc* pulling-together of men from the Special Air Service and the Special Boat Squadron to carry out missions deemed too dangerous for the intelligence services.

Shepherd sipped his tea. "Thanks for doing this at short notice, Major," he said.

"Not a problem," said Gannon.

"I didn't think they allowed live firing here, it being in the centre of London and all," said Shepherd.

"We're not training here," said the major. "We'll be in Stirling Lines."

Shepherd's heart sank. It had taken him the best part of an hour to drive from Ealing to Central London, and this meant retracing his route plus an extra four or five hours westward to Hereford. They wouldn't get to the barracks until evening, so they probably wouldn't start training until tomorrow. A whole day wasted.

Gannon looked at his watch. "Transport's on the way," he said.

"Great," said Shepherd.

"I've been reading up on SO19 procedures," said the major. "I've already briefed the guys in Hereford and they'll have the Killing House set up for us."

The Killing House was where the SAS rehearsed its hostage rescues. Shepherd had spent hundreds of hours there when he was in the Regiment, firing live ammunition at targets while colleagues played the part of hostages, often smoking and cracking jokes as the bullets flew.

"Have you done much firing recently?" asked Gannon.

Shepherd carried a pistol when he was undercover and the operation warranted it, but he'd never had to fire it in anger. Apart from a yearly range assessment, there was no requirement for him to do any live firing. It was different for the officers in SO19: their shooting skills were constantly tested and assessed, hence the need for Shepherd to get in some practice.

The windows rattled and Gannon looked over his shoulder. A large green helicopter settled slowly in the middle of the parade-ground. Its rotors slowed and the turbine settled back from a deafening roar to a juddering growl.

"Our chariot awaits," said the major. He stood up. "You can bring your tea with you, if you like." He grinned at Shepherd's confusion. "One of the perks of the job," he said.

There were three troopers behind Shepherd, their feet shuffling in the darkness. There were no lights in the Killing House, and the troopers hadn't been given night-vision goggles. Their Heckler & Koch MP5s had been fitted with 1003 Aiming Projectors, which shone a tight beam of intense light from a fifty-five-watt halogen bulb directly along the gun's line of fire. The light could be used to blind targets temporarily but because the beam was so focused it didn't affect the user's night vision.

Shepherd had the retractable stock version of the weapon, the MP5A3, which was favoured by the SAS because they often used their weapons covertly. It was also in general use by SO19.

Shepherd had memorised the layout of the Killing House by glancing at a hand-drawn map for less than five seconds. His memory gave him an advantage over the troopers he was with, but they spent up to three hours a day practising there and knew all of its permutations. The corridor they were in had three doors off it as well as the one they had just come through. There was a door at the end, facing them, another on the right three paces ahead and a third on the left a little further on.

Shepherd's eyes were stinging from the cordite in the air and his ears were buzzing. They were using live ammunition and the floor had to be swept clear of dozens of empty cartridges after each scenario had been played through. They weren't wearing gas masks because armed police were generally not permitted to use tear gas or thunderflashes, unlike the SAS who used pretty much any ordnance they needed to achieve their objective.

Shepherd flashed his light at the door on the right, then kicked it open and went in low to the right. Two troopers behind him followed, one to the left, one to the right, while the third stayed in the corridor. Lights flashed. There were two targets in the room, one sitting at a desk, the other standing in the far corner. "Armed police, drop your weapons!" shouted Shepherd, as he pulled the trigger and sent three slugs thudding into the chest of the desk target, a diving suit filled with straw. MP5s ratt-tatt-tatted behind him and the target in the corner was hit in the chest and head.

More flashes to confirm that the room was clear, then back out into the corridor. The formation changed: this time Shepherd brought up the rear and waited in the corridor while the three troopers burst into the second room. There were three short bursts of fire. One target, another padded diving suit. The briefing had specified six targets and one hostage. That meant the hostage and three targets were in the last room.

Shepherd led the way down the corridor. He flashed his light at the door then went through, keeping low as he swept his MP5 around the room, stabbing at the light button. Flash, flash, flash. There were more flashes behind him. One hostage, four targets. The briefing had been flawed to catch them out, but the troopers with Shepherd were old hands and one snorted just before Shepherd yelled, "Armed police," and the firing started.

Bullets thudded into the four padded diving suits and within seconds it was over.

"Clear," said Shepherd.

The hostage was sitting on a straight-backed wooden chair holding a transceiver. He spoke into it. "Lights," he said.

The overhead fluorescent bulbs flickered into life. Major Gannon surveyed the targets. "Not bad," he said. Like Shepherd and the three troopers, he was wearing black overalls and a Kevlar vest. "You might have given me a new parting, but I'm not bleeding so that's a good sign."

Shepherd smiled. None of the bullets had gone anywhere near the major. It was traditional for troopers to play the part of hostages in the Killing House. It demonstrated trust but it also gave them the chance to experience being under fire. The major had had more than enough experience of gunfire and that he had decided to sit in on Shepherd's initial exercise was a better demonstration of his faith in Shepherd's ability than any written evaluation.

"It's interesting without the night-vision gear," said Shepherd.

"The cops aren't trained in it," said the major. "Nine times out of ten they wouldn't go into a no-light situation. Too risky."

Shepherd had read the SO19 manuals and it was clear that the police followed different procedures from the SAS. They went in hoping that the incident could be resolved without shots being fired. They identified themselves as armed police and would charge in shouting that the targets were to drop their weapons. They were only to fire if they were under attack or if civilian lives were at risk. The SAS went in as a last resort and went in hard. There was no shouted identification, no need to tell the bad guys to give up. They went in intending to shoot and kill. The chest and the head were the only targets. Double tap, triple tap, it didn't matter: all that mattered was that the target went down and stayed down. If Shepherd stood a chance of being accepted as a member of an armed-response unit he'd have to forget most of what he'd learned as an SAS trooper.

There was a further problem, which Hargrove had made clear to him when he'd accepted the assignment: once an SO19 officer had fired his weapon he was immediately removed from firearms duty until the incident had been investigated. That could take months. If there had been a fatality, it could take years. If Shepherd fired his weapon, the undercover investigation would be over.

The major stood up and stretched. "Your marksmanship is spot on," he said. "Can't fault you on that. But we're going to have to slow your reaction time a bit." He grinned. "Crazy, I know, but at the moment you're moving at twice the speed of a cop. You're identifying yourself and firing at the same time and that'll get you drummed out the first time it happens in the real world."

Shepherd nodded.

"On style, I'd keep your weapon high, stock to shoulder," said Gannon. "I know we fire from the hip, but the cops train that way. Generally they don't go up against multiple targets so intimidation is the name of the game. They hope the bad guy will back down. Most armed cops go through their whole career without ever firing their gun in anger."

"Got it," said Shepherd.

"What you just went through is as tough as it will get," said the major. He gestured to a small CCTV camera in the corner of the room. "We'll review the

156

tapes, then run through a few exercises, just to get you more in tune with the cop way of doing things."

"I appreciate it, Major."

Gannon waved away his thanks. "It's an interesting exercise," he said. "Like detuning a high-performance car. Come on, let's get some fresh air while they're getting the tapes ready."

They walked away from the Killing House to the barracks memorial garden in front of the Regimental church. The SAS had moved from its old barracks in May 1999, and taken over the former RAF Cledenhill base. They had brought the Killing House with them and the clock tower from the old Stirling Lines barracks had been rebuilt in the garden. Engraved on it were the names of all the members of the SAS who had been killed in action.

"You know there's always a place for you here, Spider," said the major.

"On the clock tower? Thanks a lot, but I don't plan to shuffle off this mortal coil just yet."

The major ignored his jibe. "With the Regiment," he said.

"I'm a bit long in the tooth to be abseiling out of helicopters," said Shepherd.

"You're thirty-four. Hardly over the hill. And the Regiment could use you on the directing staff. We lost three instructors last month. They're in Iraq pulling in two grand a week."

"I appreciate the offer, but I was never cut out to be an instructor. Besides, as a cop I can spend more time with my boy."

"An undercover cop?" said Gannon. "That means being away for days at a time, maybe weeks, doesn't it? If you come back to us you'd be based here and have most weekends off. House prices are a darn site cheaper than London, too. Your in-laws are still in this area, aren't they?"

"Born and bred," said Shepherd. "They're taking care of Liam until I get my situation sorted. It'll be okay."

"The offer stands," said the major. "You change your mind, let me know." They headed towards the administration block. "These rogue cops, aren't they going to be suspicious when you turn up out of the blue?" asked Gannon.

"Alleged rogue cops," said Shepherd, with a smile. "That's the thing about being a cop — we have to bother with things like proof and evidence."

"But presumably they wouldn't be sending you in unless they were pretty damn sure."

"Like my boss says, knowing and proving are two different things. But my legend'll be watertight."

"It had better be," said the major. "Bad cops with automatic weapons. Not a pleasant mix."

"I'll be okay," said Shepherd.

Gannon slapped him on the back. "I don't doubt it for one minute," he said.

The Saudi knew that he would be lucky one day. That was all he needed. One lucky day when Allah smiled on him. He'd been at university in London when the IRA had almost killed the then prime minister, Margaret

Thatcher. They'd exploded a huge bomb in her Brighton hotel and she had been pulled from the rubble, shaken but alive. The Saudi had never forgotten what the IRA had said afterwards: Margaret Thatcher had been lucky, but she would have to be lucky for ever; they only had to be lucky once. The Saudi felt the same.

He had been unlucky three times already. He had planned the perfect operation in Manchester. Five men in Manchester United's Old Trafford stadium all fitted with explosive vests, ready to blow themselves up shortly after kick-off. The tickets had been acquired, the volunteers had been selected, but even before the explosives had arrived in the country a careless conversation on a mobile phone had been picked up by an electronic monitoring station at Menwith Hill in Yorkshire. Within days the five volunteers, all Iraqis with British citizenship, had been arrested.

Then he had arranged for a truck filled with fertiliser explosive to be driven to the base of the London Eye by the river Thames. They had been betrayed by an old man who had overheard a whispered conversation in an East London mosque. He had spoken to his *imam*, who had made a phone call. Two days later a rented garage in Battersea was raided and four men were taken to Belmarsh prison. The Saudi had been on his way to the lock-up to collect the truck when the police went in. Five minutes later, and he would have been arrested with the others. Allah had smiled on him, but it had not been his lucky day.

The Saudi had next planned to detonate a car bomb in Trafalgar Square, but the day he was due to strike there had been a trade-union protest and the square was sealed off. The Saudi and another man had driven the explosive-laden car around the West End for the best part of two hours before they had abandoned the mission. The Saudi had told his associate to take the car back to the house in St John's Wood that they were using as a base, but again he had been betrayed. The house was raided that night and the associate was arrested. He, too, was now in Belmarsh. The authorities hadn't released details of the arrest or the car bomb. The Saudi knew why: if the public were aware of how close al-Qaeda had come to detonating a massive bomb in Trafalgar Square they would lose all confidence in the security services.

The Saudi ran his hands down the canvas vest. It fitted well. He had made it himself, stitching it by hand. It was woman's work, but no woman could be trusted to know what he had planned. He had been unlucky three times but he would not be unlucky a fourth.

The four other men who had given themselves to the mission did not know each other. They knew only the Saudi, and only he knew that they were involved. Even if one of the others was caught or went to the authorities, they knew nothing of any value. They didn't know what the target was. They didn't know when they would be deployed. And they didn't know who else was involved. They would be told only hours before it was due to happen.

The Saudi only ever spoke to the men in person. He never used the telephone, he put nothing in writing. There were no computer files, no letters, no written instructions, just whispers and nods. All four men were highly trained and all had made their preparations. They were ready to die, happy even to give up their lives. They craved the opportunity to die killing infidels. And if the Saudi's plan worked, and if he was lucky, many hundreds of infidels would die. Soon.

Shepherd borrowed a car from the SAS pool and drove from the Stirling Lines barracks to Tom and Moira's semi. He phoned from the car to let them know he was on the way. "I wish you'd let us know you were coming, Daniel," Moira said. "I could have aired your room."

Shepherd hadn't known he was going to Hereford until the helicopter had landed on the parade-ground in London. "It's a flying visit, literally," he said. "I'm only here for two days and then I'm back to London."

Shepherd heard Liam shouting in the background. "Is that Dad?"

"Liam wants to talk to you, as you probably heard," said Moira.

"Dad, where are you?" Liam asked excitedly.

"On my way to see you," he said. "I'll be there in fifteen minutes."

"Are we going to London?"

"Not yet. Soon, though."

"But you can stay here for a while?"

"For tonight, at least," said Shepherd. "Let me talk to your gran."

Liam put his grandmother back on the line. "You don't have to go to any trouble, Moira. I can bunk down at the barracks."

"Nonsense," she said briskly. "You'll spend the night with us and that's the end of it. And you shouldn't be using the phone while you're driving. That's how accidents happen."

She cut the connection before he could explain that he was using the hands-free kit.

When he pulled up in front of the house, Liam was in the garden, waiting for him. Shepherd picked up his son and swung him round. "I missed you, kid."

"Put me down!" squealed Liam.

Shepherd lowered him to the ground and tickled him. Liam ran giggling into the house and Shepherd chased after him. They stopped short when they saw Moira in the kitchen doorway, her arms folded across her chest. "No running in the house, Liam," she said.

"Sorry, Gran."

"Sorry, Moira," said Shepherd. He winked at Liam and his son giggled.

"Don't forget your homework," said Moira.

"Gran . . ."

"It's got to be done. You either do it now or you do it after supper. And I'm sure after supper you'll want to play with your father. Why not pop up to your room and get it out of the way?"

Liam looked up at his father. "You're staying?"

"Of course."

Moira took Shepherd into the kitchen and made a pot of tea. "Just two days, you said?"

"Today and tomorrow. I'll head back to London Thursday evening, but I'll be here at the weekend."

"And you're doing something with the Regiment?"

Shepherd could hear the suspicion in her voice. She'd never been comfortable with the fact that he was an SAS trooper, and Shepherd realised she thought he might be planning a return to soldiering. She had no need to worry because that was the furthest thing from his mind. "Just some technical training," he said, "to do with a police job."

She poured milk into his tea and handed him the cup and saucer. There were no mugs in Moira's house.

She sat down at the kitchen table. "Tom and I have been talking," she said, "about Liam. He's settled in so well with us. The school was prepared to take him on a temporary basis because of the circumstances, but I've already spoken to the headmistress and there's a permanent place for him if we want it. We'd have to move quickly, though, it's a popular school . . ."

"He's my son," said Shepherd. "He belongs with me."

"Of course he does," she said. "No one's trying to take him away from you. But he's been with us for most of the past four months, and when you do come it's usually a flying visit. It's not as if your job is nine to five, is it?"

Shepherd opened his mouth to reply but shut it again when he heard a key in the front door. He stood up and smiled when Tom Wintour walked in. "Dan, good to see you," he said. "I was wondering whose car that was out front. Where's the CRV?"

"It's a loaner," said Shepherd. "The CRV's in London."

Tom shook hands with him, then dropped his battered leather briefcase under the kitchen table. "Are you staying?" he asked, as he sat down at the table next to Moira. He was portly with receding grey hair and thick horn-rimmed glasses. He was a bank manager and looked the part in his dark blue pinstriped suit, starched white shirt and inoffensive tie.

Moira poured him a cup of tea. "Of course he's staying," she said.

"I was going to bunk at the barracks, but Moira insisted," said Shepherd.

"You'll be able to have breakfast with Liam," said Tom. He sipped his tea. "Did Moira tell you we've been talking about Liam's future?" he said.

"Yes," said Moira.

"We love having him here," said Tom. "There's plenty of room. There's the garden. The school is only ten minutes away."

"I was telling Daniel about the school," said Moira.

"I appreciate the offer, Tom, really I do, but I want Liam with me."

"Absolutely," said Tom. "That's where he belongs. But until your situation is a bit more stable, why not let him stay with us?"

"I don't see him enough as it is," said Shepherd.

"But how is that going to change if you take him back to London and get a housekeeper?" asked Moira.

She and Tom were facing him and Shepherd felt as if he was being grilled in a police interrogation room. He toyed with the idea of refusing to say anything until his lawyer arrived.

"He'll be in the care of a stranger most of the time. The agencies that fix up housekeepers can be a nightmare. Half the time they don't even know the girls they're dealing with. At least here Liam is with family," Moira added.

"I'm his family," said Shepherd.

"We're his grandparents, Daniel. We have rights, too."

Shepherd didn't want to argue with them. He knew they only had Liam's best interests at heart. And, besides, they were right. "I'll make sure I get someone decent," he said. "I'll check references and stuff. It'll be fine."

"And what happens if you're sent away from London?" said Moira. "Susan said you were away all the time."

"Not all the time," said Shepherd, defensively. But, again, he knew she was right. He could as easily be assigned to a case in Aberdeen as London. And while he was always free to turn down an assignment, he doubted that Hargrove would keep him on the team if he only accepted jobs close to his home. "Even if the case is outside London, I'll be able to get home at night and at weekends more often than not."

"Daniel, you've been in Manchester for the past week," said Moira, patiently.

Shepherd took a deep breath. It would have been easier if his mother-in-law had been shouting at him but she was calm and reasonable, the logic of her argument forcing him into a corner. "I want to try," he said. "If it doesn't work out, I'll rethink my situation. But I was a good father when Sue was alive, and I don't see that I'm going to be a bad one now that she's gone."

"Nobody's suggesting that," said Tom. "We just want the best for your boy." He sighed and ran his finger around the rim of his cup. "Have you thought about moving jobs within the force?"

"Pounding a beat, you mean?"

"There are jobs, surely, that would allow you to spend more time at home."

It was something Sue had raised a few weeks before she'd died. Shepherd had said he'd think about it, but in his heart of hearts he knew he'd never ask for a transfer to a desk job. He'd given up his army career without hesitation when Sue had become pregnant with Liam. Life in the SAS was dangerous at the best of times and he had narrowly escaped death in Afghanistan after taking a sniper's bullet in the shoulder. But it was only after he'd been recruited into Hargrove's undercover unit that he'd discovered police work could be every bit as dangerous as serving with special forces. At least when he was in the SAS he had had a pretty good idea of who was going to be taking pot-shots at him. Now that he mixed with the criminal fraternity, he never knew who might decide to stick a knife in his back, both literally and figuratively. It was what gave the job its edge. There were times when it was considerably more stressful than going into battle with men you trusted with your life. But he couldn't tell Tom and Moira that. He always downplayed his police work with them, as he had with Sue.

"I can't be stuck in an office," said Shepherd, and immediately regretted the words — that was exactly where Tom Wintour had been for the past thirty years. "I need to be out and about . . ." he added. Tom was a good man and had done a sterling job in raising Sue and taking care of Moira. While it wasn't a life that Shepherd could have lived, he respected the man as a good father and husband. ". . . there are fewer perks when you're office-bound. I get travelling expenses, overnight expenses, lots of overtime. It makes a big difference to my pay cheque."

"Money isn't everything, Daniel," said Moira.

Shepherd forced himself to smile. "No, but it'll make our life easier," he said.

"Just think about it," said Tom. "He'd have stability here, and he wouldn't have the problems you get in inner-city schools these days."

"What problems?" asked Shepherd. "I live in Ealing."

"Oh, come on, Daniel, we read the papers," said Moira. "Drugs, shootings, classrooms full of asylum-seekers."

"You don't want to believe everything you read in the *Daily Mail*."

"It's not about what paper we read," said Moira. "It's about the quality of education. The schools in London, the state ones anyway, are dire, and you can't argue with that."

"Liam's school is fine," said Shepherd. "Sue went to a great deal of trouble to make sure we were in the right catchment area. Anyway, it's not about schools. I'll send him private if I have to. It's about my son being with me, and I'm sorry, but that's not negotiable." His stomach was churning and his heart pounding. "I don't want to fight, I really don't."

Tom smiled sympathetically. "It's not a fight, it's a discussion about what's best for Liam."

"I know," said Shepherd.

"Let's just leave it for the moment, shall we? You're here, Liam's here. Moira can cook us some supper and I'll open a bottle of wine."

"Maybe I'll go and help Liam with his homework."

"Good idea," said Tom. "Red or white?"

"Whatever you're having is fine," said Shepherd. He saw Moira and Tom exchange a worried look as he left the kitchen. Despite Tom's conciliatory words he knew that there had been only a temporary cessation in hostilities. The war would continue.

Sewell flicked through the TV channels. Comedy shows, gardening, a quiz hosted by an effeminate comic. A leaflet on top of the TV explained how to access the paid-for system. A dozen new-release movies were on offer, with four pornographic films. The hotel charged ten pounds each, but Sewell decided that the police could pay for an orgasm or two. At the bottom of the leaflet a brief note informed guests that the hotel was equipped with wi-fi, allowing guests to access the Internet without connecting through a phone line.

168

"Thank God for four-star hotels," muttered Sewell. He sat down at the dressing-table, opened the laptop and tapped his fingers impatiently as the computer booted up. He flicked the wi-fi switch and waited while the machine searched for a frequency to lock on to. A bubble appeared at the bottom right of the screen. WIRELESS CONNECTION AVAILABLE. Sewell was online.

He launched Outlook Express and waited as more than forty emails dropped into his inbox. There were a dozen from contacts on the dating service he'd joined. He didn't bother reading them. Most of the rest were junk, offering everything from penile extensions to American university degrees. There were a dozen emails from clients and four from people at work. Nothing from Hendrickson, of course. Sewell cursed under his breath. He was looking forward to sitting in court the day Hendrickson was sentenced. Fifteen years to life, Hargrove had said. Sewell intended to give Hendrickson a piece of his mind before they took him away.

There were two emails from clients he often played golf with, asking why he hadn't turned up on Saturday, and one from his stockbroker, tipping a couple of shares. Nothing urgent.

He closed Outlook Express and opened Internet Explorer. He was able to access his two personal bank accounts online and checked them both. There had been no withdrawals, but Sewell hadn't expected to see any. There was no way Hendrickson could access them, even if Sewell was declared dead. It was the office accounts he was worried about, but he couldn't get to them online.

He went to the company website and logged on, typing his user ID and password. Nothing much had changed since he'd been in the office. A few more orders had been placed. He went through to the accounts section and flicked through it. Everything was as it should have been. But Sewell was worried about the company bank accounts. He sat back and chewed his lower lip. He hated not knowing what Hendrickson was doing.

He closed Internet Explorer and opened Outlook Express again. He wrote an email to John Garden, swearing the lawyer to secrecy and asking him to check the status of the company bank accounts. Garden ran the company's legal department as well as acting as Sewell's private legal adviser and had been with him even before he'd set up the company. Sewell hesitated before he sent the email. The superintendent had been unequivocal about him not making contact with anybody until Hendrickson was in custody. "So sue me for not obeying your every word," Sewell said, and pressed send.

Shepherd tucked the quilt under Liam's chin. "Good night, sleep tight, hope the bedbugs don't bite," he said, and kissed his son on the forehead.

"Will you be here tomorrow?" asked Liam, sleepily.

"Sure. I'll have breakfast with you and drive you to school."

"And will you pick me up?"

"I'll try," said Shepherd. "I've some work to do at the barracks. Some training."

"Secret Squirrel?"

Shepherd laughed. "Yes. Secret Squirrel."

"Are you going back in the army?"

"Definitely not."

"So you're going back to London?"

"In a day or two."

"Can I come with you?"

"I've got to get us an au pair fixed up first, but as soon as I've done that you can be back in your old room."

"Soon?" Liam's eyes were half closed and Shepherd could see he was struggling to stay awake.

"Soon," said Shepherd.

"Promise?"

"Promise."

"Okay." Liam's eyelids fluttered and closed.

Shepherd stroked his cheek. "Sweet dreams, kid," he said.

Shepherd woke up and tried to work out where he was. He relaxed when he remembered he was in Moira and Tom's house, in the double bed he had shared with Sue whenever they had stayed over. He looked at his watch. It was seven thirty. He could hear Moira downstairs in the kitchen, getting breakfast ready.

He slid out of bed, shaved, showered and changed into a clean shirt and jeans. Liam was sitting at the kitchen table, spooning porridge into his mouth. "Hiya, kid, what time do we have to leave for school?"

"Half past eight," Liam replied.

"Liam, not with your mouth full," admonished Moira. "Egg and bacon, Daniel?"

"Lovely," said Shepherd. His mother-in-law was a first-class cook and served a great fry-up. "Egg and bacon" was her shorthand for eggs, bacon, sausage, fried bread, tomato and baked beans. He helped himself to coffee. "Where's Tom?" he asked, sitting next to Liam.

"Tom leaves at seven on the dot," said Moira, ladling beans on to his plate. "He likes to be first in. Makes a point of it. He hasn't had a day off sick in twenty-seven years. What about you? What are you doing today?"

"It's Secret Squirrel, Gran," said Liam. He took a couple of gulps from a tall glass of orange juice.

"Just training," said Shepherd. "Nothing exciting." He didn't want to tell his son or Moira that he was going to spend all morning firing handguns to get his accuracy up to the level expected by SO19.

He tucked into his fry-up, and Liam went upstairs to get ready for school.

"Shall I pick him up this afternoon?" asked Moira, and poured herself a cup of tea.

"What time does he finish?"

"Half past three."

"Thing is, I'm not sure what time I'm going back to London."

"But you'll be here this evening?"

"I hope so, but it's not up to me. The Regiment's handling transport."

172

"This coming and going doesn't do Liam any good at all," said Moira. She sighed. "I'm sorry, I don't mean to nag."

"I'll phone you when I'm done," said Shepherd, "and, whatever happens, I'll be back at the weekend."

Liam reappeared with his schoolbag. Shepherd wolfed down the last of his breakfast, picked up his overnight bag and took his son to the car. Liam gave him directions, and Shepherd realised he'd never even seen the school his son went to. He had no idea who his teacher was. He started to ask questions about it, but Liam was monosyllabic. "It's not my school, Dad," he said eventually. "My school's in London."

"I know," said Shepherd.

"London's where my friends are."

"I know."

"So don't keep asking me about it. I won't be here long."

"Okay."

"Will I?"

"I hope not."

Shepherd pulled up and Liam unclipped his seatbelt. "I'll see you tonight, yeah?"

Shepherd nodded.

"You will be here, won't you?" asked Liam.

"I'll do my best, kid," said Shepherd.

"Promise?"

"Cross my heart."

Liam beamed, slung his bag over his shoulder and ran to the gate. Shepherd knew he'd been playing with words and was suddenly ashamed. He had promised he'd try to be there, but that was not how Liam had understood it. So far as Liam was concerned, Shepherd had promised to be there, and that was a promise he couldn't make. Telling people what they wanted to hear was part of working undercover, but it was no way for a father to talk to his son.

Larry Hendrickson was sitting with his feet on the desk and sipping his second cup of coffee when his intercom buzzed. It was his secretary telling him that Norman Baston was outside and wanted a word. Hendrickson told her to send him in. Baston was the firm's IT team leader, a nerdish computer geek with slicked-back hair and two PhDs. He rarely left the computer room so Hendrickson realised it had to be important. Either something was wrong with the system or he had received another job offer and wanted his salary bumped up again. He was already earning six figures, but was worth every penny. The problem was, he knew it.

"How's it going, Norm?" asked Hendrickson, swinging his feet off the desk.

"Have you heard from Roger?" asked Baston. He had few social graces and never made small-talk. He was far more comfortable with his computers than he was with people.

"Not since last week," said Hendrickson.

"Any idea where he is?"

"What's the problem?"

"Maybe nothing, but he logged on yesterday and went through the accounts system. I just wondered if something was wrong."

Hendrickson fought to stay calm. "If there was a problem, I'm sure he'd mention it to me."

"When's he coming in?"

"Like I said, I haven't spoken to him since before the weekend, but he didn't say he was going anywhere."

"We had a meeting fixed up today. Thursday, ten fifteen. His secretary says he hasn't been in all week."

"You know what Roger's like."

"He hasn't even spoken to Barbara."

"It's only Thursday, and it's not as if the ship will sink if he's not at the helm, is it? Have you tried his mobile?"

"Goes straight through to voicemail."

Hendrickson's mind was whirling from the ramifications of what Baston had said. Sewell couldn't have logged on because he was in a shallow grave in the New Forest. So who had got hold of his User ID and password? The only person that came to mind was Tony Nelson. Had he decided to make some extra money by stealing from the company? He might have tortured Sewell before he killed him, forced him to hand over details of the company bank accounts. Hendrickson tried to appear calm. As far as anyone in the company was concerned, Sewell had gone AWOL for a few days. It wasn't unusual, and it was far too early for Hendrickson to show signs of concern. "Email?" he suggested.

175

"I'll send one now. I just thought maybe he'd said something to you."

Hendrickson shook his head. "I'm sure it's not worth worrying about."

Baston put his left thumb to his mouth and began to gnaw at the nail. He ambled out of the office.

Hendrickson stood up and began to pace. Everything had been going exactly as planned. Sewell was dead and buried. Hendrickson had yet to call in the police, but when he did they'd find the house empty. They'd check the hospitals, maybe the ports and airports, run a check on Sewell's credit cards. It would become a mystery that they'd never solve. Hendrickson knew Sewell liked to meet women through online dating agencies and chatrooms: at some point he'd suggest that maybe he had met someone online and either run off with them or been murdered. After a respectable amount of time he'd tighten his control over the company, sack Sewell's people and bring in his own. There'd be no need to sell the company, not when he was in sole control. That was the plan — but now Nelson was threatening to ruin everything. He wanted to scream with frustration and hurl his coffee mug at the wall, but he fought to stay calm. Now was not the time to lose his temper. He had to stay in control. He'd hired one killer. Now all he had to do was find another and get him to take care of Nelson. It was just a question of money, and Hendrickson had more than enough of that.

He walked down the corridor to Sewell's office, where Barbara was busy on her word-processor. He tapped on the door. She looked up and smiled when she saw him. "Larry, how can I help you?" She was an attractive brunette in her late forties.

"Any sign of Roger?"

She shook her head. "He's not answering his phone either."

"He didn't say where he was going, did he?"

"I was expecting him on Monday."

"He mentioned going to Florida. Did he say anything to you?"

"He didn't ask me to get him tickets."

"And there've been no emails from him?"

"Not this week."

"No contact at all?"

"Do you think something's wrong, Larry?"

Hendrickson tried to look relaxed. It was too soon to start raising red flags, but it was only natural to be concerned if his partner had gone missing. "No — you know what he's like. He'll probably turn up tomorrow with a sore head. Anything urgent I can take care of for him?"

"He's right up to date. He worked late last Thursday to clear his desk."

Hendrickson frowned. That wasn't like Sewell. He was forever behind with his paperwork. In fact, he left much of the day-to-day administration to Hendrickson. "I'm the ideas man," he'd always say. "You're the bread-and-butter guy, Larry." Hendrickson had to chase him to sign contracts and cheques.

"Thursday night?"

"He was still here when I left. That's why I wasn't worried when he didn't come in on Friday. I assumed he had a long weekend planned. I'm sure he's fine."

"You're probably right," said Hendrickson. "If he does phone in, ask him to give me a call, will you?"

Hendrickson headed back to his own office. He didn't think for a minute that Sewell would call. Not unless they had phones in hell. But he needed to know who'd been using Sewell's ID and password to log on to the company system. And what they wanted.

The major walked with Shepherd across the grass to the outdoor shooting range. Four troopers in fatigues were firing three-round bursts of their MP5s at metal cut-out figures of terrorists, the sound of gunfire echoing off the nearby barracks buildings.

"The Trojan units favour the Glock," said the major. "You used the SIG-Sauer, right?"

A sergeant was loading ammunition into magazines at a wooden bench and he nodded at Shepherd. His fingers were slipping rounds into the magazine quickly and efficiently, working purely by feel.

"Started with the Browning Hi-Power but, yeah, the fifteen-round magazine gives the P226 the edge every time," said Shepherd.

"The cops use the Glock with a ten-round magazine. The pros put eight in the mag so that the spring doesn't get over-strained. Two point five kilogram trigger pull. Not my favourite short, but you're stuck with it." Gannon picked up one of the pistols on the bench and handed it to Shepherd.

"They say it never jams, right?" said Shepherd.

Gannon pulled a face. "No guns jam," he said. "Ammunition jams. Put a crap round in a Glock and it'll jam. If you want jam-free, stick with revolvers, and live with having only six shots. The cops don't bother putting tracer rounds at the bottom of the mag. We do, because in situations where we need constant firepower it lets us know when to change mags. Cops make every shot count so they should always know how many they've got left. That's the theory. Now, let's see what you do at ten metres."

Shepherd picked up one of the magazines and slotted it into the butt of the Glock. Gannon stood slightly behind him as he adopted the classic firing stance. Left foot slightly ahead of the right, right hand around the butt, left hand around the right. The targets were simple ringed bullseyes, about two feet in diameter. He fired eight shots in four groups of two at one of the targets, then lowered the gun. All eight shots had gone through the centre of the target; the holes could have been covered by a fifty-pence piece.

"Show-off," said the major, grinning.

"Like riding a bike," said Shepherd. He ejected the empty mag and slotted in a fresh one.

He walked with the major to stand in front of the second target. This one was twenty-five metres away. Shepherd fired four groups of two in quick succession. His accuracy at the longer distance was virtually unchanged.

The major nodded approvingly and walked with Shepherd to the third target. This one was fifty metres away, the upper limit for a handgun. Beyond fifty metres, hitting a target with any degree of accuracy was down to luck more than training. He took a few seconds to get comfortable, forced himself to relax, then fired eight shots. All were within the centre three rings and could have been covered by a saucer. Eight killing shots at fifty metres was good shooting by anyone's standards. He ejected the mag, opened the breech to check that it was clear, locked the top slide in place and handed the gun to Gannon.

"Your accuracy's spot on, Spider, can't fault you on that," said the major. "Technique-wise, the double tap is fine for the range, but it's single shots when you're on the street. Remember, with the boys in blue every shot counts and has to be accounted for. The big difference between us and the cops is that we shoot until the target goes down. Cops shoot when only absolutely necessary to neutralise the threat."

"Got it."

"I bloody hope so, Spider, because if you revert to your Sass training and empty a magazine into a bad guy, you go to jail and don't pass go. Cops can only fire if life is in imminent danger. As soon as the bad guys drop their weapons, you stop firing."

"Okay."

"What we're going to do now is to take you back into the Killing House and run you through a series of drills, using blanks. We'll throw dozens of civilian situations at you. Teenager with an airgun, angry husband holding wife hostage, armed bank robbers, the works. We'll be testing two things — your marksman-ship and, more importantly, your judgement calls. You can't afford to make a mistake."

Just then his mobile phone rang. Shepherd grimaced. "Sorry," he said to the major. "I've got to keep it on in case the job needs me."

"Go ahead," said Gannon.

Shepherd walked away and took the call. It was Miss Malcolm from the au pair agency. "I haven't caught you at a bad time, have I, Mr Shepherd?" she asked.

Shepherd wondered what she'd say if he told her that he was about to go into the SAS Killing House to practise hostage-rescue techniques. "No, it's fine, Miss Malcolm."

"I've had four girls arrive in London at short notice and I thought I might show you the pick of the litter, so to speak."

"That's good news," said Shepherd. "The sooner the better, as far as I'm concerned."

"I was wondering if I could have one pop along to see you on Friday morning."

"That would be fine," said Shepherd. There was a burst of automatic fire from the far end of the range.

"What on earth was that?" asked Miss Malcolm.

"Nothing," said Shepherd. "Just a car backfiring." He realised that the major was listening. Gannon mimed firing a burst at him with an MP5 and Shepherd waved him away. "Thanks for your call, Miss Malcolm," he said and cut the connection. It was only when he put away the phone that he realised she hadn't told him the girl's name or where she was from.

"Sorry," he said to Gannon. "I've got to get an au pair fixed up sharpish."

"Couldn't get one for me, could you? I could do with something to keep me warm at night."

"She'll be cooking, ironing and babysitting Liam. That'll be her lot," said Shepherd. "She'll probably turn out to be a twenty-stone Romanian weight-lifter, but looks are pretty low on my list of requirements."

Shepherd spent all morning in the Killing House under the supervision of the major and a counter-terrorism instructor, a grizzled sergeant whom Shepherd remembered from his days in the SAS. They broke for lunch at one and the major took Shepherd to the mess. A special-projects team, a captain and fifteen troopers, were at an adjoining table and clearly curious as to who the major was with.

"So, what do you think of the new place?" asked Gannon, as he started on a plate of sausage and chips.

"More space than the old barracks," said Shepherd. "Food's the same as it ever was, though."

"Funnily enough, it used to be the RAF's catering school," said Gannon, stabbing at a sausage. "They didn't leave any chefs behind so we're stuck with our old guys. Still, it's only fuel, isn't it?"

"That was one of the first things I noticed when I left the Regiment," said Shepherd. "The weight started to go on. I put on ten pounds in the first month."

"All the coffee and doughnuts you cops eat, I suppose."

"Soldiering burns up the calories. Police work is less physical, certainly the sort I do."

182

"Stressful, though."

"Yeah, I suppose so. Long-term stress. In the Sass, the stress comes in bursts mainly. Bang, bang, bang, then it's all over and you wait for the shit to hit the fan again. In undercover work it's constant. Even when a case is over there's still the worry that someone might find out who you are and what you did."

"Revenge, you mean?"

Shepherd buttered a chunk of bread. "You're on your own if it goes tits up," he said. "In the Sass you've got the Regiment to take care of you. Safety in numbers."

"Cops take care of their own, don't they?"

"Uniforms, maybe, but I'm in a special unit. Most people don't even know I'm a cop."

"Armed?"

"If it goes with my cover. But as Dan Shepherd, no, I'm not supposed to carry a gun."

"Not supposed to?"

Shepherd chuckled. "Some rules are meant to be broken," he said. "Anyone sneaks into my home in the middle of the night, they'd better be wearing body armour."

They finished their lunch and walked back to the Killing House, past the ammunition stores and the briefing room they called the Kremlin. As always Gannon was carrying his sat phone.

"How much longer will you be heading up the Increment?" asked Shepherd.

"It's open-ended," said the major. "Apparently I'm doing such a good job they want me there until I retire or kick the bucket."

"All this al-Qaeda activity must keep you in the firing line," said Shepherd.

"You don't know half of it, Spider. Five is asking us to do some pretty heavy stuff, these days. Stuff we'd never have got away with in the old days."

"Difficult to get a handle on what they want, isn't it?"

"You knew where you were with the Provos — Brits out, a united Ireland. Simple. Everyone knew what they wanted, and why the British wouldn't give it to them. What the hell does al-Qaeda want? No one really knows. Death to infidels? The Yanks out of Saudi? Every woman in the world wearing a veil? And the way they wage war is so alien. Suicide bombers? Killing women and children? The Provos could be evil bastards at times, but the al-Qaeda lot are something else. How the hell are you supposed to deal with a suicide bomber?"

"It's a sick business, all right."

"It's going to happen here, Spider. Sooner or later. Five are working overtime to keep the lid on it, but there's only so much they can do. And when it happens it'll be big."

"Spectaculars, the IRA called them," said Shepherd. "Always hated that. Almost glamorised what they did. A bomb's a bomb. Casualties are casualties."

"But even they drew the line at planes. Or trains. They could have put a bomb on a British Airways flight whenever they wanted. The Dublin to Belfast train was a sitting target. But they never went for it. You know why?"

184

"They followed rules, I guess," said Shepherd.

"They regarded it as a war and they followed the rules of war. Most of the time. But al-Qaeda has no rules. The end justifies the means, no matter what the means are. They'll blow up a school if it serves their purpose. A football ground. The more horrific the better. They've got guys out in North Korea trying to buy uranium to build a dirty bomb. They were in Russia for anthrax. They've got cells all over the world stockpiling explosives. It's like trying to treat cancer. You take out one tumour and another one grows somewhere else. You're always one step behind, trying to catch up. At least with the Provos we knew who the bad guys were. We had the RUC on our side and we had real intel. You know how many Arabs they had working for MI5 on 9/11?"

"I'd guess none."

"You'd guess right. They had a few Arab speakers but they were white Oxbridge graduates. It's no wonder intelligence in that area is so weak. Still is, as far as I can see. Most of what's in the MI5 files that go across my desk is guesswork." He lifted the sat phone. "I just carry this around and wait for it to ring."

They reached the Killing House. "Question," said Shepherd.

"Fire away."

"How do you handle a suicide bomber?"

"You don't," said the major. "You can't. They want to die, so there's nothing you can say to them, no way you can apply pressure. You have to take them out with as few casualties as possible."

185

"So you slot them, end of story?"

"Head shot because the explosive is generally strapped to their body. But even then, chances are they'll go bang. They normally hold the trigger and all they have to do is press it. Even with a clean head shot the hand can spasm and set it off. Plus there's plan B."

"Plan B?"

"Whoever sends the bomber into play usually has a fall-back position. Either a timer or a remote-control trigger. They often use mobile phones."

"So slotting the guy doesn't necessarily make the bomb safe?"

"The guy can be dead on the ground and you still can't go near him, not before the bomb-disposal guys. The only way to deal with them is to take them out before they get to their target area. Once they're in place, you're screwed. The Israelis deal with them on a daily basis and the only defence they've got is public vigilance. You see a Palestinian wearing a bulky jacket, you scream like hell and run for it."

The sergeant was at the entrance to the Killing House, carrying an MP5. He nodded at Shepherd. "You ready for round two, Spider?"

Shepherd grinned. He relished working with professional soldiers again. Undercover work was solitary. He met Hargrove, he occasionally worked with other agents if the particular job required it, but generally he was alone. The comradeship of the Regiment was one of the things he missed most about it.

"We'll run through some group hostage situations," said Gannon. "Then I've arranged for sniper training."

"Excellent," said Shepherd. That was another thing he missed about the SAS. The chance to play with big boys' toys.

When the sergeant called time on the exercises in the Killing House Shepherd was exhausted. He'd been working with four troopers from the counter-terrorism wing and they'd pushed him hard. He drank from a plastic bottle of water and spat on the ground. "Nothing like the taste of cordite, is there?" said Gannon.

"How did it look?"

"You'll fit right in to SO19," said Gannon. "Not quite up to our high standards, of course."

"Of course," said Shepherd. He handed his weapon to the sergeant.

"We're going to have to leave the sniping," said Gannon. "I've got to head back to London. Chopper's ready now."

Shepherd looked at his watch and groaned. He hadn't realised how long he'd been in the Killing House. He pulled out his mobile phone and called Moira.

"Daniel," she said, and Shepherd could tell she was annoyed with him.

"Hiya, Moira. Look, I'm not going to be able to pick Liam up."

Moira sighed. "I collected him from school half an hour ago. A teacher phoned me to say that Liam was waiting at the gates."

Shepherd's heart sank. "Oh, God, I'm sorry."

"And I don't think that taking the Lord's name in vain is going to make things any better," said Moira.

"Can I talk to him?"

"He's very upset, Daniel."

Shepherd gritted his teeth, unable to believe he'd screwed up again. Why hadn't he kept a closer eye on the time?

"You can't keep doing this to him," said Moira. Her voice was flat: she wasn't accusing him, simply stating a fact.

"I know. Can you just tell him I was held up?"

"He knows that. He knows you don't do it deliberately."

The fact that she was being so understanding made Shepherd feel worse. "I'm sorry, Moira."

"I know you are. You're always sorry when you let him down. But you can't keep doing it."

"Please, Moira, can I speak to him?"

"He's crying. He won't want to speak to you. Not for a while."

Shepherd felt as if he'd been punched in the solar plexus. He squatted with his back to the wall. "Look, can you get him into the back garden in fifteen minutes?"

"What on earth for?"

"Please, Moira, just do as I ask, will you?"

"Daniel . . ."

"Fifteen minutes," said Shepherd. He cut the connection and banged the back of his head against the wall. "Shit," he said. "Shit, shit, shit."

188

Moira knocked on the bedroom door. "Liam?" she said. There was no reply so she knocked again. "Liam?"

"I'm not hungry," said Liam.

"I haven't made supper yet," said Moira. "I want you to come outside."

"Why?"

"I just do."

"I want to stay here."

"Listen to me, young man, you'll do as you're told. Open this door now."

Moira heard him slide off the bed and pad across the floor. He opened the door and looked up at her, cheeks wet with tears. "It's not fair," he said. "Dad always does this. He always says he'll be there and then he's not."

Moira bent down so that her face was level with her grandson's. "Your father loves you very much, but sometimes he's busy."

"He thinks his work's more important than me."

"No, he doesn't," said Moira. "You're the most important thing in the world to him. Now, don't be silly and come out into the garden."

Liam followed his grandmother down the stairs and out through the kitchen door. Moira took him to the end of the garden where Tom had planted a clump of rosebushes. A light wind blew through the branches of a weeping willow close to the shed.

"What are we doing, Gran?" asked Liam.

Moira wasn't sure, but she'd heard the insistence in her son-in-law's voice and could tell how upset he was. If he wanted them in the garden, then that was where they would be. They heard the helicopter before they saw it, a thudding whup-whup-whup to their right. Moira shaded her eyes with her hand and peered into the sky. There were large cumulus clouds dotted around, as white as cotton wool. She made out a black dot, no bigger than an insect, highlighted against one, and pointed at it. "There, Liam, see it?"

Liam jumped up and down. "Is it Dad?"

Despite herself Moira smiled. "Yes, I think it probably is."

The helicopter flew lower and gradually they could make out the rotor and the tail. Then they saw a figure in the open hatchway.

"It's Dad!" yelled Liam.

The helicopter was too far away for Moira to make out the man's features, but she had no doubt that it was her son-in-law. It was a grand gesture, indeed, but he didn't seem to understand that being a parent wasn't about making grand gestures, it was about providing security, and being there for your child, day and night. Liam needed a father who helped him with his homework, played football with him in the garden, tucked him up at night, not an action hero who flew in by helicopter to prove how sorry he was.

The helicopter circled the garden, the rotor wash squashing the grass flat. The man waved from the open door. Liam waved back excitedly. "Dad!"

The man blew a kiss.

Liam blew one back. "Look, Gran!"

Moira patted his shoulder. "Yes, I see him."

190

The helicopter banked, flew off to the east, towards London. Liam watched it go. "He does love me, doesn't he, Gran?"

"Oh, yes," said Moira, quietly. "He does."

Norman Baston bit into his cheeseburger and checked his email inbox for the tenth time that evening. There was no reply from Roger Sewell. Baston had tried Sewell's mobile twice and both times it had gone straight to voicemail. Sewell hadn't logged on again. The first time he'd come in remotely: he hadn't accessed the system from within the company. Baston wiped his mouth on the back of his sleeve. The meeting Sewell had missed that morning had been an important one. Baston knew that Sewell was vehemently against Hendrickson's ambition to sell the company. If he succeeded, Baston would never realise the true value of his share options. He wanted Sewell to agree to a new contract that would make up for the money he'd expected to get when the firm was sold. It was Sewell's company and Baston had no quarrel with that, but he knew what a crucial role he had played in its success. It was time for Sewell to pay the piper.

Baston knew exactly what was going on at the company. He had access to the company's computer records and could monitor all internal and external emails. Sewell was fanatical about his staff not talking to his competitors, and he also wanted to know what they said to each other. Every Monday Baston provided him with a breakdown of Internet usage and a summary of the more interesting email traffic. He knew exactly who Hendrickson was talking to, and what he stood to make if the sale went through. He'd seen all the arguments that Hendrickson had put forward in his attempts to convince Sewell to sell. And he'd read all Sewell's objections.

Baston also knew what Sewell got up to in his free time, how he liked having sex with women he met through the Internet. Sewell used pictures of male models to lure in young women, then offered them money for kinky sex. Ninety-nine per cent turned him down, but a one per cent success rate was more than enough when he was getting several hundred replies a month. Baston knew where Sewell took the women, what he did with them, and he knew where on the system Sewell stored the digital photographs he took of his escapades. Baston was sure that Sewell would agree to his pay demands. Blackmail was an ugly word. But so was transvestite. And dildo.

Baston took another bite of cheeseburger and slotted a handful of French fries into his mouth. He chewed with relish. It was almost eleven o'clock at night but he was in no rush to go home. Home was a two-up, two-down terraced house in Salford that wouldn't have been out of place in an episode of *Coronation Street*. He'd inherited it from his parents after they'd died in a motorway pile-up outside Preston on the day before his seventeenth birthday. He hadn't changed anything in the house and still slept in a single bed in the second bedroom. He hadn't been in his parents' room since the day they'd died. He hadn't even opened the door. His father's pipe was still in the ashtray next to the wing-backed chair by the gas fire. Baston never sat in the chair, or in his mother's space on the sofa. He never cooked in the house. His mother had never let him make so much as a cup of tea, and all he ate now were takeaway meals and breakfast cereal. Home was just a place where he slept and ate.

His office was where he preferred to be, working on his beloved computers. He preferred the machines to his colleagues. Computers never lied, or sneered at you because you had spots or because you would rather read a software manual than talk about soccer or women's breasts. The money Baston earned wasn't important, other than as a means of keeping score. There was nothing he wanted to buy. He didn't drive, he didn't drink or do drugs, he had all the clothes he needed and the company paid for all the equipment he wanted. But money gave him status. He had access to the payroll program — he'd designed it, and he knew what everyone in the company earned. There weren't many who earned more than he did, only Hendrickson, Sewell and the sales manager, Bill Willis. If Sewell met Baston's latest demands he'd overtake Willis. Then it would be Baston who did the sneering as he walked through the car park and saw Willis climbing into his convertible Saab, dressed in his made-to-measure suit and carrying his calf-leather briefcase. Willis always said, "Good evening," when he saw Baston heading towards the bus stop, and sometimes offered him a lift, but Baston knew he did so only to ram his success in Baston's face. Well, soon the tables would be turned. Baston knew about Willis's affair with one of the secretaries in accounting. He was married and so was she, and Baston had kept copies of all the lovey-dovey emails they sent each other. One day he'd send Willis's wife an envelope stuffed with hard copies. That would serve Willis right.

Baston checked his inbox again, but there was nothing from Sewell. It wasn't like his boss. Sewell checked his emails every hour or so, and his mobile was rarely off. Baston had sent him half a dozen emails asking him to get in touch either online or by phone. Now he logged on to the company's email system and checked Sewell's mailbox. The mail hadn't been read since Sewell had logged on to the system on Wednesday night. The six emails he'd sent him were all there, unread.

Baston sat back and stared at his monitor. Sewell wasn't picking up his office email, but he had a personal account, one he used on his laptop. Baston could access the laptop whenever Sewell was online. A couple of years earlier Baston had put in a keystroke program and set up backdoor access that allowed him to roam through the laptop's hard drive whenever the machine was connected to the Internet. He knew that Sewell would go apeshit if he ever found out, but he'd gone to a great deal of trouble to cover his tracks. His fingers played across the keyboard. Sewell wasn't online.

Baston took another bite of his cheeseburger and chewed thoughtfully. Okay, so Sewell wasn't online. And he wasn't picking up his emails. But maybe he'd sent emails last time he was online. He wiped his greasy hands on his trousers and tapped on the keyboard. He ran a search program, looking for any emails sent to company employees within the last forty-eight hours. There was one, to the head of the firm's legal department, John Garden. Sewell had sent it on Wednesday night and Garden had read it first thing that morning. It was still in his inbox. Baston chewed as he read it. Sewell didn't say where he was or what he was doing. In capital letters he told Garden on no account to tell Larry Hendrickson that he'd been in touch, and asked him to check if there had been any unexpected transfers from the company bank accounts and to send a reply to Sewell's personal email address.

"What the hell are you up to, Roger?" Baston muttered. He hated mysteries. And Roger Sewell was certainly behaving mysteriously.

Shepherd opened the fridge and groaned when he saw there was no milk. He took a sip of black coffee, then sat on the sofa and phoned Moira. Liam answered. "I knew it would be you, Dad," he said excitedly. "Did you fly all the way to London in the helicopter?"

"All the way."

"In the clouds and stuff?"

"We flew under the clouds. You can't see where you're going when you fly through clouds so it's dangerous."

"Can I go in a helicopter one day?"

"Sure you can," said Shepherd.

"Why didn't you land?"

"You have to stay away from trees and buildings. I'm sorry I didn't pick you up from school today. I was busy. I wanted to, but it didn't work out."

"That's okay."

"Are you sure?"

"Course."

"Gran said you waited outside."

"I was at the gate. Mrs Mowling asked me who was picking me up and she rang Gran. It was okay."

"But you were cross with me, yeah?"

Liam didn't say anything.

"I'll see you at the weekend, right?" said Shepherd.

"In the helicopter?"

"I'll probably drive."

"And I can come back to London with you at the weekend?" asked Liam.

"Maybe."

"You always say 'maybe' when you mean 'no'. It's not fair," said Liam.

"If I can make it happen, I will," said Shepherd, "but I have to get things sorted first. I haven't even got any milk in the fridge so how could I make you breakfast?"

"Toast," said Liam.

"No bread."

"I don't need breakfast."

"Most important meal of the day," said Shepherd.

"Says who?"

"Says everyone. Your gran for a start."

"I don't care about breakfast. I want to live at home."

"I know you do, kid. I'm only teasing. Let me get some help fixed up and then you can move back in."

"Okay." Liam sounded wretched.

"I mean it," said Shepherd.

"Okay."

"What are you doing now?" asked Shepherd.

"Talking to you."

"Before I phoned?"

"Watching TV."

"And you've done your homework?"

"I did it before supper."

"Good lad."

"Dad?"

"Yes?"

There was a long pause. "Nothing," said Liam, eventually.

"What?"

"Nothing. See you at the weekend. 'Bye." The last few words tumbled out and Liam cut the connection before Shepherd could say anything else. He wasn't sure if his son had been about to cry or if he was rushing off to do something. Shepherd thought about ringing back, then decided against it. If Liam was upset, a phone conversation wouldn't help.

When the doorbell rang Shepherd was in the shower. He cursed, grabbed a towel and peered down through the bedroom window. His visitor was a young woman, shoulder-length brown hair, raincoat with the collar up. Shepherd frowned, then remembered that Miss Malcolm had promised to send a potential au pair for him to interview. He opened the door and smiled apologetically. "I'm in the shower — give me a minute to get dressed," he said. "Why don't you make us both a coffee? The kitchen's down there." He pointed, then padded back upstairs where he finished drying and pulled on a grey turtleneck pullover and black jeans.

As he walked into the kitchen the woman handed him a mug of black coffee. "I didn't know if you wanted milk or sugar," she said.

"Black is fine," he said. "I'm out of milk anyway." He sipped the coffee. "So, where are you from, then?" he asked.

The woman frowned. "Hampshire, originally."

"You're English?"

"That surprises you?" she asked.

"It's just that Miss Malcolm said most of the girls in your line of work were from Eastern Europe."

The woman's frown deepened. "Who do you think I am?" she said.

"You're from the agency? The au pair?"

Now the woman's eyes sparkled with amusement. "You've been giving me the runaround for the past week."

Shepherd groaned. "The psychiatrist?"

"Psychologist."

"I'm sorry, but I'm busy."

"I just want a few minutes of your time, DC Shepherd."

Shepherd glared at her. "How long have you been with Hargrove's unit?" he asked.

"Six months."

"Okay, first rule of this business, we never use ranks or honorifics."

"We're in your home."

"It doesn't matter where we are. You get in the habit of using ranks or saying 'sir' and one day you do it in front of someone who gives a shit and puts a bullet in my head."

"I'm sorry," she said.

Shepherd looked at his watch.

"Really, this won't take long," she said. "I'm not going to ask you to lie on a sofa and talk about your mother. I just want a quick chat."

"You want to evaluate my mental state to see whether or not I'm suitable for undercover work," said Shepherd. "I don't mean to sound paranoid," he added.

"Just because you're paranoid doesn't mean we're not out to get you," she said. She smiled and took a sip of her coffee. "Dan — it's okay if I call you Dan, is it?"

"Anything's better than Detective Constable."

One of his mobiles rang. It was Hargrove. "I've got to take this," he said. "Can you wait for me in the sitting room?" He went out into the garden before he took the call. "If you're calling to check whether she's here, the answer's yes," he said frostily.

"Excuse me?" said Hargrove.

"The psychologist. She's here."

"Ah," said Hargrove. "That's not why I'm calling, but I'm glad you two are talking."

"Because you don't think I'm up to the job?"

"Because we all deal with stress in different ways, and she can help you cope with what's going on in your life."

"And what if I refuse to talk to her?"

"That in itself is a sign that something's amiss," said Hargrove. "It's like a guy with cancer refusing to see a specialist. Denial doesn't solve anything."

"I don't have cancer, and I'm not in denial," said Shepherd.

"Spider, will you cut me some slack here? You have to see a certified psychologist at least twice a year. You know that. All agents do."

"This is different, and you know it is. She's here to see if I'm firing on all cylinders or if I'm a few sandwiches short of a picnic. And I know I'm mixing my metaphors."

Hargrove chuckled. "Just have a chat with her, and that'll be the end of it."

"Unless she discovers I'm suicidal."

"Are you?"

"Of course not," said Shepherd, then flushed as he realised the superintendent was joking. "If you're not calling about her, then what's up?" he asked.

"Angie Kerr," said Hargrove. "Good news, bad news. The good news is that the CPS wants to do a deal with her."

"And the bad?"

"They want you to make the approach. Because you were on the original case, the Hendrickson one, they want continuity of investigation. If someone else takes over now it'll be harder to show the chain of the investigation down the line. Charlie Kerr could scream entrapment if a new officer makes the approach. If you do it, it becomes part of the ongoing investigation. You were pursuing the case against her but offered her the option of giving evidence against her husband."

"I hope you told them no," said Shepherd. "There's no way I want a gangster like Charlie Kerr knowing I was on his case. And it'll all come out in pre-trial disclosure if I make the approach."

"I'm ahead of you, Spider," said Hargrove. "I told them in no uncertain terms that your security is paramount."

"They actually thought I'd go to Angie Kerr and tell her I was an undercover cop? How stupid are the CPS?"

"They just want to make the best case they can," said Hargrove. "You can see their point. I've suggested we fix up another meeting, then we move in and arrest you and her at the same time. She'll think we have you in custody and that you'll roll over on her. We give her the out of rolling over on her husband and that should be that."

"I'm due to start with SO19 on Monday," said Shepherd. "You know how hard it is to stay in character on a job. Am I supposed to hold down two now?"

"It would just be a meet. You can say you want to go over a few details."

"I'm not sure about this," said Shepherd. "We already have the evidence against her. Manchester CID can bust her for conspiracy to murder on that, and they don't have to tell her I was undercover. Bearing in mind what her husband will do to her, she'd be a fool to turn down any deal."

"If she sees you arrested, she'll know it's over."

Shepherd sighed. "Okay. When? I'm on duty all next week, two until ten every day. I can hardly tell them I'm taking a day off to go to Manchester."

"What about this afternoon?"

Shepherd cursed. There was time to fix up a meet in Manchester, but it was a long drive and the weekend traffic would be a nightmare. "I'll phone her and get back to you," he said.

"Thanks, Spider. I've got your SO19 legend ready and a vehicle. I'll get them to you this afternoon."

Shepherd cut the connection, left the mobile on the kitchen table with the two others and went through to the sitting room. The woman was sitting in one of the armchairs. She had taken a clipboard out of her briefcase and was sitting with it on her lap. Her coffee was on a side table. Shepherd headed for the sofa, then stopped himself and sat in one of the armchairs instead. "Don't read anything into my choice of seat," he said. "I can let you finish your coffee but then I've got to drive up to Manchester. Hargrove's orders. If you have a problem with that, take it up with him."

"Fine," she said. "By the way, I'm Kathy Gift. It's Dr Gift, actually, but I take your point about not using honorifics."

"Gift?"

"As in present," she said. "It used to be longer. My great-grandparents were German. They cut off a few syllables when they moved to England." She crossed her legs. She was wearing a dark blue skirt that rose above her knees, a matching jacket and a cream shirt. There was a gold necklace with a Star of David round her neck. "Did you meet my predecessor?" she asked.

The previous psychologist had been a sixty-year-old man who wore tweed jackets and smoked a briar pipe. He had a clutch of professional qualifications and was one of the most humourless men that Shepherd had ever met. "Only when I had to."

"And you weren't impressed?"

"He was a clever guy, but unless you've done what we do it's hard to understand what's involved."

"The pressures?"

"I'm not saying you can't empathise, because of course you can. But that's a world away from understanding what we go through."

"Is it possible to explain what it's like?"

"You've spoken to other agents, haven't you?"

She brushed a lock of hair behind her ear. "They all say the same thing initially," she said. "Unless you've done it, you can't understand what it's like."

"There you go, then."

"But after a few sessions, they realise I'm there to help, not to be judgemental or make career decisions. I'm just someone you can unburden yourself to. Someone who can offer an objective view on how to deal with problems that arise."

Shepherd's brow creased. "But you're more than that, aren't you? You've a direct line to Hargrove, and if you think a guy's going over the edge you're duty-bound to tell him."

"Is that how you're feeling — that you're about to go over the edge?"

Shepherd chuckled. "You don't miss a trick, do you?"

"I'm not trying to trick you. I just want to know what makes you tick. Superintendent Hargrove is concerned, that's all. You've been under a lot of stress lately and he wants reassurance that all's well."

"I can do the job. Isn't that all that matters?"

"Short term, of course results are important. But think of a racing car belting along at top speed and developing a fault. Until it blows apart everything probably seems fine."

"Does he think I might fall apart?"

"Don't read too much into that analogy," she said. "And he thinks highly of you. You know that."

"But he still wants me to talk to a shrink."

"Think of it as preventive maintenance."

Shepherd sipped his coffee. "Okay, let's talk technique. You've read my file?"

"Of course."

"So you know about my trick memory."

"Photographic, it says in the file."

"Whatever. I can recall pretty much everything I see or hear. It fades eventually if I don't use the information, but short term it's infallible. It's because of my memory that I have few problems in maintaining my cover stories. I'm able to compartmentalise the roles I play. I put them on and take them off like I change clothes."

"As easy as that?"

"It's not easy, but it's easier for me than it is for a guy who has to try to remember what he said to whom and where he was when he said it. I can cross-reference everything without thinking about it."

"You're lucky."

"I guess."

"But you've been less lucky on the home front." She was watching for his reaction.

"I'm handling it," he said.

"How?"

"My boy's staying with his grandparents and I'm interviewing au pairs. As soon as I've found one Liam can move back in with me."

"That's not handling what happened, is it? You're dealing with practicalities, not your feelings."

"My feelings don't come into it. My wife died, it was a damn shame, but life goes on."

"You miss her." It was a statement, not a question.

"Of course I miss her."

"And Liam?"

"He lost his mother."

"Does he talk about it?"

"No."

"Have you raised it with him?"

"I don't want to upset him. He's a child."

"He has to talk about it, Dan. And so do you."

"In time."

She smiled sympathetically. Shepherd was an expert at reading faces, but he still couldn't tell if her smile was genuine or not. "There's nothing wrong with grief," she said. "It's part of the process."

"I know, eight stages," said Shepherd. "Denial, anger, bargaining, guilt, depression, loneliness, acceptance and hope."

"And what stage are you at?"

"I know Sue's dead, there's no one to be angry with, there's no one to make a deal with to get her back, it wasn't my fault so I don't feel guilty, I'm too busy to be depressed, I don't get lonely, I accept that she isn't coming back. So where does that leave me? At hope? Hoping for what?"

"It's interesting that you say there's no one to be angry with."

"It was an accident. She was driving Liam to school and went through a red light. A truck hit her. End of story."

"You don't have to be angry with a person. You can simply be angry with the unfairness of it. Why your wife? Why not some other woman on the school-run?"

"Shit happens."

"Yes, but when it does, don't we wonder why it's happened to us?"

"Thinking about it won't bring her back."

"So you block it."

"You're putting words into my mouth."

"So tell me what words you'd use. At the moment all I'm getting is negatives. You're not guilty, you're not angry, you're not depressed. What are you?"

"I really am going to have to get my skates on," said Shepherd. He stood up. "I don't want to be rude but I have to go."

"What you really mean is that you want me to go."

"That's right."

She stood up and handed him her mug. "I want to schedule a meeting with you over the next few days."

"I'll let you know."

Gift's eyes hardened. "I don't think you understand, Dan. I'm not asking, I'm telling. I have the authority to remove you from active service if I'm not completely satisfied that you're up to the job."

"Bollocks."

She flashed him a tight smile. "Check with the superintendent if you like, but he'll confirm what I'm saying."

"The case I'm on is more important than whether or not I cry myself to sleep at night." He held up his hand quickly. "Not that I do."

"Have you cried at all since your wife died?"

The question stopped Shepherd in his tracks and he lowered his hand. He hadn't cried when he'd learned that Sue had died. And he hadn't cried at her funeral. Or afterwards, when he lay alone in the double bed, still able to smell her perfume on the pillow. He wasn't the crying sort. He'd lost friends, seen two blown to bits by a landmine in Kuwait, but he'd never cried for them. If you saw action you saw death, and there wasn't time to stand over a grave bawling your eyes out. But friends and fellow soldiers weren't wives, and it was only when Gift asked the question that Shepherd saw something was wrong when a husband didn't weep for his dead wife.

Gift touched his elbow. "I'm not the enemy, Dan. I'm here to make your life easier."

"I can't come into the office," he said quietly.

"No one's asking you to," she said. "I can come to you."

"And all we do is talk?"

"Just talk. What about Monday?"

"I start the new job on Monday," he said. "I don't need any distractions."

"Tuesday, then? Or Wednesday?"

"Wednesday," said Shepherd. "I'll be here most of the morning." He had already checked with SO19 and he was on the two until ten shift for the first week.

He accompanied her to the front door and let her out. He watched her walk to her black Mazda sports car. He wondered what her choice of car said about her. He had been telling the truth when he told her he could slip into and out of his roles without difficulty. What he hadn't told her was that he was often more comfortable when he was playing a role than when he was being himself. And even he knew that that wasn't a good sign.

As the psychologist drove away, Shepherd saw a girl walking briskly towards his garden gate. She was in her twenties, dark hair dyed blonde, wearing a knee-length black leather coat. She walked down the path. "My name is Halina, from the agency," she said. She had high cheekbones, green, cat-like eyes, gleaming white teeth and a slight American accent.

Shepherd shook her hand. Her nails were painted red but bitten to the quick and she had silver rings on most of her fingers. "Where are you from, Halina?" he asked as they went inside.

"From Poland," she said. "Warsaw. I have my references here." She handed him a large manila envelope. "My name, it means 'light' in English."

Shepherd opened the envelope. There was a letter from a factory manager in Warsaw saying that she was a hard worker and good timekeeper, another from an American couple who said she had done a great job taking care of their six-year-old daughter during their year-long stay in the Polish capital. There was also a photocopy of the application form she had filled in to join Miss Malcolm's agency. Everything seemed in order. Halina spoke good English, had a clean driving licence and a consistent work history. But something was not right about her. He didn't know what it was, but he knew she wasn't to be trusted. His policeman's instinct had kicked in and he had been in the job long enough to know that, more often than not, he could rely on his gut feelings. He made small-talk with her for fifteen minutes, then sent her on her way with a promise that he'd call Miss Malcolm on Monday. He didn't want her within a mile of his son, no matter how glowing her references.

He phoned Miss Malcolm and explained that the girl she'd sent wasn't suitable. She promised to call as soon as she had any other prospects, but pointed out that it was a seller's market. "Like plumbers or electricians," she said, "sometimes you just have to take what's available."

Shepherd thanked her and rang off. His personal opinion was that the welfare of his son was a hell of a lot more important than a leaking tap or a blown fuse, but he knew there was no point in picking a fight with her. If he was going to find someone suitable, he needed Miss Malcolm on his side.

He picked up the Tony Nelson phone and took a deep breath. He had to stop being Dan Shepherd, single parent and undercover police officer. Everything he said on the phone had to be in character. Cold, efficient, ruthless. He focused on what he was about to do. Then he rang Angie Kerr. Her voicemail kicked in and Shepherd cut the connection. He'd try later.

He changed into his running gear and picked up his weighted rucksack. He did a fast ten kilometres and by the time he got back to the house he was drenched with sweat. Two cars were parked in the road outside the house, a new red Rover and a three-year-old white Toyota. Two men were standing at the front door, one with a clipboard, the other with an A4 manila envelope. Shepherd didn't recognise either but they both had the short hair and stout shoes that marked them out as police officers in plain clothes. "Dan Shepherd?" said the man with the clipboard.

"Yeah," said Shepherd. He slipped off the rucksack and dropped it on the path.

"Compliments of Superintendent Hargrove," said the man, nodding at the Toyota. He held out the clipboard and a pen. "Sign at the bottom, please." The car would be registered, taxed and insured in the name of the legend he was using as an SO19 officer.

"The gear's in the back, sir," said the man, handing him the keys. "You can check it if you want."

"I'm sure it's fine."

210

"Second page, sir."

Shepherd signed for the equipment he'd need for his SO19 duty: bulletproof Kevlar vest with ceramic plate, black Nato-style ballistic helmet, Kevlar gloves with leather trigger finger, equipment belt with plastic retention holster for the Glock, Sure-Fire combat light, CS spray, plastic handcuffs, retractable baton, radio pouch and magazine pouches.

"And page three is for documentation, sir." The man fished a white envelope out of his coat pocket and handed it to Shepherd, who signed on the third page, then handed the clipboard back to the man.

The second man gave him the manila envelope. "Background files, no need to sign for them," said the man. He had a Northern Irish accent. "Normal procedures apply." They went back to the Rover and drove off.

"Normal procedures" meant memorise and destroy. Shepherd opened the boot of the Toyota, took out the black nylon equipment bag and let himself into the house. He dropped the bag and the rucksack in the kitchen, then showered and changed back into his grey pullover and black jeans. He made himself some coffee before he opened the manila envelope.

It contained a CD disk and a dozen sheets of paper in a clear plastic file. Shepherd dropped down on to his sofa and swung his feet on to the coffee-table. The file contained his SO19 legend. He scanned the sheets, committing them to memory. He was Stuart Marsden, armed cop. Three years on the beat in Glasgow followed by four years in a Strathclyde armed-response unit. Two commendations for bravery, promotion on the horizon, single with no children. No emotional baggage. It was a far cry from Shepherd's own situation.

Marsden's date of birth was his own. That was par for the course: the people who put together the legends stuck as close as possible to the operative's own history. It was the small things that could trip up an agent. Getting his birth sign wrong. Forgetting the name of the station in the town where he was born.

He'd worked undercover in Glasgow on several long-term operations so he knew the geography of the city, and an hour or two with a guidebook and map would fill in any gaps.

When he'd finished he closed his eyes and ran through the details. It was all there. He had no idea why he had almost total recall while most people struggled to remember their own telephone number, but it had saved his life on at least two occasions. Once he'd been tied to a chair in a basement faced with three men with axe handles and it had only been his memory that had convinced them he was an art thief who specialised in early-nineteenth-century religious works. The second time he'd been helping to load a yacht with several hundred kilos of Moroccan hashish when one of the crewmen recognised him from a previous operation. He had pulled a gun and threatened to shoot. Shepherd had been using a different identity on the first operation but his faultless memory had pulled up enough detail from the original legend to persuade the sailors that he'd switched identities because he was being pursued by the DEA. He'd ended up drinking brandy with them all night, their new best friend.

He tossed the plastic file on to the coffee-table, then slotted the CD into the laptop. It contained the personnel files of Sergeant Keith Rose and two dozen members of SO19. Shepherd didn't want to read the files: it felt like eavesdropping on colleagues. It was one thing to target drugs-dealers and armed robbers, quite another to go against fellow police officers. Keith Rose might well be a bad cop, and there might well be others among the files on the CD, but the majority of the men Shepherd had to read about would be good, honest officers. Shepherd knew how he would hate another cop to read his personnel file — with information about Sue's death, or what Kathy Gift thought of the way he was dealing with stress. He wouldn't want a fellow officer to look for signs that he was corrupt.

He stood up and paced around. It was always up to him whether or not he accepted an assignment, but the only reason he had for saying no to this case was that he didn't want to investigate other cops. And Shepherd knew that wasn't a good enough reason. He sat down again and started to read.

Norman Baston ambled down the corridor towards Larry Hendrickson's office. He grinned amiably at Hendrickson's secretary. "Is your lord and master in?"

"Good morning, Norman," she said. "Let me check."

She picked up her phone and spoke to her boss, then nodded for him to go through.

Hendrickson looked up from his terminal as Baston walked into his office. "What's up, Norm?" he asked.

Baston closed the door behind him. "Have you and Roger got a problem?"

Hendrickson frowned. "What do you mean?"

Baston sat down in one of the two chairs facing Hendrickson's desk and stretched out his legs. "You still want to sell the company, right?"

"You know I do. If it wasn't for Roger, we'd have done the deal six months ago, but he's the majority shareholder."

"Do you think he might be trying to force you out? And by you, I mean us."

"What the hell are you talking about?"

Baston took a typed sheet from his jacket pocket and slid it across Hendrickson's desk.

Hendrickson blanched as he read it.

"If everything's rosy, why is he asking John to check the company accounts and not say anything to you?"

Hendrickson fought to keep calm. "He's maybe got a better offer on the table and wants to juggle the figures." He stared at the heading on the email, then glanced at the calendar on his desk. The email had been sent on Wednesday night. Five days after Roger Sewell had been shot and buried in the New Forest. And Sewell *was* dead: Nelson had shown him the photographs. Hendrickson dropped the sheet of paper on to his desk. "There's no way anyone else could have sent that, is there?"

Baston's brow creased into deep furrows. "What do you mean?"

"Someone messing about with Roger's email address."

"Not unless he gave someone his password. And why would he do that?"

Hendrickson's heart was pounding and he had a headache. If Nelson was accessing the computer and sending emails under Sewell's name, what was he hoping to achieve? And why would he email John Garden? If it was money that Nelson wanted, he could have forced Sewell to sign a few cheques before he put a bullet in his head. None of this made any sense. Unless Sewell wasn't dead. A cold shiver ran down Hendrickson's spine. And if he wasn't dead, how had Nelson got the Polaroids?

He tried to keep his voice steady. "Has John replied to Roger's email?"

"Not yet. What do you think Roger's up to?"

"He's the boss, Norm. He can do what the hell he wants."

"But I get the feeling he's cutting you — and me — out of the loop."

"Now you're being paranoid."

Baston tapped the sheet of paper. "He wants John to check the company accounts, get back to him on his personal email and not tell you. That's being devious. He's up to something. For all we know he could be selling his stake to some multinational and we'll get sod all."

"Roger wouldn't do that." Hendrickson was close to throwing up. "Look, he's taken a few days off and he wants to keep a check on things. He probably doesn't want me to know he's looking over my shoulder." Hendrickson got up, came round the desk and opened the door. "It's nothing, Norm."

Baston scratched his neck. "I've got a bad feeling about it," he said.

"It's all that junk food you eat," said Hendrickson. "Go on, I'll give you a call as soon as I hear from him."

Baston didn't seem convinced. Hendrickson patted his shoulder and eased him out of the room. He closed the door, then rushed over to the desk, picked up the sheet of paper and reread it. If Sewell wasn't dead, what had Nelson been playing at? And why hadn't Sewell turned up at the office?

Sewell *had* to be dead. What was happening now was the prelude to some blackmail attempt. He took out his mobile and called Angie. Her phone went straight to voicemail. Hendrickson didn't like to leave a message but he couldn't spend all day calling her. "Angie, hi, it's Larry. Look, I need to talk to you. It's urgent. Your husband — don't do anything until you've talked to me, okay?" He cut the connection, then realised he hadn't said anything about Tony Nelson. Maybe he should have warned her about him. He put his thumb on the redial button but had second thoughts. He didn't want to sound too worried — it might spook her. Besides, she'd know what he meant. He had to stay in control. A plan was already forming in his mind. He'd get Angie to fix up a meeting with Nelson, then he'd turn up and force the man to tell him what he was playing at.

★　★　★

Charlie Kerr closed one eye, sighted along his cue, and hit the white ball. It clipped the red into the corner pocket and pulled back behind the brown. "Nice," said Eddie Anderson. He was standing by the scoreboard, balancing his cue on his left foot.

Angie appeared at the door in her pale blue towelling robe, with a glass of orange juice. "I'll be by the pool, babe."

"Don't forget we're out tonight," he said. Two members of the Carlos Rodriguez cartel were coming over to finalise a cocaine deal he'd been putting together. The plan was to take them out to dinner with a couple of high-class escort girls. Dinner at an upmarket Thai restaurant followed by a visit to one of the city-centre casinos, then straight to Aces where they'd get the full VIP treatment.

"I'll look good for you, babe," she said. She walked up and kissed his cheek. "Don't worry."

Kerr patted her backside. "You always look good," he said. He grinned at Anderson. "What do you think, Eddie? She looks good, yeah?"

"A sight for sore eyes," said Anderson.

Angie flashed him a smile and headed for the pool. Kerr bent over the table and potted the brown. "Nice shot," said Anderson.

Kerr went for another red but it hit the edge of the pocket and spun across the table. He swore. "I need a coffee. Angie!" he shouted. There was no answer. "I don't know why we even have a pool," he said. "She never bloody swims in it, just lies down next to it. Angie!"

"I'll make it," said Anderson.

"Your coffee tastes like shit," said Kerr.

He went through to the kitchen and switched on the kettle. Angie's mobile was on the black marble work surface, plugged into a mains socket. Kerr picked it up. It was switched off. He pressed the power button, then spooned coffee into the cafetière. He picked up the phone. There was a single voice message. Kerr played it. Who the hell was Larry?

Shepherd took the black nylon equipment bag up to the bedroom and laid out the contents on the bed. It had his Stuart Marsden cover name scratched into it and looked as if it had been in use for years. The equipment was all labelled, too. Police officers were as bad as SAS troopers when it came to liberating or souveniring equipment. A name-tag was sewn into the inside of the bullet-proof vest and the belt, and "Marsden" had been scratched into the side of the holster. A printed name-tag had been sellotaped to the stem of the flashlight and the CS spray, while "SM" was painted inside the helmet. All the equipment was in good condition but had clearly been used. It was the little things that mattered when it came to maintaining a cover. If he turned up at SO19 with brand new gear, questions would be asked.

He hauled on the vest. It was similar to the one he'd worn in the SAS. It weighed several kilograms, with the ceramic plate in the front pocket to protect the heart and vital organs. He slid the belt round his waist, then slotted the CS spray and retractable baton into their holders.

He took off all the equipment and repacked it in the nylon bag, then sat down on the bed and opened the white envelope. He had destroyed the CD files Hargrove had sent, then burned the sheets of paper. But the white envelope contained the documents he'd need as Stuart Marsden: there was a warrant card, and a driving licence, both with a recent photograph, a Bank of Scotland debit card and a Barclaycard. The credit cards would function, Shepherd knew, but every pound would have to be accounted for at the end of the operation. He had a spare wallet into which he slotted the cards and the licence, with half of the banknotes from his own wallet. He put it into his bedside cabinet. He had the weekend to himself before he stepped into the shoes of Stuart Marsden, armed policeman. Not shoes, he reminded himself. Boots. SO19 officers wore regular army-issue black leather boots, and the ones Hargrove had sent were brand new. Shepherd would have preferred to wear his own, but they were brown. He'd have to go running in the new boots, wearing two pairs of thick wool socks to protect his feet until they were broken in.

He got changed and went downstairs with the boots. Before he left the house he phoned Angie Kerr again. The call went through to voicemail, but Shepherd didn't leave a message.

Angie stretched out on the sun-lounger, then pulled her Marlboros and lighter from the pocket of her robe. She lit a cigarette and she looked at the back of the house. It didn't feel like a home, even though she'd lived there for more than five years. Charlie had bought the place without telling her. He hadn't even told her he was putting their old house up for sale. The first she'd known of the sale was when an estate agent had walked in while she was in the shower.

Angie took another pull on her cigarette. She'd decided to sell this house, once Charlie was out of the way, and all the furniture. She'd walk away with just her clothes. She didn't want anything that would remind her of him. She'd have to wait until a decent interval had passed — play the grief-stricken widow for a few months — but then she'd be set for life. The house was worth at least two million, there was almost a quarter of a million in their joint account, and she had access to three safety-deposit boxes in various banks containing cash and Krugerrands worth well over half a million. She didn't know where Charlie kept all his money but she had no doubt he had millions stashed in overseas accounts. He'd made a will shortly after they'd married so she was pretty sure that his lawyers would tell her where the money was. But even if they didn't she had more than enough to live in luxury for the rest of her life.

She flicked ash and lay back on the sun-lounger, enjoying the feel of the sun on her face. She'd sell the villa in Marbella too and buy a place in France. Charlie hated France. He hated the food, he hated the people, he hated not being able to speak the language. He felt comfortable in Spain. He was a face there, he was known, feared. He was ushered into the best nightclubs without queuing or paying, he got the best seats in all the restaurants, and young women lined up to sleep with him. Once Tony Nelson had done his job, she'd never go to Spain again. She'd buy an apartment in London, Chelsea maybe, and a farmhouse in France. She'd make new friends. Real friends. The only friends she had now were the friends Charlie chose for her.

It hadn't always been like that. He'd been charming when they'd first met. She had been seventeen and a virgin, he was six years older, with money in his pocket, a green MGB and his own house. He had known the men on the doors of all the city's top clubs. Angie worked at a city-centre hairdresser's and was only six months away from being a fully qualified stylist when Charlie had walked in, wearing his Armani suit and Gucci shoes. He flirted with her and asked her out, and she had said yes. He was charming, generous and made her laugh. Her parents had been against the marriage but she'd been looking for a way to leave home since she was fourteen and eloping was the perfect excuse.

The first year had been a dream. She'd never asked where Charlie's money came from, and hadn't really cared. He hadn't started hitting her until the second year. He was on his way out one night and she'd asked where he was going. He slapped her, hard, then immediately apologised. He'd hugged her and promised he'd never hit her again, and the next day he'd given her a gold Rolex. He'd hit her again the following week when he saw she wasn't wearing the watch. She reached over and touched the Rolex. She wore it all the time now, even in the shower. She wouldn't wear it after they'd buried Charlie. She was going to have it buried with him. She smiled at the thought of him spending eternity with the watch she loathed.

She took another drag on her cigarette, held the smoke deep in her lungs, then exhaled. She'd never smoked before she'd met Charlie. Now she smoked two packets a day. When Charlie was out of the way, she'd stop.

She shivered, although it was a warm day, and opened her eyes. Her husband was standing at the bottom of the sun-lounger. Angie was wearing her sunglasses up on her head and she dropped them down so that she could see his face. He was smiling at her, the cold, humourless smile that was usually the prelude to a beating. Then she saw that he was holding her mobile phone in his left hand.

"In the house," he said. "Now."

"Charlie, what's wrong?"

"You and I are going to have a little chat," he said coldly. "About Larry."

Larry Hendrickson walked out of the changing room and threw his towel over his shoulder. He went through the weight-training area. Exercise was the last thing on his mind but he wanted to see Angie Kerr and she was often at the health club during the week. It was where he had met her, where he'd noticed the bruises. She'd first told him about her abusive husband in the club's fruit juice bar, where he'd talked about Sewell and how his dog-in-the-manger attitude was damaging the

222

company and the prospects of everyone who worked for it. Now he needed to talk to her again, about Tony Nelson. She hadn't returned his call and he didn't know where she lived so the health club was his best chance of finding her.

He looked through the glass panel in the door to the aerobics room. A couple of dozen plump housewives were trying to keep up with a lithe ponytailed blonde from New Zealand. Angie wasn't among them. Hendrickson walked on to the treadmills. There were two blondes at the far end, watching *Sky News* as they jogged up steep inclines, but neither was Angie Kerr. She wasn't on any of the exercise bikes, either.

Angie was a keen squash player but she wasn't on any of the squash courts. And she wasn't in the sauna or at the juice bar. He ordered an orange and carrot juice and sat down at an empty table. He didn't know what car she drove and he didn't want to draw attention to himself by asking at Reception if she was in today. He'd just hope she showed up.

His mobile rang and he looked at the display. It was her. "Jesus, Angie, where the hell have you been?"

"What's wrong?"

"Have you spoken to Nelson yet?"

Angie didn't reply.

"Angie, have you spoken to Nelson yet?"

"Not since Monday, no."

"Have you paid him yet?"

"What's wrong, Larry?"

"I don't know. I don't think we can trust him, that's all."

There was another long pause.

"Angie, are you listening to me?"

"I have to see you, Larry," she said. She sounded close to tears.

"I know," he said. "I'm at the health club. Can you get away?"

"You can come here, to the house."

"What about your husband?"

"He's away," said Angie. "He won't be back until next week."

"Where do you live?"

"Hale Barnes, about ten minutes' drive from the club. Can you come now?"

"No problem," he said. "What I've got to say is best not said over the phone. Give me the address."

Hendrickson stopped the car at the roadside and looked at Angie's house. It was big and modern with huge picture windows and tall chimneys. A long drive wound through sprawling lawns dotted with clumps of well-tended trees. It must have been worth a fortune. Hendrickson could see why she didn't just walk away from her husband.

There were large black wrought-iron gates at the entrance but they were open. A single car was parked in front of the double garage: Angie's Jaguar.

It was the first time Hendrickson had been to Angie's house. She'd be alone and emotionally vulnerable, especially when he told her what Nelson had been doing. Hendrickson could be a shoulder for her to cry on, and maybe, just maybe, it would lead to something else. He'd fancied Angie the first time he'd seen her in the health club. Slim and blonde with full breasts and long legs. Now he'd tell her what had happened and she'd be scared and he'd take her in his arms and tell her it was all right, he'd take care of her, and then he'd cup one of those wonderful breasts. He'd kiss her on the cheek, and then he'd find her lips, and then he'd whisper that maybe they'd be more comfortable in bed.

He took a deep breath and put his Mercedes in gear, rolled slowly up the drive and parked next to the Jaguar. He climbed out and walked to the front door, whistling softly. He rang the bell and shifted from side to side as he waited for the door to open. He heard high heels clicking on a hard wood floor and his stomach turned over. High heels and stockings, her on top, tossing her blonde hair and urging him on.

The door opened. Hendrickson's smile hardened when he saw that Angie in the flesh was a far cry from the sexy siren of his fantasy. Her face was tear-stained and there was a red blotch on her left cheek as if she'd been slapped. Her hair was pulled back into a tight ponytail and her lipstick was smeared as if she'd been roughly kissed. "Hello, Larry," she said, avoiding his eyes. "Come on in." She held open the door, looking at the floor.

"Are you okay?" said Hendrickson. It wasn't how he'd imagined it. She had on wooden sandals, baggy jeans and a pink sweatshirt.

"Come inside," she said.

Hendrickson stood at the threshold. He had a sudden urge to get back into the Mercedes and drive away. But he knew he had to find out what Tony Nelson was up to and the only way to do that was to talk to Angie. He had to find out how far she had gone with Nelson. And he had to get her to arrange a meeting with the man so that he could catch him unawares.

He stepped into the hallway and she closed the door behind him. She pressed her back against the door, her hands flat against the wood. She started crying, big, gasping sobs. Hendrickson didn't know what to do. In his fantasy he'd held her and tried to kiss her, but sex was now the furthest thing from his mind. "What's wrong?" he asked.

She didn't say anything, just stood shaking her head and sobbing.

"Is it Nelson? Has something happened?"

Angie wrapped her arms round her stomach and slid down the door until she was crouched on the floor. Tears streamed down her cheeks.

Then Hendrickson heard a sharp laugh and whirled around. Two men were standing in a doorway. One was short with tight, black curls and the other was shaven-headed and had the build of a wrestler. He wore a sovereign ring on his wedding finger and a thick gold chain on his right wrist. As he stared at Hendrickson he cracked his knuckles, like pistol shots. It was the smaller man who had laughed. He was carrying a large kitchen knife and swished the blade from side to side. Hendrickson swallowed and took a step back. "Who are you?" he stuttered. "What do you want?"

226

"We want a chat," said the man with the knife.

"What about?" said Hendrickson. He took another step back. "This isn't m-m-my house," he stammered. He pointed at Angie, who was still sobbing, her forehead resting on her arms. "I'm just visiting. I'm not her husband."

"No," said a voice to his left. A third man walked out of the sitting room. He was tall with receding hair and, like the other big man, he was holding a knife. Its blade glinted under the hall light. The man smiled — a cruel smile, the smile of a man who enjoyed inflicting pain. "I am," he said.

It took less than five minutes for Larry Hendrickson to tell Kerr everything he knew about Tony Nelson. There had been no need to torture him, or even to hurt him, but Kerr had done it anyway and taken pleasure in it. Wates and Anderson had taken him down to the wine cellar and tied him to a chair while Kerr had taken Angie up to the bedroom. Angie had cried and kept repeating that she was sorry, but it didn't mean much when she'd hired a hitman to murder him.

Kerr had taken her to the bedroom, made her undress and raped her on their king-sized bed. She didn't protest and she didn't struggle. He swore at her when he came and slapped her face. Then he used two Kenzo ties to bind her wrists and ankles and pulled the phone out of its socket. She lay on her side, sobbing into a pillow.

He showered, changed into a fresh polo shirt and khaki chinos, then went downstairs. He walked through the kitchen to the garage and took a pair of bolt-cutters before he headed down to the basement. Kerr could smell the acrid tang of urine as he walked down the wooden steps. Hendrickson had wet himself.

"This is a mistake," quavered Hendrickson.

"Couldn't agree with you more, Larry," said Kerr, swinging the bolt-cutters.

"I don't know what she told you, but it was all her idea," said Hendrickson.

"My wife, you mean?" asked Kerr.

"Please —" said Hendrickson.

"Please what? Please don't hurt me? Please don't kill me?"

"Look, I've got money —"

"Not as much as I have, Larry." Kerr slapped the bolt-cutters in the palm of his hand. "This Nelson, how did you get in touch with him?"

"I phoned him."

"I meant the first time. I'm assuming you didn't get his name from the *Yellow Pages*."

"A friend of a friend. He knows people, he said he'd put the word out, and Nelson got in touch."

"What's he look like?"

"Dark brown hair, just under six foot. He looks . . ." Hendrickson struggled to find the right word. ". . . normal," he said eventually. "He looks like everyone else."

"What does he drive?"

"A Volvo. A grey Volvo."

"I don't suppose you know the number?"

Hendrickson shook his head.

"Because it'll save you a toe if you do."

Hendrickson started to plead but Kerr knelt down next to the chair. He rolled up Hendrickson's left trouser leg. "Nice material," said Kerr. "Armani?"

"I don't know, please, God, I don't know!" screamed Hendrickson.

"Looks like Armani," said Kerr.

"The number of his car. I don't know the number of his car. Why would I know the number of his car, for God's sake?"

Kerr slipped the bolt-cutting blades on either side of the little toe on Hendrickson's left foot. Hendrickson struggled but his ankle and knee were tied to the chair. He rocked the chair backwards and forwards but Wates grabbed his shoulders to hold him still.

Kerr pressed hard on the handles of the bolt-cutters and Hendrickson screamed as the blades bit into his flesh. Kerr felt resistance as the blades hit the bone but he forced the handles together and the toe fell to the floor. Hendrickson's screams went up an octave. Kerr straightened up, grinning. Anderson had turned away but Wates was grinning as widely as Kerr, relishing Hendrickson's shrieks. The wine cellar was soundproofed and the nearest neighbour was a hundred yards away so there was no possibility that anyone would hear what was going on.

Gradually Hendrickson's screams subsided. He was breathing heavily, and his eyes glazed over. Kerr realised he was going into shock. "Get him some water," he said to Anderson, who hurried up the stairs.

"How did you meet my wife?" he asked.

Hendrickson coughed. "The gym," he said.

"What — you just walked up and asked if she wanted her husband dead?"

Hendrickson shook his head. Kerr grabbed his hair. "Don't you pass out on me, you shit," he said.

When Anderson returned with the water he put the glass to Hendrickson's lips and he gulped the water. "Thank you," he gasped.

"When was the last time you saw Nelson?"

"Last Friday."

"And he killed your business partner?"

Hendrickson nodded.

"How much did you pay him?"

"Thirty grand."

"How did he do it?"

"Shot him and buried him in the New Forest."

"Nice," said Kerr. "And you thought he could do the same to me, did you?"

"That's not what —"

"You calling me a liar, Larry?"

"It's not that — I just gave her his phone number."

"What did I ever do to you? Did I ever cause you any grief? Did I run over your cat? Because if I did, I'd rather you told me now."

"I just gave her his number, that's all."

Kerr opened his eyes wide. "Oh, that's all right, then. All you did was give my wife the phone number of a contract killer. It's all been a misunderstanding, then."

"Look, please, there's something you need to know —"

"I think I have the gist," said Kerr, slapping the bolt-cutters against his palm.

"There's something else," said Hendrickson. "If I tell you, will you let me go?"

"I don't think there's anything else I need to know. My darling wife has told me everything."

"No, this Nelson, he's up to something. That's why I called Angie. He's trying to stitch me up."

"What do you mean?"

"If I tell you, will you let me go?"

"If you don't, I'll start work on your hands," said Kerr.

"I don't want to die," said Hendrickson.

"No one wants to die," said Kerr. "So talk."

Hendrickson looked at Anderson.

"Don't look at him, Larry, look at me. What about this Nelson guy?"

"He's been using Roger's email address to get information about the company."

"Who's Roger?"

"My partner. The guy I wanted out of the way."

Kerr frowned. "You're not making any sense. This Roger guy is dead?"

Hendrickson nodded. "Nelson showed me photographs. Polaroids."

"Of what?"

"Of Roger. Dead."

"But you didn't see the body?" asked Kerr, thoughtfully.

"I didn't want to be there. I just wanted him out of the way."

"So Nelson did the dirty and showed you Polaroids and you gave him the cash?"

"Yes. But a couple of days later someone logged on to our company website using Roger's password. And sent an email about the company accounts."

"And you think it was Nelson?"

"It couldn't be anyone else. That's why I was trying to get hold of Angie. To warn her about Nelson."

Kerr considered what Hendrickson had said.

"So, can I go?" said Hendrickson. "Please. I'm sorry about what happened, but all I did was give your wife a number."

Kerr ignored him. Nelson must be an amateur to start using a victim's email. A professional would do the job he'd been paid for, then vanish. Messing around with emails was a risk, and a true professional wouldn't take risks. Kerr was getting a bad feeling about the mysterious Tony Nelson.

"I just want to go home," pleaded Hendrickson.

"You're starting to annoy me now, Larry," said Kerr.

Hendrickson began to cry and the damp patch around his groin darkened.

"Christ, I hate it when they piss themselves," said Kerr.

He took off four of Hendrickson's toes and both his thumbs before he got bored with the torture. Hendrickson had stopped screaming and was passing in and out of consciousness. Kerr dropped the bolt-cutters on the floor and stood back. He nodded at Wates, who pulled a large plastic bag over Hendrickson's head and used electrical tape to seal it round his neck.

Hendrickson struggled for a couple of minutes, then went still.

Kerr went upstairs to the bedroom. Angie was still lying on the bed, crying. Kerr untied her ankles and stroked her hair. "Stop crying," he said.

Angie took a ragged breath.

Kerr helped her sit up. "Come on, there's something I want you to see," he said. "In the wine cellar."

Shepherd phoned Hargrove just before midnight and explained that he'd had no luck in contacting Angie Kerr. Every time he called it went straight through to voicemail, which meant that her phone was switched off so his number wouldn't show up as a missed call. He'd left one message, short and to the point, asking her to call him, but she hadn't got back to him.

He went to bed and lay awake for most of the night. He kept thinking about Sue, replaying her accident. He missed her smell, her touch. He missed arguing with her and making up. He missed being inside her and holding her as she gasped. As dawn broke he went downstairs and poured himself a large measure of Jameson's, then tipped it down the sink. Alcohol wasn't going to solve anything.

He changed into a pair of faded army shorts and a tattered T-shirt, pulled on two pairs of wool socks and the black army boots, then hefted the brick-filled canvas rucksack on to his shoulders. He ran for the best part of an hour around the streets of Ealing, his boots thudding on the pavements, the rucksack straps chafing his shoulders, taking a perverse pleasure in the pain. By the time he was back home he was close to exhaustion. He took off the boots and socks and examined his feet. No blisters.

He showered, then changed into jeans and a black pullover and walked down to the local shops. He bought copies of the *Daily Mail*, the *Daily Telegraph* and the *Sun* and, on a whim, a ticket for that night's lottery draw, letting the machine choose his numbers. He picked up a carton of milk and two freshly baked croissants from the delicatessen, then headed home.

He made himself a cup of coffee and took it with the croissants into the garden. There was a wooden table with two bench seats and he sat down. He and Sue had built the table and seats from a kit they'd bought at their local garden centre. The instructions had been in some Oriental language and half the bolts were missing. Shepherd broke one of the croissants into small pieces. Sue had been seven months pregnant and she'd never looked sexier as she'd brushed her hair out of her eyes and laughed at his D-I-Y attempts. He looked up at the rear of the house. He'd stripped and repainted all the bedroom windows while Sue had done the ones on the ground floor. She'd changed the layout of the garden, putting in two rockeries, a couple of flowerbeds and a dozen fruit trees. The kitchen was her design too, and so were the two bathrooms. She had put her heart and soul into the house and there was no way he could bring himself to sell it. In time, maybe, but not yet.

He finished the croissants and coffee and carried his empty mug back into the house. He looked at his watch. Almost midday. Miss Malcolm had assured him

234

that a girl from the agency would drop in before noon. He had planned to interview the girl, then drive to Hereford to spend the weekend with Liam. While he was up in his bedroom packing an overnight case the doorbell rang.

The girl standing on the doorstep barely came up to his chest, had black hair and wore no makeup. She smiled up at him. "Mr Shepherd?"

"Yes?"

"I am Katra. The agency said I was to come and see you." She was holding a similar manila envelope to the one Halina had shown him. "I hope now is not an inconvenient time for me to call." She said each word slowly and precisely, as if she had memorised the sentence, and nodded when she'd finished.

"Come on in," he said, and held the door open for her. She was wearing a green parka with a fur-lined hood, sand-coloured cargo pants and scuffed Timberland boots. He showed her into the kitchen. "Tea or coffee?"

"Just water," she said. "Please."

Shepherd gave her a glass of tap water and opened the envelope. There was a copy of her agency application, which he scanned. She was twenty-two, although she looked less. She had left school at sixteen and had only worked in a shoe factory. There was a letter on headed notepaper from a police inspector in Slovenia saying that Katra did not have a criminal record. Shepherd frowned. Miss Malcolm hadn't mentioned she was sending a Slovenian — in fact, she had left him with the impression that she didn't trust them.

"You've not worked as an au pair before?" he asked.

"I have five younger brothers," she said.

"Five?"

"Five. The youngest is Rufin and he is twelve and can take care of himself now so my father says I can come to England. I want to study English. And work."

"You helped raise your brothers, is that it?"

"My mother died when Rufin was born. My father worked in a steel mill so I had to take care of them all."

Shepherd did the maths in his head. "You were ten when she died?"

"She was bleeding and the hospital didn't have enough of her type of blood."

"I'm sorry."

"I was very sad but it was a long time ago."

"And your father never remarried?"

"He said he never wanted another wife, that no one could take her place. I cooked and cleaned and took care of them when they were sick. It wasn't too difficult. I had aunts to help me sometimes and the teachers at school did what they could."

"Your father was lucky to have a daughter like you."

Katra grinned. "He knows that. He tells me all the time that I'm just like my mother."

"Your English is good but it says here you left school at sixteen."

"I studied at home. One of the teachers gave me some books and sometimes she would come to the house to help me practise."

"And then you worked at a shoe factory?" There was a reference letter from the manager, who said that

Katra had been a diligent worker and that after six months he had promoted her from the production line to the quality-control department.

"My father had an accident at the steel mill so I went to work."

"You were working and taking care of your family?"

"The boys were older so they helped. It wasn't so hard." She sipped her water.

"Miss Malcolm explained my situation?"

"She said you are a widower and you have a young son."

Widower. It was the first time Shepherd had heard himself described like that. It sounded Victorian, as if he should have been wearing a frock coat and top hat. But it was what he was. A man whose wife had died.

"Where is your boy?" asked Katra.

"Liam is with his grandparents. I'm on my way to see him now. I need someone who can take him to and from school. You can drive, right?"

"My father taught me. I have a licence."

"An international licence?"

Katra nodded.

"And I need someone to do laundry, clean the house and cook."

"You need a wife," she said.

At first Shepherd thought she was being funny or sarcastic, then realised she was not, just factual. It was exactly what he needed. He needed Sue. "You're right," he said.

"I can take care of you both," she said. "I cook good."

"I bet you do," he said. He glanced at his watch. "Look, what are you doing today?"

"I come to see you. Then Miss Malcolm said I should call her. That is all I do today."

"Where are you staying?"

"I share a room in a house in Battersea," she said. "Some Slovenian girls who have been here for a year are letting me stay with them until I have a job. One hundred pounds a week. That's good, no?"

It seemed expensive to Shepherd, but he smiled and said that it sounded like a good deal. "Why don't you come with me? We'll go and see Liam."

She beamed up at him. "I have the job?"

Shepherd looked at her. His life often depended on his ability to read people, and he trusted his instincts. Katra seemed open, honest and without guile. "Let's see how you get on with my son first."

Katra grabbed him around the waist and hugged him, then released him and apologised. "I'm sorry, it's just that I'm so happy."

Shepherd couldn't stop a grin. "Let's see what Liam thinks," he said. "He'll be spending more time with you than I will." He picked up his car keys and tossed them to her. "You can drive. It'll give me a chance to see how you handle the car."

"Where are we going?" she asked.

"Hereford. It's near Wales. Over to the west."

She frowned. "Do I need a visa? I have my passport but my visa is for the United Kingdom only."

Shepherd laughed. "No, love, you don't need a visa for Wales."

He told her to get the car started while he fetched his bag. As he went into the bedroom he caught sight of himself in the mirror. He was smiling, and felt guilty suddenly, as if he had been disloyal in some way to Sue. He sighed. "She'll be good for Liam, love," he whispered. "She'll make him laugh. She might even bring some happiness back into the house. God knows, we could do with some." He picked up his overnight bag, then went downstairs and locked up.

The engine was running as he climbed into the CRV. Katra was already wearing her seatbelt. He fastened his. "Let's go then," he said. "You can tell me the story of your life as you drive."

Wates rolled Hendrickson's body over on the plastic sheeting. Kerr pointed to a severed toe. "You've missed a bit, lads," he said.

Anderson picked it up, tossed it next to the body and grimaced. "What's the story, boss?" he asked.

"Wait until it's dark and bury it where it'll never be found. If we knew where the partner was we could bury them together."

"What's the plan about this Nelson guy?"

"We'll have a word in his shell-like. Find out what the score is."

"Can I say something, boss?" Anderson looked pained.

"What the hell's crawled up your arse and died?" said Kerr.

"This is not a good idea, that's all, you taking this personal."

"For fuck's sake, Eddie, this guy was talking to my wife about putting a bullet in my head."

"I don't mean him. I mean Nelson."

"I've got to find out what he's up to. Angie's given him fifteen grand and he's not made a move, but he's pissing around sending emails under a dead guy's name. That's a mystery and I hate mysteries."

"You've always said, right from the first time I started with you, that you never go near the gear or the money. You let Muppets take the risk, you take the reward."

"The Gospel according to Charlie Kerr," said Kerr.

"Right, so why are you taking risks with this? What you did to Hendrickson, that was fair enough, he came to your house. But this Nelson, if you're going to do something, why do it yourself? There's guys who'd do it for you as a favour, you know that."

"Because this is personal, Eddie." Anderson still looked uncomfortable. Kerr patted him on the shoulder. "It'll be easy-peasy," he said. "Angie'll make a call to arrange a meet and when he turns up we'll play *Who Wants To Be A Millionaire?* — he just won't get to phone a friend."

Shepherd and Katra arrived in Hereford as the sun was dipping below the horizon. The traffic had been heavy, with holidaymakers heading to Wales for the weekend, and there had been long tail-backs. Shepherd had been impressed by Katra's driving. She accelerated smoothly and used her mirrors constantly. He had felt relaxed

240

with her at the wheel and knew he could trust her with Liam in the car.

He gave her directions to Moira's house, and on the way briefed her on what to expect from his in-laws. With the best will in the world Moira was certain to view Katra as an interloper and would probably give her a hard time. Tom would be more easy-going but he wouldn't be comfortable with a stranger taking care of his grandson. "Just be yourself," concluded Shepherd. "They won't be fooled by flattery. I tried that when I first met them." He shuddered at the memory. "Shot me down in flames."

He'd worn a suit and tie and smiled so much that his face had ached. He had seen the suspicion in Moira's eyes as soon as he told them he served with the Special Air Service. There was constant friction between the Regiment and the locals, especially in the town's drinking establishments. The SAS lads needed to blow off steam from time to time, and the local men weren't happy that the town's girls made a beeline for the super-fit, self-confident soldiers. Evidently Moira wasn't going to allow Shepherd to take her beloved daughter without a fight, and her interrogation was as bad as anything he'd faced on his selection week.

Her observations had echoed the views of Shepherd's own parents when he had told them he wanted to drop out of university, although she had made her point more succinctly. Why would anybody give up a promising academic career for a job whose ultimate aim was to kill people?

Shepherd had drunk a couple of glasses of Tom's best whiskey and tried to explain that being in the SAS wasn't about killing people, it was about being the best of the best. It was about testing yourself to breaking point, and defending your country, standing up against the bullies of the world be they terrorists or dictatorships. He never convinced Moira, but he won over Tom. And while they'd both been dubious about an SAS trooper courting their daughter, it was clear that they respected his honesty.

Katra parked the CRV in front of Moira and Tom's house and looked up at it. "It's nice," she said. "Well cared-for."

"Yeah, she's house-proud, is Moira," said Shepherd.

"What shall I call her?"

"Mrs Wintour," said Shepherd. "Her husband is Tom but you'd better call him Mr Wintour unless he says otherwise."

"And is it okay to call you Dan or shall I call you Mr Shepherd?" she asked.

Shepherd took his hand off the door handle. It was a good question. Moira would notice the informality if she used his first name, and it might be better to make it clear from the outset that Katra was an employee and not a family member. "Mr Shepherd's a good idea, Katra," he said, "but only while they're around. Everywhere else it's Dan."

The front door opened as Shepherd reached for the bell. "Dad!" Liam shouted. Shepherd picked him up and hugged him. Liam looked at Katra over his shoulder. "Who's she?" he asked.

"Manners," said Shepherd.

"I'm Katra," she said.

"Are you my dad's girlfriend?"

"Liam!" said Shepherd.

Moira came down the hallway. "What's this about a girlfriend?" she said.

"Liam's overactive imagination," said Shepherd, putting his son down. "This is Katra. She's an au pair."

"I thought you were getting a housekeeper," Moira said frostily.

"Housekeeper, au pair, it's pretty much the same, isn't it?"

"Pleased to meet you, Mrs Wintour," Katra said.

Moira shook her hand. "How old are you?" she asked.

"Katra's twenty-two. Can we do this inside, Moira?"

Moira sniffed pointedly.

"Where are you from?" Liam asked Katra, as they walked down the hallway towards the kitchen.

"Portoroz," she said. "In Slovenia."

"Where's that?"

"It's in Europe," she said. "Near Russia."

"I've never heard of it."

"We're a quiet country," she said, smiling. They went into the kitchen.

Moira closed the front door. "You said you were getting a housekeeper, Daniel. That girl looks barely old enough to take care of herself."

"She's the oldest in her family and she practically raised her siblings single-handed," said Shepherd. "She won't have any trouble with one eight-year-old boy."

"Totally unsuitable," she said, folding her arms.

"Moira, she'll be fine."

"When you said housekeeper, I imagined someone more my age, with experience, someone reliable."

"She's got references and I'll make some checks of my own on Monday. Liam's taken to her already."

"Liam doesn't know any better. And what about food? What do they eat in Slovenia?"

Shepherd started to laugh, but stopped when Moira's eyes narrowed. "I'm sure she'll cope with egg and chips," he said. "That's still Liam's favourite, isn't it?"

"Fine, if you won't take me seriously," said Moira. She headed for the kitchen, and Shepherd followed her. He knew it wasn't Katra personally that Moira was against: it was the idea of anyone other than herself taking care of Liam. He could have turned up with a fifty-year-old Cordon Bleu-trained Scot and Moira would have given her the cold shoulder.

Liam was sitting with Tom at the kitchen table while Katra was spooning coffee into a cafetière. Liam was repeating something she'd said.

Katra laughed. "No, you say 'prav zadovoljen sem' because you're a boy. I'm a girl so I say 'prav zadovolna sem'. It's only a small difference, but it's important." She repeated "zadovoljen", stressing the final syllable.

"Prav zadovoljen sem," Liam said, slowly and carefully.

Katra clapped. "Well done! You sound like a Slovenian already."

244

Liam beamed. "Katra's teaching me Slovenian," he said to Shepherd. "*Prav zadovoljen sem*," he said. "It means I'm happy."

"Well, if you're happy, I'm happy," said Shepherd.

"Let me do that," said Moira, reaching for the cafetière.

"Let the girl be, Moira," said Tom. "Be nice for the two of us to be waited on for a change." Moira glared at him, clearly annoyed at what she saw as a betrayal. He put up his hands in surrender but grinned at Katra, which only made Moira angrier.

"Tom, this is my kitchen, always has been and always will be," she said.

"And no one keeps a better kitchen than you, my angel," said Tom, "but if Katra is going to look after Liam and Dan, we should at least let her show us what she can do."

Moira stood wringing her hands, then sat down at the table.

Liam kept up a torrent of questions while Katra made the coffee. What was her family like? Where had she gone to school? How long would she be staying in England?

"Maybe five years," said Katra. "I want to earn enough money to start my own business and learn English."

"Your English seems pretty good to me already," said Tom.

She poured the coffee and carried it over to the table, along with a jug of milk and the sugar bowl. She sat next to Shepherd and watched expectantly as they all sipped. Shepherd and Tom nodded approval, then looked at Moira. She shrugged. "Lovely, Katra. Thank you."

"How about we give Katra a trial run?" said Shepherd. "She could cook dinner for us."

Moira's jaw dropped. "Oh, no, I'm doing a roast. I've got everything planned."

Tom put a hand on her arm and gave it an encouraging squeeze. "It's a good idea," he said. "It'd give you a night off. We could have a nice bottle of wine and let Katra get on with it."

"Go on, Gran," said Liam. "It'll be fun."

Katra smiled. "I'd be happy to cook for you all," she said.

"There you are, then," said Tom.

Shepherd looked at his watch. "The lottery," he said. "I bought a ticket today." He fished it out of his wallet.

"Daniel, really! The lottery's nothing more than legalised gambling."

"It's for good causes," said Shepherd. "Come on, you can check the numbers with me."

Moira glanced at Katra, who had opened the refrigerator and was checking the vegetables. "I'll stay with Katra," she said, but Tom took her arm and eased her out of the kitchen.

They went through to the sitting room and he switched on the television. Within five minutes the winning numbers were on the screen. Only two matched numbers that Shepherd had chosen. He scowled and tore his ticket in half.

"Serves you right," said Moira primly.

"I was going to give you half if I won," he teased.

"I don't believe that for a second," said Moira.

"Well, you'll never know now," he said.

They watched television until eventually Liam appeared in the doorway. "It's all ready," he said.

Katra had prepared the kitchen table with silverware and napkins, and had placed two candles in the centre. There was a wooden basket filled with chunks of bread, and a bowl of sautéed potatoes that smelt strongly of garlic.

"I did the potatoes," said Liam.

Moira looked worriedly at the sink but gleaming pans were stacked on the draining-board and Katra had polished the stove until it shone.

Katra opened the oven and took out a casserole dish.

"I was going to roast the chicken," said Moira, "with stuffing."

"I know, but Liam said he wanted to try Slovenian food so I showed him how to make *kurja obara*. It's a sort of chicken gumbo."

"It smells great, Gran," said Liam.

"It's a recipe from my aunt," said Katra, "with parsley and celery."

"You're right, Liam — it does smell good," said Tom, sitting down and rubbing his hands.

Katra placed a stainless-steel bowl full of steaming dumplings on the table. "*Metini struklji*," she said. "I took some mint from the garden," she told Moira. "I hope you don't mind. The dumplings are traditional Slovenian food but not all English people like them and

Liam said you liked sautéed potatoes so I did them as well. Except Liam cooked them."

"You told me what to do," said Liam. "She's a great cook, isn't she, Grandma?"

Moira looked at Liam for several seconds, then she smiled. "Yes, she is," she said. She patted Katra's arm. "It looks lovely, dear. And if it tastes half as good as it smells I think my husband will be fighting to keep you here!"

Katra blushed and giggled. She sat down and served Moira first, then heaped spoonfuls of the chicken on to the plates in front of Shepherd, Tom and Liam. When she'd helped herself, she reached over and took Moira's hand. "Perhaps I could say a grace," she said.

Moira nodded enthusiastically. "That would be wonderful," she said, and gave Shepherd a meaningful look.

Shepherd smiled but didn't rise to the bait. The fact that he had no religious leanings was one of the many reasons his mother-in-law had thought him an unsuitable husband for Sue. They had been married in Tom and Moira's church in Hereford but he had had to bite his tongue during their pep talks with the local vicar. He had seen and been through too much to believe in God.

Moira took Liam's hand and Shepherd took the other. They all bowed their heads as Katra prayed. When she raised her head she said, "I hope you all enjoy it."

They did. Several times during the meal Shepherd caught Moira looking wistfully at Katra. He knew what she was thinking. Katra was physically different from Sue, but her smile and laugh were similar. Liam seemed to have picked up on it, albeit subconsciously. He behaved as if he had known her for years. When the meal was over he helped her clear the table and wash up.

"What do you think, Moira?" asked Shepherd, as they went back through to the sitting room for coffee.

"She'll do, I suppose," she said grudgingly, but Shepherd knew that Katra had won her over, big-time.

The explosives came into the country with some hand-carved furniture that had been ordered by a minor diplomat who was related by marriage to the Saudi royal family. The consignment carried diplomatic privilege and wasn't even looked at by Customs. It wouldn't have mattered even if they had inspected the container because the explosives were so well hidden they would never have found them. The furniture was taken to the diplomat's five-bedroomed house in Mayfair where the Saudi used an electric saw to reduce a mahogany chest to firewood. In the process he retrieved forty plastic-wrapped packages of Semtex. It had been manufactured by the Czechs and shipped to Libya. A Libyan captain with two expensive mistresses had smuggled twenty kilos of it out of his barracks and sold it to a Palestinian, who paid in brand new hundred-dollar bills and took the explosives overland to Saudi Arabia, hidden in a false compartment in a four-wheel drive.

The Saudi already had the detonators. They had been brought into the country by a pilot with Emirate Airlines, hidden in a false compartment of his flight case. The pilot was sympathetic to the aims of the Saudi and his compatriots. He was a Palestinian and two of his teenage cousins had been killed by the Israelis for not stopping quickly enough at a roadblock. The boys were unarmed, just children, and the Israelis hadn't even offered an apology.

The Saudi was able to buy the rest of the equipment he needed in London. Wire, digital alarm clocks, electrical switches, batteries and a soldering iron. The four vests were tight-fitting with ten pockets, each pocket a perfect fit for one of the packages of Semtex. He sewed the vests by hand, pricking his fingers so often that they were spotted with his blood.

He unwrapped the plastic packages, then used Sellotape to wrap dozens of two-inch nails around each block of explosive and placed them in the pockets. The explosions would be devastating but the shrapnel would do most damage.

He tested the electrical circuits on his dining-table, using flashlight bulbs in place of the detonators. Each vest had three detonators, all connected to one electrical switch. Pressing the electrical switch connected the detonators to the battery. Three was overkill, the Saudi knew, but the detonators couldn't be tested in advance.

A second circuit ran parallel to the first. It connected the battery to the detonators via a digital alarm clock. Irrespective of whether the electrical switch was activated, the clock would close the second circuit at two minutes past five p.m. The men had been told to trigger their devices at five p.m. If they failed to do so, to the bombs would detonate of their own accord. The men would not be told of the secondary circuit.

It was standard operating procedure, the Saudi knew. Most of the hijackers in the planes that had been flown into New York's World Trade Center had not been told the true nature of their mission. Only the pilots had known. Until the last few seconds the majority of the hijackers had thought that they would be landing at JFK airport and the hostages held until America agreed to al-Qaeda's terms. As far as the Saudi's men in London were concerned, they would be the ones in control. They would decide if and when to press the switch. But the Saudi knew that the human element was the weak link in any operation. If the men were captured or injured they might not be able to press their switches. If they had a change of heart, the clock circuit would take over and override the switch mechanism. It was a necessary subterfuge, the Saudi knew. The operation was more important than the operatives.

Shepherd let Katra drive the CRV back to London. Liam wanted to sit in the front but hadn't argued when Shepherd insisted that he was in the back. He wanted to learn more Slovenian words and Katra taught him a couple of songs. When they got back to Ealing he was singing on his own and could count up to twenty.

Shepherd had tried calling Miss Malcolm from Hereford to confirm that he wanted to hire Katra but had only reached the agency's answering-machine. He decided that there wouldn't be a problem and told Katra that she was hired. Katra had beamed.

Moira hadn't been happy about Shepherd taking Liam to London. There had been tears in her eyes as she'd said goodbye and as the car drove away she'd collapsed into Tom's arms. Shepherd told himself that his son belonged with him, and Liam was thrilled to be going back to London, especially when he realised that Katra would be taking care of him.

They drove via Battersea, where Katra picked up her suitcase and said goodbye to her friends.

Shepherd let them into the house and switched off the burglar alarm as Liam rushed upstairs with Katra to show her his room. He went into the kitchen. There was a photograph of Sue and Liam on the refrigerator door, held in place by a magnet in the shape of an apple. It had been taken at Hallowe'en the previous year. Liam had been invited to a schoolfriend's fancy dress party and Sue had made him a pirate's outfit. Shepherd had been away on an assignment in Bristol and the job had kept him away overnight so Liam had insisted that he and his mother take a photograph. It was the best photograph he'd ever seen of his wife and child: Sue's arm was around Liam's shoulders and they were both grinning from ear to ear.

He heard Liam and Katra laughing upstairs and suddenly felt guilty. He kissed the first and second fingers of his right hand and pressed them to his wife's face. "I'll always love you, Sue," he said softly. "She's just here to keep us together as a family."

A wave of sadness rushed over him. He was never going to see her again. The photographs and memories were all he had now.

"Dad!"

Shepherd jumped.

"Dad, come here!"

Liam was standing at the top of the stairs, one hand on the banister, the other pressed against the wall, swinging his legs backwards and forwards.

"I've told you not to do that," said Shepherd. "It's dangerous."

Liam stopped. "Where's Katra sleeping?"

"The spare room."

"Can't she sleep with me?"

"It's not a sleepover party, Katra's here to work," said Shepherd. "Anyway, boys and girls don't share rooms."

"You and Mum did," said Liam.

"Well, if you and Katra ever get married, you can share," laughed Shepherd, "but until then she has the spare room."

Katra came up behind Liam and stroked his hair. Liam giggled. "Will you marry me, Katra?"

"Of course. When you are old enough."

Shepherd went up the stairs and opened the door to the spare room. "Have a look, Katra, see what you think."

There was a double bed and a built-in wardrobe with mirrored sliding doors and a small teak dressing-table. "It's lovely," said Katra. "Perfect."

"You'll have to share the bathroom with Liam, I'm afraid."

"That's fine," she said. "In Portoroz we had one bathroom for the seven of us."

"Seven?" said Liam.

"My father and me and five brothers."

"What about your mother?"

"Katra's mum died when she was young," said Shepherd. He patted Liam's shoulder. "That's something you've got in common."

"Was it an accident?" Liam asked Katra.

"She was sick."

"I'm sorry," said Liam. He slipped his hand into hers and squeezed it.

"It was a long time ago," she said.

"It's not fair, is it, when things like that happen?"

She looked down at him and nodded. "No, it's not fair."

"I'll keep the bathroom tidy," he said.

"Thank you."

"It'll be a first," said Shepherd.

"Dad!"

Shepherd went back outside to fetch Katra's suitcase and his overnight bag, then took them upstairs. Katra was sitting on her bed. "This is so nice," she said. "Thank you." She pointed at the two black plastic bags at the foot of the bed. "What are they?" she asked.

"My wife's . . ." began Shepherd, but Sue wasn't his wife, not any more. How was he supposed to refer to her now? "They're Sue's clothes," he said finally. "I wasn't sure what to do with them. I'll find somewhere else for them." He picked them up, one in each hand, and took them down to the garage. He put them under the tool bench, then showed Katra the freezer, which was packed with ready meals. "You eat these?" she said, picking up one of the ice-encrusted boxes.

"Only if I can't get a takeaway," he said.

"Takeaway?"

"You know. Chinese or Indian food. You buy it and take it away."

"I will go shopping tomorrow for real food. And you have herbs in your garden?"

"Are weeds herbs?"

She either didn't understand the joke, or ignored it. "I will need garlic, parsley, marjoram, tarragon and horseradish," she said.

"I guess the supermarket will have them," he said. "We can go tomorrow. We'll drop Liam off at the school, then we'll shop and then I've got to go to work. I start at two and my shift finishes at ten so I'll be back at eleven."

They headed back to the kitchen. "What time does Liam go to bed?"

Shepherd shrugged. "So long as he's up for school, I leave it to him. What do you think? Ten?"

"Nine might be better."

"Nine it is," said Shepherd.

Back in the kitchen she opened the fridge and checked the sell-by date on a box of eggs. Then she opened a carton of milk and sniffed it. "I can make omelette tonight," she said. "With chips."

"Great," said Shepherd.

He switched on the kettle and reached for two coffee mugs, but Katra beat him to it. "You relax," she said. "I will make coffee."

Shepherd moved out of her way. "That grace you said at dinner yesterday, what was it?"

Katra turned pink. "Ah," she said. "I was hoping you wouldn't ask." She busied herself spooning instant coffee into the mugs.

"What's wrong?" asked Shepherd.

"Actually, my family isn't religious," she said. "My mother was, but after she died my father refused to set foot inside a church and threw out my mother's Bible and crucifix."

"What about the grace?"

"I thought Mrs Wintour might like a prayer, so I said a poem."

"A poem?"

"Well, it was a traditional Slovenian song."

"What does it mean?"

"You really want to know?"

Shepherd was enjoying her embarrassment. "Oh, yes," he said. "I think it's important that I know."

Katra looked as if she was in pain. "Well, it's about a young man who is planning to visit his three girlfriends.

256

The first is a waitress and she will give him something to drink. The second girl is a cook and she will give him something to eat. And the third . . ."

"Yes?" said Shepherd, encouragingly.

"The third is the one he really loves and she will take him to her room."

Shepherd bit his lower lip to stop himself laughing. "Her room?"

Katra looked even more uncomfortable. "You know," she said. "She loved him, so . . ." She shrugged.

"And you pretended to be saying grace?"

"You're not angry, are you? I am so sorry. I just wanted to please her."

"No, Katra, I'm not angry." He couldn't contain himself any longer and burst out laughing.

Liam came in from the sitting room. "What's wrong?" he asked.

Shepherd grinned at Katra. "Nothing," he said. "Everything's fine."

One of the mobiles in his jacket pocket rang. He was carrying three and he fished them out. It was Hargrove, and he went through to the sitting room to take the call. The superintendent wanted to know if he'd spoken to Angie Kerr.

"I've tried every hour but her phone's off. I don't want to leave a message."

"What do you think?"

"I don't know. If she's had a change of heart she'd have got back to me. It could be as simple as a lost phone."

"I'll check to see if she's reported it," said Hargrove. "I'll put a tail on her as well. But if all else fails you'll just have to go up and front her."

"I'm starting with SO19 tomorrow," said Shepherd. "Two until ten, it won't give me much time."

"You could get your mates to helicopter you."

Shepherd grinned. "You heard about that."

"I wish I had SAS resources," said Hargrove. "Worst possible scenario, you could call in sick and drive up. We've got to nail her, and soon."

"Let me know about the phone," said Shepherd.

"You got the Stuart Marsden legend?"

"Sure. It's fine."

"And everything went okay at Hereford?"

"I'm up to speed. I don't expect any problems."

"I meant with your boy. Is he okay?"

"Yeah, he's fine. He's back here now." Liam came running into the sitting room. "Can I play football in the garden with Katra?" he asked.

Shepherd waved him away. "I've got some father stuff to do," he said to Hargrove.

"Enjoy it while you can." Hargrove laughed. "Teenagers are a whole different ball-game."

Shepherd cut the connection and went back to the kitchen. Katra and Liam were running around the garden, chasing a football. Liam was whooping and waving his arms. Shepherd hadn't seen him so happy for a long time. It was good to have a woman back in the house, even if she was an employee.

★　★　★

258

Shepherd woke up with a start. He looked at the bedside table and cursed. He hadn't set the alarm. He grabbed a dressing-gown and rushed down the hallway to Liam's bedroom. He wasn't there. Shepherd hurried downstairs. His son was sitting at the kitchen table, washed, dressed in his school uniform and demolishing a plate of scrambled eggs and cheese on toast. His favourite. Katra was pouring coffee.

"Look what Katra made for me," said Liam through a mouthful of egg. "I showed her how to do it, but she uses water instead of milk."

Katra handed Shepherd a mug of coffee. "There's no need to get up," she said. "I can take him to school."

"I said I'd show her where to go," said Liam.

"Are you sure?" Shepherd asked Katra, and sipped his coffee. She'd made it just as he liked it.

"It's no problem," said Katra.

Shepherd forced a smile. It was the first time he'd entrusted his son to anyone other than family, and he barely knew Katra. "Okay," he said.

"Is the white car yours too?" asked Katra.

"It's for work," said Shepherd. "You can use the CRV." He hadn't told Katra the exact nature of his work, but she knew he was a police officer.

Liam finished his breakfast and Katra helped him put on his coat. Shepherd kissed him. "You be good, yeah?" he said.

"I'm always good," said Liam.

"I'll do the shopping on my way home," said Katra.

Shepherd took out his wallet and gave her two fifty-pound notes. Then he knelt beside Liam. "I won't be here when you get home," he said. "My shift finishes at ten, so I won't be back until you're in bed."

"I could stay up," said Liam.

Shepherd laughed. "You'll be in bed by nine, young man."

"But you'll come in and see me, even if I'm asleep?"

"Sure," said Shepherd.

He stood at the front window and watched Katra and Liam climb into the CRV. Panic gripped him and he fought to control it. Liam had been in the back of the car when Sue had jumped the red light and crashed into a delivery truck. He'd emerged from the accident unscathed but he'd seen his mother die and Shepherd couldn't imagine what that must have been like for an eight-year-old boy.

Liam waved. "Seatbelt," mouthed Shepherd. Katra turned and said something to the boy, then Liam clipped on his belt.

The CRV was a big four-by-four with airbags and antilock braking system and it was high off the ground, more crash resistant than the VW Golf Sue had been driving when she'd died. Even so, Shepherd had to fight the urge to run out and tell Katra he'd drive Liam to school. It was ridiculous, of course. Moira had been running Liam to and from school in Hereford and Shepherd hadn't given it a second thought. Sue's accident had been a stupid mistake, coupled with bad luck. Liam was no more at risk in the CRV with Katra than any other child on the school-run that morning. He'd be fine. Katra beeped the horn and Shepherd raised his coffee mug in salute. Suddenly he

260

remembered that he hadn't given Katra a mobile phone so that she could contact him in an emergency. "Relax," he whispered. "He's in good hands."

He stood at the window until the CRV was out of view, then changed into his running gear and the black army boots. He ran on auto-pilot, barely aware of his five-kilometre route through the streets of Ealing and on to Scotch Common, skirting three golf courses, a circuit he'd run almost a thousand times during the four years since he'd bought the house. Sue had suggested he joined the local gym or even put a treadmill in the garage, but Shepherd wanted the ground beneath his boots and the wind in his face — the smell of grass and trees, or even car exhaust, was preferable to the perfumed deodorants that pervaded the gym. He wanted to run outdoors and he wanted to run hard; he wanted peace and quiet so that he could think. He had to become Stuart Marsden.

By the time he got back to the house he was in character. He shaved, showered and changed into his off-duty policeman clothes: blue denim shirt, black jeans and leather jacket. He put the boots into the black nylon bag with the rest of the SO19 equipment, set the burglar alarm, locked the front door and headed for the Toyota.

He called Miss Malcolm as he drove along the A40 towards the SO19 base at Leman Street and told her he wanted to hire Katra. She said she'd put the paperwork in the post to him.

He reached Leman Street at midday. He'd been told to report two hours before his shift was due to start so that he'd have time for a briefing with Rose. There was a confusing one-way system and he passed Aldgate tube station twice before he got on to the northern end of Leman Street. He found a space and bought a pay-and-display sticker that gave him an hour's parking.

The nondescript building halfway down the street looked as if it had once been a police station but the only indication that it was a Metropolitan Police building was a sheet of paper stuck to the glass door that had the force's blue and white logo in one corner. It was a six-storey concrete and glass block, bland and featureless except for a forest of radio antennae on the roof. Three Vauxhall ARVs were parked in front.

Shepherd pulled open the glass door and went over to the reception desk to find out where he could park for the duration of his shift. A bored uniformed constable checked his warrant card and gave him directions to an underground car park.

After he'd moved the Toyota, he walked back to Leman Street with his kit-bag and went in search of Keith Rose. A civilian secretary told him he was in the indoor range in the basement. Shepherd had to ask for directions and felt like the new boy at school.

As he went down the stairs he heard the sharp cracks of an MP5. He let himself in. Six men in black overalls were standing twenty-five metres from bullseye targets. They were all wearing bright orange ear-protectors. Shepherd took out a small plastic case containing yellow foam earplugs and fitted them as he headed towards the group. He recognised Keith Rose from the photographs in the file Hargrove had given him. He was just under six feet tall and broad-shouldered. His head was shaved and he had a sweeping Mexican moustache. He was talking to one of the men who had been shooting at the targets.

They looked over at Shepherd. "Stuart Marsden," said Shepherd. "I'm looking for Sergeant Rose." He had to pretend he didn't know what Rose looked like.

"Guilty as charged." Rose stepped forward and held out his hand. Shepherd shook it and dropped his kit-bag. Like the rest of the men, the sergeant had an MP5 hanging off his shoulder on its nylon sling. "Stuart's here to show us how the Jocks do it."

"I'm not Scottish, sir," said Shepherd.

Rose frowned. "Strathclyde, they told me."

"That's right, but I was born in London."

Rose handed his MP5 to Shepherd and gestured at the targets. "Show us what you can do, then." He grinned.

Shepherd checked the weapon, then slid the safety selector to fire. He swung the gun smoothly up to his shoulder and fired six single shots into one of the targets. His grouping was good, all within the two inner circles.

"Nice," said Rose. Shepherd gave him back the carbine. "Let's go into the canteen for a chat. Then we'll get you fixed up with a Glock."

Shepherd picked up his kit-bag. Rose held open the door and took him along a corridor. "Word is you were in the army," he said.

"For a few years. The Paras."

"Why did you leave?"

Shepherd smiled easily. "Didn't realise I was being interviewed for the job. Thought I was being transferred here."

Rose didn't smile. "In the Trojans it's all about knowing your team," he said. "If we go into a building and there's bad guys with guns, we all have to be on the same wavelength and that's down to knowing everything about each other. No secrets."

"Same in the army," said Shepherd.

"So why did you quit?"

"Difficult to answer. Boredom, for one. The training got to me, running up and down mountains, waiting for the shit to hit the fan. And when the shit hits, it's pretty shitty. Afghanistan wasn't much fun."

"What about Ireland?" They reached the canteen.

"A couple of tours, but the IRA had pretty much called it quits when I was there."

Rose pointed at an empty table. "Drop your gear and we'll grab some food. You hungry? No haggis but the chef can probably stuff a sheep's stomach for you if you ask him nicely."

"I guess I'm stuck with the Scottish jokes."

"For the foreseeable future, yeah. Until we find something else to pick on. Newbie syndrome."

"No sweat," said Shepherd. He dropped his bag and joined Rose in the queue for food.

"So, you reckoned the cops was a cushier number?" asked Rose.

"I wouldn't have to sleep in a barracks, and I'd be dealing with real people. The army's a closed community — you're either in it or you're an outsider. I was fed up with the same old faces, day in, day out."

"It's not that different in the Trojans," said Rose. "We're tight. Have to be."

"But they don't make you run up and down mountains with a Bergen on your back."

"SO19 isn't a soft touch."

"Didn't mean to suggest it was," said Shepherd. "I've been a cop for seven years, and carrying a gun for most of that time."

"I don't see why you'd want to move south," said Rose. "The London weighting might be attractive, but property's still twice the price you'd be paying north of the border."

"My dad's in hospital down here, I wanted to be closer to him." They reached the front of the queue. Rose took steak and kidney pie and chips and Shepherd the same. They collected mugs of coffee and headed back to their table.

"What do we call you?" asked Rose, as he poured brown sauce over his pie.

"Up to you. The guys in Glasgow called me Irish."

Rose frowned. "You're not a Paddy, are you?"

"Irish Stew. They thought it was funny." It was one of the details in his legend that served no other function than to add colour to his cover story.

"Stu it is, then. I'll leave it up to the lads to give you a nickname. They call me Rosie in the pub, Sarge or Skipper when we're on duty."

"Yes, Sarge."

"Cards on the table, Stu. I was hoping to get someone local in our vehicle. Mike Sutherland's one of the best drivers in the Met and I ride shotgun, so it's a map man we're short of."

"I'm up to speed," said Shepherd. "I was born in London, remember."

"You've been in Scotland for almost a decade and things change," said Rose. "Last thing I need is for you to take me the wrong way down a one-way system."

"My dad was a black-cab driver," said Shepherd. More colour. "Used to test me on the Knowledge when I was still in short trousers. But we've got GPS, right?"

"Computers don't always know the quickest way," said Rose, "and sometimes they crash. If that happens I need someone in the back who knows where they're going."

"Try me," said Shepherd.

Rose grinned. "Okay," he said. "We get a call to Grosvenor Road, which is the quickest way to get there?"

"I'd guess you mean Grosvenor Road in Pimlico in which case I'd head over Vauxhall Bridge. But there are Grosvenor Roads in Upton Park, Forest Gate, Leyton and Wanstead, so I'd ask first."

Rose raised an eyebrow. "Grantully Road," he said.

"Maida Vale. One way, entrance from Morshead Road. Runs parallel to Paddington recreation ground."

Rose nodded. "Had a suicide there three months ago. Guy blew off his head with a shotgun. Okay, you're my map man." He stabbed at a chunk of steak. "Why did you join the Strathclyde cops and not the Met?"

It was a good question, and was also covered in the Stuart Marsden legend. "Had a mate in the Paras who was from Glasgow and his dad was a chief inspector. He put in a good word for me."

"But you didn't fancy London?"

Shepherd looked uncomfortable. "Long story, Sarge. My mum died when I was a kid and my dad remarried. Turned out to be the stepmother from hell. That's why I joined the army. When I got out, I wanted to be as far away from her as possible."

A police officer in black overalls and bulletproof vest walked over to their table carrying a tray. Rose grinned up at him. "Hiya, Mike, say hello to our new map man, Stu Marsden. Stu, this is Mike Sutherland. Our driver."

Sutherland nodded at Shepherd and sat down opposite him. He had a plateful of bacon and sausage and four slices of bread and butter. "The Jock, yeah?" said Sutherland.

"Nah, he's not Scottish," said Rose. "He was just explaining."

"Family stuff," said Shepherd, "but my dad's on his own now and he's not doing so well, so I want to be around when he needs me."

"And it was easy to transfer to the Met?" asked Sutherland.

"I'd been asking for a move and the SO19 vacancy came up."

"You must have friends in high places. There's a long waiting list for ARV slots." Sutherland stabbed a sausage and bit off the end.

"I was lucky."

"Just don't get me lost."

"He's fine," said Rose. "His dad was a black-cab driver."

"Funny, he doesn't look black," said Sutherland.

Rose flashed Sutherland a tight smile. "PC Sutherland is one of the least PC of our officers. We try to keep him in the car as much as possible."

Kerr got the early-morning flight to Heathrow and took a taxi to the Kings Road. He had made a phone call the previous evening and Alex Knight was expecting him. He told the taxi driver to wait.

"The meter's at sixty quid already," said the man.

Kerr pointed at the black door between an antiques shop and a hairdresser's. "I'll be in there ten minutes at most. Then we're straight back to the airport."

The driver beamed at the thought of a double fare.

Kerr got out and walked along the pavement to the black door. A small brass plaque read "Alex Knight Security" beside a bell button and a small grille. He pressed the button and was buzzed in. He took the stairs two at a time and when he reached the top Knight's secretary had the door open for him. "Charlie, we can FedEx orders, you know," she said.

Kerr kissed the striking brunette's cheek. "Just wanted to see you, love."

"He's expecting you," she said, and opened Knight's office door.

He looked up from his computer terminal and grinned boyishly, stood up and shook hands with Kerr. He was several inches taller than Kerr, but stick-thin with square-framed spectacles perched high on his nose. "We do deliver," he said.

"Yeah, Sarah said, but I wanted you to talk me through the gear."

Knight waved him to a seat. He pulled a cardboard box from one of his desk drawers and pushed it across the desk. "This is the kit you wanted. The transmitter's linked to a GPS so you get position information accurate to six metres."

Kerr opened the box. Inside he found a small metal cylinder with a three-inch wire protruding from one end and a handheld GPS unit.

"There's an on-off switch on the transmitter. Best bet is to connect it to the car's electrical circuit. Then it'll run and run. If you can connect its aerial to the car aerial, you're laughing."

"Won't have time for that," Kerr said. "Best we'll be able to do is get it under a seat."

"You'll have about twelve hours, then. Maybe a few more. But once the battery starts to go, the strength of the signal drops."

"That'll be enough," said Kerr. "What's the range?"

"Unlimited for the locator. The transmitter connects to the nearest satellite and the GPS unit logs on to the signal. You'll only lose the signal if either unit is underground or in a shielded area. But the voice transmitter is good for about two hundred metres, line of sight. Less in a built-up area."

Knight showed Kerr how to switch on the GPS unit. A map of Central London flickered on the screen. He flicked the switch and a couple of seconds later a red dot appeared on the Kings Road. "The switch there gives you the voice. It's a neat bit of kit."

"Two gizmos in one. Just what I need," said Charlie.

"It's from my mate in Kiev. Based on a KGB model."

Kerr repacked the equipment and gave Knight an envelope filled with fifty-pound notes. "Fancy lunch?" asked Knight.

Kerr stood up. "I've got to dash, mate. Mountains to climb, rivers to cross. Next time." He hurried outside and got back into the cab. Now he had everything he needed to get his claws into the mysterious Mr Nelson.

After lunch, Rose took Shepherd to the armoury where a lanky sergeant with receding hair issued him with a Glock, four magazines and a box of ammunition. The gun would be Shepherd's while he was based at Tango 99, the call sign for the Leman Street headquarters, but when he wasn't on duty it would stay in the armoury. The MP5s were a different matter: they were assigned to the ARV rather than to individual officers.

Rose and Shepherd went down to the range where they donned ear-protectors. Rose watched as Shepherd fired several dozen shots at targets ten metres away. Shepherd checked the grouping, altered the sights and fired another two dozen shots. All were in the centre ring of the bullseye.

He noted the number of shots fired in the range log, then Rose took him up to the locker room where they changed into their working gear. Shepherd loaded his three clips with 9mm ammunition and slotted them into the nylon holders on his belt. He slid his Swiss Army knife into his trouser pocket.

Rose cast a professional eye over Shepherd's equipment. "Not too far behind the times north of the border, then?"

"Aye, it was a great relief to us all when they stopped us using flintlocks, the noo," said Shepherd, in an over-the-top Scottish accent.

Rose grinned. "Come on, let's get you fixed up with a radio." He took Shepherd along a corridor to an office with "COMMS" on the door. There was a rack of radios in chargers. Rose took one for himself and signed the log with his name and the number of the unit. Shepherd followed his example, then fitted the radio into the holder on his belt. He threaded the wiring spaghetti under his vest, clipped on the microphone and put on the black plastic earpiece.

Rose talked him through the local frequencies, then they went back to the armoury. Sutherland was waiting for them. Shepherd returned his unused Glock ammunition to the sergeant and signed for the bullets he'd fired. The sergeant issued them with two MP5s, both with retractable stocks, and ammunition. More ARV crews arrived to collect their weaponry, and Rose, Shepherd and Sutherland went out to the car park.

As they left the building, Shepherd's radio crackled. "MP to all Trojan units, intruders at the Houses of Parliament. Possible Operation Rolvenden." MP was the call sign of New Scotland Yard's control centre: Operation Rolvenden was the call sign for a terrorist incident.

Rose confirmed over the radio that they were *en route* from Leman Street. "There's luck for you, Stu," he said. "First day on the job and we get a bloody terrorist incident. We'll be calling you Jonah next."

They got to their car, a Vauxhall Omega, white with a red fluorescent strip down the sides and a three-letter identifier on the roof. Shepherd got into the back and put his carbine into the metal carrier in the centre of the rear seat. Sutherland climbed into the front and fastened his seatbelt. "You know where the Houses of Parliament are, I suppose," said Sutherland. "I wouldn't want to get lost, your first day and all."

"If you need directions, just ask," said Shepherd. "I'd have thought a top driver like you would have known where the mother of all parliaments was." Rose gave Shepherd his carbine, climbed into the front seat and slammed the door.

Over the main radio more call signs came in from cars heading towards the incident. Two Trojan units were on the way, but Shepherd wasn't sure how effective armed police would be against suicide bombers. The black metal gate rattled back and Sutherland edged the car out into East Tenter Street, which ran behind the Leman Street building.

"You're up to speed on the six Cs?" asked Rose. The ARV accelerated as Sutherland turned on to Mansell Street and headed south, towards the Thames.

Shepherd couldn't tell if he was being sarcastic. The six Cs were on a card given to all police officers, explaining how to deal with a suicide bomber. "Sure,"

272

he said. "Confirm, cover, contact, civilians, colleagues, check."

It was something of a joke among serving officers, a case of stating the obvious if ever there was one. Confirm — the location and description of a suspect. Cover — withdraw fifty yards from the suspect to a point where it is possible to maintain visual contact. Contact — your supervisor and request more police assistance. Civilians — direct to a place of safety but not if this is likely to compromise or further endanger the public or other officers. Colleagues — prevent other officers coming into the danger area. Check — for further suspects or devices.

"We'll probably be going with the six Ss," said Rose. "See the bugger's got a bomb, shit yourself, say a prayer, shoot him dead, stand by your mates and say nothing."

"Definitely," said Sutherland, hitting the blues and twos and accelerating past a double-decker bus. He tapped co-ordinates into the onboard computer.

"We were on a course a few weeks back," said Rose. "How to spot a suicide bomber in a crowd. Signs of sweating, mumbling and possibly praying."

"And ten kilos of Semtex strapped to their chest is always a bad sign," said Sutherland. "Who writes that shit? Some graduate entrant who's spent his whole career sitting behind a desk?"

Rose ignored the interruption. "Well, the good news is that any blast from a suicide bomber is only lethal within about thirty feet. Severe injuries up to fifty yards. And beyond a hundred and fifty yards you're safe as houses."

"And this is good news because . . .?" asked Shepherd.

Rose jerked his thumb at the gun-holder. "Because those little beauties are dead accurate up to a hundred yards, which is as close as we're gonna get to any ragheads on a mission."

"Er, Sarge, ragheads is on the list of terms likely to cause offence," said Sutherland. "IC Six, please. Or camel jockeys."

They roared alongside the Thames, the London Eye in the distance. As they headed for Westminster Bridge they spotted the honey-coloured Big Ben tower next to the Houses of Parliament. "See anything?" asked Rose.

Shepherd had binoculars to his eyes but the west side of the tower seemed clear. "Nothing yet, Sarge."

Rose clicked his radio mike. "MP, Trojan Five Six Nine, any update on Operation Rolvenden at the Houses of Parliament?"

"Negative, Trojan Five Six Nine."

"Be handy to know if they were IC Six or not."

"Trojan Five Six Nine, soon as we know, you'll know. If the info is not suitable for RT transmission we'll call direct on the car phone."

"Who's in charge at the scene?" asked Rose.

"Chief Inspector Owen. But Assistant Commissioner Hannant is *en route*."

"Well, if Owen's on the case we can all relax and go home," said Sutherland, sarcastically.

274

Rose flashed him a withering look. Banter was all well and good between colleagues, but not when there was an open mike in the vehicle. It was a well known fact that assistant commissioners had had their sense of humour surgically removed and the AC would be monitoring all radio traffic. "Trojan Five Six Nine is three minutes away," said Rose.

"You'll be the first ARV on the scene," said the MP controller. "Report to Chief Inspector Owen on arrival."

Rose replaced the mike.

"You know Owen?" asked Shepherd.

"Couldn't make a decision to save his life," said Sutherland. "Ask him if he takes sugar in his tea and he reaches for a manual."

"He's graduate entry, accelerated promotion," said Rose. "Not thirty, but tipped as a potential chief constable. That means everything he does has a political dimension to it. He's more concerned with not making mistakes than he is with catching villains. The crack in his arse is from sitting on too many fences. Hannant's a good copper, though. Let's hope he gets there soon."

They were driving along Victoria Embankment when Shepherd saw the first of the three figures on the tower. "I've got one," he said. "Just below the clock face." He could make out a figure in a blue anorak with the hood up and a bulky pack on his back. Not necessarily a he, Shepherd corrected himself. There were as many women as men prepared to blow themselves to kingdom come.

Shepherd scanned down the tower. Two more figures were some way below the first. "I see all three," he said. "They're carrying backpacks."

"Shit," said Rose. "Backpacks mean a bigger bang. You can put thirty kilos of high explosive in a backpack with ballbearings or nails and that's the equivalent of a car bomb."

Traffic was heavy but the siren and flashing lights carved a way through for the ARV. They reached Westminster Bridge and Sutherland swung right. A traffic patrol car, its blue light flashing, had parked across the bridge and two uniformed constables were turning back southbound traffic.

Rose clicked on his radio. "MP, Trojan Five Six Nine, I see crowds all around College Green. Isn't someone moving them out of the area?"

"Trojan Five Six Nine, we have units evacuating the Houses of Parliament."

"That's fine, but the threat's outside."

Sutherland brought the car to a halt.

"MP, Trojan Five Six Nine is at the scene," said Rose, into his mike. "Break out the guns, Stu."

"Yes, Sarge." Shepherd unlocked the metal case between the two rear seats, handed one of the MP5s to Rose, then slotted a magazine into the second weapon. He climbed out of the car. All around people were staring up at the clock tower. A group of Japanese tourists was snapping away with digital cameras. Mothers with babies in pushchairs were watching the climbers, shading their eyes with their hands. Workmen in overalls were shouting catcalls up at the three, daring them to jump.

"This is bloody madness," said Rose. "Why aren't these people being moved out of the way? Where the hell's Owen?"

Shepherd let the gun hang on its nylon swing as he scanned the clock tower through his binoculars. He focused on the climber second from the top. He had turned and was watching the crowds. Shepherd got a glimpse of his face. "Looks like an Arab," he said.

"You sure?" asked Rose.

"Fairly."

Rose clicked on his transceiver mike. "MP, Trojan Five Six Nine, confirm that we have visual on three intruders. One is definitely IC Six."

Chief Inspector Owen was standing with half a dozen uniformed constables in yellow fluorescent jackets. One of the officers had a megaphone and raised it to his mouth to ask the three men to return to the ground.

"I don't believe this," said Rose. "Come on."

Shepherd followed him to the group. The constable lowered the megaphone and looked at Owen for further instructions. The workmen jeered at the officers.

Rose nodded at Owen. "Trojan unit, sir. We need authorisation from you to fire."

Owen seemed stunned by his request. "Hold on, Sergeant," he said. "All we have at the moment is three guys climbing Big Ben."

"It's down as a possible terrorist incident, sir," said Rose, "and I don't want to start telling anyone their job but we should be getting civilians out of the immediate area."

"But we don't know that there's a threat," said Owen.

"Three men with backpacks climbing one of the nation's monuments, I think it's safe to assume the worst, sir," said Rose, with emphasis on the "sir".

"Could be base jumpers," said the chief inspector.

"Base jumpers?"

"The guys who parachute off tall buildings," said Owen.

"I know what base jumpers are, sir, but at least one of them's an Arab and those aren't parachutes on their backs. MI5 has said there are specific al-Qaeda threats against the House of Commons. If we don't react decisively it'll be down to us."

"It's not a question of being decisive, Sergeant. It's about making the right decision."

Owen beckoned to the constable with the megaphone. "Start moving people back. Establish a perimeter a hundred and fifty yards from the base of the tower. And be tactful, man, we don't want a bloody stampede."

Shepherd was looking at the three climbers through the binoculars. One was only feet from the top of the tower.

"Sir, we have to take action now," said Rose.

"I'm not sure, Sergeant."

Two police cars arrived, lights flashing but sirens off.

"If they're carrying high-explosive charges they could demolish the tower. If there's shrapnel, people could be killed, even with a cordon."

Owen wiped his forehead on his sleeve. "Where's the goddamned AC?" he asked.

"It's your call, sir."

"You're sure you can reach them?"

"No question," said Rose.

Indecision was etched into Owen's face. A sergeant and three constables jogged over from the newly arrived vehicles. Over the megaphone, the constable was asking for people to move away, but no one paid him any attention. All eyes were on the men on the clock tower.

"If they destroy Big Ben, we'll look bloody stupid standing here letting them do it," said Rose. "Sir," he added, as an afterthought.

"And if they're thrill-seekers, we'll have shot three innocent men," said Owen.

Shepherd focused on the second figure on the tower. The man was looking over his shoulder and smiling. He was to the bottom right of the clock face, close to the V numeral.

"Sir," said Rose, "we need a green light from you."

Owen glanced up and down the Embankment. Two ambulances had arrived and parked close to the police cars. Owen took a deep breath. He clicked his radio mike. "MP, this is Chief Inspector Owen, can you patch me through to AC Hannant."

His radio buzzed. "I'll try, sir."

Rose sighed with exasperation.

"Hang on," said Shepherd. "I think I know him."

Owen turned towards him. "What?"

"I think I know him," repeated Shepherd. He pointed up at the figure by the V. "I don't remember his name but he's a British citizen, Pakistani descent. His wife did a runner with his two sons and he's been fighting for custody. He was in the papers last year, did the protest on Blackpool Tower with a couple of other guys." In fact, Shepherd had recalled his name — Kashif Jakhrani — but he didn't want it generally known that he had an almost perfect memory. It was best kept secret so that he could use it to his advantage.

"What protest?" asked Rose impatiently.

"Fathers for Children," said Shepherd. "Divorced dads who've been refused access to their kids. They draped the banner over the tower."

"Are you sure?" said Owen.

"That's him. I read about it in the papers."

"So on the basis of a newspaper photograph that you may or may not have seen last year, you're saying that man's an angry father and not a terrorist?" said Rose.

Shepherd put the binoculars to his eyes and focused on the man's face again. He flicked through his mental filing system and found the newspaper article he'd scanned the previous year. In the photograph, Jakhrani was wearing a Superman costume. "It's him," said Shepherd. "No question. He married an English girl and she refused him access to their two kids after they divorced. He's no terrorist."

Owen's radio crackled. "AC Hannant here. Everything okay, Paul?"

Owen clicked his mike. "Fine, sir. Just wanted to see what your ETA is. Seems to be a protest. We're keeping a watching brief and we'll pick them up when they climb down." He looked at Shepherd. "Are you sure?"

"I'm sure," said Shepherd.

"God help us if you're wrong."

Again Hannant's voice crackled over Owen's transceiver: "Are the TV people there yet?"

"No, but they'll probably be here soon, sir," said Owen.

"You handle the press, Paul. You'll know what to say. Public protests are a right, but public safety is paramount, we don't want to be heavy-handed, blah-blah-blah. The usual waffle."

"Will do, sir."

Owen waved at Rose's MP5. "The guns can go back in the car, Sergeant."

"I'd be happier if we remain armed," said Rose.

"Sarge," said Shepherd. Rose followed his gaze. Two of the three men had reached the top of the tower and had taken off their backpacks. As the third joined them they unfurled a huge banner. It billowed in the wind. "FATHERS HAVE RIGHTS, TOO!"

"Stupid bastards," Rose muttered.

Shepherd headed back to the car. Rose went after him and clapped him on the shoulder. "Nice call."

"Just lucky."

"It was more than that. To remember something you saw in the paper a year ago! I'd have slotted them without a second thought."

"And you would have been right," said Shepherd. "They could just as easily have been al-Qaeda. If I hadn't recognised the guy and we'd been ordered to shoot, I'd have done it."

"And the media would have crucified us," said Rose.

"Yeah, well, they want it both ways, don't they? They want the UK safe from terrorists yet they accuse us of being heavy-handed when we do what's necessary. Can't bloody win. Journalists and politicians — don't know which are worse."

"Throw in senior police officers and I'll agree with you."

They got into the car and stowed the MP5s. Rose picked up the radio and called in that they were back on watch.

Sutherland was peering up at the tower. A second banner had been dropped so that it covered the north face of the clock. "KIDS NEED THEIR DADS." "Do you think they know how close they came to getting shot?" he mused.

"They just want to make their point," said Shepherd.

"They were lucky," said Rose. "And you must have one hell of a memory."

"Nah, story just interested me."

"You've got kids?"

"Not that I know about," Shepherd joked. He hated denying Liam's existence but Stuart Marsden didn't have a family. "These guys get a raw deal. Most of them pay child support and want to be good fathers, but their wives get vindictive. What about you? Have you got kids?"

Sutherland flashed Shepherd a warning look, but Rose didn't seem perturbed. "A daughter. But if my missus ever tried to take her away from me, you wouldn't find me climbing Big Ben with a banner." He stretched and sighed. "I hate false alarms," he said. "All foreplay and no orgasm."

"Can't help you there I'm afraid, Sarge," said Sutherland. He looked over his shoulder at Shepherd. "Besides, that's up to the new guy."

"Didn't see that in the job description," said Shepherd.

"Don't worry, Stu," said Rose. "You're not my type."

The car radio crackled. "Trojan Five Six Nine, armed robbery in progress at Speedy Pizzas in Battersea high street."

Sutherland put the car into gear and switched on the siren and flashing lights.

Rose picked up the mike. "MP, Trojan Five Six Nine *en route*," he said.

Cars were pulling to the side of the road to let the Vauxhall through. "Hopefully we'll get you an orgasm this time, Sarge." Sutherland laughed as he stamped on the accelerator and tore past an open-topped tour bus. There was still a road-block leading to Westminster Bridge but the uniformed police waved them through. They sped across the empty bridge and through the road block on the south side.

The controller filled Rose in on what was happening. Two IC Threes, black males, had gone into the pizza shop and produced sawn-off shotguns. A customer had decided to have a go and grabbed for one of the guns. It had gone off and the noise had alerted passers-by. Three had phoned 999 on their mobiles, and within two minutes a local ARV had been on the scene with two area cars. They had contained the situation but the two robbers were now holding the customers and staff hostage.

"Why the hell would anyone stick up a pizza place?" asked Sutherland. "How much cash would they have at this time of day?"

"Could be druggies," said Rose.

"Druggies with shotguns? They're more at home with blood-filled hypodermics or knives," said Sutherland.

Shepherd felt the blood pounding through his veins and the elation that came from the body's release of adrenaline. This was no false alarm: there were men with guns and they were prepared to use them. And it was up to him and his colleagues to stop them. He focused on his immediate task, of finding the most efficient route to the crime scene, but his mind was already whirling through the ramifications of a hostage situation. There would be no gunfight while the men were inside the building with hostages. The officer in charge would play it by the book and negotiate for as long as he could. The SO19 officers would be there to contain and control, but to shoot only as a last resort. The hostage-takers would be hoping for safe passage, but Shepherd knew that wouldn't happen. The police would keep a dialogue going until the robbers realised that the siege would end only one way — with them in custody.

Sutherland cut through the south London streets. A second local ARV called up that it was on its way to the scene, and the officer in charge called in to request a hostage negotiator, then an ambulance. A customer had been hit by the shotgun blast and was bleeding heavily.

That changed the situation, Shepherd knew: if the life of a hostage was in immediate danger, there was a chance that the armed police would be ordered in.

Trojan Five Eight One called in that it was *en route* with an ETA of six minutes. It was one of SO19's black vans with trained snipers among its eight-man crew. It added to the likelihood that the building would be stormed. Shepherd's pulse raced. He remembered Major Gannon's briefing in Hereford. The way armed police took a building was a complete contrast to the SAS method. The SAS went in hard, thunderflash grenades to stun, multiple shots to make sure that the targets went down and stayed down. They stopped only when the object was secured. When the SAS did their business there were usually no cameras around, no witnesses to scream about overkill and human-rights violations. But the police had to follow procedures, many of which had been drawn up by men who had never seen a gun fired in anger, never had cordite sting their eyes, never felt the paralysing punch of a bullet hitting home.

The officer in charge was a chief inspector from Battersea. Sutherland and Rose said they didn't know him but his voice was calm. He confirmed that the street had been cordoned off and that offices and apartments were being cleared. He suggested that vehicles enter the high street from the east. Shepherd's eyes flicked over the map and he called out an alternative route to Sutherland.

They powered past an ambulance that was also Battersea-bound, siren wailing. Shepherd wondered how badly hurt the customer was. Sawn-off shotguns were lethal at close range but the shot dispersed so much once it left the barrel that the damage could be superficial beyond fifty feet or so. Shepherd had taken a bullet once and almost died, but he had been a soldier fighting a war. The customer had expected no more than a boring wait in a queue and now he was a victim in an armed robbery. There was an unfairness about crime, the way it struck without warning. If you were in the wrong place at the wrong time you became a victim. At least in a war you knew what to expect.

"Here we go," said Sutherland. Two area cars were ahead of them, their bumpers together across the road. A single uniformed constable in a yellow fluorescent jacket pointed to the left and Sutherland parked. Shepherd was already unlocking the gun-holder.

Rose took one of the MP5s and Shepherd followed him to the uniformed constable. At the far end of the road there were two more police cars, blue lights flashing. One had saucer-sized yellow stickers in the corner of the windows, which showed it was an ARV. Half a dozen uniformed policemen were kneeling behind the cars, watching the front of the building. Two had MP5s aimed at it.

"Where's the OIC?" asked Rose.

The uniformed constable indicated an estate agent's office. "Chief Inspector Cockburn," he said.

Shepherd looked up at the rooftops as he followed Rose across the road. The street had shops on both sides, with two floors of brick-built apartments above them. On the roof of the apartments opposite two policemen were scrutinising the pizza place, one through high-powered binoculars. Rose and Shepherd went into the estate agent's. A uniformed sergeant and two constables were standing by the window. Chief Inspector Cockburn was sitting at a desk, a transceiver in front of him next to his cap. His right hand was drumming on the desk and sweat glistened across his bald scalp.

"Keith Rose, sir. SO19. This is Stuart Marsden."

"Any sign of the Specialist Firearms team?"

"On its way from Leman Street, sir. What's the story?"

"We've a customer bleeding to death on the floor and two nervous young men with shooters. They were on their way out when they saw the local ARV. They took a couple of shots at it, then ran back in. I've two men on the roof opposite who can see inside. Someone's trying to stem the bleeding but it doesn't look good."

"Where do you want us, sir?"

"We're going to have to move quickly, Sergeant. I know I'm supposed to wait for a negotiator, but if we do, that customer could die. Do you have any suggestions?"

"Is there a back entrance?"

"There's a fire exit that leads into the kitchen and we have two armed officers outside. I doubt you could get in without the robbers hearing you, though."

"Have you spoken to them?"

"The negotiator's on his way. We're just keeping a lid on it until then."

It was the right thing to do, Shepherd thought. Hostage situations could easily go wrong and had to be handled by experts.

"I could get two of my men above the shop," Rose said. "They could drop down outside, on ropes. They wouldn't see them coming. Your men on the roof opposite can tell us when we've a clear run."

"Okay, Sergeant. Get them in position, but wait for my say-so."

A constable had pinned a large sheet of paper to one wall and a young man in a grey suit was helping him draw a ground plan of the pizza place. There was a large kitchen at the back, with a counter in front of it. There was a toilet and washroom to the side, but it was for staff only and was reached from behind the counter. There were a few stools and a shelf where customers could eat but it was more of a home delivery operation than a restaurant.

Rose turned to Shepherd. "How are you at abseiling, Stu?"

"It's been a while but I can handle it."

"You and Mike see if you can gain access to the roof across the way."

Shepherd hurried over to the car, opened the boot and took out two nylon ropes, karabiners and nylon harnesses. "Sarge wants us up top," he said. He slung the carbine over his shoulder and jogged to a door between a chemist and a travel agency. Sutherland followed him.

"They should try Kylie," said Shepherd.

"Kylie?" said Sutherland, frowning.

"There were these drugs guys holed up with hostages in South America, I forget where, and the local cops got them out by playing Kylie Minogue singing 'I Should Be So Lucky' non-stop for three days."

Sutherland chuckled. "Urban myth, right?"

"True as I'm standing here, Mike."

"I'll let you pitch it to the sarge."

To the right of the door there was a rusting intercom with two buttons and Shepherd pressed both. There was no reply. "I'll get the Enforcer." He went back to the Vauxhall and opened the boot. It was packed with equipment, including a first-aid kit, Kevlar ballistic blanket, ballistic shield, a firearms make-safe kit, to preserve weapons for forensic analysis, a ballistic bag for safely unloading weapons, and the red hammer-like ram nicknamed the Enforcer. Shepherd grabbed it and returned to the door.

"I'll do the honours," said Sutherland. "The paperwork's a bitch but I've got the forms in my desk." He took the ram from Shepherd and slammed it into the door by the lock. The wooden frame splintered and Shepherd finished the job with a hard kick.

Beyond the doorway was a narrow staircase. On the first floor a door led to a flat and the stairs twisted to the left up to the second floor. Sutherland was about to use the ram on the second-floor flat when Shepherd pointed to a hatch in the ceiling.

Sutherland propped the Enforcer against the wall and nodded at Shepherd to give him a leg up. Shepherd grinned. "Mike, I'm ten kilos lighter than you and about six inches narrower around the waist. If you get stuck in that hatch we'll be all day getting you out. I'll go first." He put the ropes and his carbine on the floor. Sutherland made a step with his hands and pushed Shepherd up to the ceiling. The hatch was just a piece of plywood painted the same colour as the ceiling and lifted easily. Shepherd wriggled through. The walls were bare brick covered with cobwebs, there were dusty wooden beams supporting tiles, and thick layers of yellow fibreglass insulation padding between the floor beams.

Shepherd lay down on a beam and took the equipment from Sutherland, then leaned down and pulled up his colleague. It was indeed a tight fit but Sutherland got through. He wiped the dust off his overalls and grinned. "See? I didn't even need to take the vest off."

Shepherd handed him his MP5 and picked up a rope. There were two windows in the roof, encrusted with pigeon droppings. Shepherd tried to open one but it had been painted so many times it was jammed tight. The second was looser and he slid it open. He clicked his transceiver to transmit. "We're in, Sarge," he said. "We have a window to get on to the roof."

"Get above the pizza joint and sit tight," said Rose. "The Specialist Firearms team's arrived and we've got two snipers moving into position across the road from you."

"Will do," said Shepherd. He stood to the side so that Sutherland could go through the window first. "What did I say wrong earlier?" he asked.

"About what?"

"About the sarge having kids."

"Rosie's daughter's sick," said Sutherland. "It's not something he talks about, and you being the new guy and all . . ."

"Shit," said Shepherd.

"It's okay — we should have warned you. We ask him how she's getting on but it's not good."

"Poor guy."

"Yeah, tell me about it."

"What is it? Leukaemia?"

"Some sort of tumour on her spine. Inoperable."

"Christ."

"Yeah. She's a sweet kid, too, Kelly. Cute as a button. Seven years old."

"And she's dying?"

"Don't let Rosie hear you say that — he'll tear you a new one."

"Sorry. Thanks for setting me straight."

Sutherland pulled himself through the window and Shepherd pushed him up, then handed him the ropes and followed. A lead-lined rain gully ran the length of the roof, below a waist-high brick parapet. Sutherland knelt down and looked over at the buildings opposite. Shepherd joined him. Down below, close to the road block on their left, was the black high-sided van of the Specialist Firearms team. A tall thin man with close-cropped bullet grey hair was standing with an MP5 slung over his shoulder, talking to a uniformed constable. "That's Ken Swift, the inspector in charge of Amber team. Bloody good guy."

Swift turned away from the constable and spoke into the microphone clipped to his bulletproof vest. Shepherd looked at the rooftops opposite and saw the two uniformed officers who had the pizza place under surveillance. Two armed policemen appeared, bent low behind the parapet. He glimpsed the barrel of a sniping rifle. He dropped down and called Rose on his radio. "I see the shots opposite, Sarge," he said. "They know we're here, right?"

"Affirmative," crackled Rose's voice.

Shepherd peered over the parapet again. The two snipers had taken up position at either side of the surveillance officers. Shepherd waved, then indicated that he and Sutherland were going to move along the roof. One of the snipers nodded. Shepherd flashed Sutherland an "OK" signal and they headed down the gully, bent double, carbines clutched to their chests. They stopped when they were directly opposite the snipers. Shepherd hooked a rope round a chimney and attached a karabiner. Sutherland did the same. Shepherd radioed to Rose that they were in position, then the two men settled behind the parapet.

"Have you been in hostage situations before?" asked Shepherd.

"A few times," said Sutherland. "Usually domestics, though. Criminals tend not to take hostages. They know it always ends badly and the judge will throw away the key."

"Sounds like they were forced into it this time," said Shepherd. "With any luck they'll be talked out of it."

"Don't bank on it," said Sutherland, laconically. "There's a punter bleeding on the floor, remember. That could be attempted murder. Life if the guy dies."

Shepherd's earpiece crackled. "Negotiator's arrived, but it's not looking good," he said. "They're refusing to send the injured man out until they get a coach or a minibus. They want to take the hostages with them."

Down below, more area cars were arriving. Sutherland popped a stick of gum into his mouth and offered the pack to Shepherd. Shepherd took a piece.

"I've got a bad feeling about this," said Sutherland.

Shepherd chewed thoughtfully. Rose's plan was for the two of them to drop down the front of the shop. But there were two sawn-off shotguns below and at close range they could do a lot of damage. The robbers would see them and the first shots from the MP5 would only smash the windows. It was impossible to fire through glass with any accuracy. They could use the snipers to smash the windows and, hopefully, the robbers would have their heads down but even so Shepherd and Sutherland would be facing two men with shotguns who knew they were under attack.

"Negotiators know what they're doing," said Shepherd. "They're professionals."

"So are we, mate, but things sometimes turn to shit no matter how well trained you are."

"Two shots from Amber team are going to be joining you," said Rose in Shepherd's earpiece. "How did you get access?"

Shepherd told the sergeant about the hatchway.

To their right an ambulance arrived. Two paramedics opened the rear doors, took out a trolley and pushed it to the road block.

"What about going down?" said Shepherd.

"Not until Rosie gives the say-so," said Sutherland.

"I mean downstairs. See if we can get into the flat below. Not so far to jump. We might even be able to get through the ceiling. You saw what it was like in the attic."

"Bounce it off the sarge, if you like. He can put it to Cockburn."

Shepherd called up Rose, who told him to stay put.

A minute or so later Cockburn was on the radio. "Chief Inspector Cockburn here, Marsden. What's your plan?"

"It's not really a plan, sir, it's just that we've less of a drop if we go from the first floor instead of the roof, and there's an outside chance that there might be a way in through the ceiling."

"You can get access to the first-floor flat?"

"We've an Enforcer with us, but the lock didn't look too strong so we could probably shoulder it."

There was a long silence. "Okay, give it a go," Cockburn said, "but keep the noise to a minimum. The negotiator isn't making much progress so it's likely we'll have to go in."

"Will do, sir." Shepherd nodded at Sutherland. "Let's get to it."

They untied their ropes, coiled them and shuffled back along the gully. As they reached the window, they met the two armed police from the Specialist Firearms team. Sutherland knew them and introduced them to Shepherd as Brian Ramshaw and Kevin Tapping. Both were in their late thirties, calm and unruffled. Shepherd briefed them on what they were going to do.

The four men went back down through the hatch into the hallway, picked up the ram and hurried down to the first floor. Shepherd examined the lock. It was a simple Yale with a metal plate to protect it from being jemmied. Sutherland prepared to use the ram but Shepherd called up Rose and asked him to get one of the area cars to rev its engines, so that the men in the pizza place would be distracted.

A couple of minutes later, when the engine was revving, Shepherd kicked the door hard. It crashed inwards, and a few seconds later the engine went quiet.

Shepherd tiptoed into the flat. It was cheaply furnished with worn carpets and woodchip wallpaper painted a pale yellow. In the hallway there was a teak-effect low table with a phone on it and a framed print of a bowl of fruit above it. The furniture in the sitting room was shabby, and an ashtray overflowed with the butts of hand-rolled cigarettes. The faint smell of marijuana hung in the air.

Sutherland grinned. "Whoever lives here is going to piss themselves when they find out that the Old Bill's been in," he said.

Shepherd was already pushing the sofa towards the television. "Roll back the carpet — let's see what we've got," he said to Ramshaw and Tapping.

The two men ripped away the carpet from the wall. Instead of underlay newspapers lay on the floorboards, dated ten years earlier. Sutherland went to the sash window and opened it. He flashed an "OK" sign to the snipers opposite, then called up Rose and told him they were inside the flat.

Shepherd studied the floorboards, which were in as bad a condition as the carpets. He knelt down and used his Swiss Army knife to lever one up. Ramshaw and Tapping helped him take up several more. Thick beams ran the length of the room from the window to the doorway, about shoulder width apart. If the men went through side on, there should be room to spare, even wearing their bulletproof vests. Shepherd used his knife to make a small hole in the plasterwork and bent down to peer through it. He couldn't see anything so he widened the hole and took his torch from his belt and shone it through. There was a space almost a foot deep, then sheets of plasterboard. He widened the hole so that he could stick his head through. Close to the walls he could make out air-conditioning ducts and electrical wiring.

He sat up and switched off the torch, then signalled for the three men to keep quiet.

He went back into the hallway outside the flat to radio Rose. "It's definitely a goer, Sarge," he said. "They've put a suspended ceiling below the plaster. It'll be a tight fit but I reckon we can crash through, two of us with guns, two playing out the rope. If we get the positioning right we'll drop down behind them."

"Sit tight while I bounce it off the OIC," said Rose. "Good work."

"I need to know where the targets are. We'll be going in blind."

"Got that," said Rose.

A couple of minutes passed before he came back on the radio. "Do the prep," he said. "Negotiator's going around in circles."

"Affirmative," said Shepherd.

"The surveillance guys say they're both behind the counter, which is eighteen feet back from the wall and four feet wide. The customer who was shot is being attended to by a female hostage. One of the robbers is covering her with a gun. Everyone else has been taken behind the counter and the second guy's guarding them. The kitchen's empty."

Shepherd closed his eyes and recalled the ground plan in the estate agent's. "Give us five minutes and then have the cars hit the sirens. We'll be lifting the floorboards."

"Affirmative."

Shepherd waved for the three officers to join him in the hallway, whispered instructions to them, then went back to the window and paced eighteen feet. It took him into the bedroom at the rear of the property. Ramshaw and Tapping moved the bed and rolled back the carpet. As soon as they heard the sirens, all four men eased up the floorboards. Shepherd poked another hole in the plaster and checked with his flashlight. The layout was the same as it was below the sitting room. Outside the sirens died.

Shepherd carefully hacked away chunks of plaster with his knife and placed them on a sheet he'd taken from the bed. When he'd finished they were staring at the back of a plasterboard ceiling.

"It'll be a tight fit," said Sutherland.

"Best if you let me and Kevin go down," said Shepherd. "We're the thinnest."

"Are you saying I'm fat?"

"You're not fat, but we're thinner."

Sutherland patted his bulletproof vest. "It's the vest. Makes me look fatter than I am."

"You're not fat," repeated Shepherd. "Kevin, you up for it?"

"Absolutely," said Tapping.

"Lose the equipment belt."

"Including the Glock?"

"If the MP5s don't do it, the Glocks won't be any use."

"Everything okay?" asked Rose, in Shepherd's earpiece.

"We're in position," Shepherd whispered into his mike. "I'm going down with Tapping."

"Hang fire until I give you the green light," said Rose. "The negotiator's still talking."

Shepherd and Tapping removed their equipment belts and stood by the gaping hole in the floor, their MP5s close to their chests. They were about eight feet apart.

"The counter should be there," whispered Shepherd, pointing down between two of the joists. He pointed four feet to the left. "That's where the kitchen starts. Dropping in won't be pleasant."

"I'll do it," said Tapping.

"No offence, but I'm a bit smaller. Less chance of me hitting something."

Tapping nodded. "Go for it."

Ramshaw was holding the rope attached to Shepherd's waist and Sutherland had Tapping's.

"Brian, let me go five feet down, then take the strain, just in case there's an oven or something below. Give me a count of two to get my bearings, then let the rope go." Ramshaw flashed him a thumbs-up. Shepherd winked at Tapping. "Okay, Kev?"

"Just want to get it over with," whispered Tapping.

"We'll be fine," said Shepherd. "It's the last thing they'll be expecting. Just so long as Mike and Brian don't let go of the ropes."

They heard sirens in the distance, and overhead the thudding beat of a helicopter rotor. Then silence.

"They're still demanding a coach in return for letting the injured hostage go." Rose's voice crackled in Shepherd's earpiece. "We've got a vehicle ready to go, but there's no way we're letting them drive away. We reckon one target will come out with hostages to check the coach, with the other remaining inside until he's sure everything's okay. As soon as Target One is at the door and the snipers have a clear shot, I'll green-light you two. You take out Target Two, and we take out Target One."

"Affirmative," said Shepherd.

"Affirmative," echoed Tapping.

"Good luck, guys," said Rose. "Once things start moving, I'll talk you through it."

The radio went quiet.

"There's got to be more to this than pizzas," whispered Shepherd.

"What do you mean?" said Tapping.

"If it was druggies they wouldn't have shotguns and they wouldn't be giving the negotiator a hard time. They'd be freaking out by now."

"So."

"So why knock over a pizza place? There are three building societies and a jeweller in the street."

Tapping frowned. "You think they're selling drugs, is that it?"

"I don't think they went in with guns to steal a few pepperoni pizzas. Drugs or money-laundering would be my bet."

Shepherd's earpiece crackled. "We have more details of what's going on inside," said Rose. "Targets are IC Three males. Not masked. Both have sawn-off shotguns, one appears to be double-barrelled but let's not make any assumptions. The wounded customer is about six feet from the door being attended to by an IC One female wearing a dark blue coat. One of the targets is between the counter and the door, but keeps the woman as a barrier. The second target is in the doorway that leads from the kitchen to the area behind the counter. He has three employees with him, all in uniform. There are two customers also behind the counter, both IC One males in their early twenties, casually dressed."

There was no need to spell it out. Shepherd would take the man behind the counter, Tapping the other.

"The coach is driving towards the shop," said Rose. "We have two men on board plus the driver. They're moving through the road block now."

Shepherd's heart beat faster and a surge of adrenaline entered his system. Time seemed to slow, as it always did when he faced combat. All his senses became more alert, more focused.

"The coach is going to park in the middle of the road to give the snipers a clear shot," said Rose, "but we want to do this inside if we can."

"Affirmative," said Shepherd. He nodded at Tapping and pressed his MP5 close to his chest, finger outside the trigger guard.

They heard the hiss of air brakes. Then silence.

"The negotiator's talking to them," said Rose.

There was a long silence. Shepherd spat out his chewing-gum and took a deep breath.

"Okay, they're going to move to the coach," said Rose. "Target One is going to go outside with one hostage to check the coach. Target Two will remain inside. As soon as Target One opens the door, you move. Target One is still in the kitchen doorway. All the hostages are lying down."

Shepherd nodded at Tapping again. Tapping grinned and spat out his gum.

Shepherd played it out in his head. He would drop down behind the man in the doorway. He would shout for the man to drop his weapon. If he complied, it was game over. If it looked like he was going to fire, Shepherd would fire first. Tapping would drop behind the man at the front of the shop. The biggest risk, so far as Shepherd could see, was of the man in the doorway shooting Tapping in the back.

"The coach door has opened," said Rose, in Shepherd's earpiece. "Target One is moving towards the door. The hostage is an IC One male wearing a black-leather motorcycle jacket. Go, go, go!"

Shepherd stepped forward, keeping his elbows tight against his sides. He dropped and his feet broke through the plasterboard with the sound of tearing paper. There was a jolt around his waist as the rope held but he continued to fall. His instinct was to close his eyes but he forced himself to keep them open. He saw stainless-steel ovens, a hotplate, a large refrigerator, work surfaces thick with flour, plastic containers full of tomato sauce, green peppers, sliced pepperoni and the man standing in the doorway, starting to turn. There was a second ripping noise as Tapping broke through the ceiling.

The rope bit into his waist and Shepherd jerked to a halt. He was hanging a few feet from a metal preparation table with half a dozen pizzas ready to go into the oven. "Armed police!" he yelled. "Drop your weapon."

The man kept turning. The barrel of the shotgun was pointing at the ceiling.

"Drop your weapon!" Shepherd yelled.

"Armed police!" shouted Tapping, from the front of the shop. There was the deafening sound of a shotgun blast followed by the crack of a 9mm round. A woman screamed and a man yelled.

Almost immediately Ramshaw let the rope slide and Shepherd dropped to the floor. He bent his knees to absorb the impact but his eyes never left the man in front of him. He caught a glimpse of a hostage just behind the target, a man in his twenties wearing a blue baseball jacket, but he kept focused on the man with the shotgun.

The shotgun barrel swung down. The man's mouth was open in surprise, eyes wide and staring. Shepherd slid his finger inside the trigger guard. One pull and he'd hit him dead centre. His finger tightened on the trigger, but he could see how frightened the man was. Shepherd rushed forward, the rope trailing in his wake, and slammed the stock of the carbine against the man's chin. His eyes turned up in their sockets and he fell to the ground. Shepherd kicked the shotgun to the side and rushed through the door. He shouldered the man in the baseball jacket to the side, his MP5 at the ready, but it was all over.

The air was thick with dust from the ceiling. The second target was on the floor, the shotgun several feet away, blood oozing from his left thigh. He was clutching his leg and wheezing. Through the shop window Shepherd saw two armed police running from the coach, handguns held high.

Tapping was standing by the counter, breathing heavily.

"You okay, Kev?"

Tapping nodded.

Shepherd spoke into his radio mike. "All clear, Sarge. Two targets, one unconscious, one bleeding from a leg wound. We need paramedics."

"They're on their way, Stu. You okay?"

"We're fine."

The two armed officers burst into the shop. One picked up the shotgun and made it safe.

"There's another in the kitchen," said Shepherd.

Two paramedics arrived with a trolley. Tapping and Shepherd ushered the hostages outside. One of the members of staff, a middle-aged West Indian, was insisting that he be allowed to stay but Tapping told him it was a crime scene and pushed him outside. The woman who had been looking after the injured hostage was sobbing and a WPC took her to an ambulance.

The paramedics dealt with the injured hostage who was bleeding from the stomach and barely conscious. Shepherd knelt beside the robber Tapping had shot and used his Swiss Army knife to cut away the man's bloody trouser leg. There was an entry wound six inches above the knee and a larger exit wound at the back. It was bleeding but Shepherd could see it wasn't life-threatening.

Two more paramedics rushed in. Tapping and Shepherd moved away to give them room to work on the man's injured leg. Sutherland and Ramshaw appeared at the shop doorway. "Everything okay?" asked Sutherland.

"We're fine," said Shepherd.

The armed officer who'd gone into the kitchen reappeared with two uniformed officers who'd come in through the fire exit. They had handcuffed the robber Shepherd had knocked out. The man was still dazed but he could walk.

"How did you manage that?" asked Sutherland.

"He was slow," said Shepherd, "and I almost landed on top of him."

"Mine fired by mistake," said Tapping. "Shat himself when I dropped through and the shot went into the ceiling but I couldn't take the chance of him firing again."

"I'd forget the 'by mistake' bit if I were you," said Shepherd, keeping his voice low. "He fired, end of story. There were too many civilians around to take chances."

Rose appeared at the door. "You guys okay?"

"Not a scratch," said Tapping. "The one on the ground shot at me so I fired. Stu here didn't bother with his gun, took his guy out with a flying drop kick."

"I hit him with the stock," said Shepherd.

Rose clapped him on the shoulder. "Not bad for a first day on the job," he said.

Swift jogged down the street. He stood aside for the paramedics to wheel out the injured hostage. "Is he going to be okay?"

"Stomach and intestine perforated and he's lost a lot of blood," said a paramedic. "It doesn't look good."

"No one else hurt?" asked Swift.

"Just a leg wound," said Rose, indicating the robber on the floor.

"Brilliant, lads," said Swift. "Might have a photocall for you later, turn you into heroes."

Shepherd grimaced. "If it's all the same to you, sir, I'd rather keep a low profile. A guy did stop a bullet. He might have relatives who'll take offence if they see us grinning on the front page of the *Evening Standard*."

"Maybe you're right," said Swift, "but the OIC's going to be putting you up for a commendation."

Shepherd forced a smile. He knew he wouldn't be getting a commendation for ending the siege. Stuart Marsden didn't exist. If Shepherd got a commendation it would be for exposing the bad apples in SO19. And he doubted that Ken Swift or any other cop would be lining up to shake his hand when that happened.

"You know the drill, Kev," said Swift, putting his hand on Tapping's shoulder. "SOCO will take the weapon and you'll have to talk to the Internal Investigation Command. You're removed from firearms duty, pending the result of the investigation, but it looks righteous to me. I don't see you having any problems."

"I do my job and I get to ride a desk for six months," said Tapping, bitterly.

"You saved lives today," said Swift, "but there's a procedure, you know that. You did well, and you'll be back on duty before you know it."

"Might be worth giving this place a going-over, sir," said Shepherd. "The owner seemed pretty keen to stay and it seems a funny place to stick up with shotguns."

A uniformed constable picked up a red nylon bag with a Nike swoosh that had been lying behind the counter. He unzipped it and whistled softly. It contained rolls of banknotes and a Ziploc plastic bag filled with polythene packages of white crystals.

Swift walked over and picked up the Ziploc bag. "Crack cocaine," he said. He looked at Shepherd. "You were right."

"Explains the artillery," said Shepherd.

"There must be thirty grand there," said Sutherland.

Swift put the drugs back into the nylon bag and zipped it up. "It just gets better and better for you two," he said. "You rescue the hostages and bust a major drugs operation."

"All in a day's work." Shepherd grinned and winked at Tapping. Then he looked at Rose. The sergeant was gazing at the nylon bag with a thoughtful look on his face.

Shepherd glanced over his shoulder to check that no one was paying any attention to him, then slipped the three mobile phones out of his locker and into the pockets of his jacket. He didn't want anyone asking why he was carrying so many. When he worked undercover among villains it was common practice to have numerous mobiles, usually with pay-as-you-go Sim cards that were thrown away regularly. But cops weren't villains. Most of them, anyway.

Shepherd left the building and headed for the underground car park. He took one of the phones out of his pocket and switched it on.

Rose and Sutherland caught up with him and slapped his shoulder. "Drinks," said Rose.

"Right, Sarge," said Shepherd.

"First round's on the new guy," said Sutherland. "Tradition."

"Where?"

"Bull's Head, down there on the left," said Rose, pointing along Leman Street. "Landlord used to be in the job so we can have a lock-in whenever we want. Tonight's gonna be a heavy night."

"I'm driving, Sarge."

"That's what minicabs are for." He pointed down the road. "Second left."

"I'll catch you up," said Shepherd. "I just want to check my messages."

Rose and Sutherland headed down the road, deep in conversation. Shepherd looked at the mobile. A voicemail message was waiting on the Tony Nelson phone. Shepherd put it to his ear and listened. It was Angie Kerr, asking him to call her back. Her husband was away for the night so he could call any time.

Shepherd dialled her number.

"It's me," he said, when she answered. "Is it okay to talk?"

"He's away all night," she said. "When are you going to do it?"

"This isn't the sort of conversation I want to have on the phone," said Shepherd.

"I've got some details of where he'll be over the next few days," said Angie. "I thought it might help to meet up."

Shepherd raised his eyebrows. He'd thought he was going to have a problem persuading her to meet him, but now she was the one pressing for a face-to-face.

"Okay," he said. "That works for me."

"Tomorrow?"

"Morning should be okay." Shepherd did a quick calculation in his head. He could get to Manchester in four hours, but getting back to Leman Street for two o'clock would be a taller order. A helicopter would be the fastest way, but even Major Gannon would draw the line at Shepherd using the SAS as his personal taxi service. If he drove he'd have to leave Manchester at ten to stand a chance of getting to Leman Street in time for his shift. He'd have to talk to Hargrove and see if they could come up with a suitable reason for him being late on his second day with the unit. "How about early?"

"Nine? Same place as before? The supermarket?"

"Okay," said Shepherd.

"And you won't do anything before then, will you?"

"As soon as I'm ready to move I'll let you know. That way you can get your alibi sorted. Anyway, like I said, this isn't a conversation for the phone." Shepherd cut the connection and phoned Hargrove.

"I hear you've had a busy day," said the superintendent.

"It's helped me bond, that's for sure," said Shepherd. "Angie Kerr's been in touch. She wants a meet and I've fixed up for tomorrow at nine. The supermarket car park again."

"She wanted the meet?"

"Said she wanted to give me some info about his movements."

"That's perfect. We'll have the Volvo wired again, get her on video handing you the info then bust you both. She gets taken to the nick and you go back to SO19."

"I'm going to need a reason for getting to Leman Street late. Medical, maybe. Can you fix it up?"

"I'll take care of it. What's your plan now?"

"I'm off for some more bonding with the guys, then I'll drive up to Manchester. The flat's still free, isn't it?"

"Sure."

"I'll catch a few hours' kip there. Just hope tomorrow's a quiet shift."

Shepherd put away the phone and walked to the pub. He heard booming laughter and clinking glasses as he went into the main bar. He wasn't proud of what he was doing: he was lying to fellow cops, and that made him feel sick. There was a good chance that Keith Rose was bad, but he had no way of knowing who was helping him, which meant he had to lie to everyone. He forced himself to smile. He was Stuart Marsden and he was among friends.

Ken Swift was standing at the bar surrounded by half a dozen men from Amber team. Rose was in a booth with Sutherland, the two men deep in conversation. The sergeant looked up as Shepherd walked in and raised his glass in salute. Shepherd nodded and headed for the bar.

Ken Swift had bought a round and ordered lager for Shepherd. "Nice work, Stu," he said. "You done that falling-through-the-ceiling trick before?"

"I've abseiled, but never gone through a ceiling."

The inspector introduced Shepherd to Amber team. Shepherd shook hands with them all, committing to memory the names and faces he hadn't already memorised from Hargrove's files. They were all easy in each other's company, men who had worked and drunk together for months, if not years, but they made sure he felt at home, including him in their conversation and

310

jokes. They were a good mix: a couple were older than Shepherd, the old hands of the team, but the rest were about his age or younger. They all worshipped Swift, deferring to him whenever he spoke, watching him even while they were joking and knocking back their pints. Ramshaw and Tapping came in together. Everyone cheered Tapping and Shepherd took the opportunity to buy a round, dumping his first pint in the process. With the drive to Manchester ahead, he didn't want to drink more than a few mouthfuls.

He stood with Amber team for half an hour, but kept a watchful eye on Rose and Sutherland. The two men were still deep in conversation, Rose doing most of the talking and Sutherland nodding.

Swift came to stand next to Shepherd. "How are you getting on with Rosie?" he asked.

"So far, so good," said Shepherd.

"What about the map work? Must be a lot harder than Glasgow."

"No problems," said Shepherd.

"You ever use the rifle?"

"Not really," said Shepherd. "I never liked the long-distance stuff. Always seems too impersonal."

"A good sniper can take out a problem without putting lives at risk," said Swift.

"No argument there," said Shepherd. "I just prefer to be up close and personal, that's all. Why do you ask?"

"One of our snipers has just made sergeant and he'll be moving from SO19. I'm looking for someone to fill the slot."

Shepherd took a sip of his pint. The last thing he needed was to be moved from the ARV. "I prefer to be on the ground," he said.

"Yeah, but you get all the false alarms as well. The Specialist Firearms teams only get called out for the big stuff."

"Horses for courses," said Shepherd.

Rose came over to the group by the bar and put his arm round Swift. "Don't let this guy talk you into joining Amber," he said to Shepherd. "You'd hate it, driving around in a furniture van, turning up late."

"Don't listen to him. It's his lack of ambition that's kept him a sergeant all these years," said Swift.

"I didn't kiss the right arses, is what he means," said Rose. He ordered a round. Shepherd took the opportunity to slip his three-quarters full glass on to the bar.

"There's a lot to be said for military training," said Swift. "Maybe we should be recruiting more ex-army guys."

"Were you army?" asked Shepherd, although he knew that Swift had never been in the armed forces. His file had been on Hargrove's CD.

"Nah, I was a fireman, way back when. Got fed up with climbing ladders. I was at Hendon the same time as Rosie here. A few years older and a lot better-looking."

"That's why you've been divorced three times, I suppose," said Rose.

"The grass is always greener," said Swift. "That's been my problem."

"You married now?" asked Shepherd. The file had said Swift was being sued for divorce by his third wife.

"Just about to get loose from wife number three," said Swift. "Good riddance. What about you? Bitten the bullet?"

Shepherd grinned. "I'll give it a few years before I settle down."

"Wish I'd done that," said Swift. "My first wife got her claws into me when I was eighteen. Dragged me kicking and screaming down the aisle a year later. Still, we had three good years."

"You got divorced after just three years?"

"Nah," said Swift. "The three good years were followed by five hellish ones. Then she divorced me."

Rose groaned. Clearly it was a joke he'd heard many times before.

Sutherland was sitting on his own now, legs stretched out, staring up at the ceiling with his beer glass balanced on his stomach. Shepherd walked over and sat down next to him. "All right, Mike?" he said, clinking his glass against Sutherland's.

"Ace," said Sutherland, sitting up. "One hell of a day. Like Rosie said, you might be a Jonah. You can go a week without a big one breaking and you get two in one day."

"You'd rather spend all day dealing with false alarms? Kids with airguns and robbers with cucumbers in brown-paper bags?"

"Oh, Christ, an adrenaline junkie." Sutherland groaned. "Just what we need."

"We're trained to deal with armed criminals," said Shepherd. "Anything else is a waste of our time." He stretched out his legs. "I'll sleep well tonight," he said. "Damn near broke my hip dropping through that ceiling."

Tapping was being toasted noisily by Swift and half a dozen members of Amber team. "It's Kev I feel sorry for," said Sutherland. "That's him off firearms duties until the shooting's investigated."

"It was by the book." Shepherd grinned. "At least it was once we bust through the ceiling."

"Doesn't matter if it was by the book or not. He's on desk duties until it's investigated. We've one guy who's still on hold four years after a shooting."

"Shit," said Shepherd.

"Shit's right. Shot an armed robber during a raid on a supermarket. Robber's gun turned out to be a replica and now he's trying to sue the Met for everything from lost wages to infringement of his human rights. He was terrorising a pregnant woman, for God's sake, yet he's the one suing us. Until it's resolved, our guy isn't allowed to pick up a gun."

"Lucky I didn't get off a shot," said Shepherd.

"I'm serious, Stu. The world's gone bloody mental. You have to work your balls off to get into SO19, then you train and train to do the job right, but the minute you fire your weapon you're treated like a criminal. In fact, the criminals get more leeway than we do." He drank some lager. "You know Swift's serious about getting you and Kev a commendation?" he said.

314

"Screw that. I'd rather have a pay rise," said Shepherd. "You can't spend a commendation."

"You short?" asked Sutherland.

"Who isn't, these days?"

"I can bung you a few quid until you're sorted."

"Cheers, Mike, but I need more than that." He leaned closer to Sutherland and lowered his voice to a whisper. "That thirty grand would have come in handy."

"What thirty grand?"

"In the pizza place. The drugs money. There was thirty grand in that bag."

Sutherland looked stunned. "Fuck me, Stu, don't even say that as a joke."

"Come on, it's drugs money. What's going to happen to it? Unless the Drugs Squad can make a case against the guys running the pizza place, they get the money back. How sick is that?"

"So crime pays. What's new?"

"I'm just saying, I could do a lot with thirty grand."

"I think we should drop it, mate. Walls have ears, right?"

Shepherd shrugged carelessly. "Okay, forget I said anything. What happened to the guy I took over from? What was his name? Hornby?"

"Ormsby. Andy Ormsby. Good guy."

"Did he move on to better things?"

Sutherland shifted in his seat and took several gulps of his lager. Shepherd tried to appear relaxed. It was a reasonable question and he waited to see what Sutherland would say.

"Bit of a mystery," said Sutherland, eventually. "He just went."

"Walked off the job?"

"Just went. No one knows what happened. Some say it was girl trouble, some say he had a nervous breakdown. You know the stress that comes with the job. He was quite young."

"Couldn't take the pressure?"

"I guess."

"But he was in your vehicle, right? Didn't you see the signs?"

"You a psychiatrist now?"

"You can tell when someone's not handling the pressure — you don't need a degree in psychology to spot the signs. Short temper, loss of appetite, nail-biting, all the usual clichés."

"He was a good guy," said Sutherland.

"Yeah, you said. You don't think there'll be a problem, me stepping into his shoes?"

"It's not like you pushed him out of his job, is it?"

"Yeah, I know, but some guys are a tough act to follow."

"You carry on like today and no one'll have any problems with you," said Sutherland. "You're a bloody hero, you are."

Shepherd didn't feel like a hero. He felt like a man who was being friendly to a fellow police officer so that he could betray him. He felt like a rat.

★ ★ ★

Rose dropped his kit-bag by the kitchen door, went over to the sink and drank from the cold tap.

"That's disgusting," said his wife, coming up behind him.

Rose straightened and wiped the back of his mouth with his hand.

"Sorry, love."

"You've been drinking."

"Celebrating."

"You drove like that?"

"Three pints, love. It's not a crime."

Tracey folded her arms. She was wearing her pink dressing-gown but it had fallen open at the front and he could see she was naked underneath. "Actually, it is a crime. And you know that."

Rose held out his arms. "It was a one-off. Two big jobs today and we came out covered in glory."

"I saw the Houses of Parliament thing on the news. Those men were lucky they weren't shot."

"Give me a hug," said Rose.

"I can smell you from here."

"Ditto," said Rose. He stepped forward and took her in his arms. She slipped her arms round his neck and he kissed her.

"You were a hero, were you?" she said, as she broke away.

"My guys were," said Rose. "How's Kelly?"

Tracey's lips tightened. "She didn't eat much. And she says her back hurts. I just wish I could take the pain away."

"I'm working on it," said Rose.

"It's so bloody unfair. She's only seven — she hasn't even started her life. It should be me lying up there. I'd die happy knowing she was okay."

Rose pressed his face into her long, dark hair. He knew exactly how his wife felt. When Kelly had first been ill he'd knelt at the side of her bed and promised God anything if He'd just spare his daughter. But his prayers had been ignored, and as his daughter's health had deteriorated he'd lost faith in God. "I'll get it sorted. I promise."

Tracey hugged him and Rose kissed her neck. "I'll just check my emails, and then I'll see you in bed," he whispered.

Tracey pinched him. "You'll shower first and clean your teeth," she said. "I'll bring you up some cocoa."

Rose went upstairs and crept into Kelly's room. His daughter was lying on her back, her mouth open. For a few seconds she was totally still and Rose's heart pounded as he waited for her to breathe. When she did, the quilt barely moved. Rose checked the drip, then sat on the edge of the bed. The local hospital had said it was okay for Kelly to be at home — a tacit admission that there was nothing else they could do for her. She'd get gradually weaker until one day they'd take her back into hospital, the intensive-care unit with its paintings of teddy bears and balloons, the smell of bleach and death, and they'd wait for the end.

Rose took his daughter's hand and pressed it to his cheek. "It's not going to come to that, sweetheart," he said. "Daddy's going to make it better."

318

He kissed her forehead, then went along the hallway to the boxroom he used as a study. He sat down at his computer and switched it on, twiddling a Biro as he waited for the machine to boot up. He scanned the emails in his inbox and saw one from the surgeon in Chicago. He had a slot in three weeks' time and wanted to know if Rose could get Kelly to America by then. He specialised in tumours of the spine and had pioneered a new treatment that used chemotherapy to shrink the tumour, then laser surgery. The chemotherapy was experimental but had been successful in more than eighty per cent of cases, and the computer-controlled laser would destroy the tumour without damaging the spinal cord. Rose had discovered the doctor on the Internet and had already sent him the NHS X-rays and reports. Unlike the doctors in the UK, the Chicago surgeon was optimistic that he could save Kelly. He couldn't make any promises, but he stood by his eighty per cent success rate. However, his expertise didn't come cheap and the NHS had refused to pay.

Rose checked his bank account online. He had a little over fifteen thousand pounds in his savings account, a few hundred in his current account. His drugs money was wrapped in polythene bags and tucked away behind the water tank in the attic. A hundred thousand euros.

He looked at the figures he'd jotted on the notepad. Getting Kelly to Chicago, paying for the treatment and the surgery, then the month's recuperation and monitoring, was going to cost a minimum of two hundred thousand dollars. And that was if there were no complications. He tapped on his calculator, converting the currencies. He was about sixty thousand pounds short. He was close, so damn close. They'd bought the house just six months before Kelly had fallen ill so he only owned about twenty thousand pounds' worth of it. If he sold he'd lose a big chunk of that in estate agent and legal fees. He'd already asked the bank to increase his mortgage but they'd turned him down, even when he'd explained why he needed the money.

Rose sat back in his chair. There was no way round it. He needed a big score. Forty grand was the minimum, but to make sure Kelly got the shot she deserved he'd want a hundred grand. He chewed the ballpoint pen. A hundred wasn't impossible. He just needed a plan.

He sent an email to the surgeon, telling him to expect Kelly in three weeks.

Shepherd let himself into the house and went upstairs. Liam was asleep. Shepherd kissed him and tucked the quilt under his chin. He went across to his own bathroom where he showered and changed into a clean pullover and jeans. Then he went down to the kitchen and made himself a mug of black coffee. He was okay to drive — he'd drunk less than a pint. In one of the kitchen cupboards he had a stack of pay-as-you-go Sim cards. He took one out and slotted it into one of his spare mobiles, a fairly new Nokia, then stored the number in one of his own mobiles.

He went back upstairs and knocked on Katra's door. She didn't answer and he knocked again, louder this time. He heard her get out of bed and the door opened. She looked at him bleary-eyed. "Is Liam okay?"

Shepherd was touched by her concern and realised once more that he'd made the right choice in hiring her.

"He's fine," he said, "but I have to go to Manchester tonight. I won't be here when he wakes up."

"I'll tell him," she said. She brushed her hair out of her eyes. "Drive carefully."

"I will," said Shepherd. He winked. "Thanks." He gave her the mobile and told her there was a charger in the kitchen. "So I can call you while I'm out," he explained.

He went downstairs, finished his coffee, then went out to the Toyota.

Angie Kerr lay on her back, staring at the ceiling. Her husband was beside her, snoring softly. She felt like crying but she knew that if she did he would wake and hurt her. He'd raped her again before he fell asleep. He'd put his hands round her throat as he came and she had seen the hatred in his eyes.

He was going to kill her, she was sure of it. It was just a question of when. He'd dragged her down to the wine cellar and shown her what he'd done to Larry — he'd pushed her down so that her face was only inches from the plastic-wrapped corpse. "See what happens to anyone who crosses me," he'd hissed. "See what you made me do? This is down to you."

He'd kept her in the house all day. Anderson had driven him away first thing in the morning, then returned an hour and a half later. He and Wates had followed her around the house, standing guard outside the bedroom door when she went to lie down, sitting at the kitchen table while she made them coffee. She'd tried to go down to the shops but Anderson had said no, Charlie didn't want her to go out. She knew there was no point in trying to press the point. Charlie's word was law.

Anderson had gone out at four o'clock and returned with Charlie, who had brought a box with him. He didn't tell her where he'd been. He'd ordered pizza and made her eat two slices, even though she wasn't hungry. They'd sat in the main dining room, underneath the chandeliers he'd imported from Italy, and he'd opened a bottle of Dom Pérignon, made her match him drink for drink. Afterwards they'd watched TV while Wates and Anderson stayed in the kitchen. At just after ten, he'd ordered her to phone Nelson. He'd told her what to say and had stood by her while she made the call. Then he'd taken her upstairs and raped her.

Angie rolled over and pulled her knees to her stomach. He'd killed Larry, he was going to kill Nelson and then he'd kill her. There was nothing she could do, no one she could turn to for help. Even if she could get to the police, what could she tell them? That her husband had gone on the rampage because she'd hired a hitman to kill him? Besides, he always boasted that he had the police in his pocket. He'd once taken her out

322

for dinner with a chief inspector and his wife, followed by a night's drinking in the VIP section of Aces. Twenty grand a year he paid the man, Charlie had said. Brown envelopes every few months. Charlie said he paid off half a dozen cops regularly and that, as far as the law was concerned, he was untouchable. Angie didn't know who she could trust. Any cop she spoke to might be on Charlie's payroll. The tears ran down her cheeks and she bit her lip hard so that she made no sound.

Shepherd had four hours' sleep before the alarm woke him at eight thirty. He made a call to Hargrove to check that everything was geared up for the surveillance. Hargrove told him he'd arranged for New Scotland Yard's personnel department to call SO19 and tell them Stuart Marsden had to report for a medical that morning; he wasn't expected at Leman Street until late afternoon.

Shepherd changed into Tony Nelson's clothes, drank two cups of black coffee, then went into the bathroom and stood in front of the mirror. He was a hired killer. A man who took lives for money. A man with no conscience. He ran through his legend, checking and cross-checking all the information he'd given Angie. One mistake could ruin everything.

The Volvo was where he'd left it in the underground car park. He did a quick check of the cameras and transmitters, then drove to Altrincham and parked in the corner of the supermarket furthest from the entrance. The blue Transit van was already in place.

Shepherd switched off his engine. "Sound check," he said.

The Transit's lights flashed once. Shepherd settled back in his seat. The clock in the dashboard said 8:55. He put on his black leather gloves.

A couple of dozen other vehicles were in the car park. Shepherd couldn't see where the armed police were but he knew they'd be close by. They'd make it look as real as possible, moving in with guns and shouts, and he'd be dragged out of the car and thrown face down on the ground. They probably wouldn't have been told that Shepherd was a cop. The fewer people who knew he was undercover, the better. He'd be taken into custody, then Hargrove would make sure he was released quietly while the CPS put together a deal with Angie.

He saw Angie's Jaguar enter the car park and drive slowly towards him. Shepherd took a deep breath. It was the end phase of the operation. He only had to be in Tony Nelson's skin for a few more minutes. He'd be glad to leave the character behind.

Angie saw the grey Volvo at the far end of the car park. Tony Nelson was sitting with his hands on the steering-wheel. She drove slowly towards him, parked and got out of her Jaguar. Charlie had told her to get into Nelson's car and plant the transmitter under the seat. She knew what he would do to her if she let him down.

She grabbed the door handle and slid into the passenger seat. Nelson looked as calm as ever, jaw set tight, eyes like flint. He was the opposite of Charlie, who wore his emotions on his face: when he was angry his cheeks flushed and his lips vanished into slits. When he was happy he grinned from ear to ear. Nelson's face was a blank mask. "Thanks," she said.

"For what?"

"For coming."

"You said you had his movements for me."

"Yes. That's right." She opened her handbag, took out a folded sheet of paper and handed it to Nelson.

Nelson looked at it.

Charlie had told her what to write. It showed that he was in London and would be returning the next day. That he would be at a football match on Wednesday night, and having dinner with her on Thursday. Friday he was going to be at Aces.

"Can I smoke?"

"Sure," said Nelson.

Angie took out her cigarettes and lighter. She fumbled with her bag and the contents spilled into Nelson's lap. "I'm sorry," she said. Nelson grabbed for the bag but a perfume spray, breath mints and a comb tumbled on to the floor. "It's okay," he said. He bent down and picked up the items. Angie slipped her left hand into her jacket pocket and pulled out the transmitter her husband had given her. She lowered her hand between the door and the seat and flicked the metal cylinder sideways.

Nelson straightened and handed her her things. She thanked him, lit a cigarette and offered him one. He shook his head. "You've never smoked?" she asked.

"It's a drug, the nicotine," he said. "I don't have an addictive personality."

"Do you have any personality at all?" she asked quickly.

Nelson raised an eyebrow. "Is something on your mind, Angie?"

She looked out of the side window. Charlie had said he would be close by, listening to everything she said. She couldn't see him, but she knew he was there. "When will you do it?" she asked, still looking out of the window.

"Wednesday maybe. Or Friday, if you're not going to the club. I'll call you in advance to give you a chance to get your alibi fixed. The casino's still the best bet. So make sure your mobile's on."

Sweat was beading on Angie's forehead. She took out a tissue and dabbed herself with it.

"You're going to have to relax," said Nelson. "At some point the police are going to talk to you."

"I'll be okay."

"You'd better be because they'll be looking for signs that there's anything fishy."

"Even with my alibi?"

"The cops aren't stupid," said Nelson, "but if you keep calm, they'll have to believe you."

Angie took a deep breath. She couldn't go to the police because she didn't know if she could trust them. But Nelson was a hired gun, whose sole motivation was money. Provided she paid him enough, she could trust him.

"Do you have a gun, Tony?"

"Of course I've got a gun."

"I mean now? In the car?"

"Why?"

Angie took a long pull on her cigarette. Charlie was listening so she had only one chance, and she needed an immediate answer from Nelson. They'd have to drive — and drive fast. She'd throw the transmitter out of the car and they'd have to leave Manchester. But how much money would a man like Nelson need to become her protector? Five hundred pounds a day? A thousand? The only money she had was in joint accounts and it wouldn't take Charlie long to close them. And he would cancel her credit cards. She had her watch and her jewellery, but once those were gone she'd have nothing. What could she offer him? He hadn't shown the slightest interest in her as a woman. She was a client, nothing more. The only thing he'd ever expressed an interest in was her money.

A white van drove into the car park and headed towards them. Angie opened the passenger side window and blew smoke out of the car. "Sorry," she said.

"It doesn't bother me," said Nelson. He was looking at the white van. He put his gloved hands back on the steering-wheel.

"I keep trying to give up, but sometimes I just need a smoke, you know?"

"I guess so."

The van was slowing. Angie looked at Nelson. If she was going to ask him, she'd have to do it now. If he said no, she was finished. She took another pull on the cigarette. She was finished anyway. Charlie had killed

Larry. He was going to kill Nelson. And she knew everything, which meant he'd kill her. Eventually. He'd kill her in the wine cellar, wrap her in a sheet of polythene and bury her somewhere, then shack up with one of the teenage waitresses from the club. Charlie was using her now to get Nelson, but once he had Nelson he'd have no further use for her. Not after what she'd tried to do. And what she knew. She had no choice. She had to run.

"Tony?" she said, her heart pounding.

"Yes?" He turned to her, his hands still on the steering-wheel.

She opened her mouth to speak but before she could say anything the white van screeched to a halt and the back doors were flung open. Four men dressed in black, waving handguns, jumped out and surrounded the car. "Armed police!" shouted one. "Keep your hands where they are."

"It's the police!" shouted Angie.

"Just do as they say," said Nelson, calmly.

"Oh, Christ, I'm dead," said Angie.

"Armed police!" shouted another officer.

Slowly Angie raised her hands. "Don't shoot, please don't shoot," she whispered.

An officer yanked open the door on the driver's side and pointed his weapon at Nelson's head. "Keep your hands on the steering-wheel where I can see them," he said.

"I'm not moving," said Nelson.

Another officer opened the door on Angie's side with his left hand while keeping the gun in his right aimed at her head. "Hands in the air, don't make any sudden moves!" he shouted.

Two officers were standing at the front of the Volvo, both hands on their weapons, one aiming at Nelson, the other at her.

Two police cars roared into the car park and pulled up on either side of the white van. Uniformed officers piled out of the cars and stood waiting for the armed police to finish their job. They were followed by two dark saloons each containing three big men in plain clothes, cheap suits and dark raincoats.

Angie's hands were shaking. She looked at Nelson. The armed officer grabbed him by the collar of his jacket and pulled him out of the Volvo. "I'm sorry," said Angie. "I'm so sorry."

"What the hell is this?" said Kerr. In the distance an armed policeman was pointing a gun at Nelson who was on his knees by the side of the Volvo. Another cop was pulling Angie out of the car.

"Cops," said Anderson. He was sitting in the front of the Range Rover, with Wates in the passenger seat.

"I can see it's the fucking cops, shit-for-brains. What the hell are they doing here?"

One of the cops used a plastic tie to bind Nelson's wrists behind his back, then he was hauled to his feet and over to one of the police cars.

"Shall we do a runner?" asked Anderson.

"Sit tight," said Kerr. "We're far enough away. If it was anything to do with us there'd be armed cops here too."

The cops made Angie stand against the Volvo with her hands on the roof as they patted her down. A uniformed inspector walked up to her and said something to her. Kerr had the receiver in his lap but the cop was too far away from the transmitter for him to hear what was said. He was probably giving her the caution in case she said something stupid on the drive back to the station.

Another officer used a plastic tie to bind her wrists, then took her to one of the patrol cars. He helped her get into the back and slammed the door. The armed police were returning to the white van, laughing and joking.

A plain-clothes officer in a dark blue raincoat took the ignition keys out of the Volvo and locked the car.

"What's on your mind, boss?" asked Anderson.

"I'm just wondering who the cops were there for."

"What do you mean?" asked Anderson.

"Were they there for Angie or Nelson?"

"Does it matter?"

Kerr sighed. Of course it mattered, but there was no point in explaining it to Anderson or Wates. If they were there to arrest a hired killer and his wife had been caught up as an innocent bystander, that was one thing. But if they had arrested Angie and Nelson for conspiring to kill him, it was another. Something wasn't right, but Kerr couldn't work out what it was. He was getting a headache.

"Let's just sit here for a while, boys," he said. "We'll see what develops."

330

The two patrol cars drove out of the car park, followed by the dark saloons. The armed cops climbed into the back of the white van, then it, too, drove away, heading in the opposite direction to the patrol cars.

Kerr lit a cigarette and stared at the Volvo. It was almost as if it had never happened, as if it had been a figment of his imagination. A huddle of customers stood at the entrance to the supermarket, staring after the patrol cars and gossiping, but after a few minutes they went inside. A blue Transit van drove out of the car park. Kerr blew smoke, and frowned. Something was lurking on the edge of his consciousness but every time he tried to focus on it, it evaporated. It was like grabbing mist.

Shepherd sat in the back of the patrol car. There were two uniformed cops in the front and a plain-clothes detective on his right. He said nothing. He didn't know if the cops knew he was an undercover officer, but reckoned they probably didn't. As far as they were concerned he was Tony Nelson, hitman for hire, and he preferred it that way. The fewer people who knew who he was, the better.

He looked over his shoulder, just once, and saw the car containing Angie Kerr following some distance behind. They were being taken to the same police station, but that was to be expected. Hargrove would want her to see Nelson taken into custody. He'd want her to know that he was in an interview room being grilled by detectives, and that her only chance of avoiding prison would be to co-operate. Hargrove would probably go in heavy first, play her the recordings from the Volvo, tell her she was going to prison for a long time and then, finally, he would offer her the way out. He'd probably start talking about her husband, asking her why she wanted him dead. Then he'd suggest there were other ways of dealing with Charlie Kerr that didn't involve her spending a dozen or more years in a prison cell.

Shepherd took a deep breath. It would soon be over and he could turn his back on Tony Nelson.

The plastic tie was cutting into his wrists but he knew there was no point in saying anything to the detective sitting next to him. Once fitted, the ties couldn't be loosened, only cut off.

He sat in silence until they reached the police station. A metal gate rattled back and the two patrol cars rolled into the car park. The detective manhandled Shepherd out of the car and up a concrete ramp to the entrance. He looked at Angie. Tears were streaming down her face, but he glared at her, playing the part. Tony Nelson, killer for hire, would probably blame her for the police raid. And if she thought Nelson was angry with her, she'd be more likely to take any offer the police made.

A uniformed officer opened a metal door and stood to the side to allow Shepherd through. The detective took him along a corridor and put him into an interview room with a single barred window. There was a tape-recorder with two slots for tapes and an alarm strip running along two of the walls. A metal table stood against one wall, two chairs on either side of it.

The detective pointed at a chair and Shepherd sat down. "Any chance of a coffee?" he asked.

"About as much chance as I have of giving Britney Spears one," said the detective.

"She's a looker all right, but a bit young for you," said Shepherd. He sat down. All he could do now was to wait.

The detective grinned at him. "Okay, how do you want it?"

"Thanks. Black. No sugar."

The detective's grin widened. "Got you," he said, laughed harshly and left the room.

Kerr stabbed out his cigarette. "They didn't check the fucking car," he said.

"Sorry, boss?" said Anderson.

"They didn't look in the Volvo. Good news for us because they didn't find the transmitter, but Nelson's a hired killer so why didn't they toss the car looking for a weapon?"

There were deep furrows in Anderson's brow and he scratched his chin.

"Because they were told to take the two of them in, full stop," said Kerr. "They were just following orders. Take the two of them in, forget the motor. Why? Because he's going to come back for the motor."

It had all clicked into place. It had been there, right from the start, staring him in the face, Kerr thought. Nelson was a cop. He hadn't killed Larry Hendrickson's partner. The Polaroids had been faked. The partner wasn't dead, but he'd screwed up and gone roaming the Internet. The cops must have put him on ice because Hendrickson had introduced Nelson to his wife. They were letting the job run and today they'd moved in. Nelson was a cop and Angie had hired him, thinking he was a hitman. They had all they needed to put her away on conspiracy to murder. Kerr lit another cigarette. Except that Angie Kerr wasn't just a wife with a chip on her shoulder. She was *his* wife. She knew how he earned his living *and* where a good chunk of his money was hidden. If the cops could turn Angie, she'd do him a lot of damage.

He lit another cigarette. It was all clear now. From A to B to C. Hendrickson had been set up by an undercover cop pretending to be a hired killer. At some point Hendrickson had passed the cop on to Angie. The cop had decided to run with Angie so Hendrickson hadn't been arrested. The problem was, where did the cops go from there? Did they charge Angie and pat themselves on the back for performing a public service? Would they send a couple of Manchester's finest to his house to tell him they'd saved his life and ask for a donation to the widows and orphans fund? Or would they try to turn Angie because what they really wanted was to put Charlie Kerr behind bars? The cops had been after his scalp for years. He had a detective sergeant in the Drugs Squad on his payroll so he always knew when they were gunning for him, but whoever was running Nelson must be doing it without telling the local boys. This had come out of the blue.

Kerr stared at the Volvo. What to do? He could run away with his tail between his legs. A few minutes on the phone would be all it took to clear out his bank accounts and he could be on a plane to Spain or South America that afternoon. He had more than enough to buy himself a new identity and all the protection he needed, and even with Angie's co-operation it would take them months to put a case against him. If he left the country, they'd probably decide not to go after him. That would pretty much screw up any deal Angie made. If he ran, they'd probably make do with putting her away.

"Are we going to sit here all day?" asked Wates.

"Yes, Ray, that's exactly what we're going to do," said Kerr. "If that's okay with you."

Wates said nothing but looked anxiously at Anderson. They were clearly uneasy, but he couldn't be bothered to explain the situation to them. They were just the hired help.

He wasn't going to run. If he did, everything he'd built up in Manchester would count for nothing. He had respect in the city, he was a face, and he was damned if he was going to throw that away just because Angie had turned against him. At the moment the police had nothing: they'd have to get her to agree to co-operate. Angie's father had died of a heart-attack three years ago but her mother was living in Lytham St Anne's in a nice little flat with a sea view. Angie had a sister, too, a sour-faced cow who'd married an estate agent. They lived in a pokey terraced house in Stretford with their two young sons. Angie would have a few home truths explained to her: if she helped the police, Kerr would stamp on her relatives — hard. And if she still sided with the filth, she'd only be useful if she stood in the witness box and gave evidence against him: she'd have to take a bullet in police custody. Difficult, but not impossible. It was just a question of paying the right man the right amount of money.

Kerr relaxed and took a long drag on his cigarette. Things weren't as bad as he'd first thought. The cops must have reckoned he was stupid, and Kerr resented that. How dare they assume they could get his bitch of a wife to roll over on him? He wanted to teach them a lesson they'd never forget.

Shepherd looked up as the door opened and grinned when he saw a familiar face. It was Jimmy "Razor" Sharpe, a twenty-year police veteran who had worked with him on several undercover cases. He was a small, heavy-set Scotsman with a mischievous grin. "You've been a naughty boy again, have you, Nelson?" said Sharpe.

Shepherd caught sight of two uniformed constables in the corridor behind him. "I've nothing to say," he said.

"I don't give a monkey's either way," said Sharpe. "Come on, it's back to Glasgow for you." He pulled Shepherd to his feet and held his arm as he took him along the corridor. They were joined by a second detective and went out into the car park. A blue Vauxhall was waiting, engine running. Sharpe climbed into the back with Shepherd.

336

Shepherd waited until the Vauxhall was away from the police station before he spoke. "How's it going, Razor?" he asked.

"Bloody fed up with babysitting you," said Sharpe.

"Where's Hargrove?"

"Talking to your woman in there. He wanted me to tell you the tapes are fine."

"Are you going to keep me like this all day?" said Shepherd.

"I was waiting for you to ask nicely," said Sharpe, taking a small penknife from his pocket.

Shepherd twisted to the side and pushed his bound wrists towards Sharpe. "Pretty please," he said.

Sharpe cut the plastic tie, and Shepherd massaged his wrists. "Those things hurt," he said.

"Cost effective," said Sharpe. "Have you got time for a drink?"

"I wish," said Shepherd, "but I've got to get back to London."

"No rest for the wicked," said Sharpe.

Eddie Anderson looked at his watch. "Eddie, if you do that one more time I'll chop your bloody hand off," said Kerr. He opened the Range Rover's window and flicked out the cigarette butt. The Volvo was where the police had left it, in the far corner of the supermarket car park. Kerr had phoned one of his police contacts and asked him to check out the registration number. The officer had promised to get back to him but said it might take a while. All checks on the Police National

Computer were recorded so he'd wait until he could get on using another officer's log-on.

They'd been sitting in the Range Rover for the best part of two hours when a blue Vauxhall parked next to the Volvo. After thirty seconds or so Tony Nelson climbed out, waved to its occupants and got into the Volvo.

"What the fuck . . . !" exclaimed Anderson.

"Boss, did you see that?" said Wates.

Kerr looked at the GPS unit in his hand. "Follow him, Eddie, but keep your distance."

"What's going on?"

"We'll see where the rat runs to," said Kerr.

"Why did they let him go?" asked Anderson.

"Just drive, will you?" said Kerr, tersely. "Leave the thinking to me."

Shepherd drove into the underground car park and reversed the Volvo into the space next to the white Toyota. He took the lift up to his apartment and changed into his Stuart Marsden clothes. He left the Volvo keys in the kitchen, went back to the car park and got into the Toyota. He was dog-tired but he had to get back to Leman Street and report for duty. He'd left his kit-bag in the boot so he could go straight to work. It would be at least eleven o'clock before he got home.

He slotted his mobile into the hands-free kit, then drove out of the car park and headed for the M6. He called Katra first. She said Liam was fine, that she was cleaning the bathroom and planned to do the kitchen. Later she was going food shopping.

338

His second call was to Hargrove. "Nice work, Spider," said the superintendent.

"Has she rolled?"

"She's thinking about it," said Hargrove. "She's asked for a lawyer so until he turns up we can't question her."

"You can't let her see a lawyer — he'll just report back to Kerr."

"We can't stop her," said Hargrove. "We've explained that we'll need her to gather evidence against her husband, and that he can't know what's going on, but she says she wants a lawyer to advise her on the legality of any deal we make."

"I don't like this at all."

"We've no choice. And you can see her point of view — she's got no reason to trust us. We could be planning to use her, then throw her to the wolves. She called her own lawyer, a guy who doesn't work for her husband. We're waiting for him to come in now. We've told her you're spilling your guts and that we've got the whole thing on tape anyway."

"She doesn't know I'm a cop?"

"Absolutely not. I can't see her lawyer advising her to do anything other than co-operate with us, so as soon as she agrees the Drugs Squad and the CPS move in. Your name won't come up."

"And Hendrickson?"

"We'll pick him up this evening. It's open and shut so I can't see him doing anything other than copping a plea. Job well done, Spider."

Shepherd thanked the superintendent and ended the call. Technically it *had* been a job well done. Hendrickson was a scumbag who had deserved what was coming to him, but Shepherd was less convinced about Angie Kerr. Her husband had beaten her and threatened to have her killed. What sort of man would stub out a lighted cigarette on his wife's breast? Charlie Kerr was the villain, but his wife was going to be punished.

Keith Rose sat down opposite Mike Sutherland, who was working his way through a fry-up and a stack of bread and butter. "Do you ever measure your cholesterol?" said Rose.

"There's good and bad cholesterol, so there's no point. Six of one, that's what I figure."

"Shot in the dark, I think sausages are probably heavy on the bad sort."

Sutherland jabbed his fork at Rose's plate. "Cornish pastie and chips is healthier, is it?" He looked around the canteen. "Where's Stu?"

"Some sort of medical. He never had a chest X-ray up in Strathclyde but the Met insists on it."

"He's not a smoker, shouldn't be a problem."

"Rules is rules," said Rose. "Dave Bamber will be map man today. Stu'll report to Ken and Amber team when he gets in." Rose leaned across the table. "The guy in Chicago's given me a date for Kelly's operation."

"Brilliant," said Sutherland.

"Three weeks," said Rose. "I'll put in for the leave and we'll all fly out together."

"That's great," said Sutherland.

"Yeah, but I'm still short, money-wise."

"Fuck."

"Yeah."

Sutherland leaned across the table, a chunk of sausage on the end of his fork. "If there's anything you need, Rosie, all you have to do is ask."

Rose nodded. "Thanks, Mike."

They almost lost the Toyota just outside Birmingham. The M5 split off the M6 and they were too far away to see which fork the Toyota took. "Head for London," said Kerr. It was a gamble, but they caught up with Nelson just before the junction with the M42.

There were two other cars on the Toyota's tail: a BMW driven by two brothers from Chorlton-cum-Hardy who worked for Kerr when he needed extra muscle, and Sammy McEvoy, who ran security at Aces, in his Audi T4. The Audi was a conspicuous car so the Range Rover and the BMW did the close work with the Audi either hanging back or overtaking and staying half a mile ahead of the Toyota. They kept in touch by mobile, switching position every few minutes. The man pretending to be Tony Nelson was either an undercover cop or worked for one of the intelligence services. Either way he'd be trained to spot a tail so they gave the Toyota a lot of space.

He was a conscientious driver, never exceeding the speed limit and only using the outside lane to overtake, so they could keep well back until they were near an intersection. Twice the Audi took a wrong turn while it was ahead of the Toyota but McEvoy was able to get back on the motorway and make up lost ground.

"Looks like London all the way," said Bill Wallace, in the BMW. He was a couple of hundred yards behind the Toyota in the inside lane.

"Looks like it, but stay on your toes," said Kerr. "If we lose him he's gone for good."

Kerr had phoned his police contact and told him not to bother checking the registration number of the Volvo. No undercover cop would be stupid enough to use his own vehicle on a job, and if his man discovered that the Volvo was a plain-clothes police car alarm bells would ring.

Kerr had called in McEvoy and the Wallace brothers when he'd seen the Volvo drive into the underground car park of the city-centre warehouse conversion. His first thought was that Nelson lived in the block but when he drove out in a second vehicle he realised it was merely a staging-post. As soon as the Toyota had driven on to the motorway, Kerr knew Nelson wasn't local. He was going home.

Shepherd swiped his ID and pushed through the revolving door into the main building. The inspectors who headed the Specialist Firearms teams shared an office at the rear of the building, and Ken Swift was sprawled in his chair with his feet on his desk when Shepherd opened the door. "I'm to report to you, sir," said Shepherd.

"How was the medical?" asked Swift, looking up from the tactics manual in his lap. He was wearing his black overalls and rubber-soled boots.

"Just an X-ray," said Shepherd. "The docs in Scotland were supposed to give me one two years ago but it slipped by. Personnel department at the Met spotted it and said I couldn't be active until it was sorted. All done now, anyway."

"The guys are at the range," said Swift. "Get changed and join them."

"Anything happening?" asked Shepherd.

"We've got a briefing from British Transport Police about an operation in Central London. Other than that, it's all quiet on the Western Front."

"This is getting bloody weird, boss," said Anderson, scratching his head. They had pulled in at the side of the road when they saw Nelson drive into the underground car park, and when he'd walked out he'd been carrying a large black kit-bag. From where they'd parked they'd seen the building Nelson had walked into. "That's a cop shop, right?"

Kerr nodded. The six-storey concrete and glass building looked like a seventies police station, but there was no sign on the front. There was no wheelchair access either, which was virtually compulsory in the politically correct twenty-first century. It wasn't a regular police station, that was for sure. Two police cars, white with orange strips down the middle, were parked in the roads. Jam butties, they called them in Manchester. In the corners of the windscreens there were yellow dots the size of a saucer. Kerr knew what they meant: the cars were armed-response vehicles, so the cops inside the building carried guns, which meant they were SO19, the SWAT-type units that went up against armed criminals. Why would they use an armed policeman to work undercover? It didn't make sense. "Okay, let's go home. We know where to find him now." He called McEvoy and the Wallace brothers and told them to go back to Manchester. He'd deal with Tony Nelson in due course, but first he was going to sort out his wife.

Shepherd and the men on Amber team filed into the briefing room. Yellow team were already there. One of the Yellows was a woman, her face devoid of makeup and her hair cropped short. She was chewing gum, her Glock in a holster high on her hip. Shepherd was surprised to see an armed woman, not because they were less capable than men, but because most of the women he knew would have hated the idea of carrying a weapon.

A man in plain clothes was standing next to Ken Swift at the front of the room. On a table behind them were a television and a video-recorder.

Swift waited until the last man was in before he raised his hand. "Okay, guys," he said, then nodded at the female officer. "And girl."

She flashed Swift a humourless smile.

"This is DS Nick Wright of the British Transport Police. He's running Operation Wingman," said Swift. "He's going to fill you in on the details, but basically we've got a gang of armed thugs running riot on the tube. BTP want us to provide armed back-up so it'll be a joint operation. The big problem is that Met radios don't work down the tube. When we go in, each group will have to be shadowed by a BTP officer." There were several groans. "I thought you'd like the sound of that."

Wright was in his late thirties with dark hair, greying at the temples. He was wearing a tweed jacket with leather patches on the elbows, dark brown trousers, a grey flannel shirt and a featureless brown tie. To Shepherd he looked like a uniformed cop trying to dress like an accountant on his day off.

"It's something we're stuck with, I'm afraid," said Wright.

"You're saying that our guy up top has to talk to one of your guys, who relays the message to your guy underground, who tells our guys?" The question had come from a sergeant standing by the door.

Wright shrugged apologetically. "We think it's as crazy as you do," he said.

"Bloody madness, is what it is," said the sergeant.

"It's a budget issue, I'm told. The Met thinks London Underground should pay for the upgrade to the system. My bosses want the Met to pay. It's going to cost millions so God knows when it'll be resolved. Until then, one of our guys has to shadow you wherever you go."

"And what happens if shots are fired?" said Swift. "I can't have my people looking over their shoulders worrying if there's a BTP officer about to get his balls shot off."

"We can issue them with protective vests," said Wright, "and they'll be told to keep out of the way."

"It's a recipe for disaster," said Swift.

Wright didn't respond. Shepherd felt sorry for the guy. He'd turned up to give a briefing and ended up taking the flak for departmental budgeting constraints.

Wright took a deep breath. "I've got some CCTV footage of the suspects." He pressed play and the screen flickered into life. A group of youngsters was huddled on a tube station platform, casually dressed in cargo pants, football shirts and flashy trainers. The oldest was barely out of his teens.

"This is the leader of the group," said Wright, tapping a girl in a combat jacket whose hair was tied in a ponytail and fed through the back of a baseball cap. "IC One female, five six or seven, blue eyes. She usually wears her mobile phone on a camouflage strap around her neck." He grinned at the assembled armed officers. "The less politically correct of our officers refer to her as Snow White, and her gang as the Seven Dwarfs. Sometimes there are seven, but there have been as many as two dozen in some of the attacks. To date, she's the only female involved. She's been at each incident we've looked at."

There was another ten seconds of footage from the cameras on the platform, then the viewpoint changed. This time it was footage from a camera in a busy shopping centre. It was obviously taken on a different day because the blonde girl was wearing a pink top now. "They gather at the Trocadero in Piccadilly Circus, then head for one of the tube stations. They've

346

been seen going into Piccadilly Circus, Leicester Square and Tottenham Court Road. That gives them direct access to the Piccadilly, Bakerloo and the Northern Lines. We don't have video of them in action because they only strike on trains."

On the screen the teenagers were working purposefully towards the exit. The picture jumped to a viewpoint from a camera in Piccadilly Circus, the statue of Eros in the background. Dozens of tourists, mostly backpackers, were sitting on the steps at the base of the statue, munching fast food from Burger King and KFC. The picture jumped again, and now the group were hurrying down the steps into the tube station, elbowing an elderly couple out of the way.

There was a view of a platform. The group was gathered together at the far end, close to the tunnel entrance. Wright froze the picture. "This is them at Leicester Square." He tapped the screen with his pencil. "Here's Snow White. This is a Bangladeshi guy. These three are IC Threes who are always with her. This is a twelve- or thirteen-year-old of mixed race. The IC One male has been involved in at least half a dozen robberies and is always wearing an Arsenal shirt. These two are also of mixed race and have been identified at several robberies. The two IC Threes here have been involved in at least two steamings. Ten minutes after this was taken they boarded a southbound train. Between Leicester Square and Charing Cross they attacked two girls, stole their mobiles and bags. One girl was slashed across the face with a Stanley knife, the other was punched repeatedly in the face and almost lost an eye. That's what makes this so bloody nasty. It's not about theft — they get a few quid out of the bags but next to nothing for the phones — they get their kicks from terrorising people. And they've been getting progressively more violent. We think they've been responsible for fifteen separate attacks over the past month."

He ran the video for a few seconds. The view changed to a different platform and a different group of youngsters, although the blonde girl was still at the centre. Wright tapped the face of a tubby young man in a light blue hooded jacket. "He's been involved in several incidents and we believe he has a gun." He froze the picture. "We haven't seen anything on video, but three of the victims say he had one. A woman who was robbed ended up with a broken jaw and says she was pistol-whipped. We've no idea if it's a real gun or a replica."

He pressed play again and the video showed the group getting on to a train. Another station. Another group of youngsters. "There's Snow White again," said Wright. He paused the video and tapped the girl's face. "Their attacks start in different ways. If there's a large group they steam along a train, terrorising everyone, shouting, screaming and grabbing what they can. Sometimes they target individuals. One ploy is for this young lad to start a conversation with the victim." He tapped the face of a young mixed-race boy. "While he's distracting them, the rest pile in. They put an American tourist in hospital last week — beat him to a pulp and didn't even steal anything. A lot of the time it's not

348

about theft, it's about humiliation. They slash clothing, slap and punch."

Wright faced the SO19 team. "We don't know where they'll strike — that's our main problem. They don't seem to have a game plan. Snow White is their focus, but she doesn't give orders. They act like a pack of hyenas. We'll have an undercover team in the Trocadero so we'll be able to follow them down into the system, then we can track them with CCTV. We'll know which train they board, but it's a question of getting our guys on to the same train and calling it in once they attack. That's when we'll be needing SO19 assistance. We'll stop the train between stations and crack on there's a mechanical problem, just long enough to get you guys in position at the next station. Then we let the train roll and arrest them."

Wright opened a briefcase and handed out a stack of sheets of photocopied stills taken from the CCTV footage. "These are the fifteen guys we've seen with Snow White. Two already have criminal records for assault and theft, Foday Gbonda and Leeroy Tavenier. They are the only two we can identify by name."

The SO19 officers passed round the sheets.

"We plan to start this afternoon in the Trocadero. We have six male officers and three females on standby. They'll follow the group if and when they leave and notify our control room which station they go to. We'd like two of your guys with us in plain clothes in case the gun is produced."

"What about our teams? Where should they lie up?" said Swift.

"I'd suggest they stay mobile," said Wright. "One should be near Piccadilly Circus because that's closest to the Trocadero, and of the fifteen attacks we know the group has carried out, they boarded at Piccadilly Circus in nine cases."

"Do they attack as soon as the train moves off?" asked Swift.

"Unfortunately not," Wright said. "On one occasion, they went as far as Hammersmith and on another to Caledonian Road."

"So the idea is that the Specialist Firearms teams shadow the train above ground?"

"That would be our game plan," said Wright. "By holding up the train in a tunnel we should be able to give you time to get in position."

"You're going to lock down a train after a robbery has been committed when there's a chance that a firearm might be involved?" asked Swift.

"We'll have our officers on board, plus your plain-clothes armed officers."

"And if they start shooting? You want a firefight in a train in a tunnel?"

"I'm assuming there won't be a firefight," said Wright, "and that our officers will be able to contain the situation. If there is a firearm, the presence of armed officers should prevent it being used."

"Should, would, could," said Swift. "If it goes wrong, civilians may get caught in the crossfire."

"Like I said, if the boy has a gun, he hasn't fired it yet."

Brian Ramshaw passed the photographs to Shepherd, who took a set and passed the rest to the officer on his left. The pictures were grainy but clear enough to aid in identification. Shepherd memorised the faces.

"That's the state of play," said Wright. "We'll kick off at about six this evening. BTP will have six plain-clothes officers, including myself. There'll be a chief inspector running the operation at our Management Information and Communications Centre in Broadway just opposite New Scotland Yard. He'll have access to all the CCTV cameras and can liaise with us in the tunnels and with your guys above ground. Two uniformed officers with radios will be here later today and they can ride with the Specialist Firearms teams. Any questions?"

Heads shook.

"I'm going to suggest Stu Marsden and Brian Ramshaw as the undercover officers from SO19," said Swift. "Have you guys got suitable casual clothes?"

Shepherd was already wearing a leather jacket and jeans with a blue denim shirt. He glanced at Ramshaw, who was nodding.

"That's it, then," said Swift.

"Don't suppose I can take my Heckler, can I?" asked Ramshaw.

"Only if you can hide it down the front of your trousers," said Swift, dead-pan.

A uniformed WPC opened the cell door and smiled at Angie. "Your lawyer's here."

"Thanks," said Angie. The WPC took her along a corridor to an interview room. When the woman opened the door and Angie saw who was sitting at the metal table her face fell. It wasn't the lawyer she'd phoned. It was Gary Payne, who worked for Charlie. She hesitated but Payne got to his feet and held out his hands, a broad smile on his suntanned face. He spent a lot of time in his villa in Marbella, a stone's throw from Charlie's. "Angie, love, what a nightmare," he said. She took his hand, and he squeezed it hard enough to make her wince. His lips were smiling, but his eyes were flint hard. "Sit down and let's see what we can do to get you out of here."

"Would you like some tea or coffee?" asked the WPC.

"Tea with milk and two sugars," said Payne. "Bit of a sweet tooth. Angie'll have the same." He swung his slim Gucci briefcase on to the table.

"I don't want anything," said Angie.

"Nonsense," said Payne, jovially. "Hot sweet tea will do you the world of good."

The WPC left the room, closing the door behind her.

The smile vanished from Payne's face. "You stupid, stupid, cow," he said.

Angie put her head in her hands.

Payne leaned over her, so close she could smell the garlic on his breath. "Did you think you'd get away with it? That Charlie wouldn't find out?"

"Can you tell him I'm sorry?" Tears poured down her face.

352

"You're sorry?" Payne sneered. "Sorry doesn't cut it, Angie. Don't you understand what you've done?" He sat down opposite her, interlinked his fingers on top of his briefcase and waited for her to stop crying.

She wiped her eyes with the back of her hands, and Payne handed her a crisp white handkerchief with his initials in one corner. "Use this. What have they said to you so far?"

"Gary, please, I've got my own lawyer coming —"

Payne's grey eyes burned into hers. "Listen, you stupid bitch, your life is over, the trick you've tried to pull. All we're trying to do now is minimise the damage you've done. If you don't help Charlie you're going to bring more grief on your family than you can believe."

Angie felt as if she'd been slapped across the face.

"What did they offer you?" he snapped.

"They said they'll forget what I did if I help them put Charlie away."

"Specifically?"

"Deals he's done. People he's met. Where his money is."

"You know the guy you paid was a cop?"

Angie's jaw dropped.

"You paid off an undercover cop."

"No."

"Yes."

"He killed someone else. There were photographs."

"It was a set-up, Angie."

She slumped in her chair.

"The cops set you up because they needed you to help them put Charlie away. You were never going to get what you wanted. The game was rigged from the start."

"Oh, God."

"He can't help you now. No one can. Do I have to spell it out for you, Angie? There's your mother, your sister, your nephews. Do you want them hurt because of your stupidity? It's over for you. Charlie won't let you take him down. You know that. The cops will end up putting you on trial for trying to have him killed. If you get sent down, Charlie will have you done in jail. And if you don't go down, you know what he'll do to you. Heads or tails, Angie, it's over for you. You paid a guy to kill Charlie. He can't let that lie."

Angie nodded.

"You know what you've got to do, don't you?"

Tears rolled down her cheeks and she blew her nose.

"Look at me, Angie." Her eyes locked with Payne's. "You do know what you have to do, don't you?" he repeated. "You have no choice."

She nodded again.

"Better to get this sorted now, rather than dragging it out. Because if you do drag it out, others are going to get hurt."

"Okay," she whispered.

Payne reached into his pocket and took out a small polythene bag, containing two dozen capsules. He slid the bag across the table. "These are barbiturates, Angie. Sleeping tablets. When you get back to your cell, take them with that cup of tea. Flush the bag down the toilet. Then lie down, go to sleep and everything will be okay."

354

Angie reached for the bag. She picked it up and slipped it into her pocket.

"You know it's for the best, don't you, Angie?"

"Yes," she said, her voice barely a whisper.

"Good girl," said Payne. He stood up, picked up his brief-case and patted her shoulder. "Your will's all sorted. Your mum will want for nothing, there's money for your nephews, your sister gets your jewellery. Everything will be neat and tidy. Don't worry about a thing."

Payne opened the door. The WPC was waiting there, her back to the wall. "Everything okay?" she said.

"Everything's fine," said Payne, cheerfully. "Mrs Kerr might need a few seconds to get herself together. She's had an emotional time."

"Superintendent Hargrove would like a word with you on your way out, sir," said the WPC. "Third door on the left."

Payne walked down the corridor, knocked on the door and opened it without waiting for a response. There were three men in the room. Payne knew one, Christopher Thornton, a portly lawyer who worked for the Crown Prosecution Service. "Christopher, hi, I'm looking for Superintendent Hargrove."

"That would be me," said the tallest of the three. He was in his mid-forties, his hair greying at the temples, a professional smile on his lips. He was wearing a dark blue pinstripe suit with a pale blue shirt and gold cufflinks in the shape of cricket bats. His grip was firm when he shook Payne's hand. "Christopher Thornton you know, and this is Chief Inspector Wainer of the Drugs Squad."

"I've heard of the chief inspector, of course," said Payne.

Wainer nodded curtly, but didn't offer his hand.

"May I assume that your client will be co-operating fully?" said Hargrove.

"She wants to sleep on it."

"I was hoping for something a bit more concrete," said the superintendent. "We'd like to put things in motion as quickly as possible."

"I have a question, actually," said Thornton. "You are acting for Mrs Kerr and solely for Mrs Kerr?"

"What are you suggesting?" said Payne.

"Because any deal we make with Mrs Kerr depends on us proceeding in secrecy," said Thornton. "We'll need her to help collate evidence."

"You want her to wear a wire?"

"Possibly," said Wainer. "It's one of our options."

"You know what her husband will do if he finds her with one?"

"It might not come to that," said Hargrove. "She could give us the numbers of any mobiles he uses and we could access them through GCHQ."

"But back to the point I was making," said Thornton. "Anything you've heard today has to stay within these four walls. Angie Kerr's life is on the line."

Payne gave Thornton a withering look. "I'm well aware of the danger my client is in," he said, "and I don't need to remind you that it was the police who put

356

her in the firing line. What you've done was perilously close to entrapment."

"What do you mean?" asked Hargrove.

"Please don't insult my intelligence, Superintendent," said Payne. "You have my client and the hitman on tape, which means you knew about the meeting in advance. That suggests either very long-term surveillance of the man in question, or that he was co-operating with you. Either way, you were clearly giving my client enough rope to hang herself."

"She paid fifteen grand up front to have her husband killed," said Wainer.

"Which begs the question, why didn't you arrest her then?" said Payne.

"This isn't getting us anywhere," said Hargrove, impatiently. "Your client is on tape commissioning a murder. If she co-operates with us, she can walk away from that. But she has to help us nail her husband. The ball's in your court and, frankly, I'm losing my patience."

"And, as I've already told you, my client will sleep on it. We'll talk again in the morning." Payne smiled. "Maybe things will be a little clearer then. Now, I've got another meeting so I'll bid you farewell." He left the room. Things would definitely be clearer in the morning.

The two teenage girls blasted away at the Zombies, cheering as skulls exploded and green slime splattered across the screen. "Die, you bastard!" yelled one. She was a blonde in khaki cargo pants and a tight black top, clearly braless. Her friend was a brunette, hair cropped. Shepherd watched. The girls were skilled at the game, chatting to each other as they fired. Flying monsters swooped down and the girls blew them away, giggling as they exploded into bloody segments.

"You want something, Granddad?" said the blonde, looking over her shoulder at Shepherd. She couldn't have been more than fourteen but even so he thought it was an unfair thing to say.

"Enjoy yourselves, girls," he said.

"Wanker," said the brunette.

Shepherd walked away, his hands in his pockets. At the far end of the amusement arcade there was a line of football video games. Shepherd walked slowly along them, scanning the faces of the teenagers playing them. None matched those on the CCTV pictures. One scowled at him, and he headed for the exit. He knew that a man in his thirties prowling around an amusement arcade could easily have people drawing the wrong conclusions.

He popped in his radio earpiece, then walked out to a mezzanine area where he could look down at the ground floor. A mother and father were buying ice creams for their three children, the whole family wearing backpacks decorated with the Stars and Stripes.

His earpiece crackled. "I have a visual on Snow White," said a voice. It was Nick Wright. "She's with two IC Three males on the second floor."

There was another huge amusement arcade up there. Shepherd headed for the escalator, slipping out the earpiece. He found Wright at the entrance to the arcade. He looked as out of place as Shepherd felt. The Trocadero was a known haunt of paedophiles and rent-boys, and several teenage boys had smiled invitingly at Shepherd as he'd been wandering around.

Shepherd took a ten-pound note out of his wallet and went to a change machine. As he fed in the note he looked around casually. Snow White was watching two black teenagers dancing to a rap tune on a dance machine, matching their movements to instructions on two video screens. She was wearing the same camouflage top she'd had on in one of the CCTV pictures and her phone was on a strap round her neck.

Shepherd scooped up his pound coins and walked round the arcade, looking at the games machines. He strolled out and saw Brian Ramshaw at the far side of the mall, eating an ice cream.

Shepherd took the escalator to the first floor. According to Wright, the gang waited until they were at critical mass before they headed into the tube station. He found a spot where he could watch the escalators and propped himself against a guardrail. His Glock was in a nylon shoulder holster, pressed against his left side. A BTP radio that would operate throughout the Underground system was clipped to his belt; it was connected to his earpiece and a microphone in his cuff.

Another BTP plain-clothes officer was on the ground floor. Tommy Reid was a detective sergeant, the same rank as Wright, but a good ten years older. He'd dressed down for the operation and was wearing a shabby coat tied at the waist with a piece of string, scuffed workboots and a shapeless Burberry-pattern hat with a red fishing fly stuck into the side. He was carrying a brown-paper bag that looked as if it held a bottle. A uniformed security guard had twice asked him to move away from shop fronts and now he was standing just inside the main entrance.

He made brief eye-contact with Shepherd and raised his bag in salute, then sat down with his back against the wall. Reid's disguise was faultless, and the broken red veins on his nose suggested he was no stranger to strong drink.

Then Shepherd stiffened. He had recognised two boys on the escalator. One was an IC Three male in an Arsenal T-shirt. The other was the mixed-race thirteen-year-old. The youngster was wearing a light blue top with the hood up but Shepherd had glimpsed his face. He raised his cuff to his mouth. "First floor, two suspects on the escalator heading for the second floor," he whispered.

"I have them," said Wright.

At the bottom of the escalator, also going up, was a young woman in tight jeans and a black leather motorcycle jacket. She was one of the BTP's undercover officers.

Shepherd stayed where he was for five minutes, then wandered around checking reflections in shop windows. He saw another female undercover officer walking out of an amusement arcade.

"They're on the way down," said Wright's voice in Shepherd's ear.

A few seconds later Shepherd saw Snow White and half a dozen young men standing in a group on the down escalator, blocking it so that no one could walk past them. They were laughing and Snow White was smoking a cigarette.

Down below, Reid got to his feet and walked out of the mall.

As the group reached the ground floor they were joined by two white teenagers in casual sports gear, Nike sweat-shirts, tracksuit bottoms and gleaming white trainers. They both had thick gold chains round their necks and wrists. They gave Snow White high fives, then the group moved towards the exit.

Shepherd walked towards the escalator. Wright was already on his way down and Shepherd saw another plain-clothes BTP officer walk out of a mobile-phone shop, pretending to read a brochure.

The group left the Trocadero and walked through Piccadilly Circus, threading their way through crowds of tourists having their photographs taken in front of Eros.

"They're heading for Piccadilly Circus station," said Reid, over the radio.

"This is Control. We're ready for them," said a Scottish voice in Shepherd's ear. The BTP chief inspector in the Management Information and Communications Centre was a Glaswegian. He was sitting at a work station that allowed him immediate access to any of the six thousand CCTV cameras on the London Underground system.

Shepherd walked out of the Trocadero. Nick Wright followed him into the street without acknowledging him. The two female BTP officers fanned out to either side and worked their way purposefully towards the station.

"They're at the entrance now," said Reid.

Shepherd started to jog. He put the microphone close to his mouth. "Brian, where are you?"

"Twenty metres behind you," said Ramshaw, in his earpiece.

Shepherd upped the pace. It was vital that at least one armed officer was close to the group in case a firearm was produced on the tube.

"They're inside the booking hall now," said the chief inspector over the radio, "passing through the barriers."

Shepherd reached the tunnel entrance at the same time as Wright, who already had his tube pass in his hand. Shepherd cursed under his breath. He didn't have a ticket. He stuck his hand in his pocket and grabbed a handful of change, but Wright pointed at a blue-uniformed member of staff to let him through.

"Down escalator heading for the Piccadilly Line," said the chief inspector.

"I'm on the Piccadilly platform, southbound," said Reid, over the radio.

Shepherd was impressed. Either the DS was lucky and had played a hunch, or he'd assumed that the Piccadilly Line was the most likely place for the gang to go. Either way, he was ahead of the game.

Shepherd walked down the escalator behind Wright. Below he could see Snow White talking to the kid in the light blue top. Shepherd took out the earpiece. Now that he had them in sight he didn't need the chief inspector's commentary.

Shepherd and Wright reached the foot of the escalator. Snow White and her gang were standing in the hallway as if they weren't sure whether to go north or south. Shepherd headed north. So did Wright.

Shepherd glanced over his shoulder. Ramshaw was on the escalator, trapped behind a slow-moving student with a massive rucksack. He nodded almost imperceptibly. He could see that Shepherd was going north, so he'd go south.

Shepherd waited halfway down the platform, close to the tunnel that led to where Snow White and the gang were waiting, laughing and pushing each other around. He looked up at the electronic sign that announced the train arrivals. There was one minute to go before the next train arrived. Wright was pacing up and down, arms folded, head down, as if he was deep in thought. Surreptitiously Shepherd slid the earpiece back in. "Suspects are in the hallway," said the chief inspector. "No way of knowing which way they'll move."

"Ramshaw, I'm on the south platform," said Ramshaw.

Shepherd raised his cuff to his mouth. "Marsden, I'm on the northbound platform."

He felt the breeze of an approaching train. One of the female undercover officers walked on to the platform. She was in a long coat, holding a Marks & Spencer carrier-bag.

The rails rattled and the train burst out of the tunnel into the station. Shepherd caught a glimpse of the driver, then the carriages flashed by. The brakes shrieked and the train juddered to a halt. The doors slid open and several dozen passengers got off. Shepherd caught Wright's eye.

"North, north, they're heading north," said the chief inspector.

Shepherd walked to the train, and as he stepped on board Snow White and her gang ran on to the platform and jumped on. Wright got into the adjoining carriage and took a seat close to the connecting door. The female officer got in and sat down, her carrier-bag on her lap. The doors clunked shut and the train lurched along the platform.

Shepherd was at the far end of the carriage. Snow White and her gang were standing at the mid-point, swinging from the handles set into the roof. They were looking around and laughing, and even from where he was sitting Shepherd could detect the predatory look in their eyes. He sat with his arms folded. He could feel the gun pressing against his side. Could he draw it against children? He took a deep breath and said a silent prayer that it wouldn't come to that. The plan was to stop the train as soon as the gang struck and to get Ken Swift and his team into position at the next station.

The train rushed into the tunnel. Shepherd counted the passengers in the carriage. Most were sitting, but three businessmen in dark suits were standing to his left, discussing a sales conference. A West Indian woman sat opposite, with a wicker shopping basket on her lap. Next to her a teenage girl was listening to a Walkman as she ate a Sainsbury's salad with a plastic fork. On the other side of the West Indian woman a workman in paint-stained overalls and a floppy hat was reading the *Sun*.

Shepherd glanced at the gang. The youngster in the light blue top was bending over a middle-aged woman, his face only inches away from hers. "Give me a kiss, darling," he said. She was sitting next to a little girl of seven or eight. Same age as Liam.

The woman looked embarrassed.

"Come on, darling, slip me the tongue," said the teenager. He opened his mouth and waggled his at her.

The little girl laughed, but the teenager glared at her. The woman put her arm round her daughter and drew her close.

Two black teenagers moved to stand behind the young thug. "Go on, give him a kiss," said one. "He don't have Aids or nuffink."

"Please, leave me alone," said the woman. The little girl looked scared now.

The teenager reached out to stroke her cheek. The woman flinched, and glanced round the carriage, but no one met her gaze. No one wanted to get involved. Shepherd knew that was why the gang had been so successful in their attacks. They picked on one victim and focused all their attention on them; the rest of the passengers were relieved that they weren't under attack and did nothing.

Snow White and one of the white teenagers moved to join the group who were intimidating the woman.

Shepherd saw Wright stand up and move towards the connecting door.

"Give us yer bag, darling," said Snow White.

"Please, I don't want any trouble," said the woman, close to tears.

The teenager pulled out a Stanley knife. So did Snow White. "Give me your fucking bag, you bitch!" screamed the teenager.

Snow White lashed out with her knife and cut the woman's coat. "Come on, come on!" she shouted.

Shepherd saw Wright talking into his radio microphone, notifying the control centre that the attack had started.

The little girl screamed and pressed herself to her mother. The teenager grabbed her blonde hair and twisted it savagely.

"Leave her alone!" shouted the mother.

Snow White slapped her face. "Let go of the bag, bitch!"

Shepherd stood up. One of the black teenagers stared at him menacingly. The woman BTP officer also got to her feet, waiting to see what Shepherd would do.

The mother released her bag and Snow White tossed it to one of the gang.

The rest of the passengers were frozen now with horror.

Shepherd took a step towards the group. Three of them moved to block his way.

Shepherd took out his warrant card and held it up. "Police!" he shouted. "Put down those knives!"

The teenager with the Stanley knife pulled the little girl to her feet and held it to her throat. "I'll cut her!" he yelled.

The mother screamed and Snow White punched her in the mouth.

"No, you won't," said Shepherd. The little girl struggled but the teenager held her tight.

Wright was trying to open the connecting door but two of the gang members were pushing against it.

The train roared out of the tunnel and into Leicester Square station. Faces flashed by but Shepherd concentrated on the teenager. The blade of the Stanley knife had pierced the little girl's neck and a dribble of blood ran down her shirt.

The doors opened and the passengers scattered. Shepherd moved to allow an overweight businessman to waddle by, clutching his briefcase to his chest, but kept his eyes on the boy with the knife. "Just drop the knife on the floor and this will all work out just fine," he said.

The boy pulled back the little girl's hair. "I'll cut her!" he yelled again.

"No, you won't," said Shepherd. Passengers started to get on to the train but stopped when they saw what was happening. The teenager stabbed the knife into the child's throat and blood spurted.

The mother screamed, her hands over her face.

Snow White ran out on to the platform, cursing at passengers to get out of her way. The two black teenagers ran after her. The boy with the knife spat at Shepherd, then pushed the child down the carriage and bolted on to the platform. The little girl staggered against Shepherd. Her shirt was soaked with blood but she was still conscious, eyes wide with fear. She tried to speak but all that came out was a gurgle. Her mother ran towards Shepherd, arms outstretched. She fell to the floor and grabbed her daughter.

Shepherd looked at the teenagers running full pelt down the platform, then at the child. It was no contest. "Put her down gently," he said to the mother. He examined the cut. It was about two inches long and deep, but blood wasn't pumping out, which meant that a major artery hadn't been severed. The mother was sobbing.

Wright burst through the connecting door. "I'll radio for a paramedic."

"Go!" said Shepherd. Wright hurried on to the platform.

The female officer was preventing passengers getting on to the train.

The child coughed and blood splattered out of her mouth. Shepherd needed something to stem the bleeding. She coughed again and more blood spurted over her chest. Shepherd's medical training was basic, and mostly concerned with broken limbs and bullet wounds. The way her mouth kept filling with blood suggested he should get her head up. He propped her against a seat, then took off his leather jacket and the holstered Glock.

Wright appeared at the carriage door. "Paramedics on their way," he said.

"Okay." Shepherd tore off his shirt and pressed it to the little girl's throat. He smiled at her. "The paramedics will be here in a minute. It's going to be okay." Blood seeped into the shirt and he increased the pressure on the wound.

The child stared wide-eyed at him. Her mother stroked her hair. "Hang on, honey, you're going to be all right," she said. She turned to Shepherd, eyes brimming with tears. "What can we do? We've got to stop her bleeding."

"What's your daughter's name?" he asked.

"Emily. Emily McKenna."

Emily coughed and more blood gushed from her lips. Her chest heaved and Shepherd could see she was having trouble breathing. Blood was flowing down her windpipe and Shepherd knew he had to do something quickly.

"Where are the paramedics?" he asked Wright.

Wright shrugged helplessly. "They know the situation," he said. "They said they'll be right here."

"We need them now."

"The chief inspector said they're on the way."

Emily's chest was heaving as she fought for breath. She was choking to death. "Have you got a Biro?" Shepherd asked.

Wright fumbled in his pocket and pulled one out. "Are you sure about this?"

"The blood's running into her lungs," said Shepherd.

"What are you talking about?" said Mrs McKenna.

"We have to help your daughter breathe," said Shepherd. He put his hands on Emily's shoulders. He could see the panic in her eyes. "Listen, Emily. You have to lie down again, okay?" She nodded. "Then I want you to close your eyes and imagine you're somewhere else."

Emily made a gurgling sound as her mouth tried to form words. "Don't talk," said Shepherd, and lowered her to the floor.

"What are you doing?" said Mrs McKenna.

"Close your eyes, Emily," said Shepherd. He reached into his pocket and took out his Swiss Army knife, flicked out a blade and wiped it on his shirt. There was no time to worry about infection — they could pump antibiotics into her later. If he didn't fix her breathing Emily would be dead within minutes.

"Oh, God, no," whispered Mrs McKenna.

"It has to be done," said Shepherd. "It won't hurt, I promise, and it will save her life."

Emily coughed and more blood gushed from her lips.

"Hold her hands, Mrs McKenna. Keep talking to her — keep her calm." He pulled the ink cartridge out of the Biro and tossed it on to the seat behind him.

Mrs McKenna looked wildly at Wright as if he might have an alternative suggestion.

"Do it now!" said Shepherd.

Mrs McKenna knelt down beside her daughter and took her hands. "It's okay, sweetheart, I'm here."

Shepherd took the child's throat in his left hand and gently squeezed the windpipe.

"I'll check where they are," said Wright. He ran on to the platform, talking into his radio.

"You can't stick that in her throat!" said Mrs McKenna.

"She won't feel it," said Shepherd, "and if we don't let her get air into her lungs . . ." He pressed the tip of the blade between the cartilage ridges of her windpipe until it popped through, pulled it out, then pressed with his fingers. The hole opened wide. He put the knife on to the seat and pushed the plastic tube into the hole. Air sucked in through the tube and Emily's chest stopped juddering.

"It's okay, darling," said Mrs McKenna.

Emily's mouth moved soundlessly. Her chest was moving up and down, and air was whistling through the tube.

Shepherd sat back on his heels and wiped his forehead on the back of his arm.

Wright appeared at the carriage door. "They're here," he said. "One minute."

"Do you have a clean handkerchief, Mrs McKenna?" asked Shepherd.

Mrs McKenna didn't take her eyes off her daughter but fumbled in her pocket and pulled out a white handkerchief.

Shepherd took it and wrapped it round the base of the Biro tube.

"Hang on, precious," said Mrs McKenna.

Emily's breathing had settled down. Blood was still trickling out of her mouth but she wasn't choking now.

Shepherd heard rapid footsteps. Two men in green and yellow fluorescent jackets dashed into the carriage. He stood up to give them room to work. "Throat wound, no major arterial damage. Her mouth was filling with blood so I did a tracheotomy," he said.

One of the paramedics checked the tube. "Good work."

The second paramedic felt for a pulse while the first went to work on Emily's neck.

Shepherd helped Mrs McKenna to her feet. There was blood on her hands and smeared across the front of her coat. "She'll be okay," he said.

Tears were running down the woman's face. "How could they do that to my little girl?" she asked.

Shepherd said nothing. It was a question he couldn't answer.

The hatch in the cell door clanged open and a face appeared in the gap. It was the WPC who'd taken her to see Gary Payne. "Are you okay, Mrs Kerr?" she asked. She had a sweet face, thought Angie. Her eyes were a blue so pale that they were almost grey and she had used mascara on her lashes.

"I'm fine," said Angie, in a monotone.

"I'm off my shift in a few minutes. Do you want me to get you some food before I go?"

"I'm fine," repeated Angie.

"It'll be your last chance before morning. And the night custody officer is a bit of a grouch."

Angie forced a smile. "Really, I'm fine."

"What about some tea?"

Angie nodded at the polystyrene cup on the floor. "I've still got the one you gave me before."

"That was hours ago," said the WPC. "It'll be stone cold."

Angie shrugged. "It'll do."

The WPC smiled and closed the hatch. Angie opened her right hand and counted the barbiturate capsules. Twenty-four. She put them on the grey blanket, then picked up the polystyrene cup. A brown scum had formed on the tea. She took a sip and grimaced. She didn't take sugar.

She sat down on the bed, popped one of the tablets on to her tongue, took another sip of tea, flicked her head back and swallowed. One down, twenty-three to go. She sipped the cold tea. It wasn't so bad.

Ken Swift tossed the T-shirt to Shepherd. It was grey with NYPD on the front. "Got this on an exchange visit with the New York SWAT guys," he said. "I wouldn't mind having it back."

"Thanks, sir," said Shepherd.

"Shift's over," said Swift. "It's Ken."

Shepherd pulled on the T-shirt. The paramedics had taken his shirt when they wheeled away the little girl. They'd stabilised her and put her on a saline drip.

"Where did you learn to do that throat thing?" asked Swift.

Shepherd shrugged. "Army, first-aid training. I'm just glad I was paying attention that day."

"Saved her life," said Swift.

"The way the world is, the mother will probably sue me," said Shepherd. "I still don't know if I did the right thing by not pulling my gun."

"They only had knives — you couldn't have shot them. Not without a shit-load of trouble from the civil-liberty groups, and the press would have had a field day."

"They were kids, but the way they behaved . . ."

"Animals," said Swift.

"The one who stabbed the little girl wasn't more than thirteen. What was he doing with a knife? Why aren't his parents asking where he is?"

"They probably don't care," said Swift. "Father's probably run off. Mother's got no money. Schools are too busy maintaining order to get involved."

"Have you got kids?"

"Three — and no matter what happened to the marriages I was always a father to them. Saw them whenever I could, went to school events, took them on holiday. When there were problems, I nipped them in the bud. I was a good dad, Stu. A shit husband, I'll put my hands up to that, but I was always there for my kids."

"I can't believe they got away," said Shepherd. "We were there on the bloody train. I was six feet away. If they hadn't stabbed the little girl . . ."

"That's why they stabbed her. They knew you'd have to stop and help."

The chief inspector was right: they'd made a calculated decision to knife a child because anyone with humanity would help her rather than give chase. It was the sort of behaviour Shepherd would expect from a professional criminal or a soldier, not from teenagers.

"By the time we got to Leicester Square they were well gone," said Swift. "CCTV footage shows them getting the Northern Line to Charing Cross. They left the station, probably walked back to their stamping ground."

"So what next?"

"BTP want to try again in a couple of days. Thursday evening, maybe, or Friday. All we have to do now is find them. With you and the BTP detectives as witnesses, we have a case."

"I'm up for it," said Shepherd. "I want another crack at them."

Swift slapped him on the back. "Job's yours," he said. "Now, let's go get a pint. We've earned it."

Shepherd set his alarm for seven thirty so that he could have breakfast with Liam before he went to school, but he was awake before the alarm went off. He heard Katra get up and go down to the kitchen, and later he heard her getting Liam ready. He grabbed his dressing-gown and went downstairs. Liam was sitting at the kitchen table, eating toast and drinking orange juice.

Katra had a mug of coffee ready for him.

"What time did you get home, Dad?" asked Liam.

"About eleven," said Shepherd. "I came in to say goodnight but you were asleep. Did you do your homework?"

"Katra helped me," said Liam.

"It was maths," said Katra. "I was always good at that."

"Thanks," said Shepherd. "I'm working late all this week, but I'll be able to do my bit at the weekend."

"What was work like yesterday?" asked Liam.

Shepherd shrugged. "Boring office stuff," he lied.

"Why do you have to work at night, then?"

"There's office stuff to do all day," said Shepherd. He didn't like lying to his son, but he certainly didn't want to tell him he'd stuck a knife into a little girl's windpipe. "Did you manage the drive all right?" he asked Katra.

"She's great, Dad," said Liam. "Better than you."

"Thanks, kid."

"Come on, Liam, it's time to go," said Katra. She helped Liam on with his blazer and handed him his bag. "I'll cook breakfast for you when I get back," she said to Shepherd.

"That's okay, I'm fine with coffee," said Shepherd, raising his mug.

"It's the most important meal of the day," said Liam, and grinned.

Katra giggled and they left.

Shepherd went through to the sitting room and waved as they drove off. Then he went upstairs, shaved, climbed into the shower and turned it on cold, gasping as the icy water washed over him.

The doorbell rang as he was rinsing shampoo from his hair. Shepherd swore, grabbed a towel and wrapped it round his waist as he rushed downstairs. It was Kathy Gift. He'd forgotten she'd said she'd be round on

Wednesday morning. He wanted to ask her to reschedule but he knew that if he avoided her she'd tell Hargrove. All he had to do was sit down and talk to her. He could do that. And he could show her he was on an even keel, that all was well with the world. He spent half of his undercover life pretending to be something he wasn't.

"I seem to be making a habit of getting you out of the shower," she said.

"It isn't even eight yet," he said.

"The early bird," she said. "Is someone with you? Is this a bad time?"

Shepherd smiled ruefully. "No. I'm alone."

"Liam's still with his grandparents?"

"He moved back in at the weekend but he's just gone to school."

"So you solved your au pair problem?"

"Looks that way," he said. He held the door open for her. "I've just had coffee, but if you want one, you know where everything is."

He hurried upstairs, dried himself and put on a grey pullover and black jeans. When he got back downstairs she was studying the framed photographs in the bookcase. There were two mugs of coffee on the table by the sofa.

"He's a good-looking boy," she said, peering at a snap of Liam in his school uniform.

"Takes after his mum," said Shepherd.

Gift smiled at a silver-framed photograph of Shepherd and Sue standing in the garden, their backs to the house. Liam had taken it the previous year on

Sue's birthday and he'd kept them smiling at the camera for almost two minutes before he eventually pressed the shutter. Sue had burst out laughing just as Liam took the picture and her eyes were full of life, full of joy. It felt like a lifetime ago.

Gift sat down in an armchair and opened her briefcase. She took out a clipboard with a ballpoint pen.

"No tape-recorder?" he asked.

"It's my impressions I want to record, rather than what you say."

"The opposite of a police interrogation," said Shepherd.

"That's one way of looking at it." She crossed her legs and rested the clipboard on her knee. "But I'm not trying to trap you or get you to admit anything that you don't want to."

"Just a chat between friends?"

The psychologist chuckled. "I'm here to help, Dan," she said. "I just want to get a feeling for how you're handling the job. I talk to everyone on the unit at least once a year."

But Shepherd knew her visit wasn't just an annual service. Hargrove had asked her to talk to him, which meant the superintendent was concerned.

"I couldn't help noticing the scar on your shoulder when you answered the door."

"I stopped a bullet a while back. It was nothing."

"Before you joined the police?"

"In my previous life."

"Do you mind talking about it?"

378

"Being shot, or being in the SAS?"

Gift looked at him with a slight smile on her face. "Which do you feel most comfortable talking about?"

Shepherd folded his arms, then realised she might think his body language defensive. He put his hands on his knees but that felt too posed so he moved them to his lap. "That's such a psychologist's question," he said.

"I didn't mean it to be. I'm just interested."

"In what specifically?"

"What it was like to be shot, I guess."

Shepherd rubbed his chin. "It doesn't hurt, if that's what you mean. Not at first, anyway. It's like been punched really hard. The endorphins kick in and you're aware that you're losing blood and you just go weak."

"Who shot you?"

"He didn't leave a card," said Shepherd.

"You didn't see him?"

"He was over a rise. We weren't in combat, he just took a shot."

"A sniper?"

"Or a coward. One shot and he was off. It was in Afghanistan. Never found out if he was a soldier or just a villager with a gun."

"You were lucky."

"Everyone says that, but if I'd really been lucky I wouldn't have been shot in the first place," said Shepherd.

"I meant lucky you weren't killed."

"It hit bone and went downwards, missed an artery by half an inch. I was in a four-man team and the medic did his stuff. I was helicoptered to hospital and a

379

week later I was back in the UK." There were other details he didn't want to tell her. Like the fact that he had been cradling a dying SAS captain who had lost a good-sized chunk of skull and brain when the sniper's bullet had slammed into Shepherd's shoulder.

"You didn't leave the SAS on medical grounds, though, did you?" she asked.

"That's in my file, is it?"

She smiled reassuringly. "I'm not trying to trick you, Dan," she said. "Your file only says you spent six years in the regiment before leaving to join the police. It wasn't a bad enough injury to have you RTUd?"

RTU. Returned to Unit. It was every SAS trooper's worst nightmare: being told that the Regiment didn't want or need them any more and they were to return to their original unit. Shepherd hadn't been RTUd. He'd walked out for Sue. "I heal quickly," said Shepherd.

"What's it like, being in a firefight?"

"It wasn't a firefight, it was an ambush."

"But when you're under fire, what's that like?"

"If you have to ask, you'll never know," he said.

"That's an easy answer," she said.

"It's a difficult question. Unless you've had bad guys blasting away at you you're never going to understand what it feels like."

"But you're scared?"

Shepherd frowned as he tried to find words to explain. It wasn't fear: he had fought alongside regular soldiers and he'd seen fear in their eyes when the bullets were flying but he'd never seen it in the eyes of SAS troopers. The men of the SAS relished combat: it was what they trained for, what they lived for. They had the same look when they prepared to jump from a Hercules two miles up. Excitement. Elation. Adrenaline pumping, heart pounding. "It's like they say, you're never so alive as when you're close to death."

"They say, too, that time seems to slow down?"

Shepherd nodded. "It's not that things go slowly, more that everything is clearer. Sounds are sharper, colours more vibrant."

"It sounds like a drug."

"I've never taken drugs so I wouldn't know."

"Really?"

"Really. Not so much as a whiff of a cannabis. And even if I had I'd be pretty damn stupid to tell a police psychologist, wouldn't I?"

She nodded slowly. "But combat is addictive, I suppose?"

Shepherd wondered where she was heading.

"It enhances sensation," she said. "That's what many drugs do. Even runners feel the same effect, don't they? The chemicals released during a marathon run induce a feeling of euphoria."

"Have you ever run a marathon?"

"Three times. Twice here in London and once in New York. I don't run as much as I used to, but in my twenties you'd have been hard pushed to keep up with me."

Shepherd took a quick look at her legs. She crossed them and when he looked back at her face she was smiling. "So, am I right?" she asked. "Does combat give you a similar high?"

It was, Shepherd realised, another good question. But Kathy Gift was paid to ask searching questions and evaluate the answers she was given. "For some people, I suppose it is."

"It's an interesting thought, isn't it?" she said. "Most people would be scared witless if they were shot at. But for some maybe the excitement outweighs the fear. Wouldn't they be the ones selected to join the SAS?"

Shepherd shook his head emphatically. "The selection process weeds out the thrill-seekers and the wannabe James Bonds. The ones who make it aren't adrenaline junkies."

"So what sort of people do make it?"

"You've got to be physically fit, but it's mental toughness that gets you through."

"There's a type, is there?"

"I guess so. Most are working class, from pretty tough backgrounds, and they're all driven."

"Driven?"

"To show that they're the best. That's what keeps you going through selection. You reach a point where you're physically exhausted. From then on it's a matter of willpower."

"And having gone through all that, having shown that you're among the best of the best, you walked away?"

"I was a father."

"There are married men in the Regiment, aren't there?"

382

"Some. But it puts the marriage under strain. We're off having adventures around the world and the wives sit at home changing nappies."

"Is that how you see life in the SAS, having adventures?"

Shepherd sat back and folded his arms, no longer caring about his body language. He could see where she was going. She wanted to show that he was hooked on the excitement of dangerous situations. "I think that's how the wives see it," he said. "They think it's all fun and games, and that's partly our fault — we tend to downplay the dangerous aspects."

"Because you don't want them to worry?"

Shepherd nodded.

"But your wife was still worried. Was that why she wanted you to leave the SAS?"

"It wasn't so much the danger, more that I was away for long periods. She had a point."

"So you agreed to leave?"

"We talked about it and decided it was for the best."

"And you went straight into undercover work?"

"That's right." It would all be in Shepherd's file. He'd applied to join the Met, but his potential had been spotted almost immediately. Instead of being sent to the Police Training College at Hendon he'd been interviewed by Superintendent Hargrove and offered a place on his unit.

"Out of the frying pan into the fire?"

It was a phrase Sue had used. An armed criminal could be every bit as dangerous as an Afghan tribesman or an Iraqi soldier. "I got to spend more time at home," he said.

"And what about you? Was the job as challenging?"

Another good question. Kathy Gift had the knack of getting to the heart of the matter. "It's different," he said, choosing his words carefully. "In the Regiment you're part of a team. There's the Regiment, then your troop, then your four-man brick. You always have mates to rely on who'll pull your balls out of the fire if necessary. Working undercover, most of the time you're on your own. You might be under surveillance, but they're always on the outside, looking in."

"It must be stressful."

Of course it was stressful. She was a psychologist who worked with a specialist undercover unit: she knew exactly how much stress there was in the job. What did she expect him to say? Ask for some Valium? "You deal with it," he said eventually.

"How?"

"I run."

"Running clears the mind, doesn't it?"

"It can."

"It must be difficult, being undercover for long periods."

"Sure. But that's the job."

"Not everyone can deal with the stress for ever."

"I know." It wasn't unusual for undercover agents to turn to alcohol, or even drugs, to relieve the pressure. Shepherd wasn't averse to a drink, but he never drank to excess.

"Do you find it getting easier or harder?"

"The more time I spend undercover, the better I get at it."

Gift brushed a stray lock of hair behind her ear. "I meant the stress," she said. "Is it easier to deal with it?"

Shepherd exhaled slowly. "I don't know," he said. "It's not something I think about."

"But do you sleep okay, for instance?"

"Like a baby."

"Panic attacks, shortness of breath, dizziness?"

"Never," said Shepherd, emphatically.

"Do you lose your temper easily?"

"No."

"Loss of appetite?"

"I eat like a horse."

"So, you're fine?"

"That's what I've been telling you."

"No problems?"

"None."

"And the new job?"

"I'm not supposed to divulge operational details, you know that."

"Of course I do. I was just asking how it was going. Is it straightforward? Is it stressful? How are you coping with it? That was all I meant."

"It's as straightforward as undercover assignments ever can be, no more stressful than previous jobs and I'm coping just fine."

"Okay," she said. She stood up and bent down to pick up the briefcase.

Shepherd found himself looking at her legs again. He could believe she was a runner. "That's it, then?" he asked.

"For the moment." She slipped the clipboard and pen into the briefcase, then snapped the twin locks shut. "I'd like to see you again in a few days. I'll phone."

"I'm really busy on this case," he said, as she left the room. He hurried after her. "I have to work shifts, two till ten this week, and I'm on nights next week."

"I'm flexible time-wise," she said. "I'll try not to catch you in the shower next time."

Shepherd got to the front door before her and opened it. She flashed him a smile and walked towards her black Mazda, high heels clicking on the paving-stones. Shepherd closed the door and leaned his forehead against it. He took a deep breath. He'd been on his guard throughout the interview, wanting to appear co-operative but without giving away too much of himself. The psychologist was there to help, but she also had the power to remove him from operational work if she felt he was a danger to himself or others. The interview had gone well, he thought. He had answered most of her questions truthfully. But the one thing he'd been expecting her to talk about she hadn't mentioned: Sue's death and how he was dealing with it. Shepherd knew she was too smart to have forgotten to bring it up. That meant she'd deliberately avoided it — for the time being at least. But Shepherd had no doubt that Kathy Gift would be back and that she'd want him

386

to open up about it. It wasn't something to which he was looking forward.

Rashid Malik was British. He had been born in Britain and he had a British passport. He spoke English with a Birmingham accent and supported Birmingham City Football Club. He even had a season ticket to the St Andrews stadium. The British state had educated him, looked after his health, even paid him when he didn't feel like working. But now Malik was prepared to die to strike at the heart of the British establishment. And to kill as many people as he could.

He lay down in the bathtub and allowed the warm water to rise over his face. He held his breath and pretended he was already dead. It felt good. He was at peace, relaxed.

Malik had only been in London for two days and he hadn't left the studio flat. There was food in the cupboard, fruit juice and bottled water in the fridge, a prayer mat and a copy of the Qur'ān in the corner of the room. That was all he needed while he prepared himself.

Malik had been starting primary school in a lower middle-class suburb of Birmingham when the Palestinians announced their first *intifada* and began sending suicide bombers against the Israelis who had stolen their land. When he was ten he watched the news as the American and British forces invaded Kuwait in Operation Desert Storm and listened to his father curse the Saudis for allowing the infidels to use their soil as a base from which to attack a Muslim nation. Malik moved to his secondary school during the civil war in Bosnia, and watched television in horror as the Serbs butchered Muslims in their thousands while the world did nothing. He left school when he was seventeen. His teachers said he was clever enough to go to university, but there was nothing he wanted to study. He loathed the thought of working in an office or programming computers. It all seemed so pointless when fellow Muslims were being murdered around the world. He tried raising it with the *imam* at his local mosque but he had said only that Malik should be grateful to live in a country where everyone had a place and a voice.

Malik had spent three years either filling supermarket shelves or on the dole. He had been at home watching television when two planes slammed into the World Trade Center in New York and a third hit the Pentagon. When it was revealed that Muslims had carried out the attacks, he had cheered, then rushed to his mosque where other young men were equally excited that someone had stood up to the Americans. The older members of the mosque had tried to calm them, tried to tell them that Islam was a peaceful religion, that any form of killing was wrong and that terrorism against innocent men, women and children was a sin, no matter what the provocation. Malik would not listen.

He joined street protests calling on the government not to join in the invasion of Afghanistan, and helped make petrol bombs when it became clear that Britain was going to back President Bush. It was when he saw images of a children's hospital in Kabul destroyed by an American missile that he decided protests were not enough. He told his parents he wanted to spend time in Pakistan, discovering his roots. They welcomed his decision as an opportunity for him to find a suitable wife and even paid for his ticket. They gave him a list of the phone numbers and addresses of family and friends and cried as he walked through the departure gates at Heathrow's Terminal Three. It was the last time they had seen him.

Malik spent a week in Pakistan and didn't call any of the numbers his parents had given him. He headed north to the frontier town of Peshawar and met a group of young Muslims who were as keen to fight American imperialism as he was. He was taken to a camp where Muslims who wanted to fight the infidel were recruited and trained. There, they were desperate for recruits to send to Afghanistan to fight with the Taliban, but the men who ran the camp were suspicious of the clean-shaven young man who spoke only English. But the fact that he had a British passport intrigued them and they kept him under observation for three weeks, during which time he did nothing but study the Qur'ān, grow a beard and perform basic exercise drills. Once they were convinced of his good intentions he was trained in the use of explosives, light weapons and communications. Malik was a quick learner, and enthusiastic. He had finally found something he considered worth studying.

His instructors monitored his progress and were about to send him to join the Taliban when word came from an al-Qaeda aide that Malik was to be moved to a training camp in the Yemen. There, he was given further intensive training in terrorism techniques but he spent the bulk of his time studying the Qur'ān and the Hadiths, texts based on the life of the Prophet Muhammad. Without realising it, Malik was being nudged towards the passages that glorified martyrdom, that promised everlasting joy in the shadow of Allah for those who fought and died in the name of Islam. He was shown videos of other young volunteers who had sacrificed themselves. He was told how the *shahids* — the martyrs — would never be forgotten on earth and would live for ever in heaven. Malik watched the videos of bright-eyed men and women, some not even in their teens, eager to give their lives for the fight against the infidel.

Afghanistan fell to the Americans, and then it was Iraq's turn. Malik watched on CNN as the infidels slaughtered Muslims, then pillaged the country's resources. He saw photographs of American and British soldiers torturing Iraqi prisoners-of-war and begged his instructors to send him on a mission. He was told to wait, that his time would come, that he was too valuable a resource to be wasted. He was special, and Allah had a special place for him in heaven.

Bombs exploded in Spain and the Spanish government pulled its troops out of Iraq; once again, Malik begged his instructors to use him. Finally his time came. He was told to shave off his beard and return to the United Kingdom, not to Birmingham and his parents but to a bedsit in Derby, where he was to speak to no one other than a man who would bring him food and clean clothes. He stayed in the bedsit for two weeks and left the room only once, at night. He walked to a local graveyard and climbed over the wall. He found a space between two graves and lay there, his arms crossed over his chest, trying to imagine what it would be like to be dead. He closed his eyes under the star-sprinkled skies and realised he was at peace. Death was nothing to be scared of. Malik knew that it wouldn't lead to eternal sleep. The death of a *shahid* was rewarded with eternal paradise for himself and his relatives. Death was to be embraced.

Eventually a second man collected him and drove him to London in a van that smelt of curry. In London he was shown into another bedsit and told not to go out. He spent the days studying the Qur'ān and the nights sleeping.

One day the Saudi came to the bedsit, wearing a suit that looked made to measure and carrying a slim leather briefcase. Malik didn't know the Saudi's name, nor did he want to. The Saudi explained that Malik would be given the chance to strike at the British, to punish them for their actions, to make a statement that would be heard across the world. Malik listened to him, then hugged him and thanked him for the opportunity he was being given. "*Allahu akbar*," he said.

"*Allahu akbar*," the Saudi echoed. God is great.

The Saudi told Malik to cleanse himself and prepare for his mission. When the time came Malik would be given only an hour's notice. He was to be ready at all times, day or night.

★ ★ ★

Shepherd had three mobile phones on the seat of his Toyota. One rang as he pulled away from the house. It was Hargrove. "Bad news, Spider," said the superintendent. "Bad news, and really bad news."

"I'm listening," said Shepherd.

"Where are you?"

"*En route* to Leman Street. I'm on the two to ten shift. What's happened?"

"Angie Kerr's dead."

"What?" It was the last thing Shepherd had expected to hear.

"She killed herself."

"She was in custody. How the hell could that have happened?"

"Sleeping tablets. The custody officer thought she was asleep. They didn't try waking her until eleven and by then she was cold."

Shepherd indicated and pulled over to the side of the road. "Spider, are you there?"

"How the hell did she get sleeping tablets? Wasn't she searched when she was taken in?"

"They patted her down but I'm not sure how thoroughly. It's not as if they expected a weapon. But she had two visitors yesterday so we think it was one of them."

"Her husband?"

"Her husband's lawyer and her own lawyer."

"For God's sake, this is getting worse by the minute. Why the hell did her husband's lawyer come in?"

"We didn't know the man was his lawyer. She made a call, said she wanted legal advice before she agreed to

392

any deal with the CPS. A couple of hours later a lawyer called Gary Payne turned up and spent ten minutes with her. An hour later she spent five minutes with her own lawyer, then asked to go back to her cell."

"So Payne told her what Kerr planned to do to her and gave her the tablets?"

"That's the way I read it, but it's one thing knowing and another proving it."

Shepherd closed his eyes. He'd liked Angie Kerr and, directly or indirectly, he'd been responsible for her death. Hargrove wouldn't see it that way, of course, but Shepherd had made the decision to extend the Hendrickson investigation, Shepherd had set her up, and Shepherd had been in the car when she was arrested. If she'd never met him, she'd still be alive.

"There's more," said Hargrove. "Hendrickson's disappeared."

"He's what?"

"He hasn't been in the office since Friday."

"For God's sake, this is Wednesday. Wasn't he being watched?"

Hargrove didn't reply, which meant no.

"So the Kerr case has turned to shit, and Hendrickson's done a runner?" said Shepherd.

"With the wife dead we've got nothing on the husband," said Hargrove.

"So I've wasted the last two weeks," said Shepherd.

"If we get Hendrickson, he'll go down. Look, I know we should have had the lid on him, but the local cops have budgetary considerations. They took the decision to leave him be until we were ready to move in."

"This is a bloody nightmare," said Shepherd. "What's the point of me working my balls off if it all turns to shit down the line? Angie Kerr should have been watched — she was supposed to have been an asset. Jesus H. Christ, we were promising her witness protection and we let her husband kill her."

"She killed herself," said Hargrove.

"That's semantics, and you know it," said Shepherd, bitterly.

"There'll be an inquiry, of course, but life goes on."

"Yeah," said Shepherd. "Life goes on."

"Anything turns up on Hendrickson, I'll let you know," said Hargrove.

Shepherd ended the call. He sat in silence, staring through the windscreen with unseeing eyes. He thought about the first time he'd met her. The way she'd sat in the car, smoking and flirting with him. The fear in her eyes when the armed police had charged out of the van. And now she was dead. Not only that, she'd killed herself because of the position he'd put her in. It had been Hargrove's plan, but Shepherd had forced her into a corner with only one way out. Except that Angie had found another option. He swore under his breath. Her husband had killed her, as surely as if he'd put a gun to her head and pulled the trigger.

Shepherd was drinking a polystyrene cup of strong tea when the call came in over the main set. An IC One male with a handgun in Maida Vale. He tossed the cup out of the window as Sutherland started the car. Rose entered the address, a council estate off the Harrow

Road, into the computer while Shepherd checked it in the street directory.

"Indian country," said Rose. "The locals aren't averse to taking pot-shots out of spite."

The three men listened as a female officer relayed the details of the incident over the radio. "Neighbour saw a man with a gun enter number twenty-eight. He forced his way in. Occupant is a Sharon Jones, estranged from her husband Barry. He has convictions for assault and there's a restraining order against him." Rose scribbled on his clipboard.

"Anyone confirm that it's the husband in the house?" Rose asked.

"Negative," said the female officer. "We have no description other than IC One."

"Can you confirm that Barry Jones is IC One?"

"Affirmative," said the female officer.

Rose pulled a face. "It's like pulling teeth sometimes," he said.

"I hate domestics," muttered Sutherland. He flashed the main beams and cut in front of a double-decker bus. "Give me a Yardie with an Ingram any day of the week. You know where you are with a Yardie. Guy with a grudge against his wife can do anything. Shoot her, shoot himself, shoot us. It's like trying to second-guess a rabid dog."

"Nice analogy," said Rose.

"You know what I mean," said Sutherland. "Criminals with guns, you can generally figure what they'll do. Citizens are just plain dangerous."

They reached the Harrow Road and Sutherland killed the blues and twos. The traffic was light and there was no point in announcing their arrival.

They pulled up in front of the housing estate. There were no police cars, no paramedics. A middle-aged man was sitting on a small patch of grass in front of number twenty-eight. Rose frowned and asked the control room who else was attending.

"A local car is *en route*," said the female officer.

"Shit, we're first on the scene," said Rose. "Come on, break out the big stuff. Mike, you stay on the main set."

"Will do," said Sutherland.

The man on the grass was sitting perfectly still, his hands in his lap.

Shepherd unlocked the Hecklers and handed one to Rose, then a magazine. "Don't you think these'll spook him?" asked Shepherd.

"My experience, amateurs take one look at an MP5 and throw their hands in the air," said Rose.

"Or panic and do something stupid," said Shepherd. "It could go either way. He's got something in his hand and I reckon it's a gun."

"We have to contain the situation," said Rose.

"Let me talk to him," said Shepherd.

Rose shook his head emphatically. "No bloody way," he said. "You're not trained in hostage negotiation."

"He doesn't have a hostage," said Shepherd.

"Same difference," said Rose. "There are guys trained to talk to these psychos, and guys trained to shoot them. We wait for a negotiator."

"Sarge, the way I see it, one of two things is going to happen. He's going to pull the trigger or he's going to start waving that gun around. Either way, he's leaving here in a body-bag."

Rose stared at Shepherd. "You done this sort of thing before?"

"A couple of times," lied Shepherd.

"If he even looks like he's going to point his weapon at you, I'll take him out," said Rose.

"I'd want you to," said Shepherd.

Rose nodded slowly. "Keep out of my line of fire."

"Will do."

"And if I tell you to get out of there, you do it."

"Cheers, Sarge."

"I just hope you know what you're doing."

Shepherd put the MP5 into the boot of the Vauxhall and reached for his Glock.

"You're not going in without a gun," said Rose.

"I want to show him I'm no threat."

"So leave it in your holster."

"If it's holstered, I won't have time to draw it anyway," said Shepherd.

"You do understand why they call us armed police, don't you?"

"If he sees a gun, be it an MP5 or a Glock, he'll panic."

"Take the Taser, then." The ARVs were equipped with Taser guns capable of firing electrode-tipped wires up to twenty-one feet and delivering a debilitating 50,000-volt electric shock that would drop a man in less than a second.

"Any sort of weapon could set him off," said Shepherd. He made the Glock safe and put it into the ballistic bag in the boot with his CS spray and retractable baton. He took a deep breath. "Into the valley of death," he said, then winked at Rose. "It'll be fine, Sarge." He turned and walked towards the house, his arms out at his sides, palms open to show that he wasn't carrying.

Jones was sitting cross-legged on the grass. As Shepherd approached, he lifted the barrel of his handgun and pressed it against his right temple. Shepherd stopped a dozen paces in front of him. "Barry, I'm going to need you to do something for me," he said quietly.

"Fuck off," said Jones. He looked as if he hadn't washed or shaved for several days and Shepherd could smell the man's body odour.

"Listen to me, Barry. I need you to keep that gun exactly where it is, jammed up against your head."

Jones frowned. "What?"

Shepherd nodded at Rose. "See that guy over there? If you start waving that gun around, he'll shoot you."

"He'll be saving me the trouble."

"Just so you know," said Shepherd. "As long as you keep the gun where it is, we'll all be okay."

"Just piss off and let me get on with it," said Jones.

"You want to tell me what's made you so angry?"

"What are you? A shrink?"

"I'm the guy who's going to have to write the report if this turns to shit," said Shepherd, "and I hate writing reports."

Jones stared at him. "You're wasting your time establishing a rapport with me. I'm not interested." His finger tightened on the trigger. The gun was a Chinese knock-off of a Colt .45. It was old but it was in good condition and the barrel glistened with fresh oil.

"Where did you get the gun from, Barry?" asked Shepherd.

"Using my first name isn't going to win me over," said Jones.

"Just curious," said Shepherd. "You don't see too many of those. Practically a collector's item."

"I brought it back from Afghanistan. Souvenir."

"You were in the army?"

"Sort of. Look, piss off and let me get this done, will you?"

Shepherd sat down slowly, taking care to make no sudden movements. "I need to take the weight off," he said. "Been on my feet all day." He stretched out his legs. "The missus giving you grief, is she?" he asked.

"Ex-missus. As of yesterday."

"And what's this about? Winning her back?"

"You don't know what you're talking about."

Tyres squealed and a second ARV came round the corner. Shepherd couldn't see who was inside it. The Vauxhall braked and stopped behind Rose's car.

"Reinforcements," said Jones. "The more the merrier." He took the gun away from his head.

"Keep the gun where it is, Barry," said Shepherd. "They won't do anything while I'm here."

"You think I'm scared of a few Robocops?"

"No, but if you do anything threatening, they'll blow you away."

"So long as I'm dead I don't see it matters who does the job," said Jones.

Shepherd glanced over his shoulder. Rose was behind the Vauxhall, his MP5 targeted on Jones's chest. The doors of the newly arrived ARV opened and two men hurried over to Rose, bent at the waist.

"What were you doing in Afghanistan?" asked Shepherd.

"That's classified," said Jones. "I could tell you, but I'd have to kill you."

Shepherd smiled. So long as the man had his sense of humour, there was less chance of him pulling the trigger.

"Must have been hairy," said Shepherd.

"It was no picnic." Jones took a deep breath, then let it out slowly.

"You were in the Sass?" Jones was almost a decade older than Shepherd so it was just about possible that they had served at the same time. Shepherd was sure he'd never met the man, though.

Jones shrugged. "What's it to you?"

"I'm just trying to understand why you're doing this, that's all."

"Post-traumatic stress syndrome, is that what you think?" said Jones, contemptuously. "You really are an amateur shrink, aren't you?"

"If it's not stress, what is it? What you're doing isn't rational — you've got to admit that, right? Sitting on the grass with a gun pointed at your head."

"Quicker than hanging or slicing my wrists."

"Unless the gun jerks and you only blow off a piece of your skull. Then you spend the rest of your life being fed through a tube."

"It won't jerk," said Jones. He nodded at Rose. "Is he any good with that thing?"

"Probably not as good as you," said Shepherd.

Jones grinned ruefully. "Not fired a Five for years," he said.

"Like riding a bike," said Shepherd. "Why did you leave the Regiment?"

"RTUd. Just couldn't hack it any more."

Life in the SAS was tough, and while some troopers served virtually their whole career in the Regiment, others burned out after just a few years. Shepherd had always felt he could have done a full twenty years, but that was before Sue had become pregnant with Liam. Children changed everything.

"Couldn't hack the regular army either, not after being in the Sass. Went back to Civvy Street and it was pretty much downhill from then on."

Shepherd's earpiece crackled. "We've got you covered, Stu. Any sign that he's getting aggressive and you hit the ground." Rose's voice was close to a whisper so there was no chance of Jones overhearing.

Shepherd nodded towards the house. "Sharon's an army wife?"

"Met her after I left. She got pregnant first time we slept together and that was it. Game over."

"Boy or girl?"

"Girl. You got kids?"

"No."

"Keep it that way," said Jones. "They bring you nothing but grief and misery, wives and kids."

"You don't mean that," said Shepherd.

"You don't know what I mean."

"I know most people say that kids are what life is about."

"Yeah? And what if your wife uses your kid as a weapon to beat you over the head with? What if she poisons the kid against you so that she won't even talk to you on the phone because she's been told that you're the meanest bastard on God's earth?"

"I'm sorry," said Shepherd, but regretted the words as soon as they'd left his mouth.

"No, you're not," said Jones. "You're trying to connect so that you can talk me out of doing what I'm going to do."

"That's my job," said Shepherd. "It's what I'm paid to do."

"Yeah, well, enjoy it while you can because when they've no more use for you you'll be out on the streets." Jones took another deep breath. "You should leave now before you get blood on that nice clean Robocop uniform."

"At least tell me why you're so keen to end it all. I thought the Sass never gave up. Fought to the last man. Never give up, never leave a man behind."

Jones narrowed his eyes as he looked at Shepherd. "Do I know you?"

"No."

"What did you do before you were a cop?"

402

"Always been a cop."

"Never been in the army?"

"Never wanted to sleep in a barracks," said Shepherd.

"You look the type, that's all."

"What type?"

"The type who passes selection, gets badged."

"Is it as tough as they say it is?"

"Tougher than you can ever imagine. The Regiment has never lowered its standards. Your lot, they let anyone in now, right? Height restrictions went, then they lowered fitness levels. Now, providing you've got a pulse, you can be a cop. But the Sass, if you're not the best, don't even think about it."

"And how do you get from there to here?" asked Shepherd.

An ambulance turned into the street. No siren, no flashing lights. Softly, softly.

"You mean how did my life turn to shit? Reality, mate. A wife who thought she was marrying a hero, a daughter who thinks I hate her, a world that doesn't give a shit about who I was or what I did. You'll find out the same, once you leave the police. You are what you do, and when you stop doing it, your life stops too." He gestured at the house. A curtain flickered at an upstairs window. "Think she even cares what happens to me? She's got a restraining order against me. I'm not supposed to come within half a mile of her."

"Why's that?"

"Because she lied, told the judge I beat the crap out of her. I never did. On my daughter's life I never lifted a finger to her. I've never hit a woman. Never have and never will. Now she's got herself another man and I'm still paying her half of everything I earn. Which is half of fuck-all." Jones took a deep breath. "This is a waste of time," he said. "Mine and yours."

"I'm not going anywhere," said Shepherd.

"You talk me out of doing this now, I go to jail for a few months and I'll still end up topping myself. Might as well let me get it over with."

"What is it you want, Barry?"

"I want you to tell my daughter I loved her," said Jones. "Can you do that for me?"

"Barry —"

The gun went off and the top of Jones's head exploded. Blood splattered across Shepherd's cheek but most of the brain and skull fragments sprayed over the grass. Jones's shoulders hit the ground with a dull thud. For a second or two Shepherd thought Rose had fired but his ears were ringing and he realised Jones had pulled the trigger.

"Stu, are you okay?" Rose's voice crackled in Shepherd's ear.

Shepherd nodded but didn't say anything. The gun lay on the ground, the barrel pointing towards him. Jones's eyes were wide open. His left leg twitched once, then was still. There was a faint gurgling sound in his chest, which stopped.

Boots thudded across the grass. Shepherd felt a hand on his shoulder. "Stu, are you hit?" It was Rose, but he sounded as if he was talking through water.

404

Shepherd continued to stare at Jones. A fist-sized chunk of his skull was missing and blood pooled on the grass. There were shouts in the distance and a woman screamed.

Rose knelt in front of Shepherd, put his hands on his shoulders and looked into his eyes. "Come on, mate, it's okay."

"It's not okay," said Shepherd flatly.

"You did everything you could. It wasn't your fault."

"Who's fault was it, then?"

"He shot himself — no one forced him to pull the trigger. Just be grateful that no one else got hurt."

Rose pulled Shepherd to his feet. Two paramedics rushed across the grass with a trolley but slowed when they saw the damage to the man's skull.

Rose put an arm round Shepherd and guided him away from the body. "You need a drink," he said.

"I'm fine," said Shepherd.

"First time you've seen a kill?"

"No, but it's the first time I've seen anyone kill themselves," he said. "He was talking to me and then . . ."

"Did he mean to do it? It wasn't an accident?"

"He knew what he was doing. The gun he had doesn't have a hair trigger. You don't fire it by mistake." Shepherd looked over his shoulder at the paramedics who were zipping Jones into a black plastic body-bag. "I fucked up," he said.

"No, you didn't," said Rose. "He was hell-bent on doing it. There was nothing you could have said or done."

Shepherd wondered if that was true. Maybe if he'd told Jones that he, too, had been in the SAS, maybe if he'd made that connection Jones would have talked for longer. And if he'd kept talking maybe Shepherd could have persuaded him not to take his life. But Rule Number One of living undercover was that you never told an outsider who you really were.

Rose put his arm round Shepherd's shoulders. "You did the best you could, Stu. There aren't many guys who would have gone out there the way you did."

Shepherd gestured at the house. "The guy's daughter, is she in there?"

"Yeah. Emma, her name is."

Shepherd shook off Rose's arm and headed for the house.

"Where are you going?" asked Rose.

"I've got something to tell her," said Shepherd.

Charlie Kerr poured himself a large measure of gin, splashed in tonic water and dropped in a slice of lemon. He drained half, then poured in more gin and belched.

He took a roll of black rubbish bags from one of the kitchen drawers and went upstairs. He put the glass between the twin basins in the master bathroom, then picked up Angie's cosmetics and dumped them into one of the bags. He took her sanitary towels from the cupboard under the sink, her soap, her shampoo, her medicines, her cotton buds, everything she had ever touched, and tossed them into the bag. He took a long pull at his gin and tonic, checked that he hadn't forgotten anything, then smiled at his reflection in the mirror. He'd be able to bring back all the women he wanted now. There was no nagging wife to bitch and moan.

He carried the bag into the bedroom and dropped it on to the king-size bed. He pulled open the drawers in the dressing-table, grabbed handfuls of her underwear and thrust it into the bag with her brushes, combs and hair spray. The book she was reading — the latest John Grisham — went in, with her alarm clock and slippers. He'd barely started on her wardrobes before the bag was full. He knotted the top, opened the bedroom window and threw it out. It landed on the lawn with a thump. He cursed when he saw it had burst and the contents were strewn across the grass.

Eddie Anderson appeared from behind the garage. "You okay, boss?"

"Sort that out, Eddie." He went back to the wardrobes and filled the rest of the bags with Angie's clothing. Gary Payne had told him she was dead. But the moment she had climbed into the car with Tony Nelson, she'd signed her own death warrant. No way could he have let her live. She'd wanted him dead so badly she'd been prepared to pay a stranger to put a bullet in his head. "Stupid cow," Kerr muttered. Stupid to have thought she could ever get the better of him. Stupid not to have spotted that she was dealing with an undercover cop. Stupid to have thought he would let her live. Now she was dead and soon Tony Nelson would be, too.

He finished filling another bag with Angie's clothes and tossed it out of the window. Tony Nelson had it coming, whether or not he was a cop. He must have known who Kerr was. He must know who he was dealing with. And despite that, despite Kerr's reputation, he'd still tried to entrap Angie. That was what riled Kerr more than anything: the fact that Nelson, or whatever his real name was, thought he was so much smarter than Kerr. "I'll show you," muttered Kerr. "I'll fucking show you what happens when you mess with Charlie Kerr."

There'd be an inquest, of course, but there was no doubt that Angie had taken her own life. The cops would want to know how she got hold of the sleeping tablets and they'd be looking for someone to blame. Payne would never tell, of course. Kerr paid him handsomely for his loyalty. The custody sergeant would probably end up taking the blame for not searching her properly. And if that happened, Kerr would take pleasure in suing the police for millions. He smiled malevolently.

Sutherland drove the ARV into the car park from East Tenter Street and parked next to an undercover van belonging to the Specialist Firearms teams. It had the name of a fictitious florist on the side and a stencilled bunch of flowers that looked as if it had been done by a five-year-old.

Shepherd unlocked the gun-holder and handed the MP5s to Rose and Sutherland, then he climbed out and stretched. The heavy bulletproof vest played havoc with his spine but it had to be worn. He followed Rose and Sutherland through the rear entrance and along to the armoury. Two Specialist Firearms officers were already making their MP5s safe, the barrels pointed into Kevlar-lined metal containers with sand at the bottom while they pulled out the magazines and checked there were no rounds in the breech. The police were safety-conscious to a fault. It was a far cry from the laid-back attitude of the SAS where live weapons were carried as casually as mobile phones.

Rose and Sutherland unloaded, checked their carbines and Glocks, then handed them over to the armoury officer. As Shepherd cleared his weapons, Rose and Sutherland counted their ammunition and handed it in. "You okay, Stu?" asked Rose.

"Knackered," said Shepherd.

"You need a pint at the Bull's Head," said Rose.

"Nah, raincheck," said Shepherd. "I need some kip."

"What happened today, there's people you can talk to here. I don't know how they did it north of the border but we've got psychiatrists and occupational health advisors on tap."

Shepherd gave his Glock and ammunition to the armoury officer. "We had them in Glasgow, but they're more trouble than they're worth. I'll go for a run when I get home."

"At night?"

"Best time," said Shepherd. "Not so many cars around. A few miles will clear my head."

"What you did today, it was above and beyond, you know?"

"Didn't do any good, did it?"

"You tried, and that was more than a lot of guys would have done." Rose patted Shepherd's shoulder. "He was going to do it anyway, no matter what you said to him. He just wanted an audience."

Shepherd knew Rose was right, but that didn't make it any easier to deal with. He looked down at his bulletproof vest. There were still spots of Jones's blood on it.

Shepherd woke with a start. His heart was pounding and he swung his feet off the bed. He sat with his head in his hands, trying to work out why he had been so affected by Barry Jones's suicide. He had seen men die at close range, and some had been friends and colleagues. Jones was a stranger — yet he was the one giving him nightmares. He stood up and took deep breaths. He was wearing only pyjama bottoms and padded down the landing to the bathroom. He drank from the cold tap.

The door to Liam's bedroom was open and the glow of his nightlight seeped out. Shepherd went into the room and found Liam on his side, mouth open, hair over his eyes. Shepherd knelt beside the bed and brushed it off his face. He couldn't imagine what it was like for an eight-year-old boy to lose his mother — to see her die. He shook his head, trying to kill the train of thought.

Shepherd rested his forehead against his son's cheek and swore silently that he'd never put Liam through the pain that Emma Jones was now going through. He had lost one parent and that was enough. Liam murmured in his sleep, and Shepherd kissed him, then returned to his room and lay down. He pulled the quilt up to his chin but he doubted that he'd get any more sleep that night. Every time he closed his eyes he was back on the housing estate, waiting for Barry Jones to pull the trigger.

Eddie Anderson wasn't happy about the way things were going, but he knew there was no way he could tell Kerr. Charlie Kerr didn't listen to anyone except maybe Gary Payne, but even the lawyer had to tread carefully. Eddie drove in the outside lane at a steady ninety miles an hour, flashing his headlights at anyone in front of him. It wasn't the way he preferred to drive, but it was what Kerr wanted. Kerr hated being overtaken, so Anderson kept his foot hard on the accelerator and checked the rear-view mirror every couple of seconds.

He was sorry about what had happened to Mrs Kerr. She had never seemed the type who'd want to kill herself, but he'd never thought she'd be stupid enough to try to have Kerr killed. Charlie Kerr was a face, and anyone she hired to kill him would soon realise they'd bitten off more than they could chew.

Anderson didn't approve of the way that Kerr had treated his wife, but it wasn't his place to say anything. What Kerr had done, throwing her stuff out of the window before her body was even cold, that was wrong, too, but Anderson still hadn't said anything. Kerr had made him burn the lot at the end of the garden. He'd had to siphon petrol from the Range Rover to get it going, and he'd used a garden fork to keep turning the clothes until there was nothing left but ashes. The brushes and combs had melted and he'd smashed the perfume bottles.

Anderson had reservations about why they were driving to London, but he could tell that Kerr was in no mood to take, or even tolerate, any advice. He would have to hold his counsel. He looked across at Ray Wates. It was obvious from the way he was grinding his teeth that he was as unhappy as Anderson about what was happening. Kerr sat in the back, chain-smoking. A sawn-off shotgun and two silenced automatics were in the boot.

It was madness, thought Anderson, as the Range Rover powered past a coachload of Japanese tourists. They were driving to London to kill a cop. It made no sense at all. If Kerr wanted the cop killed, he could pay a professional, someone who could take the time to do it right. Kerr was behaving irrationally and had been since he'd watched Angie get into the car with the undercover cop. There was a glazed look in his eyes, and he kept smiling to himself. He'd been taking cocaine, too, and in the rear-view mirror Anderson saw Kerr sniff and wipe his nose with the back of his hand. Anderson had a bad feeling about the way Kerr was behaving. If they succeeded in killing the cop, the police would do whatever it took to track them down and bring them to justice. If they failed, God alone knew how it would end.

"You okay, Eddie?" asked Kerr.

"Sure, boss," said Anderson.

"Something on your mind? You're breathing like a train."

"Nothing, boss."

"Glad to hear it." Kerr opened the rear window, flicked out the butt, then lit a fresh cigarette.

It had been a quiet shift: the ARV had spent most of its time cruising around Central London. They had been called out to Hampstead Heath in the early evening by nervous gays after there had been reports of two men with guns prowling around. It turned out to be two teenagers with airguns, shooting squirrels, which had prompted Sutherland into an hour of anti-gay jokes. Towards the end of the shift they helped a team of CID officers from Paddington Green police station arrest two suspected terrorists, but the men weren't armed and went quietly, protesting their innocence.

They drove in through the East Tenter Street entrance five minutes before their shift was due to end. Sutherland noted the mileage and fuel details as Rose and Shepherd went inside. They unloaded their weapons and handed them in at the armoury, then went together to the locker room and changed into civilian clothing.

"Quick one before you head off?" asked Rose.

"Sure," said Shepherd. He wanted to go home but it was important to keep building bridges with Rose and Sutherland. Several times he had dropped hints about being short of money but he couldn't do it too often. Soon after he'd joined Hargrove's undercover unit, Shepherd had memorised a host of sports statistics going back five years and could talk knowledgeably about football, horseracing and boxing. He wasn't interested in sport but most villains were, and the information was useful to back up his legend as an enthusiastic, and unsuccessful, gambler.

They waited for Sutherland, then walked together out of the main entrance. Immediately next door was a pub called Mr Pickwick's, a green frontage with a restaurant upstairs. "What about here?" asked Shepherd.

"Too close to home," said Sutherland. "Every man and his dog walks by. Can't relax."

They headed down Leman Street and into the Bull's Head, where half a dozen Specialist Firearms officers were standing at the bar. "White team," said Rose.

Sutherland and Shepherd went over to a table and sat down. Rose carried over their drinks and they toasted each other.

"Any news of Andy?" asked Shepherd.

Sutherland frowned. "What do you mean?"

"Just wondered if there was any news, that's all."

"I don't think we're expecting any," said Rose. "He's done a bunk — I don't see how he can show his face here again."

"Strange business, all said and done," said Shepherd. He raised his glass. "What the hell? It got me back to London, didn't it?"

Anderson twisted in his seat. The Range Rover was parked down the road from the Leman Street building and they had watched Nelson and two of his colleagues walk to the Bull's Head.

"We wait for him to come out," said Kerr. He had a silenced automatic on his lap. "Then we teach the bastard a lesson."

"That pub's full of armed cops," said Wates. He was holding the sawn-off shotgun between his legs. Anderson had a silenced automatic at his feet.

"They don't take their guns home with them, Ray," said Kerr. "It's against the rules. That's the great thing about doing what we do. There are no rules." He rubbed his nose and sniffed.

Anderson wasn't happy about his boss snorting cocaine, especially not when he was going to be waving a gun around. Drugs and guns were a dangerous mix. And drugs, guns and Charlie Kerr were about as dangerous a mix as you could wish for.

Shepherd and Rose left the Bull's Head at just after eleven. They walked back to the underground car park where the SO19 officers kept their cars, arguing over who was the best boxer of all time, a conversation that had started in the pub.

Shepherd drove out first, beeping his horn and waving goodbye to the sergeant. He didn't see the black Range Rover pull away from the kerb and follow at a safe distance.

Kerr looked around. The streets were deserted. "We should do this now," he said. "He's gonna see us if we leave it much longer." He clicked off the safety. "Let's do the bastard now."

Anderson glanced at Wates. He looked as worried as Anderson felt. Attacking a cop in the street was just plain stupid, but Kerr had taken it personally, and that, with the cocaine, had pushed him over the edge. There was nothing they could say to him — or nothing that wouldn't make him as angry with them as he was with Nelson.

"Whatever you say, boss," said Anderson.

"Don't fire that unless you have to," Kerr said to Wates. "Let's try to do this as quietly as we can."

Ahead, the Toyota was stopping at a set of traffic-lights turning from amber to red.

"Okay, let's do it," said Kerr. "Let's do the bastard."

Rose was about a hundred yards from the traffic-lights when he saw the Range Rover pull up next to Marsden's Toyota. He was braking when he saw the rear passenger door of the Range Rover open and a man get out. At first Rose thought the man was going to ask directions but then he saw the gun in his hand. A large automatic with a silencer.

The man took a step towards the Toyota just as the front passenger door opened and a second man got out with a sawn-off shotgun.

Shepherd sat with his fingers loosely on the steering-wheel, deep in thought. Liam would be asleep when he got home. The way things were going, he was seeing as little of his son as he was when Liam was in Hereford with his grandparents. The sooner he got on the day shift the better, because then he could spend the evenings with him. Help him with his homework. Read him a story. Do some real father-and-son stuff.

He heard car doors open and turned. Two men were in the road, staring at him, a black Range Rover behind them. Shepherd experienced a surge of adrenaline as he recognised them. Charlie Kerr and Ray Wates. And they had guns.

Rose banged on his horn. He was reacting instinctively, not caring who the men were or why they had guns. All he knew was that Stu Marsden was in danger and he had to help. Ahead of him, the first man out of the Range Rover was bringing his gun to bear on the Toyota.

Shepherd bent down and groped under the front passenger seat for his SIG-Sauer. As he sat up again he saw Kerr turning to look at the rear of the Toyota. He heard a horn blare and an engine roar. He pushed open the door.

Kerr heard the car roar up behind them, then a squeal of brakes. He swore. Some interfering busybody was about to get what was coming to them if they weren't careful. He pointed the gun at the car and gestured with it so that the driver could see he was armed. Most people pissed themselves at the sight of a gun. In another life Kerr had been an armed robber and he'd only ever had to fire his gun once in anger. Banks, post offices, jewellers, it didn't matter: as soon as he produced a shooter everyone dived for cover.

As Shepherd opened the Toyota's door, Wates swung round the shotgun, but he was too slow. Shepherd whipped the barrel of the SIG-Sauer across his face and heard the cheekbone crack. Wates didn't go down, though, and he brought the gun up again. Shepherd grabbed at the shotgun with his left hand and brought his knee up into Wates's stomach. Wates doubled over, blood streaming from the cut on his cheek. Shepherd brought the butt of the gun down on the side of his head and kicked the shotgun under the Range Rover. Wates slumped to the ground.

Rose saw the gun in the man's hand. There was a silencer on the end. He hit the main beam sending a tunnel of dazzling light down the road. There was little an unarmed man could do against a man with a gun but he was damned if he was going to let Marsden take a bullet. He gunned the engine and moved the car forward.

Anderson watched, horrified, as Wates fell, blood pouring from his face. Now Kerr was turning towards Nelson, his upper lip curled back in a sneer, the barrel of the gun pointing up at the night sky. Anderson groped around for his weapon. He knew it had been a bad idea from the start, but now he had to see it through.

Kerr heard Wates go down and faced the Toyota. He brought up his gun. The headlights had dazzled him but he could make out Nelson standing over Wates. His finger tightened on the trigger and he aimed the gun at Nelson's head. He gritted his teeth, blinking rapidly. The gun fired but the bullet went way over Nelson's head. Kerr bellowed in frustration and took aim again.

Anderson heard a dull pop and realised Kerr had fired. He transferred his own gun to his left hand and fumbled for the door handle with the other. His bowels felt liquid and he feared that he was going to wet himself. The door opened and he stumbled out into the road.

Rose saw the man lurch out of the driver's side of the Range Rover. Marsden had hit one of the men but it was still two against one and unless Rose did something, Marsden would die. Then he realised he had a weapon he could use against the men. He stamped on the accelerator and the car leaped forward.

Shepherd heard the roar of the engine as he dropped into a crouch. The first shot had missed his head by inches and Kerr was about to fire again. Shepherd swung up his SIG-Sauer and fired twice in quick succession. Both shots hit Kerr in the chest and he fell backwards, mouth working soundlessly.

Shepherd turned sideways and saw Anderson taking aim, his face contorted by fear or hatred. Shepherd swung his gun round but Anderson had him in his sights. All he had to do was pull the trigger and it would all be over.

Rose gripped the steering-wheel and pressed his foot on the brake, not too hard because he wasn't wearing his seatbelt. The car smashed into the man with the gun, hurling him against the door of the Range Rover with such force that it broke off its hinges. The man fell back on to the door, arms flailing. The gun fell out of his hand, and he slumped to the tarmac.

Rose climbed out of the car. Marsden was leaning against his Toyota, both hands on the butt of his gun.

"What the hell's going on?" asked Rose.

"We've got to get out of here."

"You just shot a man," said Rose.

"Rosie, I can't be caught here," he said. He tucked the gun into the waistband of his trousers. "I'm not going down for this."

Rose glared at him. "Okay, follow me," he said. He got back into the car, reversed away from the Range Rover, then sped off down the road.

Shepherd followed Rose as he drove off the main road and zigzagged through side-streets, his eyes constantly checking the rear-view mirror. They weren't being followed. Rose parked behind an overflowing builder's skip, got out of the car, jogged to the Toyota and climbed into the front passenger seat. "What the hell was that about, Stu?"

Shepherd couldn't tell Rose the truth about Kerr, because Shepherd was an undercover cop and Rose was his target. "Just leave it, Rosie," he said. If Rose reported what had happened, Shepherd's assignment was over. If Shepherd told Rose who Kerr was, his assignment was over. The only way out would be to use what had happened to his advantage.

"Leave it?" said Rose. "You just shot a man and I hit one with my car."

"They attacked me, remember?"

"So why aren't we calling this in?" asked Rose. "Why did we run? And what the hell were you doing with a gun?"

Shepherd shrugged and avoided eye-contact. The pressure had to come from Rose. "Just forget it ever happened."

"What the hell is wrong with you?" asked Rose. "Have you any idea how much shit we're in?"

Shepherd's mind was racing for a workable story. It was always best to go in with the legend in place so that all contingencies could be anticipated. In a good undercover operation every move was planned in advance so that nothing could go wrong. Thinking on your feet got the adrenaline going but it could lead all too easily to disaster.

"I mean it, Stu. Tell me what the fuck you've got yourself into, or I call this in, right now."

Shepherd took a deep breath. "I owed them money."

"So they were from the Halifax, were they? You behind on your mortgage?"

Shepherd flashed him a sarcastic smile. "Good to see you've kept your sense of humour," he said.

"It must be one hell of a lot of money for them to come after you with guns."

421

"Thirty grand, and some," said Shepherd.

Rose raised his eyebrows. "How the hell did you run up a debt like that?"

"I don't want to get into this. It was my own fault, and now I've got to sort it."

"Yeah, regular Gary Cooper, you are." Rose leaned towards him and dropped his voice to a low whisper. "Think of this as a confession. You have sinned, my son, but by repenting you will be saved."

"I'm not a Catholic," said Shepherd.

Rose's voice hardened. "And I'm not a fucking priest. I saved your life back there, so spill your guts."

"It's a gambling debt," said Shepherd, slowly. "At least, twenty grand is. There's more than ten grand of juice. Interest."

"And you can't pay?"

"For fuck's sake, Rosie, didn't you hear what I just said? Thirty grand. Could you lay your hands on thirty grand cash? That's more than a year's salary after tax and insurance and all the rest of the shit they take off us."

"Haven't you got a house you could have mortgaged?"

"The only asset I've got is the car."

"How bad a gambler are you? You're what, thirty-three, thirty-four, and the only thing you've got to your name is a three-year-old Toyota?"

"I had a bad year," said Shepherd. "Okay, a couple of bad years."

"Horses?"

"Some horses. But football recently. Long-odds stuff. Liverpool to win three-one with Owen scoring twice, that sort of stuff."

"Is that why you had to leave Scotland?"

Rose had taken the bait. Shepherd had set up the story and Rose was filling in the gaps, which was always the best way. He nodded.

"And you thought by moving to London they wouldn't find you?"

Shepherd nodded again. "My father's here, though, and he does need me around. But, yeah, I thought they wouldn't be able to find me down here."

They sat in silence for a while, listening to the engine click as it cooled.

"The gun," said Rose, eventually. "Where did it come from?"

"I bought it from a guy in Glasgow. It's untraceable. I needed protection."

"Suppose I offered you a way of getting thirty grand. And more."

Shepherd knew what was coming next. "I'm listening," he said.

"We can help each other, two birds with one stone."

"What did you have in mind?"

"What happened out there, we're in this together."

"No arguments there," agreed Shepherd.

"Are you prepared to take it a step further? Become proactive?"

"If the rewards are there, sure. Depends what you have in mind."

"Remember the pizza place? Mike was saying you made a crack about the money."

"It was just that. A crack."

"But it was a good point. Drugs money is fair game. You take it, who loses out? Drugs-dealers. Do we care? Of course we don't. Does anyone?"

"What are you saying?" said Shepherd, although he knew exactly what Rose was proposing. It was what he'd been working towards over the past week. The attack on his life had been unforeseen, but it had shown Rose that Shepherd had the qualities to take Andy Ormsby's place.

"I'm saying that if the circumstances were right, we could help each other. I need a lot of cash."

"For Kelly?"

Rose's eyes narrowed. "Who told you about her?"

"Mike said she was ill."

"That was none of his business. Or yours."

Shepherd held up his hands. "It came up in conversation. But it gives you a reason for needing money, so I see where you're coming from."

"You've no idea where I'm coming from," he said. "You haven't the faintest idea."

"She's really sick?"

"She's going to die unless I do something. But that's not the issue. The issue is how far you're prepared to go. I've got the weaponry, I'm in the process of gathering the intel. All I need is the manpower."

"You mean there's more than you and me?"

"It takes a three-man team."

"You, me and . . .?"

424

Rose smiled tightly. "Let me talk to the third party first. Just in case . . ."

"Just in case he doesn't trust me?"

"It's like being in the ARV. We all have to trust each other one thousand per cent. We've all got too much to risk."

"Assuming he's okay with me, what's the next step?"

"We work out where and when."

"And we rip off a drugs-dealer?"

"That's the plan."

Shepherd whistled softly. "You are one hell of a dark horse."

"I'll fix up a meet tomorrow and call you."

Shepherd ran a hand through his hair. "How soon before we move?"

"Next week. I've got a deadline, money-wise."

Shepherd sat in his car for a while, looking at his house. His heart was still racing. He felt guilty, but not because of what he'd done to the men who'd attacked him. He'd reacted instinctively, as he'd been trained. The guilt came from having lied to Rose. He liked the man. He was a good cop, too, reliable and disciplined, and he'd crossed the line because he wanted to provide for his daughter. He'd helped Shepherd in the street, with little or no thought for his own safety. If Rose hadn't turned up there was a good chance that he would have been killed. Rose had saved his life, but Shepherd didn't want to dwell on that. Rose's reward was going to be a long prison sentence, and Shepherd didn't want to think what that would mean for his daughter.

He let himself into the house. There was a light on in the kitchen and Katra was at the sink, washing up. "Hiya, Katra," he said. She was wearing a white dressing-gown. For a moment he thought it was Sue's, but then he realised it fitted Katra perfectly and she was smaller than his wife had been. He switched on the kettle.

"I'll make you coffee," said Katra. "And I have a beef and paprika stew and baked potatoes in the oven."

"It's nearly midnight!" exclaimed Shepherd.

"You have eaten already?" she asked.

"No, but I worry about you staying up so late on my account when you've got to take Liam to school. How was he today?"

"He is a good boy," she said. "He wants to spend more time with you."

"I know. I won't always be as busy as this. These shifts are unusual." Even as the words left his mouth, Shepherd knew he wasn't telling the truth. He often worked late, no matter what case he was on, and sometimes he was away for days on end. Villains didn't work nine to five, and neither did undercover cops. "I've got to make a call first," he said. "Thanks for the food."

She beamed.

"You go to bed. I'll get it out of the oven."

Shepherd waited until she had gone upstairs, then phoned Hargrove. "I'm in," he said. "Rose tried to recruit me tonight."

426

"Excellent," said Hargrove. "That was quick work."

"I had help," said Shepherd. He explained to the superintendent about Kerr's attack and how he'd reacted.

"What state are the casualties in?" Hargrove asked.

"Kerr's dead, I'm sure. Shot in the chest. I hit Wates hard. Anderson was hit by Rose's car. I'm sorry it got so messy."

"Not your fault, Spider. I guess what we need to worry about is how the hell Kerr found out who you are."

"He could have followed me from Manchester. But if he did, shame on me for not spotting it."

"The Manchester operation was over and Angie Kerr was in custody. You were heading home."

"And I let my guard down." It was something he was going to have to think about. If Kerr had followed him to Leman Street, he could just as easily have gone to his home. His carelessness had put his son at risk. That was unforgivable.

"What happens next?" asked Hargrove.

"Rose is going to call me tomorrow and set up a meet with his partner."

"We'll arrange surveillance," said Hargrove.

"No," said Shepherd quickly. "They're cops, they'll know what to look for. I'm not even going to wear a wire for this first meeting."

"I don't think you should go in alone," said Hargrove.

"Rose is convinced I'm with him," said Shepherd. "He saw me shoot Kerr and I spun him a yarn about gambling debts in Glasgow. Tomorrow's just about meeting this other guy."

"And who do you think it is?" asked Hargrove.

"If I had to name a name I'd say Mike Sutherland, but only because he's so close to Rose. And they were both in the ARV with Ormsby."

"We could put a tail on Sutherland."

"I wouldn't," said Shepherd. "I'd rather see what they've got planned."

"Catch them red-handed?"

"Maybe not. But I'd like to know who they're planning to rip off."

"It's your call, Spider."

"As soon as I've had the meet I'll fill you in." Shepherd cut the connection, then went upstairs.

Liam was fast asleep, hugging his pillow. It scared Shepherd, how much he loved his son. He would do anything for him. He wondered if Keith Rose was sitting by his daughter, watching her sleep, wanting to be a good father, promising to do whatever it took to ensure that she'd be healthy and happy. He felt uncomfortable. He kissed his son then went to his bathroom. He felt dirty and wanted to shower.

Shepherd got up early and had breakfast with Liam, who asked his father if he could drive him to school. Shepherd said yes. "Great!" shrieked Liam.

"I could drive you both," said Katra.

"Nah, that's okay," said Shepherd. "I'll take the Toyota."

"That's a horrible old car," said Liam. "Why are you driving it?"

"It's for work."

"The Golf's much better —" Liam stopped and put down his knife and fork. His lower lip was trembling.

Shepherd laid a hand on his son's arm.

"I'm sorry," said Liam.

"I keep doing the same thing."

Liam pushed away his plate and stood up. "I'll get my bag." He ran out of the kitchen and thumped up the stairs.

"What's wrong?" asked Katra.

"His mum drove a black VW Golf," said Shepherd. "It was the car they were in when they crashed."

Katra looked horrified. "When his mother died?"

Shepherd nodded.

She wiped her hands on a tea-towel. "I'll go and talk to him."

"I will," said Shepherd. He hurried upstairs. Liam was sitting on his bed, clutching his schoolbag. Shepherd sat down next to him. "I miss her, too," he said.

"I miss her all the time."

"We'll always miss her. That's what happens when someone you love goes away."

"She didn't go away," said Liam. "She died."

"I know."

"Why do people say that? Why do they say she went away when that's not what happened? Gran says that. So does Granddad. They say she went away but if she went away she'd come back. But she's never coming back, is she?"

Shepherd felt tears prick his eyes and fought them back. "No," he said, "but that doesn't mean she's not in our hearts, because she is. She'll always be with us."

"But not really, right? She's never going to hug me again, is she?"

Shepherd felt a tear run down his right cheek and brushed it away. "No," he said. "But I'm still here. I can hug you."

Suddenly Liam reached for him, and buried his head in his father's chest. "I don't want you to die, Dad," he sobbed.

"I won't," said Shepherd. "Not for a long, long time."

Shepherd held Liam until he stopped crying, then wiped his eyes and told him to go and wash his face. He carried Liam's schoolbag into the hallway and waited until Liam was ready to go.

Katra was standing at the bottom of the stairs and ruffled Liam's hair as he went by. She looked up at Shepherd, who mouthed, "It's okay."

He went after Liam and gave him his bag. As they walked to the Toyota, one of Shepherd's mobiles rang — his Stuart Marsden phone. He told Liam to go back into the house while he took the call. It was Rose.

"Where are you?"

"Home," said Shepherd.

"You up for a meet?"

"Where?"

"Wapping High Street. Outside the tube station. In an hour."

Shepherd glanced at his watch. "I'll be there," he said.

As he put away the phone he saw Liam standing at the front door. Katra was behind him, her hand on his shoulder. Shepherd could see from the look on Liam's face that he knew what he was going to say. "I'm sorry," he said.

"Work?" said Liam.

Shepherd nodded.

"You can drive me to school, can't you, Katra?"

"Of course. I'll get changed," said Katra. She went inside. Liam walked over to the CRV.

"Liam, I'm sorry," said Shepherd.

"It doesn't matter."

"I'll take you to school tomorrow."

"Tomorrow's Saturday," said Liam.

"Well, we'll do something tomorrow. It's my day off, too."

Liam climbed into the back of the CRV. He fastened his seatbelt and deliberately avoided his father's eyes.

Shepherd waited at the front door until Katra came downstairs. She was wearing the green parka and sand-coloured cargo pants she'd had on the first time they'd met.

"I'll phone you later," he said. She waved and got into the car. Shepherd watched them drive away, hoping that Liam would wave. He didn't.

He set the burglar alarm and locked the house, then drove the Toyota across town. He found a parking space about ten minutes' walk from Wapping High Street. He sat for a few minutes, staring at his reflection in the rear-view mirror, preparing himself mentally for what he was about to do. He was going to lie to a man who thought he was his friend. It wasn't the first time and it wouldn't be the last. He put the Stuart Marsden phone into his jacket pocket and the others into the glove compartment.

He got out of the Toyota and walked slowly towards Wapping tube station. Rose was already there, wearing a long black coat over blue jeans and a black polo-neck sweater. He nodded at Shepherd and started walking down the street. Shepherd caught up with him and the two men walked in silence. Rose turned into a side-street and they went between two warehouse conversions, ornate black metal grilles over the windows, CCTV cameras covering all angles. Fortresses for City workers.

Rose made a left turn and walked up to a modern block. Concrete stairs led to the entrance. Someone had spray-painted "HOMES FOR LOCALS NOT YUPPIE SCUM" across the glass door that led into the building. A line of thirty door-bells was set into a stainless-steel intercom system, covered by a CCTV camera above the door. Rose pressed one of the bells. Flat twenty-seven. Shepherd heard a tinny voice but couldn't make out what was said. Rose smiled apologetically at him. "He wants me to pat you down."

"He what?"

Shepherd tried to look surprised — and angry. It was a narrow line to tread but one he'd trodden dozens of time in the past. A search meant a lack of trust, and anyone would take offence at not being trusted. But protesting too much could be as dangerous as not protesting at all. The trick was to call it just right: righteous indignation followed by annoyed resignation. "You approached me, remember?" said Shepherd. "I didn't come knocking on your door."

"Just humour him," said Rose. "It's his flat we're going into."

"What does he think I'm carrying? A gun?"

Rose looked uncomfortable.

"He thinks I'm wearing a *wire*? For God's sake, why would I?"

"Like I said, humour him. Please."

Shepherd sighed and raised his arms. Rose patted him down quickly and efficiently. He made Shepherd take out his mobile phone and examined it carefully.

"It's a phone, Rosie."

"They can bug them so they transmit all the time," said Rose, "with or without your co-operation." He pulled off the back, took out the battery and the Sim card, then handed the pieces back to Shepherd and continued his search. He missed nothing, even patting Shepherd's groin and running his hands up and down his inner thighs. If Shepherd had been wearing any sort of transmitter or recording device, Rose would have found it.

"Satisfied?" said Shepherd.

"Don't get ratty," said Rose. "We get caught doing this and they'll throw away the key." He went back up the stairs and pressed the bell again. "He's okay," Rose said, into the intercom. The glass door buzzed and Rose pushed it open. Shepherd followed him into the hallway. There was a lift to the right but Rose headed up the stairs. The flat was on the second floor and the door was already open.

"Out here," said a voice.

Shepherd walked through what was clearly a rented property. Cherrywood laminated flooring, a beige sofa, a glass-topped coffee-table, a small television and DVD player. There was nothing of a personal nature. The framed prints on the cream-painted walls were as bland and nondescript as the sofa. At the far end of the room, open french windows led to a large square balcony, overlooking the Thames. There were three white plastic chairs and a matching round table on which stood a cafetière, mugs, a carton of low-fat milk, a box of sugar cubes, and a basket of croissants. The occupant of the flat was standing with his back to the window. He turned as Shepherd walked out. It was Ken Swift.

"Do you want coffee, Stu?" he asked.

"That would be good," said Shepherd, casually. Swift was watching him closely, trying to gauge his reaction, but Shepherd played it cool. Swift poured coffee into the three mugs.

"Milk?" he asked Shepherd.

"Black, no sugar."

Swift poured a dash of milk into Rose's coffee and handed it to him, then he and Rose dropped on to the chairs.

"Nice place," said Shepherd.

"I can walk to Leman Street, which is a plus," said Swift. "Just the one bedroom, but the balcony makes up for it. All I can afford at the moment."

"Three divorces?"

"First wife got fifty per cent, second wife got fifty per cent of what was left. Wife number three is aiming for the house and everything in it, which doesn't leave me much. You're better off being single, Stu. And don't get me started on kids. I'm responsible for them right through university, and at the moment I'm lucky to see them twice a month."

Shepherd sipped his coffee.

"Rose says three guys attacked you. Three guys from Glasgow."

"They might have been from Manchester. I borrowed the money in Glasgow but it was a Manchester bookie."

"You were lucky."

"Rosie helped me. If it hadn't been for him, we wouldn't be having this conversation."

"You had a gun?"

"For my own protection."

"You know the guy you shot is dead?" said Swift. "There's a full-scale murder inquiry on the go."

"No one saw us. No forensics. Rosie and I can alibi each other if necessary. No way will they pin anything on us."

"And you owed them money?"

"Thirty grand."

"Gambling debts, Rosie said."

"I was a twat, I know. I just kept getting in deeper and deeper."

"So you're up for what we're planning?"

"I don't know what it is," said Shepherd. "Ripping off a drugs-dealer is all I know."

"But in principle?"

"In principle I'm more than happy to relieve them of their ill-gotten gains. So long as we don't have to go in with guns blazing."

"We don't intend to hurt anyone," said Rose. "We're not vigilantes. It's not about putting them out of business. It's solely about money. They have it. We take it."

"Count me in," Shepherd said. "But I could do with knowing one thing."

"What's that?"

"You've done this before, haven't you?"

Swift and Rose exchanged a look. Then Swift nodded. "Once. We hit a crack-dealing crew in Harlesden."

"And was Andy Ormsby involved?"

Swift's eyes narrowed to slits. "Who the fuck told you about Andy?"

Shepherd returned the man's stare. "Andy disappeared. You and Rose barely mention his name. You're a man short, which means you're a man down, and you don't have to be Sherlock Holmes to figure out that Andy's the missing link."

"He took a bullet. We did what we could but he died before we could get him to a doctor. We buried him."

"Just like that?"

"*No!*" Rose had raised his voice. "We thought long and hard about what to do."

"And if he hadn't died, would you have taken him to hospital?"

"There was nothing we could do," said Rose.

"That wasn't what I was asking," said Shepherd. "If you screw up again and I get shot, what happens to me?"

"We didn't screw up," said Swift.

"Every time shots are fired, someone's screwed up," said Shepherd.

Swift stood up. "This isn't about what happened to Andy. It's about where we go from here."

"I understand that, but I need to know exactly what I'm getting into," said Shepherd. "Where did you bury him?"

"Why do you want to know?" asked Swift.

"If there's a body out there that could lead back to me, I want to know it'll never be found."

"The New Forest," said Swift. "And don't worry, no one will find him."

"He didn't have anyone close," said Rose. "It's not like he was married or had kids."

"Like me," said Shepherd. "No one would miss me either. But that's not to say I want to end up buried in the New Forest." He sipped his coffee. "I don't mean to sound negative, but it's not every day you get an offer to take part in an armed robbery."

"We don't look at it that way," said Swift. He picked up a croissant. "We're stealing from drugs-dealers. Bad guys. The money we take is drugs money. If we didn't take it, they'd only be using it to wholesale more drugs."

"So we're sort of Robin Hoods?" said Shepherd.

"The only way it can go wrong is if someone gets hurt," said Rose. "If we get away clean there's no way they can report it."

"And three is enough?" asked Shepherd.

"Three's best," said Rose. "Two to go in, one to drive."

"And my role would be?"

"You come with me, Ken stays with the car," said Rose.

"And weaponry?"

"We've an Ingram, there's a Python .45 and a Glock. We're well sorted. Whatever happens, you should ditch your gun."

Rose drank his coffee and Swift put another chunk of croissant into his mouth.

Shepherd put down his mug. "And what would my take be?"

"Three-way split," said Swift. "How much we get depends on who we turn over."

"How much did you get from the Yardies?" asked Shepherd.

"It didn't work out as planned," Rose said awkwardly.

"In what way?"

"The cash wasn't there. They'd done a coke deal, so we took the drugs."

Shepherd raised his eyebrows. "There's no way I'm being paid in gear," he said.

"I sold it to some Paddies," said Rose.

"You did a drugs deal?"

"It was a one-off."

Shepherd was astounded. He was sitting opposite two long-serving police officers who had admitted to murder, armed robbery, and drugs-dealing. "One more question," he said.

"This is turning into *Mastermind*," said Swift.

"It's a big step," said Shepherd.

"Except that you killed a man last night," said Swift, "and put two more in hospital."

"Self-defence," said Shepherd.

"Self-defence or not, you'll be off the force if it comes out. Maybe worse."

"No argument there," said Shepherd.

"So, what's the question?"

"Knowing what I know, what happens if I turn you down?"

"After what happened last night, we know enough about each other to cause everyone a whole lot of grief."

"So if I say no, I just walk away?"

"Like I said, you killed a guy last night. Rosie and I did what we did. We don't have to force you to do anything against your will. It's your choice."

Shepherd picked up his mug. "It's good coffee," he said.

"I don't like instant," said Swift. "It's all about grinding it fresh each time."

Shepherd took a sip. "I'm in," he said.

Rose looked at Swift and nodded enthusiastically. "Great," he said.

"The three musketeers," said Shepherd. "All for one and all that shit."

Swift leaned over and shook his hand. "Good to have you aboard, Stu."

"It's just the one job," said Rose. "I need one more hit. So does Ken. One hit and we walk away."

"One hit," repeated Shepherd. "That's all I need." He put his mug on the table and stood up.

"Can you find your own way out?" asked Rose.

"Sure."

As Shepherd stepped through the french windows, Swift called after him, "Hey, haven't you forgotten something?"

Shepherd turned. "What?"

"That SWAT shirt I lent you, the one from New York. I want it back, you know. Sentimental value."

"I'll get it cleaned," said Shepherd. He went back through the sitting room and out of the front door. He knew the two men were talking about him, but that was to be expected. He replayed the conversation in his head as he walked along Wapping High Street. It had gone well. He'd played it just right. Not too keen, not too suspicious, not too eager to break the law. They thought they could trust him because of what had happened the previous night, that he was as much of a criminal as they were. A cold wind was blowing off the Thames and Shepherd shivered.

He went back to his car, taking a circuitous route to check that he wasn't being followed. He reassembled his mobile phone as he walked. As it was the Stuart Marsden phone he didn't use it to call Hargrove. When he was in his car, he took his other two mobiles out of the glove compartment and used one to phone Hargrove. "It's Ken Swift," he said, "the inspector with Specialist Firearms Team Amber."

"You met with him?"

"He's got a rented flat in Wapping High Street."

"And what's the plan?"

"He and Rosie are putting together a robbery. Drugs-dealers, same as they did in Harlesden. I'll be taking Andy Ormsby's place."

"They talked about him?"

"Shot by one of the Yardies. Died in the back of the van they were using. Buried in the New Forest."

"So that's it, then?"

"You want to move in on what I have?"

"Did they mention the Python?"

"They're going to use it on the next job."

"We need that gun, Spider. The icing on the cake. We'll get dogs looking for Ormsby's body. With what we've got, Rose will roll on Swift. You won't be involved."

"They're cops, and they're not stupid," said Shepherd. "You bust them straight after they've talked to me and they'll put two and two together."

"What are you suggesting?"

"Let it run for a few days. Rose has to move soon because he needs the money for his daughter's medical bills. Swift said they were putting something together now, so let them fill me in on it and bust us *en route*.

Take me in with them, then they'll assume I've cut a deal. That way I stay as Stuart Marsden, bent cop, and don't show my hand."

"You're okay with that?"

Shepherd grimaced. He wasn't happy about setting up Rose and Swift but he had to keep his undercover status secret. The more people who knew who he was and what he did, the harder it would be for him to operate in future. And the greater the risk to Liam. "It's the best way," he said.

"Still no wire?" asked Hargrove.

"I don't want to show out on this case," said Shepherd.

"I understand," said Hargrove. "Swift needs money, does he?"

"Two ex-wives and one on the way." Shepherd cut the connection, then tapped in another number. The major answered. "Gannon."

"It's Spider. Don't suppose you're free for a chat?"

"Where are you?"

"Wapping."

"I'm in Westminster, on my way to talk to a select committee who want reassurance that all's well with the world. It isn't, of course, but I'm supposed to sound confident that we can handle anything that's thrown at us. This afternoon I'm over at New Scotland Yard to meet their anti-terrorism guys. All good stuff."

"No sweat. If you're busy it can wait."

"If you can get to the Embankment within half an hour we'll talk before I go in to the great and the good."

442

"Do you know a guy called Barry Jones? From the Regiment? He just killed himself."

"Doesn't ring a bell. But I'll check. Is that what you want to talk about?"

"That's part of it."

Shepherd ended the call and drove westwards. He parked in a multi-storey near Charing Cross station and walked down to Victoria Embankment. It wasn't a problem for him to be seen with the major: Stuart Marsden was an armed policeman not a drugs-dealer or a gangland hitman, so it wouldn't be out of character for him to know a member of the SAS. The worst that would happen was that he'd have to lie, but lying was second nature.

Shepherd headed along the paved walkway on the north side of the river. It felt good to be out in regular clothes rather than driving around in the ARV in his combat gear. He wasn't used to working regular hours. His usual roles involved passing himself off as a career criminal, and one of the perks of the criminal fraternity was being able to choose your hours.

Shepherd spotted the major looking out over the river, a metallic attaché case in his left hand.

"Good to see you're not in uniform, Spider," he said as they shook hands. His was the size of a shovel and he wore the Regimental signet ring on his little finger.

They walked together towards Westminster Bridge.

"Thanks for this, Major."

"I was early, anyway. I hate these briefings to politicians, but at least they get me out of the barracks." He hefted the metal case. "All I do is wait for the sat phone to ring, and when it does all hell breaks loose. But until it rings, it's just me and four walls. With a staff sergeant who still can't make a decent brew."

"It's like that in the ARV. We spend hours driving around waiting for something to kick off. But when it does, there's all sorts of rules and regulations about what we can and can't do. It's like going into battle with one hand tied behind your back."

"Any idea how long you'll be undercover this time?"

"I've almost cracked it."

"Hell of a job, Spider."

"If they're bent, they deserve what's coming to them."

"I meant a hell of a job for you. Winning their trust so that you can betray them. Especially when they're cops."

"I try not to think of it that way," said Shepherd. "I'm just gathering evidence. If they weren't bad, they wouldn't have anything to worry about."

"It would do my head in," said Gannon. "We tried using our guys undercover in Ireland, but it never worked."

"Different skills," said Shepherd.

"Yeah. They grew their hair long, wore the right clothes and got the accent, but they just didn't fit."

"Everyone knows everyone else over the water. You were trying to blend into an incestuous community."

444

"The UK criminal fraternity's not that big — aren't you worried you'll be rumbled by someone you've come across before?"

"I'm good with names and faces," said Shepherd. "I can usually spot trouble before it happens. And, more often than not, I leave an operation before the bad guys are busted so no one's the wiser."

"But you're doing okay?"

Shepherd knew Gannon wasn't talking about work. Was he okay about Sue? "One day at a time," he said. "That's what they say, isn't it? You take each day as it comes, and after a while it doesn't hurt as much. Eventually life gets back to normal."

"It's easy to say, I know."

"I miss her so damn much."

"That'll never change."

"It would be easier if there was someone to blame." Shepherd took a deep breath. "There's no one I can talk it through with," he went on. "Liam's too young, Sue's parents are trying to deal with their own grief. The unit's given me a psychologist but she's more interested in knowing if I'm up to the job."

They sat down on a bench beside the London Eye. Shepherd grinned. "Let me give you a crap analogy." He pointed to the giant wheel. "That's life, in a way. We all get one circuit, then it's someone else's turn. But with the whole world to experience, most people never get beyond the pod they're born in. Once round and then off into the long night."

"Fuck me, Spider, how depressed are you?"

"Don't worry, I'm not after the meaning of life. It's just that there are times when you wonder what the point of it is."

"Life? Or the London Eye?" Gannon smiled. "The London Eye's a tourist attraction — but life? Who the hell knows?"

"The guy who topped himself in front of me — Barry Jones. We'd started on a meaning-of-life conversation before he pulled the trigger."

"He had a history of depression. That's why he was RTUd. He was a loose cannon, waiting to go off."

"His life had turned to shit, was what he said. Wife had left him, found a new man, wouldn't let him see his daughter."

"He used to knock her around. That's what I was told. Any problems he had, he brought them on himself."

"That's not the way he saw it. He said he loved his kid, that his wife was turning her against him, and that he'd never laid a finger on her."

"He had a short fuse — it was in his file. He decked an officer once but it was in the field and the officer was due to move on so nothing came of it."

"I tried to see the little girl afterwards," said Shepherd. "Jones asked me to tell her that he loved her, but her mother wouldn't let me into the house. Said I was a murderer — she seemed to think we'd killed him. I had his blood all over me."

"Probably best that you didn't see the child, then. It would have been pretty traumatic for her. The gear that

SO19 wear is as intimidating as our kit, with or without bloodstains."

"I keep having dreams that she was at the window watching her dad shoot himself. She wasn't — I know she wasn't."

"Small mercies," said Gannon. "You wouldn't want a kid seeing something like that. Probably wouldn't benefit from seeing you, either, to be honest. She's always going to remember you as the man who was there when her dad died."

"Yeah, you're probably right. Maybe I'll write her a letter or something." He scowled. "Nah, the mother would just throw it away. But she has to know her dad loved her. If I don't tell her, she'll go through life thinking he didn't."

"You're not responsible for his actions," said Gannon. "You don't owe him anything."

"He was Sass, and it was his last request," said Shepherd. "And if I don't carry it out, who will? Jeez, what state must he have been in to pull the trigger? We were talking and then, *bang*, he was gone."

"Jones lived for the Regiment. It was his be-all and end-all. When he was RTUd, he fell apart. It happens." Gannon took a packet of Wrigley's gum from his pocket and offered a piece to Shepherd. Shepherd shook his head. Gannon popped a stick into his mouth and chewed. "It's like greyhounds. They're bred for one reason. To win races. As soon as they're past their best, they're surplus to requirements. Twenty-five thousand healthy dogs are put down every year just so that the punters can bet a few quid on a Saturday night."

"It's a better analogy than my London Eye."

"It's the way it is. Greyhounds aren't bred as family pets, they're bred to win races. The Sass doesn't train men to be good fathers or husbands or to run businesses. It trains them to jump out of aeroplanes, march through hazardous terrain with back-breaking loads and kill people. Once your Sass days are over, those skills aren't especially useful. You know what most guys used to end up doing after they left the Regiment?"

"The building trade."

"Dead right. Brickies or scaffolders. I've had guys end up as gravediggers and lollipop men. Most leave thinking they're going to earn a living as mercenaries or security consultants, but most end up on building sites or guarding car parks. Iraq has thrown up job opportunities but not everyone's suitable for close-protection work. And the ones who've been out of the Regiment for a few years have lost their edge. Life's tough, and it's even tougher for our guys out in the real world. I'm sorry Barry Jones took his life, but he's one of half a dozen former members of the Regiment so far this year."

That was news to Shepherd. "And there's nothing anyone can do?"

"It's a rough old world. We're the SAS, not the Samaritans. I'm not happy about the way it is, Spider, and I do what I can. But I've enough on my plate with the Increment. So, tell me about the trick-cyclist."

"My boss reckons I might be stressed out. It was tough going undercover in a high-security prison. Then there was Sue's accident. And I've been pretty much flat out since I started with the unit."

"You seem straight and level to me."

"Thanks."

"You were never the most relaxed of guys, but that's the nature of our job."

"Thanks again. I'll tell her when I see her next."

"Ah, the plot thickens. A woman?"

"Oh, yes."

"I guess it's difficult for her to relate to, right?"

"She's a smart girl but, yeah, she's never fired a gun in anger."

"Not many people have."

"I don't see why they should expect me to spill my guts to a stranger, someone who has no conception of what it's like to be in combat or to work undercover."

"I doubt they'd be using her if she wasn't qualified."

"Oh, she's good all right. Downright bloody devious. Keeps trying to get me to talk about Sue without asking me full on."

"Why's she interested in Sue?"

"She reckons I'm not dealing with her death. I get the feeling she thinks I should be crying my eyes out."

"We all deal with death in our own way," said Gannon.

"There's nothing wrong with me just because I'm not bursting into tears every other day."

"I didn't say there was," said Gannon. "I know how much she meant to you. You gave up the Regiment for her."

449

"For her and Liam," said Shepherd. "She wanted the quiet life. Me at home with a pipe and slippers." He smiled ruefully. "Out of the frying-pan and into the bloody fire. She didn't realise the cops would have me undercover. She saw more of me when I was with the Sass."

"How's Liam handling it?"

"How does any kid deal with the death of his mum? She was the world to him."

"Have you talked to him about it?"

"It's like pulling teeth."

"Like father, like son," said Gannon.

"You think he gets it from me?" said Shepherd.

"You're his role model," said Gannon. "If you're the strong, silent type he'll try to be the same."

Shepherd stared up at the cloudless blue sky. "Maybe that's it."

"What's eating you, Spider?" asked Gannon, quietly.

High overhead a 747 banked towards Heathrow. "I'm not sure. There's something not right but I don't know what it is." He wasn't used to telling people how he felt: his whole undercover life was spent masking his true feelings.

"Maybe Jones made you aware of your own mortality."

"I'm not suicidal," said Shepherd. Too quickly: he'd sounded defensive. "And I've seen men die. Hell, I've killed them close up, too."

"Yeah, but they were the enemy. You didn't get to know them before you pulled the trigger. You had a chance to talk to Jones, to get inside his head — you let

450

him get inside yours too. And there were obvious similarities to your own situation."

"Maybe." Shepherd was unconvinced. He was no stranger to death. He'd killed on missions and slept the sleep of the just. He'd seen friends and colleagues die, too — a young trooper had died after a snake bite in the Borneo jungle during a training exercise. He'd seen another fall to his death in a climbing accident. He would never forget the men's faces, but they didn't haunt his dreams as Jones did.

"You and Jones both left the Regiment and both have one child," said Gannon. "Maybe you saw a bit of yourself in him. Seems to me that if you really want to get to the bottom of what's troubling you, you should try opening up to the psychologist."

"But you think I'm okay?"

"You keep asking me that, and you seem fine — but what the hell do I know?"

His head hurt. His throat hurt. His left knee felt as if it was on fire. His right hand ached and the slightest movement of his thumb sent pain lancing down his arm. The only good thing was that at least it meant he was alive. Eddie Anderson would have smiled except he was missing his front teeth and moving his lips was agony.

He heard movement at the side of his bed. He didn't open his eyes. A nurse came to check on him every fifteen minutes. Sometimes they changed his dressings. There was a drip in his left arm and sometimes they did something with the bag.

"You're in a right state, aren't you?"

Anderson opened his eyes a fraction and squinted up at his visitor. He expected a doctor but the man looking down at him wasn't wearing a white coat. He was wearing a black raincoat over a dark blue suit. He was a tall, thin man with close-cropped bullet grey hair and he was holding a warrant card six inches from Anderson's nose.

"No comment," said Anderson, wincing because it hurt to speak.

"I admire your loyalty but your boss is dead," said the detective.

"Dead?"

"Deceased. No more. Dead on arrival. He is an ex-boss. Am I getting through to you?"

"What about Ray?"

"Wates is in a worse state than you, Eddie. They're taking his spleen out this afternoon."

"Shit," said Anderson.

"You can live without a spleen. They say."

Anderson closed his eyes.

"Three against one and two of you are in intensive care while one's on a slab. And the other guy, not a mark on him."

Anderson said nothing.

"You knew he was a cop, right?" said the detective.

"No comment."

"This is just you and me, Eddie. There's no tape. Whatever you tell me stays in this room."

"Who the fuck are you?"

"I'm a cop who hates mysteries," said the detective. "You, Charlie Kerr and Ray Wates go charging in with guns. Kerr gets shot dead, Wates gets beaten to a pulp and you get hit by a car. That's a mystery."

"How do you know what happened?" said Anderson. He opened his eyes. "You weren't there."

"No, but I know a man who was," said the detective.

"So why no caution?" asked Anderson suspiciously. "You caution me, I get a brief. Piss off and leave me alone."

The detective leaned over the bed, his face a few inches from Anderson's. "The way things stand at the moment, they reckon you're the victim here. Crazy as it seems, the plods think you, Charlie and Ray were attacked. So, you tell me what I want to know and I walk out of here and maybe, just maybe, you get to go home to your wife and kid in Chorlton-cum-Hardy. But you screw me around any more and I'll put the plods right. You'll go down for attempted murder."

Anderson glared at the detective. "It sounds like you know everything anyway."

"The guy you attacked, you knew he was a cop?"

"Fucking right."

"And that didn't worry you?"

"It worried me and Ray, but Charlie wanted him dead." Anderson frowned. "No comebacks, right?"

"On my mother's life," said the detective.

"Nelson tried to fuck with Charlie's missus. Charlie, not surprisingly, took it personal. That's why he was there. I told him it was a mistake."

"Nelson?" said the detective. "Who the fuck is Nelson?"

"Nelson's the undercover cop. That's the name he was using anyway. Tony Nelson." A wave of nausea washed over him and Anderson closed his eyes.

When he opened them again, the detective was staring at him. "How do you know he was an undercover cop?"

"Because he was cracking on he was a fucking hitman, that's why. And we followed him to a cop shop in the City."

"Leman Street?"

"I don't know what road it was. Near Aldgate station."

"And Nelson was pretending to be a hitman?"

Anderson fought another bout of nausea. "I need a doctor," he said.

"No, you need me," said the cop. "I'm the only one standing between you and a life sentence. You tried to kill a cop, remember."

"A fucking supercop, that's what he is. Who the hell is he anyway?"

"Kerr didn't tell you?"

"When we followed him from Manchester, we thought he was a hitman. Angie had paid him to put a bullet in Charlie. We saw her and Nelson get busted, then Nelson got a get-out-of-jail-free card. We followed him to London and he reported to a cop shop."

"That was when?"

"Tuesday."

"And what time did he arrive at the cop shop?"

454

"Four o'clock. Four thirty, maybe."

"And you left it until Thursday before you made your move?"

"Charlie had things to do up north."

The ward doors crashed open and a middle-aged Chinese man in a white coat hurried over the linoleum floor towards Anderson's bed. "What the hell is going on here?" he asked, in a perfect Home Counties accent.

"I'm just having a few words with Mr Anderson," said the detective.

"He's a sick man," said the doctor.

"He almost killed a policeman."

"And once he's stabilised you can charge him. But at the moment he's my patient."

"I'm done anyway," said the detective.

"Yes, you are," said the doctor.

The detective stared at him, long and hard. The doctor tried to meet his gaze but his face reddened. He began to busy himself with the equipment monitoring Anderson's vital signs.

"So that's it?" said Anderson. "I'm in the clear?"

"Fingers crossed," said the detective. He left the ward, his black leather shoes squeaking with each step.

It was only as the detective barged out through the double doors that Anderson realised the man hadn't identified himself, and the warrant card had been too close to his face to read.

The name on the passport that the man was using was Muhammad Zahid. It was a good name, but it wasn't the name that he had been born with. The passport was

Iraqi, but the man was Palestinian. When he had joined the ranks of the *shahid* a video would be shown on Arab TV stations across the Middle East proclaiming his love for the Palestinian people and his hatred for the infidels who aided the Israeli murderers. The man calling himself Zahid hadn't been in Palestine for five years and hadn't seen his family for six. Ever since his Arab brothers had achieved martyrdom during the attacks on the World Trade Center and the Pentagon, the West's intelligence service had gone into overdrive. Suspected terrorists were watched, hunted and held without trial. Phones were tapped, emails were read, letters were opened. There was no such thing as secrecy any more. The Americans wanted to photograph, fingerprint and take DNA samples from every human being on the planet, but until they did, all that a man like the Palestinian needed was a valid passport with a valid visa. The immigration officer at Heathrow's Terminal Three was underpaid and overworked: he had only seconds to look at the passport and compare the photograph in it with the man in front of him. The resemblance was close enough and the passport was genuine, so the Palestinian was waved through. The immigration officer even welcomed him back to the United Kingdom. It had been so easy. The British were so trusting, so gullible.

The passport the Palestinian was using belonged to an Iraqi whose brother had been murdered by Saddam Hussein. The man had fled with his wife and two young sons before the Iraqi secret police could visit him in the middle of the night. The British had granted the family

456

asylum, and permanent residency in the United Kingdom. The Iraqi hated the British as much as the Palestinian did, but he was happy to take advantage of them. He had received a new hip, courtesy of the National Health Service, lived in a spacious three-bedroomed council flat in Notting Hill, with a balcony and use of a communal garden, his children were receiving a free education and would, hopefully, go to university one day. The Iraqi didn't need his passport any more. He had no plans to leave the country. Iraq was a hellish place run by the infidels, but even if it wasn't he wouldn't want to return. In Britain he was richer than he would ever be in Iraq. His children would soon be granted British citizenship, and they already spoke with British accents.

The Iraqi wasn't grateful for what the British had done for him. He saw it as his right. The British helped the Americans, who murdered and tortured Muslims around the world. He owed the infidels no loyalty. His only loyalty was to Islam and his Arab brothers. When he was approached by the Saudi one summer afternoon as he strolled through a pretty London square, he didn't take much convincing to hand over his passport. He didn't even want to know how it would be used. All he knew was that his Arab brothers were preparing to strike at the heart of the infidels and lending his passport was the least he could do. Even if the authorities ever traced it, all the Iraqi had to do was say it had been stolen. That was one of the benefits of living in Britain: it was so easy to lie to the police. Unlike in Iraq, where the secret police could torture and kill with impunity, the British police had to call him "sir" and would get him a lawyer, free of charge, if he needed one.

The Palestinian had been in the UK for two weeks, and he had spent all that time in the bedsit that had been found for him. Food and drink was brought to him by a man who never spoke. Another man — a Saudi, the Palestinian thought — came after a week, took measurements of his chest and waist and gave him some newspaper cuttings about the latest atrocities on the West Bank. Five schoolchildren killed by an Israeli rocket. A baby shot in crossfire. A student killed by a rubber bullet that hit him in the throat. The Palestinian didn't need the newspaper stories to fuel his hatred for the West. That had been forged more than ten years earlier when the Israelis had thrown him and his family out of their house, then bulldozed it. His father had fought back and been shot in the leg. The doctors had amputated it above the knee and he had never worked again. A year later, the Palestinian's elder brother had died when Israeli soldiers had fired into a crowd of protestors, and his mother had died of a broken heart six months later. The Palestinian hated the Israelis, he hated the Americans, who funded the Israelis, and he hated the British, who kowtowed to every demand the Americans made. It was time to hit the British, to show them what it was like to have people die in the streets. To make them suffer as the Palestinians had suffered.

There was a knock and the Palestinian got up off the prayer mat. He unlocked the door. It was the Saudi.

458

The Saudi opened his bag and took out a canvas vest with bulky packages in pockets spaced around it at even intervals. Red and blue wires ran from the pockets.

The Saudi helped the Palestinian fit the vest and tightened it with straps and buckles. The button to detonate the explosives was at the end of a white wire. The Palestinian tucked it away in one of the pockets. He knew how the vest worked: he'd been on a training course that was part technical, part indoctrination. He hadn't needed brainwashing: he'd welcomed the opportunity to join the ranks of the *shahid*. Once he had given his life for the *jihad*, he would be with his mother and brother in heaven, his father, too, when his time came.

The Palestinian put on his coat over the vest and fastened the buttons. The Saudi walked round him several times. He made a small adjustment to the shoulders, then handed the Palestinian an envelope. He picked up his bag and left. "*Allahu akbar*," he whispered, as the door closed. God is great.

The Palestinian opened the envelope. Inside, there was a single sheet of paper. It was a photocopy of a map of the London Underground system. One station had been circled in red ink. King's Cross. And written in the margin was a time: five o'clock.

The Palestinian looked at the cheap clock on the wall by the door. It was a quarter to one. He had plenty of time. He knelt to pray.

Ken Swift swiped his card and pushed through the revolving door. His boots squeaked as he walked down the corridor, head swivelling to left and right. He popped his head into the COMMS room and saw Mike Sutherland checking a radio. "Seen Rosie?" he asked.

"On the range," said Sutherland. "He's not happy with the sights on his Glock."

Swift turned on his heel. He heard the cracks of 9mm rounds as he went down the stairs to the range, single shots, evenly spaced. He barged through the door and saw Rose firing at a bullseye target ten metres down the range. Rose was in his black overalls, wearing orange ear-protectors.

"Rosie!" shouted Swift.

Rose carried on firing. When he'd emptied the magazine he pressed the button that brought the target closer so that he could see exactly where his shots had gone.

Swift walked up behind him and put a hand on his shoulder. Rose pulled off his ear-protectors. "What?" he said.

"Where's Marsden?"

Rose frowned. "He's with BTP this afternoon. They want him undercover on Operation Wingman. Why?"

"We're in deep shit," said Swift. "Deep, deep shit."

The Palestinian pulled the door to his bedsit shut behind him and walked slowly down the stairs. He heard loud rock music from one of the rooms on the first floor. Whoever was living there played music all day long and well into the night. Some nights the Palestinian had been unable to sleep but he had never gone down to complain. He hadn't wanted to draw

460

attention to himself. He just hoped that whoever was in the room would be at King's Cross station at five o'clock.

At the bottom of the stairs a glass door led to the street. The Palestinian pulled at it but it wouldn't open. Then he realised he had to press a button to unlock it. He stared at it. It was exactly the same as the one on his vest. It was an omen, he decided. An omen that everything would go as planned. "*Allahu akbar,*" he whispered. He pressed the button and the lock buzzed. It would be just as easy to press the other button, when the time came. Click, and he would be in heaven. He pulled open the door and walked into the street. He was just five minutes' walk from Brixton station in South London, the terminus of the Victoria Line.

The sky was overcast, another good omen. He had to wear the coat to cover the vest and it would have looked out of place on a warm, sunny day. Allah was smiling on him because what was about to happen was Allah's will.

The streets were busy with afternoon shoppers. Music blared from an open window. Reggae this time, not rock, but it was just as offensive to the Palestinian's ears. He walked past a travel agency, whose windows were plastered with posters offering cheap holidays — one for two weeks in Israel. The Palestinian shook his head sadly. Why would anyone want to holiday with murderers? he wondered. Had the Nazis offered package holidays to their extermination camps? London was full of tourists, coming to spend their money in a country that aided the persecution of

Muslims. It was time to show those tourists that they would have been better to stay at home.

He walked under a railway bridge and a train rattled overhead, making him flinch. Brakes squealed with the sound of a tortured animal. He walked along a street filled with market stalls selling cheap clothes, flimsy luggage and counterfeit batteries. Most of the shops catered to the Afro-Caribbean community, supermarkets with open boxes piled high with vegetables the Palestinian had never seen before, butchers offering halal meat, posters advertising phonecards to make cheap calls to Jamaica and West Africa. The Palestinian moved through the shoppers, trying to avoid physical contact with those around him.

He turned right on to Brixton Road. He was only yards from the tube entrance. He was so busy with his thoughts that he didn't see the two men blocking his way until he had almost bumped into them. He mumbled an apology and tried to step to the side, but a hand gripped his right arm just below the shoulder. He looked up to see two big black men. One had dreadlocks tumbling from under a red, green and yellow woollen hat. The other was shorter but wider, with a large medallion on a thick gold chain. Both stared at him with undisguised hatred.

"Give us your mobile," said the man with dreadlocks.

"Excuse me?" said the Palestinian.

"I don't want your fucking apology, I want your fucking phone. You speaka da fucking English, don't you?" He pushed the Palestinian in the chest and he staggered back against a shop window. He was facing a bus stop where half a dozen housewives and old men stood with bags of shopping. They didn't intervene: they knew from experience that it brought only grief and a trip to the local Accident and Emergency department.

The Palestinian was confused. "I understand English, but I don't have a phone."

"Everybody's got a fucking phone," said the shorter of the two men. He pulled a small knife out of his pocket, a shiny blade with a brown wooden handle. "Now, give us your fucking phone or I'll stick you."

"I don't have a phone," said the Palestinian. "Please, I have to be somewhere."

"Give us your wallet, then."

"I don't have a wallet," said the Palestinian. He had nothing in his coat pockets and only a handful of coins in his trousers, just enough to buy his tube ticket to King's Cross. He had been told to carry nothing that might identify him.

The Palestinian tried to push between the two men. "Excuse me, please," he said. The knife flashed in and out and he felt a searing pain in his side. He gasped.

"You fucking Arab piece of shit," hissed the man with the medallion. He stabbed the knife into the Palestinian's side again. And again. The Palestinian staggered back against the window and it rattled from the impact. He felt blood flow under his vest and his legs went weak. He tried to reach under his coat so that at least he could die with honour, with glory, but his arms were like lead.

"Think you're better than us, do you?" hissed the man with the knife. The knife struck again, in his chest this time. The Palestinian's breath gurgled in his throat and he sank to his knees, a red mist falling over his eyes. His last thoughts were of the shame he would bring upon his family when they heard he had died in the street, that he had failed in his mission, that he had died for nothing, murdered by an infidel for not having a phone. He slumped forward and slammed face down on to the pavement, bloody froth spilling from his lips.

Shepherd took a drink from his plastic bottle of water, sat down under a map of the Underground system and stretched out his legs. He had been walking around Piccadilly Circus tube station for the best part of an hour, moving from platform to platform. His radio was clipped to the back of his belt under his leather jacket and there was a microphone inside his right cuff.

Nick Wright, Tommy Reid and four other British Transport Police undercover officers were on the same frequency, as were Brian Ramshaw and a controller at the Management Information and Communications Centre in Broadway. She was monitoring the CCTV cameras at Piccadilly Circus, where Wright and a female BTP officer were with Shepherd, Leicester Square, where Ramshaw was with Reid, and Tottenham Court Road, where the rest of the BTP officers were staked out.

"How's it going, Stu?" asked Wright, through the earpiece.

"Bored rigid," said Shepherd.

"You can pop up for a coffee," said Wright.

"Maybe later," said Shepherd. The BTP had wanted Wright and Ramshaw on the operation because they had seen Snow White and her crew up close. But they'd decided not to stake out the Trocadero again in case the steamers recognised any of the undercover officers. Four new BTP undercover officers were hanging around the amusement arcades while the officers from Wednesday's operation were in the tube system. Shepherd was wearing his leather jacket, blue jeans and a grey pullover. Wright had been more creative and was dressed as a priest, complete with dog collar and a shabby document case with the name of an East London church stencilled on the side.

Shepherd folded his arms, and felt the Glock hard against his left side. He couldn't get over the fact that armed police were going up against teenagers, but Shepherd couldn't forget how the boy had casually knifed the little girl. There had been no fear in his eyes, no regret. He'd smiled as he stuck the blade into the child's flesh. Shepherd wasn't happy about being taken off ARV duties, but he was glad to have another crack at the Snow White gang. This time he'd be quicker off the mark.

Eric Tierney had seen it all on the streets of Brixton. On a good day it could be a heart-warming, lively place, vibrant in its ethnicity. On a bad day it was a cross between a third-world slum and a war zone. Over the six years that Tierney had been a paramedic, he'd tended teenage boys with bullet wounds, twelve-year-old girls after back-street abortions, drug overdoses, young men who'd had pub glasses thrust into their faces, underage prostitutes who'd been slashed with razors. On a bad day, Brixton was the closest thing to hell that Tierney could imagine. But it was never dull. Tierney would have hated a nine-to-five job in a factory or office. Not that he'd ever tried one. He'd joined the army from school, and trained as a medic. He'd done ten years in uniform and served in Iraq, then decided that if he didn't leave before he was thirty he never would. The Ambulance Service had snapped him up and sent him to work in South London where his skill in patching up bullet wounds was a welcome bonus.

Today Tierney had started work at two and it was only four fifteen but already he had dealt with two heroin overdoses and a toddler who had been knocked out of her push-chair by a bus driver who had the dilated pupils of a drug-user. The police had taken the man for a blood test and the little girl was in intensive care with head injuries.

The fourth call of the day was to a man lying face down in the street. That was all the information they had. He could be drunk, on drugs, or dead. The driver had the siren and lights flashing but the traffic was heavy and there was no room for the cars ahead to pull to the side, so they had to wait it out.

The ambulance crawled along the road. Eventually Tierney saw a small crowd of onlookers and a police car with its blue light flashing. He grabbed his resuscitation kit, opened the door and ran down the street. As he got closer to the police car he slowed. The body was on the pavement, close to the road. One uniformed officer was holding back the onlookers, the other was on the radio. Tierney could see why neither was attending to the man on the ground. There was a large pool of blood around him: a body couldn't lose that much and still be alive.

Tierney knelt down beside the body, taking care to avoid the blood. He couldn't see a wound, but there was no doubt that the man had been stabbed or shot. There were no cartridge cases on the pavement and the local gang-bangers tended to use semi-automatics because that was what they used in the movies. The man had probably been stabbed.

Tierney put a hand on his back, preparing to turn him over.

"CID's on the way," said one of the officers. "Best leave the body where it is."

"I've got to confirm that it *is* a body," said Tierney, "check for a pulse."

"Waste of time," said the officer.

"Them's the rules," said Tierney, although he knew the officer was right. He felt something hard and oblong under the coat, and frowned. He moved his hand round the body and felt another object, the same shape as the first. He sat back on his heels. His first inclination had been to turn the man over, but now he was having second thoughts. Something was not right — something that was making the hairs on the back of his neck stand on end.

He remembered a poster he'd seen in Iraq, one of many produced by the Americans. It warned of the dangers of suicide bombers, and on it was a photograph of a vest with pockets that held tubes of dynamite — not oblong blocks like Tierney had felt but tubes like Blackpool rock. Tierney craned his neck and looked at the man's face. It was pale but definitely Middle Eastern.

"Get those people back," Tierney said quietly.

"What's wrong?" asked the officer.

"Just move them back, get everybody as far away from here as you can."

Tierney reached for the bottom of the man's coat and pulled it slowly up his legs. Then he rolled it up to the man's waist. He saw grey canvas and knew his hunch had been right. A few more inches and he could see three pockets, each containing something oblong. Tierney swallowed. His mouth was bone dry.

"Is that what I think it is?" asked the officer, his voice a harsh whisper.

Tierney didn't reply. He eased the coat higher. It snagged on something and he cursed. He couldn't reach the coat buttons without turning the body over, and he didn't want to risk that. It was something for the bomb-disposal experts. But Tierney wanted to be sure. He eased the coat from side to side, then pulled it further up the body. He saw wires. Red and blue. Now he was sure.

Major Allan Gannon enjoyed his monthly meetings with the head of the Met's Anti-terrorist Squad.

Commander Ronnie Roberts was a career cop who'd worked his way up from the beat in South London, with stints in Special Branch and the Robbery Squad. His office on the eleventh floor of New Scotland Yard overlooked Broadway, and as Gannon stood at the window and looked through the bomb-proof curtains he saw a group of Japanese tourists photographing themselves in front of the famous triangular rotating sign.

"How does it feel to be a tourist attraction?" asked Gannon.

"It's a funny old world, isn't it?" said Roberts. "On the one hand we're supposed to be *Dixon of Dock Green* and walking guidebooks for tourists, and on the other we've got machine-guns at Heathrow and surveillance operations on terrorists trying to buy anthrax spores over the Internet."

"I blame TV," said Gannon. "Newspapers make do with words but TV needs pictures and sound. The Iranian embassy siege did it for us. Once they saw us in action they wanted to know everything. Next thing we know there's movies about us, kill-and-tell books, the works."

"I don't know who thought openness was a good thing," said Roberts, "but they should have slapped a D Notice on anything connected with you guys. Now every man and his dog knows what weapons you have and how you train."

"And everyone in the world knows where MI6 is," agreed Gannon. "Never understood that. They're supposed to be the Secret Service but they allow their

HQ to be featured in a James Bond movie. And they act all surprised when the IRA takes a pot-shot at them with an RPG."

There was a knock on the door and a secretary showed in Greig Mulhern, number three at Special Branch. He shook hands with Gannon and Roberts and sat on a sofa in the corner of the room. He was a bulky man, almost square, with a thick neck and bullet-shaped head.

"Coffee's on the way," said Roberts. The meeting had no agenda and no notes were taken. It was just an opportunity to share information without having to go through multiple layers of bureaucracy.

"Martin not here yet?" asked Mulhern. Martin Jackson was the fourth member of the group and as he had furthest to travel he was, more often than not, the last to arrive. He worked for GCHQ, the government's eavesdropping facility that monitored phone, satellite and Internet traffic around the world.

"On his way," said Roberts. "How's business?"

"We've got the Yanks on our back, big-time," said Mulhern. "They want us to put undercover guys in the London mosques. They're picking up intel that al-Qaeda's planning a big one in the UK."

"That's just them wanting to keep us on side," said Gannon. "Every time public opinion swings against what they're doing in Iraq, they crack on that the whole world's in danger. Remember what Bush said? You're either with us or against us."

Mulhern scratched at his shirt collar. He had short arms and he always had trouble finding shirts that fitted. Either the sleeves were too long or the collars too tight. "They're not talking specifics, but they rarely do in case they give away their sources. But they say there's a big one being planned and that they'll be using Muslims with British passports. Invisibles."

"That narrows it down to — what? About a million?" Gannon laughed.

"Thing is, do you know how many Arabs we have in Special Branch? Or how many could even pass for Arab or Pakistani? The answer is a big fat zero."

"Five's the same," said Roberts. "They've got Oxbridge graduates who can speak the languages and who know everything there is to know about the culture, but they're all whiter than white, so undercover operations are out of the question. We're only just getting black officers into our undercover units. We don't have a single Arab we could put into play."

"What's the nature of the London threat?" asked Gannon.

Mulhern shrugged. "No details. But there's been heavy selling short of the UK market through New York from clients out in the Middle East. That much is a fact. Someone reckons the London stock market is going to plunge."

"Not all terrorists play the market," said Gannon, drily.

"Agreed, but there was a lot of selling short of shares in the airlines whose planes crashed into the World Trade Center," said Mulhern. "But it's not just the trading, there's been phone traffic in which British Muslims were referred to."

"Do you think they've got intel they're not telling you about?" asked Roberts.

Mulhern frowned. "It's possible, but if they have they're playing it close to their chest. They might well have an undercover agent somewhere in the al-Qaeda network and don't want to expose him by giving us the full details."

"So what's the game plan?" asked Gannon.

"We've got sympathetic Muslims in most of the country's mosques," said Mulhern. "We'll put out feelers. That's about all we can do. Martin can tell us what GCHQ is doing. I'm sure the National Security Agency has already been on to them."

A harsh beeping came from the metal case at the side of the sofa. It was Gannon's satellite phone. He stood up and went to it. As he reached for it, the pager on Mulhern's belt went off. As Mulhern checked the message, one of the phones on Roberts's desk rang.

The three men exchanged a worried look. It couldn't be a coincidence that they were being contacted at the same time. Something had happened. Something big.

Rose sat deep in thought as Sutherland drove the ARV away from the traffic-lights. It was a cold day but the heater was on too high and he could feel sweat running down his back. He shifted uncomfortably in his seat and ran his hand over his shaved head.

"You okay, Sarge?" asked Sutherland.

"Huh?"

"You're a million miles away. Something wrong?"

Rose forced a smile. "Just bored. I hate these days when nothing happens."

Dave Bamber was sitting in the back by the MP5s. He was a ten-year veteran of SO19, a Welshman with a shock of freckles across his nose and cheeks. "I like a quiet day, myself," said Bamber.

"It's because we haven't got Jonah on board," said Sutherland.

"Jonah?"

"Stu Marsden. Every time we have him in the back, shit happens. First day on the job we get the call to Big Ben. Then the shoot-up at the pizza place."

"Yeah, bugger about Kev, right?"

"He'll be okay," said Rose. "The other guy let loose with a shotgun first. Kev was lucky he didn't get a face full of shot."

"He and Stu are up for commendations," said Sutherland.

Rose stared out of the window, tight-lipped. If only he hadn't driven down the road at the moment Marsden had been attacked, he would never have told him about the Harlesden job or taken him to see Swift. They'd have recruited someone else and done the second job, Kelly would have flown to Chicago and everything would have been all right. Now it was turning to shit. Unless he did something fast he was going to prison and his daughter would die.

Rose had replayed his conversation with Swift and Marsden over and over in his head as he sat in the front seat of the ARV. He and Swift had confessed to everything — the robbery, disposing of Ormsby's body, the Dublin drugs deal. They'd told him about their guns. It was open and shut.

"Commendations don't mean shit," said Bamber.

"Yeah, that's what Stu said." Sutherland laughed.

Rose and Swift had spent fifteen minutes before their shift working out their options. That they hadn't already been busted by IIC meant that the powers-that-be were waiting for something. Marsden's evidence plus the gun would be all that was needed to file charges against them both, so the fact that they hadn't already been arrested meant that IIC wanted more. Marsden hadn't been wearing a wire, so maybe that was what they wanted: he would try to get them to confess on tape. Maybe he'd even get them to talk about the next job. If that was so they had a few days' grace, a few days in which to dig themselves out of the shit they were in. They could get rid of the guns. Rose could dismantle them, screw up the barrels so that they'd get no usable forensics, then throw away the pieces where hopefully they'd never be found. They'd have to make sure they weren't being followed. It had been a big mistake telling Marsden where Ormsby was buried. The alarm bells should have rung when he'd asked where they'd put the body, but he'd seemed so bloody reasonable. He was a cop, for God's sake, an undercover cop, and they hadn't spotted what he was up to. Rose gritted his teeth.

They'd have to dig up the body and move it. Rose wasn't looking forward to that. He wasn't looking forward to any of it. The money would have to go, too. There was no way he could pay for Kelly's operation now, not without showing out. The best he could do was sit on the money until after he'd retired, and by then Kelly would be dead. Rose stamped on the thought. No way was he going to let his daughter die.

He took a deep breath. Sutherland flashed him a sideways look. "This vest is killing me today," Rose said. "Must be putting on weight."

"Take the plate out," suggested Sutherland.

"Yeah, maybe," said Rose, but he left it where it was.

So, they got rid of the guns, moved the body and took care of the money. What then? They already had cast-iron alibis for the night of the Harlesden robbery. Without a recording of the conversation that had taken place on Swift's balcony, it would be Marsden's word against theirs. Two cops against one. They could try to pass it off as a joke, claim they were just pulling the new guy's leg. That would leave Swift in the clear, but Rose's situation was more complicated. There had been the drugs deal in Dublin. He'd used his own car to cross the water. And the biggest problem was what had happened on Thursday night: the shoot-out. One man dead and two in hospital. That was the part that made no sense to Rose. If Marsden, or whoever he really was, was an undercover cop, then why had those three guys driven down from Manchester to kill him? And if Marsden's bosses had heard about the shoot-out, why hadn't he been pulled out? The big question, the one that Swift and he still had to deal with, was what to do with Stuart Marsden.

★   ★   ★

Major Gannon strode into the Management Information and Communications Centre. He was carrying his grey metal sat-phone case. Two uniformed officers were behind him and Commander Roberts brought up the rear. "Who's in command here?" shouted Gannon.

A uniformed inspector in shirtsleeves stood up at a work station. "Who are you?" asked the inspector.

"I'm the guy with a direct line to the prime minister, and as of now I'm in charge," said Gannon. "Major Gannon, SAS. I need you to do exactly as I say over the next few minutes." He looked up at a large clock on the wall behind the inspector's desk. It was four thirty-one.

Commander Roberts flashed his warrant card at the BTP inspector. "Roberts, Anti-terrorist Squad," he said. "Just follow Major Gannon's instructions."

Gannon swung his sat phone on to the BTP inspector's desk and held up his hands. There were some twenty men and women in the control room, all wearing headsets and each facing three flat computer screens. Most were talking into their microphones but all were looking at Gannon.

"Would you all please stop what you are doing, right now?" Gannon shouted. "No matter who you're talking to, cut them off."

Most of the officers did as Gannon said but some continued to talk. Gannon waved at the uniformed officers who had arrived with him. They walked over to those who were talking and unplugged their headsets.

"As of now we are dealing with a category-one emergency," said Gannon. "This has priority over everything else until I tell you otherwise. You will not answer the phones, you will not deal with any other enquiries. I can tell you that a man wearing a vest full of high explosive has been found on the pavement in Brixton with a map of the tube, and we believe that King's Cross station was the intended target."

The inspector's jaw dropped. "What?"

"It's unlikely that King's Cross would have been the only target, which means we have to assume that there are other person-borne explosive devices heading towards others." Gannon smiled grimly. "That's what we call suicide bombers these days — person-borne explosive devices. I want every CCTV camera on the tube system checked now. We are looking for Arabs wearing bulky clothing, or anyone who looks suspicious."

"You can't —" began the inspector.

Gannon silenced him by pointing a finger at his face. "If you say 'can't', 'won't' or 'shouldn't' to me again, one of the men with me will throw you through that window over there, and I don't care what floor we're on. You will listen to me, you will answer my questions and you will carry out my orders, because if you don't a lot of people will die. Are we clear?"

The blood had drained from the inspector's face. "Yes, sir."

"Good man. I need you to contact the manager of every station on the Underground system and tell them to send their staff to the platforms. If they spot anyone suspicious they are to radio in here and notify you. We will then view the person on your CCTV screens. Got that?"

The inspector nodded.

"How many stations are there on the system?"

"Two hundred and eighty-seven," said the inspector.

Gannon did a quick calculation in his head. Even if each call could be completed in a minute, it would still take one man almost five hours to contact every station. They would have to split the workload. There were twenty officers here. Even with all of them on the case, it would still take about fifteen minutes. "Split your officers into teams and divide the stations between them. Cover the ones with mainline terminals first."

"Yes, sir."

Gannon pointed at the BTP sergeant who had been sitting to the inspector's right. "Show me how this equipment works," he said, and sat in the inspector's chair. "Get me one of those headsets."

Rose looked at Sutherland. "I wouldn't mind a coffee, Mike," he said.

Before Sutherland could say anything, the main set burst into life. "MP to all Trojan units. Possible Operation Rolvenden in Central London, location unspecified. All Trojan units to report to nearest mainline rail station and await further instructions."

Sutherland frowned. "That's a bit bloody vague," he said.

"Ours not to reason why," said Rose. "What would our nearest station be?"

Sutherland looked across at his visual display.

"Six of one," he said. "Victoria, Charing Cross. Waterloo if you want to cross the water. They're all five minutes away, max."

"Victoria," said Rose. "I can get a decent coffee there." He picked up the main set microphone. "Trojan Five Six Nine, *en route* to Victoria Station."

Shepherd's earpiece crackled. It was the female control officer at the Management Information and Communications Centre. She sounded blonde and thirtyish but that might have been Shepherd's imagination in overdrive.

"PC Marsden, please switch channels to three-seven."

"Will do," said Shepherd, but that was easier said than done with the radio in the small of his back. He got up and walked to the far end of the platform where there were fewer passengers and retuned it to channel thirty-seven. "Marsden receiving," he said, into his cuff.

"Bloody hell, Spider, you said you were in deep cover but I didn't think you meant going underground literally."

"Major?" said Shepherd. "Where are you?"

"The BTP control centre. I asked what resources they had in play and when they said they had a couple of SO19 officers undercover I asked for a description and put two and two together."

"No one can hear you, can they?" asked Shepherd.

"I've got one of those headsets on and everyone's working so hard they don't have time to eavesdrop on me," said Gannon. "At four twenty-four today a suicide bomber was found on a Brixton street, knifed. He was on his way to King's Cross and we know he was looking to detonate at about five. If he was alone, all well and good and we've had a narrow escape, but if there are others the chances are they'll be primed to go off at the same time, a few minutes either way at most."

Shepherd was hardly able to believe what he was hearing. He looked at his watch. It was four thirty-five.

"We're checking CCTV cameras and station staff are checking their platforms. Where are you now?"

"Piccadilly Circus," said Shepherd.

"We think mainline stations are the most likely targets, followed by intersections. Have a look around. And forget all that PC crap spouted by the civil libertarians. We're not looking for ninety-year-old Catholic nuns. You know the profile."

"Got you," said Shepherd.

Two middle-aged women were staring at Shepherd. He walked past them, scanning the faces of the passengers waiting for the next train. He knew the profile. Young, male and Muslim. Middle Eastern or Asian. Late teens a possibility. Twenties most likely. Thirties and above, possible but unlikely. Wearing clothing capable of hiding explosives. Blinking or staring. And as the deadline drew closer, probably muttering phrases from the Qur'ān.

Malik stood up, even though there were empty seats in the carriage. The raincoat looked fine as long as he was standing but if he sat down the vest would press against the coat and somebody might notice the outline of the blocks of explosive.

The train stopped at Oxford Circus and half a dozen people got off. Two Japanese tourists got on, clutching a street directory and peering at the route map above the doors. The man was wearing a Burberry golfing hat and squinted at Malik. "Baker Street?" he asked.

Malik tried to ignore the man.

"Baker Street?" repeated the Japanese.

Malik forced himself to smile. "You need to go north."

"North?" repeated the man. He looked at his wife. "North?"

The doors clunked shut and the train lurched towards the tunnel. Several of the seated passengers were looking at Malik, waiting to see what he would say next. Malik swallowed. He wasn't supposed to be noticed. He was supposed to move unseen through the crowds until he detonated the explosives.

He tapped the Bakerloo Line map. "This is Oxford Circus. You're going south. Baker Street is here. You need to go north."

The man's frown deepened and he spoke to his wife in rapid Japanese. More faces were turning to watch.

"You need to get off at the next station," added Malik. "Piccadilly Circus. Then find the platform for northbound trains. Bakerloo Line. North. Okay?"

"North. Thank you."

A couple of teenagers in combat trousers and camouflage-patterned coats were whispering and smirking. Malik fought to keep calm. It didn't matter who saw him. At precisely five o'clock he would press the button that would activate the bomb that would send him to heaven and take with him dozens if not hundreds of infidels. He looked across at the teenagers. Maybe they would get off at Charing Cross. Maybe they would be on the platform at five o'clock. He hoped so. Malik smiled. It was all going to be just fine.

It was, thought Major Gannon, like looking for the proverbial needle in a haystack. There were some six thousand CCTV cameras covering the tube system. In any one hour a hundred and fifty thousand people were heading underground, more at rush-hour — and it was rush-hour now. There were too many cameras to monitor. With twenty work-stations in the control room, even a ten-second look at each camera would take fifty minutes. And there were no cameras on any of the trains criss-crossing the system. The bomber in Brixton had been on his way to King's Cross on the Victoria Line. If others were *en route*, they would probably be travelling by train too, so they wouldn't be visible until they stepped out on to a platform. The cameras would have to be checked every time a train pulled in. It was an impossible task. Even if they had a face recognition system they could run in conjunction with the CCTV cameras, they didn't know who they were looking for. And there was a good chance that whoever had planned the operation had recruited Invisibles, men or women who held British citizenship in their own right and who were able to move around under the intelligence service's radar.

A phone rang and the inspector answered it, then handed the receiver to Gannon. It was Commander Matt Richards, who was running the GT Ops room at New Scotland Yard, the main control room in the event of a major terrorist incident. Richards was in direct communication with COBRA, the Cabinet Office briefing room, and the prime minister.

"How's it going there, Major?"

"Ronnie Roberts and I are checking the CCTV cameras but there are too many people down there. Can we evacuate?"

"Sorry, Major, that's not an option. Every scenario we've ever run shows that evacuation causes more problems than it solves. Crowds form outside the stations and if a bomb goes off there we have more casualties than if the explosion takes place below ground."

"The good of the many outweighs the good of the few?"

"We've run the numbers, Major. Evacuation of the system doesn't save lives. If we have a specific threat, place and time, we can shut down a section of line or run trains through a station without stopping. But shutting the whole system is just not on."

"No clues on the Brixton bomber?"

"Just the Underground map. Only King's Cross was circled, so there's a possibility that he was a lone wolf," said Richards.

"If it's al-Qaeda, multiple targets are more likely," said Gannon.

"God be with us," said Richards, and cut the connection.

The commander was a regular churchgoer and fond of quoting from the Bible. Gannon doubted that God would be of much help over the next half an hour. He sat back in his chair and steepled his fingers under his chin. King's Cross was an obvious target because so many tube lines intersected at the station. But Victoria was the busiest station on the system. Gannon wondered why the man was travelling from Brixton to King's Cross when Victoria was only four stops away. King's Cross was four stops further on. Why risk travelling the extra distance? *Because someone else was going to Victoria.* Someone who would be using a different tube line.

Gannon jumped to his feet. He pointed at the sergeant. "I want Victoria station evacuated," he said.

Shepherd's earpiece crackled. "Spider, you there?" It was Gannon.

"Receiving," said Shepherd.

"Victoria station, how quickly can you get there?"

"It'll have to be on foot, there's no direct line."

"There's going to be a bomber at Victoria. I've got guys heading over from the barracks but you might get there first."

"On my way," said Shepherd.

Shepherd saw Nick Wright at the far end of the platform and jogged over to him. "Nick, I've got to get to Victoria now."

"You'll have to go through Green Park. Piccadilly Line to Green Park, then Victoria Line south."

"I don't have time, what about running through the tunnels?"

"Other than that it's pitch black and there's a live rail that'll fry you if you touch it, it sounds like a plan. Over ground is the only way."

"Cheers," said Shepherd. He rushed for the escalator and ran up the moving stairs two at a time.

Gannon put his hand on the shoulder of the young WPC and peered at her screen. On the display was a view of the southbound Victoria Line platform at Victoria station and a map of its CCTV cameras.

The platform was deserted except for a uniformed member of staff who was pacing up and down with a radio pressed to his ear.

"How's the evacuation going?" he asked.

The WPC was wearing a lightweight headset. She reached for her computer mouse and clicked on to a CCTV camera in the main ticket hall. The screen showed four staff members holding back a crowd of frustrated passengers.

She clicked to another view, this time of the escalators, both running upwards. Then a passenger walkway, which was deserted. She flicked from camera to camera. Other than a few stragglers the station was empty. "So far, so good," said the WPC. "As each train comes in the passengers are shunted upstairs." She looked up at the major. "I know it's none of my business, but why don't you just close the station and not allow the trains to stop?"

"Because if I'm right, there's a bomber on one of those trains. We need him out in the open."

"And then what?" asked the WPC.

"We just hope we can take him out before he blows himself to kingdom come."

The tube train slowed to a halt. Malik wondered what was happening. Several passengers swore. Malik glanced at his wristwatch. It was a quarter to five. The Saudi had said that Malik should be on a platform when the bomb went off. Malik wondered what he should do if the train remained in the tunnel. Should he press the button at five o'clock, or wait until the train got to the station? He counted the people in the carriage. Twenty-six. Not enough. There would be hundreds on the platform. He would wait until the train reached the station, even if it meant going over the deadline by a few minutes. The Saudi had insisted that Malik pressed the button at exactly five p.m., but he hadn't known that the train would be stuck in a tunnel. Malik was the man on the spot, and he would decide when to activate the bomb. Why kill only twenty-six when he could kill hundreds?

His pulse raced at the thought of the explosion. The Saudi had said it would happen so quickly that there would be no sensation, just the bright light, and then he would be with Allah, one of the revered *shahids*, and he would receive all the rewards that were the right of those who gave their lives for Islam. Those closest to him would feel no pain. They probably wouldn't be aware of the explosion: their lives would just wink out. There would be no place in heaven for the unbelievers. But that wasn't Malik's problem. They were infidels, no better than animals.

The train lurched and started moving again.

"Thank God," murmured a middle-aged man, cradling a briefcase.

Malik wondered if the man really believed in God. And if he did, would that God save him from what was about to happen?

The train arrived at Charing Cross. The two Japanese pushed in front of him, eager to get off. The man with the briefcase also pushed ahead. Malik let them go, then stepped slowly off the train. A housewife knocked his shoulder as she got on to the train. She gave him a bright smile and apologised. Malik watched her as the doors closed and she mouthed, "Sorry," again.

The train pulled out of the station. There were only a dozen people waiting for the next, but more were arriving. At the far end of the platform a CCTV camera seemed to look accusingly at him, but he knew he was just one of millions of passengers passing through the station every day. No one was looking for him. He had nothing to fear from the surveillance, but he didn't want to stand on the platform for too long: someone might wonder why he didn't board a train. He started to walk, following signs for the Northern Line.

★ ★ ★

Shepherd's jacket flapped behind him as he ran and he kept his arm pressed to his left side so that no one would see the Glock in its holster. His feet pounded on the pavement and he breathed deeply and evenly. Ahead of him the Mall separated Green Park from St James's Park. Shepherd upped the pace. It was virtually a mile from Piccadilly Circus to Victoria as the crow flew but Shepherd wasn't a bird and he wasn't flying. He'd run along Piccadilly, which was crowded with shoppers and office-workers heading home, then turned down St James's Street. It was no distance, compared with his normal running schedule, but he was sweating in his pullover, jeans and jacket.

He ran past St James's Palace and turned on to the Mall. In the distance he could see Buckingham Palace. The Royal Standard was flying, indicating that the Queen was in residence. A girl was throwing a Frisbee for a barking cocker spaniel. Two teenagers were kissing on a bench. A crocodile of Chinese tourists was walking down the Mall towards the palace, their faces impassive. Two policemen looked over at Shepherd, but dismissed him as just a man late for an appointment. Shepherd ran on. He was halfway there.

Malik walked on to the Northern Line platform. It was crowded and he smiled inwardly. Perfect. He looked up at the electronic board and saw that a train was due in four minutes, then another five minutes after that. Malik looked at his wristwatch. It was four fifty-one. Passengers were piling on to the platform, their faces falling when they saw how long they had to wait. Malik walked slowly to the middle, his hands in his pockets. The button was still tucked into the vest so that it could not be pressed accidentally. He wouldn't hold it until the last minute.

He moved back to stand by the wall. There was a chocolate machine to his left. Malik looked at it, his mouth watering. It would be good to taste chocolate one last time. Maybe even to have a piece in his mouth as he pressed the button. He had some coins in his pocket and ran them through his fingers. He felt the milled edges of a pound, and took that as a sign that Allah meant him to have the taste of chocolate in his mouth when he went to heaven.

He went to the machine and slotted in the coin. He chose a bar of mint chocolate, then went back to the wall. He unwrapped it and popped a piece into his mouth. There were over a hundred people along the platform.

Malik let the chocolate melt in his mouth. It reminded him of the mint tea his mother had made for him. Would there be chocolate in heaven? Yes. All his needs would be taken care of. Malik hadn't seen his mother and father since he returned to England, but when it was over and the media reported what had happened, they would realise where he had been and what he had done. Whether or not they understood why he had given his life for the *jihad*, they would know that he had earned them a place in heaven and they would thank him for all eternity.

Malik felt a tug at his coat and he flinched. Then he saw it was a little girl of five or six and smiled. Blonde curly hair, blue eyes, wearing a grey overcoat with toggles and bright pink wellington boots. "Can I have some?" she asked.

"Go away, little girl," he whispered.

"I want some chocolate."

"Didn't your mother tell you not to talk to strangers?"

The child nodded solemnly.

"Well, go away."

"I just want some chocolate."

A young woman rushed up to him. Her hair was the same colour as the child's and she had the same big blue eyes. She grabbed the child's hand. "I'm so sorry," she said.

"She wanted some chocolate," said Malik. "Is it okay if I give her a piece?"

"I don't like her to eat chocolate," she said. "It's bad for her teeth." She looked down at her daughter. "What have I told you about bothering people?"

"Really, it's no bother," said Malik.

The woman's brow creased as she looked at Malik. "Are you all right?" she asked.

"What do you mean?"

"You look hot. Like you might be ill. I have a flu powder, the sort you can take without water." She fumbled in her handbag.

"I'm not sick, but thank you," said Malik. "It's the air down here. It's always so stuffy."

"I know what you mean," she said. "I hate it but it's the easiest way to travel around, especially when you have children. So much safer than the roads."

"Yes," said Malik, quietly. "So much safer."

He felt a breeze on his cheek, heralding the arrival of the train. The lines vibrated and then he heard the train powering through the tunnel. Several passengers moved back but most stayed close to the edge, not wanting to lose their place. The little girl reached up for her mother's hand and Malik felt a surge of relief that they were getting on to the train.

"No, pet, it's too crowded," said the woman. "Let's wait for the next one." She smiled at Malik. "We're going to see my parents. It's my father's birthday." Malik saw she had a prettily wrapped package in a carrier-bag, tied with a gold bow.

The train roared into the station and its brakes squealed. Malik kept his back to the wall as the door opened and passengers flooded out. Many stayed on, though, heading south to Waterloo, and the train was still too full for those on the platform to get on. Some tried, but the carriages were filled to capacity. Malik looked up at the electronic display. Five minutes until the next train.

The little girl waved at Malik but he turned his back on her and walked away, holding the chocolate. He passed two Canadians, their rucksacks emblazoned with red and white maple-leaf logos. They were holding hands and whispering to each other. An Indian woman was sitting with three young children, her arms around them protectively. She smiled at him and looked into his eyes. For a second Malik felt as if she could see right into his mind. He averted his eyes and hurried past.

He could barely breathe. His way was blocked by a group of students standing guard over a line of suitcases. They were talking excitedly in Italian. Malik tried to get through them, apologising. One, a teenage boy, put his hand on Malik's back. Malik twisted away. More passengers were pushing their way on to the platform. Malik saw a gap by the wall and moved into it. There were hundreds of people on the platform with more arriving all the time, parents with children, businessmen carrying briefcases, couples holding hands.

He couldn't see the little blonde girl now, but he knew she was there, and that she was still holding her mother's hand. Malik's mind was racing. This wasn't how it was supposed to be. They were the enemy. The infidel. They weren't people — they were targets. But now he couldn't stop seeing them as people. Men, women and children who would soon be lying broken and bleeding on the platform. Dead and dying. Those still alive crying out for their loved ones. Begging their gods to save them.

Malik's hands were soaked with sweat and he wiped them on his raincoat. He felt the bulky packages of explosive. Three Arab women moved down the platform, clothed from head to foot in the traditional black *jibab*, only their eyes visible. They were all carrying bulging Marks & Spencer carrier-bags. Malik stared at them in horror. Muslim women. He looked around frantically. There were two Pakistani women to his left. It wasn't how he'd pictured it when he'd lain on his back in the graveyard. In his dreams he'd been surrounded by men when he'd pressed the button. Evil men, who hated Islam and everything it stood for, who murdered innocent Muslims, slaughtered women and children. But as Malik stood on the station platform he realised that he was the one who'd be killing innocents. He would be as bad as the infidels he hated. And how could he live in heaven for eternity knowing he had earned his place with Allah by killing women and children? The three Muslim women stopped next to Malik. He rubbed a hand over his face. This wasn't right, he thought. What he was doing wasn't right.

The ARV pulled up in front of Victoria station. BTP officers had drawn up a cordon and were preventing passengers entering the station. A manager was using a megaphone to tell the crowds that the station was closed until further notice. Rose radioed in that they had arrived. They were told to wait for further instructions.

"What's the story?" Rose asked the controller.

"When we know, you'll know," said the controller. "All we're being told is that it's a possible Operation Rolvenden."

"If it's those Fathers for Children nutters again, I'll shoot them myself this time," said Sutherland.

Suddenly Rose saw a man running at full pelt towards the station. He frowned. It was Stu Marsden.

"What's he doing?" asked Sutherland.

"Who is it?" asked Bamber.

"Stu, our observer," said Sutherland. "He's on attachment with BTP today. Undercover."

Rose climbed out of the ARV. "I'll have a word with him," said Rose. "Maybe he knows what's going on."

Shepherd saw the crowds at Victoria station long before he reached the tube entrance. He forced his way through, holding up his warrant card and identifying himself as a policeman. There was a uniformed BTP officer at the entrance. He checked Shepherd's ID and waved him through.

Shepherd headed for the turnstiles. A tube employee in a blue uniform and peaked cap opened a gate to let him through. He ran for the escalator. Three tube lines operated through the station: the District, Circle and Victoria lines. As he reached the top, he heard the sound of boots behind him. Shepherd looked over his shoulder. It was Rose. "What's up, Sarge?" he asked.

"I was going to ask you the same," said Rose.

The two men stood looking at each other. Rose's hand moved towards the butt of his Glock. "You're going to take me down, aren't you?"

"What do you mean?"

"You know what I mean. Don't fucking lie to me. You're an undercover cop."

Shepherd looked at Rose for several seconds without saying anything. Then he nodded.

Rose screwed up his face. "Shit."

"It's my job," said Shepherd. "It's what I do."

"You're a cop investigating cops," said Rose bitterly. "Scum of the earth."

494

"You're the first police officer I've ever gone up against," said Shepherd, "and I'm as happy about it as you are."

"I goddamned liked you, Stu," he said fiercely. "I thought you were my friend."

Shepherd didn't know what to say.

"You know why I did it."

"Sure. Your daughter."

"My daughter's got a name. Kelly. She's seven years old, Stu. Seven."

"I know."

"Have you got kids?"

Shepherd stared at Rose. As Stuart Marsden, he didn't, so the answer was no. He was in character, and it was against every rule in the book to step out of role. But Keith Rose deserved better than a lie. "A boy. Eight."

Rose smiled grimly. "So you know exactly how far a father will go to save his child. If you were in my position, you'd do whatever you had to."

"You killed two people, Keith."

"They were drugs-dealers. And they started shooting first."

"You sold drugs."

"They were on the streets anyway. I just changed their location."

"You broke the law."

"Whose law?" said Rose. "The state's? Fuck the state, Stu. My daughter's dying and the state isn't lifting a finger to help her. So I'm doing what I have to do. End of story."

"It's not like I don't understand," said Shepherd.

"*Do* you understand, Stu? Do you *really*? Do you know what's it like to see your little girl getting weaker by the day and to be told by some pen-pushing bureaucrat that there aren't the resources to treat her? And when I go hunting on the Internet and find a guy in Chicago who might save her the same fucking bureaucrat tells me that the health authority can't afford it. Can't afford it? I pay my taxes. I pay National Insurance. And the one time I need something from the state, they tell me they don't have the money. The specialist here — who we waited three months to see — says her tumour's inoperable. The guy in Chicago says he can operate and there's an eighty per cent chance she'll be okay. But will the state pay? It'll pay to rehabilitate child-killers but it won't to save my daughter."

"What do you want me to say? That life's not fair?"

"Life isn't fair," said Rose. "We cops know that better than anyone. We know that the biggest villains never go down because we don't have the resources to take them down. And they have enough cash to buy the best lawyers and pay off anyone who needs paying off. Cops, CPS, judges, juries. You know how it works. Speed cameras generate revenue, but putting drugs barons behind bars doesn't. So millions of motorists send off cheques every year while the biggest, hardest bastards live lives of luxury. The state chooses the soft targets. Always has and always will."

"So you started ripping off drugs-dealers to redress the balance?"

"By hook or by fucking crook, my daughter's going to live. I'll do whatever it takes."

"I don't have time for this," said Shepherd. "There are terrorists on the tube system. Suicide bombers."

"Bollocks there are," said Rose.

"They got one at Brixton. They think Victoria's a target."

Malik walked up to the two constables. They were deep in conversation, close to the tube-station exit. One of the policemen nodded curtly when Malik approached them. "Yes, sir?" He was young, maybe a year younger than Malik. He was good-looking, thought Malik, handsome, even. A man who would have no trouble winning the hearts of pretty girls. "I have done a terrible thing," he said.

The second constable was in his early thirties, with a square jaw and unfriendly eyes. "What would that have been, sir?" he said.

"I have followed the wrong path. I know that now. I need to repent."

The second constable raised his eyebrows at his colleague. "What exactly have you done, sir?"

Malik stepped closer to the two policemen, unbuttoning his raincoat.

"Not a bloody flasher," muttered the older policeman.

"You must take me somewhere safe," said Malik, "somewhere I can take this off." He opened the raincoat so that they could see the vest and its pockets of explosives.

The two policemen froze. "Jesus fucking Christ," said the younger constable.

"It's okay," said Malik. He held up his hands to show that he was not holding a trigger. "It will not go off."

"Jesus fucking Christ," repeated the constable, taking a step back.

"It is safe," said Malik. "I don't want to harm anybody."

"Who are you?" said the older constable.

"My name is Rashid Malik. I was to explode this bomb in the Underground but I cannot be a murderer. I cannot kill women and children."

The younger constable reached for his radio mike but the older one grabbed his arm. "No!" he said. "Radio frequencies can set them off." He looked at Malik. "How does that thing go off?"

Malik opened his coat wider so that the policemen could see the button tucked into one of the vest pockets. "I have to press that."

"What about if you take it off? Is that okay?"

"I think so."

"We're not going to touch it, are we?" said the younger constable, his voice shaky.

The older constable gripped his shoulder. "It's going to be okay, Chris. We have to start moving people back, just to be on the safe side. Can you do that?"

Chris nodded.

"Okay. I'll sit him down here."

Malik smiled encouragingly. "It is okay, really," he said. "It is safe now. Nobody is going to get hurt."

★　★　★

498

Rose's hand was still on the butt of his Glock but he made no move to take it from the holster. "Your name isn't really Stu, is it?"

Shepherd shook his head.

"What is it? Or are you undercover guys not allowed to say?"

"Dan. Dan Shepherd."

"At least I got one truthful statement out of you — but it's your job, isn't it, to get close to people and then shit on them?"

"It's not like that, Rosie."

Rose's earpiece crackled. "MP, Trojan Five Six Nine, what is your location?"

Rose kept his eyes on Shepherd as he took the call. "Trojan Five Six Nine, still at Victoria station."

"MP, we need you at Charing Cross station concourse, suspected suicide bomber."

Rose's eyes widened.

"What's wrong?" asked Shepherd.

"They've found one. Charing Cross."

Shepherd frowned. "You mean it's gone off?"

Rose shook his head. "They want us there now."

The two men stared at each other. "That's it, then," said Rose, eventually. "Whatever happens, it's over for me, isn't it?"

Shepherd said nothing. Rose started walking towards the tube entrance.

"Rosie?"

Rose stopped. "What?"

"I'm sorry."

Rose held Shepherd's eyes for two seconds, then jogged away. Shepherd watched him go. Then his earpiece crackled. It was the major. "Where are you, Spider?"

"Just got here, heading downstairs now." Shepherd ran down the escalator. A train must have arrived because passengers were heading up. Several looked at him curiously, wondering why he was the only person going down.

Major Gannon used the mouse to change viewpoints. There were tube staff and BTP officers on the platforms, and each time a train arrived they ushered the passengers quickly out of the carriages. He flicked from platform to platform. There were just too many passengers, too many possibilities. He looked up at the clock. Four fifty-six. If there were multiple bombers, they would almost certainly be under orders to detonate at about the same time. As soon as one device exploded, the authorities would have to evacuate and all advantage of surprise would be lost. If Gannon had been planning it, he'd have them primed to explode at the same time. The chances were that if there was another bomber, he would also be working to a five p.m. deadline. It meant that if Victoria was a target, he would be arriving within the next four minutes.

He flicked to the westbound District Line. A train burst out of the tunnel. There was no sound on the monitor. The doors opened and passengers stepped out, confused when they saw that the platforms were empty. Three CCTV cameras were covering the platform and Gannon skipped from view to view. When he clicked on the camera covering the rear of the train, something caught his attention. He leaned forward, staring at the screen.

The ARV pulled up in front of Charing Cross station. Bamber unlocked the MP5s. "Stay with the car, Mike," said Rose. "Monitor the main set." He stripped off his personal radio. "Dave, you stay between me and the car. I won't be able to use the radio because it might set the thing off. Anything I should know, shout. Keep at least fifty metres from me."

"Sarge, I don't —"

Rose cut Bamber off with an impatient wave. "Just do as you're told."

Bamber held out an MP5 but Rose shook his head. At the entrance to the station a uniformed sergeant was standing next to a young Pakistani man in a long raincoat with his hands on his head. He was talking animatedly to the sergeant. Rose looked at the huge station clock. It was almost five o'clock.

He put on his ballistic helmet and fastened the chinstrap as he walked towards the two men.

There were crowds on the pavement, standing and staring. "Can you all move back, please?" shouted Rose, but no one paid him any attention. "Keith Rose, SO19," he said, as he drew level with the sergeant.

"Ben Harris. Are you bomb disposal?"

"They're on their way." Rose nodded at the Pakistani. "You've seen it?"

The sergeant nodded. There was no colour in his face. "He opened his coat. I made him stay like that so he can't touch the button."

"It's okay," said the Pakistani. "I don't want to hurt anyone."

Rose was surprised at the man's nasal Birmingham accent. "What's your name?" asked Rose.

"Rashid Malik."

"Okay, Rashid. Just stay where you are. We'll get this fixed, don't worry."

Malik smiled eagerly. "It is okay. The bomb is safe."

A uniformed constable and two rail employees were trying to stop people leaving the station as they would have to walk past the Pakistani. Commuters were shouting angrily. "Ben, go and help your colleague over there. Keep everyone at least a hundred metres away."

"The bomb is safe," said Malik.

The sergeant looked as if he was going to argue so Rose pointed in the direction of the station concourse. "If more people arrive, we'll have major crowd problems over there. Find another way for them to leave."

"Everything is all right," said Malik.

The sergeant hurried off to shout at the crowds.

Rose waved at Bamber. He pointed at the crowds on the pavement. "Dave, get them moving towards Trafalgar Square."

"Right, Sarge!" shouted Bamber. He ran over to the commuters and yelled at them to move away. He was faced with a wall of blank faces. The office-workers wanted to go home and they weren't prepared to budge.

Rose took one of the plastic ties from his belt and moved behind Malik. "I'm just going to fasten your wrists, Rashid," said Rose, matter-of-factly. "It's for your own safety."

"There is no need," said Malik, but he didn't resist as Rose fastened the tie.

"Now, stand very still, Rashid. Let me see what we're dealing with."

Shepherd scanned the northbound Victoria Line platform as the passengers rushed out of the carriages and registered surprise when they saw the platform was empty. Blue-uniformed members of staff cajoled them towards the escalators. Shepherd saw two Pakistani teenagers, young men with gelled hair and gold chains, but they were wearing loose sweatshirts with designer labels. No threat.

He walked back down the platform. He saw anxious faces, nervous faces, angry faces, but he didn't see the face of a man prepared to kill himself and dozens of others. There were businessmen with briefcases, secretaries wearing drab office suits and white trainers, schoolchildren with ties at half mast, tourists looking bemused and holding maps of the Underground system.

"Spider, I have a possible. Just got off the westbound District Line," said the major in Shepherd's ear.

Shepherd started to thread his way through the passengers.

★ ★ ★

Gannon moved his face closer to the monitor. The man was an Arab and he'd been in the second to last carriage of the westbound train. He was walking slowly down the platform, wearing a brown raincoat that looked several sizes too big for him. The coat had attracted Gannon's attention, but the man's body language also suggested something wasn't right. He was tense: his eyes darted from side to side, and he was clenching and unclenching his fists. Gannon clicked on to a camera closer to the man. It was clear that the man was Middle Eastern: skin the colour of weak coffee, clean-shaven with a hooked nose. Gannon clicked back to the distant view. The man had a scrawny neck but the coat looked bulky round his chest. Or was he imagining it? Gannon had to be sure. "Ronnie," he said. "Have a look at this."

The commander came up and stood behind him.

"What do you think?" asked Gannon.

Roberts exhaled. "Maybe."

"Maybe" wasn't good enough. Gannon clicked back to the close-up. "Not a face you recognise?"

Roberts shook his head. "He's not right, though. Look at his eyes — he's hyper."

As they watched, the man began to mutter to himself. He looked as if he might be praying.

Shepherd ran through the pedestrian tunnel. Half a dozen office workers using the tunnel as a short-cut glared at him even though they were the ones heading

504

in the wrong direction. Shepherd pressed in his earpiece.

"Arab male, late twenties, wearing a long brown raincoat. Clean-shaven. He's on the platform about eighty feet from the exit tunnel."

Shepherd pulled the Glock from its holster as he ran. A middle-aged woman opened her mouth wide in astonishment and Shepherd had a glimpse of black fillings as he ran past her.

"Where are you, Spider?"

"Tunnel leading to the platform," said Shepherd.

"He's just passed it. You'll come out behind him. He's stopped."

Shepherd raised his gun so that the barrel was pointing at the ceiling. The tunnel curved to the right and ahead of him he saw the platform.

There could be no mistake, Gannon knew. If he called it wrong and an innocent man was shot in the head for no other reason than that he was an Arab, his career would be over, Shepherd's too. Gannon stared at the CCTV picture, Roberts at his shoulder. "It's a definite maybe," said Roberts.

"I think so."

The man was still muttering to himself, hands by his sides. Commuters were bumping into him as they passed but he showed no reaction.

Gannon linked his fingers and continued to stare at the screen, unblinking. The man's hands were empty, he was sure. He wasn't holding a trigger. Gannon's eyes flicked to the wall-mounted clock. It was four fifty-nine.

The timing was right. The location was right. The man fitted the profile. But was that enough? Was that enough to order a man to be killed?

The Arab stopped. Commuters passed by him like river water flowing around a rock. He raised his head until he was staring into the CCTV camera. His eyes bored into Gannon's. The Arab smiled. A cruel, knowing smile. His right hand moved to unbutton his raincoat.

"It's him," said Gannon, calmly. "Green light."

Shepherd ran out on to the platform. There were a dozen or so passengers still there: stragglers in no rush to get home, tourists who weren't sure if they were heading the right way. A woman in the light blue uniform of the station staff was hurrying them along.

Shepherd dropped into the firing position, legs shoulder-width apart, left foot in front of the right, toes turned inward. He brought up his left hand to cup the right and took aim with the Glock.

The man was fifteen feet ahead. Brown raincoat, black trousers, black shoes. His hair was jet black and glistened under the tunnel lights. Shepherd couldn't see any facial features. The man's left hand was hanging by his side; he couldn't see the right. Shepherd was all too aware of the enormity of what he was doing: he was shooting a man in the back of the head, with no warning, giving him no chance to surrender. It was a cold kill, done for no other reason than that Major Gannon was telling him to do it. Shepherd didn't even consider that the major might be wrong. He trusted him.

Shepherd pulled the trigger and the Glock kicked. The front of the man's forehead exploded in a shower of blood, brain matter and bone fragments. Immediately Shepherd fired again and this time a chunk of skull blew across the tracks.

The shots were deafening in the confined space, followed by screams of terror. Passengers scattered, bent double and running for the exit. Shepherd ignored them. He stayed focused on the target. A BTP officer rushed out on to the platform, saw what was happening and dashed back into the pedestrian tunnel.

The man's legs started to go. The right hand appeared at his side, fingers fluttering like the wings of a trapped bird. Shepherd fired a third shot, which blasted away most of what was left of the top of the skull.

As the body slumped to the floor Shepherd kept the gun trained on the man's head and started walking. He fired again. And again. He had to be sure.

The body hit the ground, blood seeping from the gaping head wounds. The legs were twitching. Shepherd pumped two more rounds into the head at close range. Gobs of brain matter splattered across the platform.

Shepherd was breathing heavily and his heart was pounding. It hurt when he swallowed. If the man he and Gannon had killed was just an innocent bystander, all hell was about to break loose.

Slowly he knelt beside the body.

* * *

The phone on Gannon's desk rang. He kept his eyes on the monitor as he took the call. It was Commander Richards at the New Scotland Yard control centre.

"The vests have timers," said Richards. "The EOD boys have defused the one in Brixton. It was set to go off at five-oh-two p.m." Gannon's eyes flicked to the wall clock. It was exactly five o'clock.

"Any other circuits?"

On the monitor, Shepherd was using his Swiss Army knife to cut the raincoat up the middle. He stripped it away as if he was skinning a rabbit.

"Just the timer and the manual switch," said Richards.

"I'll call you right back," said Gannon, and replaced the receiver. "Spider, you okay?"

On the monitor Gannon saw Shepherd's hand go to his mouth. "Good call, Major," he said.

"Listen to me, Spider. There's a secondary circuit. The EOD guys at Brixton called it in. If it's not detonated by hand, a timer kicks in."

"What do I do?" Shepherd seemed unfazed by what he had been told.

"The EOD guys say there are no booby traps so you can just pull the detonators out of the explosives. Then rip the clock out of the circuit. Easy-peasy."

The man was one of the Invisibles, but after he had fulfilled his destiny he would be invisible no longer: his name would join the long list of martyrs to the cause of Islam. He was British-born of Iranian parents who had fled their country when it was known as Persia, but the man had never felt British. He was a Muslim, first and foremost. It was as a Muslim that he lived and it was as a Muslim that he would die.

He stepped off the train and groped inside his coat for the button. He looked left and right down the platform. It was packed with commuters rushing to get upstairs and on to their trains home. Liverpool Street station, five o'clock in the evening. The place and time of his destiny. The place and time that would be remembered for ever.

He walked along the platform. People were still pouring off the train. The exits were blocked and the man heard sighs of annoyance and frustration. He was nudged in the back, his shoulders were pressed tight on either side; all around him, men and women were pushing and shoving, like cattle rushing into an abattoir.

"*Allahu akbar,*" whispered the man. His thumb was on the button. God is great.

No, he thought. It wasn't something to be whispered, as if he was ashamed of what he was doing. There was no shame. He was proud to die in the service of Allah. It was something to be shouted with pride.

"*Allahu akbar!*" he screamed. Angry faces glared at him. "*Allahu akbar!*" he cried, and pressed the button.

Shepherd ran his hands down the vest. There were four pockets in the back, each with a slab of explosive wrapped in nails. Wires led from the front to the explosives. Shepherd tugged at one and a thin metal cylinder the size of a cigarette eased out. Shepherd quickly pulled out the other three detonators, then rolled the body over. There were six pockets on the front of the vest, three on each side of the chest. Shepherd used both hands to pull out the detonators. Then he grabbed the wiring cluster and yanked it away from the vest. A digital clock emerged from a pocket. Shepherd grabbed it and pulled out the wires. He stared at the digital readout: 17:01.

The main set burst into life. "MP, Trojan Five Six Nine, are you receiving?" A man's voice.

Sutherland reached over and picked up the microphone. "Trojan Five Six Nine, receiving."

"Trojan Five Six Nine, we've just received intel on the bomb in Brixton. There is a secondary circuit attached to the device, activated by a timer."

Sutherland stared through the windscreen at Rose. He was holding the Arab's raincoat open.

"What do we do?" asked Sutherland.

"Is there an EOD team there yet?"

"Negative," said Sutherland.

"The detonators can be removed from the explosive," said the controller. "Just slide them out. What is your situation there?"

"Trojan Five Six Nine, hang on . . ." Sutherland got out of the car and waved both hands above his head. "Sarge! Sarge!"

Rose turned, still holding open the raincoat.

Before Sutherland could say more, Malik and Rose were engulfed by light. The two men were vaporised as the ten kilos of Semtex exploded. A hundred yards away, Sutherland was flung back against the car by the force of the explosion.

The Saudi watched the BBC reporter detail the casualties. Forty-seven dead, including a police officer. Over a hundred injured. Third time lucky. Only two explosions, and one had been above ground, but it had been more than enough. The TV images of the dead and dying were winging their way round the world. There would be more pressure on the British government to pull out of Iraq. More protests in the streets. More recruits eager to join the ranks of al-Qaeda, willing to sacrifice themselves in the war against the infidel.

The Saudi knew it was time to move on. He had done his work in London. He already had his ticket for Thailand. It would soon be the peak tourist season in Phuket, the island in the south of the country. Much of the population in the south was Muslim and the Saudi already had three cells in place, planning his next operation. The bar area of Patong was a prime target, packed every night with Australians, Americans and Brits. It was a soft target, the sort the Saudi preferred.

He would be travelling on a British passport so he wouldn't need a visa. He would automatically be granted a month's stay on arrival. The Saudi had held British citizenship for more than twelve years. His father had invested heavily in the country and had made large donations to both major political parties. He had offered his hospitality to MPs from across the political spectrum, and over the years several dozen had enjoyed themselves on yachts in the South of France, in hotels in Dubai and on the family's stud farm in Ireland. His application for citizenship for himself and his family had gone through smoothly, boosted by the fact he had signed a half-billion-pound contract with a British construction company. The government had bent over backwards to welcome the Saudi's father, even though in private the man made no secret of his hatred for the British. They were there to be used, he said. They granted citizenship to anyone willing to pay for it, allowed outsiders to live in their country without paying taxes, allowed foreigners to buy everything from land to their football teams. They had no pride in their country and were prepared to prostitute themselves to the world. They deserved what they got.

The Saudi had been educated at a top public school, his entrance facilitated by his father's multi-million-pound donation towards a new science wing. No bribe had been necessary to get into the London School of Economics: the Saudi had won his place on merit. With his perfect English, first-class degree and wealthy family, the world was at the Saudi's feet. But his hatred of the West matched his father's, and he had devoted his life to bringing the West to its knees.

The Qur'ān promised unlimited sex with seventy-two black-eyed virgins to the martyrs who sacrificed their lives for Islam. Virgins as beautiful as rubies, with complexions like diamonds and pearls. The Qur'ān said that martyrs went straight to heaven and that places would be saved for seventy relatives. There would be eighty thousand servants to take care of them. And they would see the face of Allah Himself. It was all nonsense, the Saudi knew. The Qur'ān also said that suicide was wrong. A sin. And it forbade the killing of women, children and old people, even for *jihad*. The Saudi didn't believe in the virgins and didn't believe in heaven. But he did believe in punishing America and her allies, striking where it hurt until they removed their forces from Muslim territories around the world.

He walked over to his prayer mat and knelt facing Mecca. For the next hour he bowed and prayed, offering his life to the *jihad* and asking to be lucky again.

Shepherd and the superintendent walked together along the path through the gravestones, some more than a hundred years old. The superintendent's driver stood by the official Rover at the entrance to the churchyard, ready to open the rear door. "It was a good service," said Hargrove.

"He was a good cop," said Shepherd.

"A good cop gone bad."

There was going to be a headstone, but there had been no coffin and no body. Rose's Kevlar vest had been found intact, and there was some metal from his weapons but not a fragment of bone or soft tissue.

"Rose did what he did for his family," said Shepherd.

"He killed two people for money."

"They were drugs-dealers and they shot first."

"That was his story," said Hargrove.

"I believe him."

"He was ripping off drugs-dealers, and because of that Andy Ormsby died along with the two Yardies, don't forget that."

"I won't," said Shepherd. "But he was still a good cop."

"And as far as the world's concerned that's all he was," said Hargrove. "His family gets the insurance, his pension and a medal for the sideboard."

"No one gets to know?"

"Just you and me. And the commissioner. He figures we should let sleeping dogs lie."

"That's one hell of a decision."

Hargrove shrugged. "Rose is dead. The money's probably hidden offshore where no one will ever find it. What's served by going public? We tell the world that the capital's armed police can't be trusted? The way it is now, Keith Rose was a hero. And the way things are at the moment, we need all the heroes we can get."

Ken Swift walked out of the church in full uniform. With him was Rose's widow, dressed in black and clutching a shiny black handbag. She had her arm through his and as they walked he bent down to whisper something in her ear.

"And Rose's daughter gets to go to America for her operation? On the insurance money?"

"The Met is footing the bill. She's the daughter of a dead hero. They didn't have a choice. So all's well that ends well."

"Depends which way you look at it," said Shepherd.

"If he hadn't died as he did there'd have been a court case followed by life in a cat-A prison and the kid would have died in an NHS hospital. Given the choice, I know which I'd prefer."

Shepherd sighed. "Maybe you're right."

Swift helped Mrs Rose towards a waiting limousine. Briefly he locked eyes with Shepherd, then nodded, almost imperceptibly, and got into the car with her.

"Swift?"

"We can't charge him without revealing Rose's wrongdoing. He's taking early retirement next week."

"Keeps his pension?"

"Let it go, Spider."

The limousine drove away.

"He told us where Ormsby was buried," Hargrove added. "Now the lad can have a proper funeral."

"What about Ormsby's family?"

"There isn't one. He was an only child. Parents died when he was a teenager. No wife."

"Swift knows who I am. And what I did."

"He can't say anything. He knows what will happen if he does. You did a good job, Spider."

"I'll take some convincing of that."

"Take some time off. Go and be a dad for a while."

"For a while? It doesn't work like that and you know it. You're either a good father or you're not. Over the last few months I've been a crap one."

"That's why I said take some time off."

"And then what? I come back to investigate more cops? Hound some other poor bastard until he decides that his only option is to kill himself."

"Keith Rose didn't kill himself. He died trying to save lives."

"You can keep telling yourself that," said Shepherd, "but we know what really happened."

"It was his choice," said Hargrove.

"I know," said Shepherd. "But you know as well as I do, sometimes choices aren't really choices at all."

The Bombmaker

Stephen Leather

Ten years ago, Andrea Hayes was the best master bombmaker in the business. Young, beautiful and deadly, she was the favourite of her Irish republican masters. Then it all went wrong. Five children were killed, when disruption was all that was intended. It all became too much, and she turned away from her trade . . .

Now, a new Andrea Hayes lives a safe suburban life, with her loving husband and young daughter. Safe in the knowledge that her past is another country. But then her daughter is kidnapped by persons unknown and the past has come knocking.

As Andrea gets blackmailed into returning to her craft and building a bomb that dwarfs any planted by the IRA, a faceless mastermind is working behind the scenes to pull off one of the most daring scams in world history . . .

ISBN 0-7531-7067-1 (hb)
ISBN 0-7531-7068-X (pb)

Hard Landing

Stephen Leather

As a detective working for an elite undercover squad, Dan "Spider" Shepherd has lied, cheated and conned in order to bring Britain's most wanted criminals to justice. When a powerful drugs baron starts to kill off witnesses to his crimes, Shepherd is given his most dangerous assignment yet. He has to go undercover in a top security prison — a world where one wrong move will mean certain death. Corrupt prison officers, lifers with nothing to lose, and hard men with something to prove are all gunning for Shepherd. The only way to survive is to play his role to perfection, twenty-four-seven, among criminals for whom violence is a way of life. As he gambles everything to move in on his quarry, he soon realises that the man he is set to trap is even more dangerous than the police have anticipated. And that he is capable of striking outside the prison walls and hitting Shepherd where it hurts most.

ISBN 0-7531-7147-3 (hb)
ISBN 0-7531-7148-1 (pb)

The Tunnel Rats

Stephen Leather

"Authentic . . . exciting stuff with plenty of heart-palpitating action" **Daily Mail**

Two murders, thousands of miles apart: one in London, one in Bangkok. The bodies brutally mutilated: an ace of spades impaled upon their chests.

In Washington, a US senator receives photographs of the corpses. And realises that his past has come back to haunt him.

Nick Wright is the detective trying to solve the mystery of the double killing. His hunt for a motive takes him to the tunnels in Vietnam, where the American tunnel rats fought the dirtiest battle of the war against the Viet Cong. But there is a killer protecting the secrets of the tunnels. At whatever cost . . .

ISBN 0-7531-7065-5 (hb)
ISBN 0-7531-7066-3 (pb)

The Solitary Man

Stephen Leather

"In the top rank of thriller writers"   **Jack Higgins**

Chris Hutchinson is a man on the run. Imprisoned for a crime he didn't commit, Hutch escapes from a British maximum security prison and starts a new life in Hong Kong. Then a ghost from his past catches up with him, forcing him to help a former terrorist break out of a Bankok prison. Or face life behind bars once more. Meanwhile the Drug Enforcement Administration wants to nail the vicious drug warlord responsible for flooding the States with cheap heroin. And decides to use Hutch as a pawn in a deadly game. Hutch's bid for freedom takes him into the lawless killing fields of the Golden Triangle, where the scene is set for one final act of betrayal . . .

ISBN 0-7531-7063-9 (hb)
ISBN 0-7531-7064-7 (pb)